Silent Battleground Reviews

'Captain Ulmer parlays his knowledge and experience gained from command of a US Navy Diesel-Electric submarine and earlier service as a Department Head on one of the first nuclear-powered Polaris ballistic missile submarines to craft a fascinating alternative history in the early part of the last decade of the 20th century ... unusual in this "techno-thriller" genre, Silent Battleground absolutely reeks of both technical and tactical credibility ... readers will find a delightful blend of elements from On the Beach, Incredible Victory, Thirteen Days and Hunt for Red October. Submariners will approve, non-submariners will learn, but all will enjoy *Silent Battleground*.'

—James H. Patton, CAPT USN (Ret)
Technical Advisor, film ***Hunt for Red October***

'*Silent Battleground* is a powerful, compelling novel. Author, D. M. Ulmer, a Navy veteran of 32 years, moves the reader through tense events with skill and expertise using his professional savvy to lace the plot with intrigue and speculation that makes the book a page-turner. Ulmer's rare talent exposes torn loyalty and self-discovery the characters endure. They serve with duty, fear, and vengeance but the human element of love and family challenges them. I found myself believing fiction to be fact.'

—**JR Reynolds**, Author
Sustenance of Courage and Woman of Courage

'Don Ulmer's *Silent Battleground* leaves me breathless at the end of every chapter. Don brings us, realistically, into the shipboard world. His wardroom scenes are so realistic that I found myself there. Don shows us a scenario that very nearly happened. In doing so, he not only gives us a view of professional Navy officers, but opens a rare glimpse into the war-fighters' personal lives–on both sides of a conflict we hope never happens.'

—**Dave Bartholomew**, CAPT USN (Ret)

BEYOND
SILENT BATTLEGROUND

John:

Many thanks for all the good times and invaluable help at most.

Best

Dm

D.M. ULMER

M. Ulmer

BEYOND SILENT BATTLEGROUND

ISBN-13: 978-0-9905724-6-6

Manager Editor, Dari Bradley
Technical Editor, Nelson O. Ottenhausen
Senior Editor, Doris Littlefield
Cover Design by Dari Bradley
Cover Photo USS *Seawolf* (SSN 21) by US Navy

This story is fiction. Use or mention of any historical events, places, names of anyone or any similarity of the storyline to persons, places or events is purely coincidental. However, the story contains true and authentic information about some United States government agencies.

Published by Patriot Media, Inc.

Publishing America's Patriots

P.O. Box 5414
Niceville, FL 32578
United States of America
patriotmediainc.com

Foreword

Nobody writes submarine techno-thrillers better than Don Ulmer, a retired naval submarine officer. Don's career began as an enlisted man aboard USS *Clamagore*, a diesel-electric submarine prior to his selection to the United States Naval Academy. His submarine experience includes seven submarines, both diesel and nuclear, uniquely culminating in command of USS *Clamagore* from 1967-69; the same submarine he earned his original enlisted submarine qualification aboard in 1949.

The mixture of his experiences uniquely qualify Don to write with authority both from the enlisted and the officer's perspective, and the yarns he spins come across as right and true to other submariners, perhaps the harshest of critics of submarine fiction.

Beyond Silent Battleground is a follow-up sequel thriller to his excellent *Silent Battleground*, and continues the story of a limited nuclear and sea war between the Soviet Union and the United States in the waning days of the Cold War to its exciting conclusion. The stories main characters, mostly submariners, are believable in their actions as circumstances take one exciting turn after another.

Anyone interested in a good techno-thriller will find this book to be a compelling and a satisfying read.

—Patrick Householder
Past National Commander,
U.S. Submarine Veterans Inc.

Dedication

For the late Kenyon L. (Bud) Hussey, USMC, a Marine's Marine. His optimism, his courage, and determination in the face of great adversity was inspiring for all who had the good fortune to know Bud. Make a place for us where you have gone, old friend, for we too shall be along.

Acknowledgements

Special Thanks To:

My wife Carol, a pillar of support.

Doris Littlefield, editor extraordinaire who continues to keep me on the straight and narrow.

Patrick Householder, past National Commander, United States. Submarine Veterans, for the kind words in his foreword.

Doris Northstrom, Creative Writer Professor, Bellevue, WA College for her generous imparting of wisdom.

Cindy and Commander Mike McLane respectively for spot on period clothing advice and making sure I got it right.

My son Matthew whose salmon river-fishing prowess and passion for the outdoors brighten the tale immensely.

Captain Jim Patton, USN (Ret.), for unscrambling all the mysteries of nuclear propulsion and inventive tactics for this old diesel boat sailor.

Las Plumas Literary Critique Group of King County, WA for yet another superb review and manuscript comments.

Nelson Ottenhausen, Dari and Ed Bradley for opening my literary door.

Cast of Characters

Anderson, Andy – Leading Torpedoman, *Steelhead*

Anikanov, Yuri – *Zampolit*

Askew, Shrew – Seaman, *Steelhead*

Baknov, Vasiliy – Russian Navy Lieutenant, *Zhukov*

Baylor, Thomas – Canadian posing as a Russian

Bentley, Tom – XO, *Steelhead*

Biddle, Warren – Baknov's fisherman alias

Bintliff, Tom – Commanding Officer, *Steelhead*

Bondini, Benito (Sparks) – Chief Radioman, *Sterlet*

Borkowski, Dmitri – *Kapitan* 1st Rank, Soviet Submarine *Lenin*

Bostwick, Hal – Former CO, *Denver;* Commodore, Bay of Fundy

Bryan, Bill – LT, Engineer Officer, *Steelhead*

Buchanan, James (Jim) – CO, *Denver*

Campbell, Jim – Captain, Woods Hole Oceanic ship, *Drifter*

Coker – Chief Sonarman, *Denver*

Danis, Eric – Rear Admiral, Commands flotilla of Attack and Trident ballistic missile submarines, wife Eve

Dempsey, Andrew – President of the United States

Dewars, Wayne – LTJG, Weapons Officer, *Sterlet*. Weapons Officer &1st LT, *Denver*

Douglass, Bob – XO, *Denver*

Giambri, Phil – Chief Sonarman, *Steelhead*

Harold – Caretaker where Vasily held prisoner

Henri, Jacques – COB, Quartermaster Chief, *Steelhead*

Hussey, Erica – Female environmentalist dubbed *salmon nazi*

Jackson, Warren – Vasiliy Baknov's derelict alias

Maddock, Brent – LT, Executive Officer, *Sterlet* ... CO, *Steelhead*

Manning, Darrel – U.S. Senator and presidential hopeful

Olsen, John (Jack) – Commanding Officer, *Sterlet*, wife Rita

Omensen, Ken – Commodore, Bay of Fundy

Painter, John & Mary Agnes – Terry Painter's parents

Painter, Terry – Torpedoman, Jeep driver

Parnell, Woodruff H. (Woody) – LT, Weapons Officer, *Steelhead*

Patrick, Dan – LCDR Pacific Northwest *Pitstop*

Rubin, Dave – Engineer Officer, *Sterlet*

Sherensky, Andrei – CO of *Tango* damaged by *Denver*, then scuttled

Smith, Al – Chief of the Boat, COB, *Sterlet*

Tania – Russian woman working for Manning

Tom, Dave, & Ron – Men who interrogated Vasiliy

Turgenev, Mikhail – Russian, former navy colleague of Borkowski

Wade, Leo – CDR, Aide to ADM Danis, CNO, Pentagon

Zane, Bea – CNO Liaison Officer, Maddock's ladylove *(then wife)*

Zane, Dave – CAPT, Pacific Northwest *Pitstop*, Bea's father

Introduction

Two years prior, a limited nuclear attack had been unleashed on the United States and survival of the planet hung by a thread. Fortunately, despite frequent United States and Soviet Union heated threat exchanges, the combatants exercised restraint. To the victor belongs the spoils and with no spoils, there could be no victor. Hence the war settled down to a conventional one of attrition.

Opening nuclear attacks took heavy tolls on both Allied and Soviet military facilities, naval bases in particular. This permitted Soviet land forces to quickly occupy Europe and for the most part left submarines to conduct the war at sea.

A major undersea warfare battle in the Bering Sea, the first significant Allied victory, diminished Soviet assets severely, but enough ballistic missile submarines survived to deter further nuclear weapons exchanges. An unknown number of Soviet attack submarines endured to interdict Allied convoys bent on resupplying a depleted Great Britain. Survival of Soviet troops occupying Europe depended upon Britain's isolation.

Experiencing more than enough conflict in the twentieth century, the people on both sides grew tired of war and expressed their dissatisfaction to governing parties. Thus the stage is set for the next conflict.

Who would blink first?

'Is life so dear, or peace so sweet, as to be purchased at the price of chains and slavery?'

—Patrick Henry

Beyond Silent Battleground

Chapter 1

North Pacific off the Washington Coast

Three United States MK 46 torpedoes struck the Soviet attack submarine *Zhukov* and shook her to her very soul.

BOOM. She could survive one hit. *BOOM ... BOOM*, but not the two more that sent her to the seabed.

Only four men escaped from the stricken submarine with no time to don life jackets. Churning arms and legs were all that kept them afloat. This coupled with sea temperatures hovering in the low fifties left little hope of their survival.

Lieutenant Vasiliy Baknov, a Soviet Navy officer, watched three of his fellow survivors from the *Akula*-class, attack-submarine slip away one by one until only he remained. A severely fractured left arm gave him use of only one arm. He knew either exhaustion or hypothermia would probably claim him, and soon, but not before his last bit of energy dissipated. Baknov had good cause to not give up. He survived on an anger that exceeded the fear being brought on by his impending doom.

He hated all things American with a deep passion, and this alone sustained his endurance beyond that of the others.

Lieutenant Baknov's festering hatred fueled his determination to stay afloat in the frigid North Pacific. A major target of Baknov's fury, his father, Yuri, a ballet dancer who defected to America shortly after Vasiliy's birth. Shame brought on the Baknov family by his father's decision plagued Vasiliy throughout his life, most significantly by preventing the young man's acceptance into the Communist Party. His father's death by Vasiliy's own hand would help to ease this raging turmoil.

But another event angered him even more. He believed that U.S. Navy Lieutenant Brent Maddock's hand launched a *Tomahawk* cruise missile against Vladivostok that took the life of the young Russian's mother.

I must remain alive. Maddock can be properly made to pay for his crime only by my hand. And pay he shall. I will track him to the gates of hell if necessary. But find him I shall and he will pay.

Zhukov's commanding officer had made a valiant attempt to save his crew. With the ship's last ounce of strength, he brought her close to the surface by blowing ballast tanks. But not close enough. Decks awash, seawater poured through hatches immediately on opening and quickly flooded the ship. *Zhukov* returned to the seabed where she and the rest of her crew would remain forever.

Saltwater burned Lieutenant Baknov's eyes, but not to the extent it prevented him from seeing a lone fishing boat heading directly toward him. *I must stay afloat a bit longer.*

Waterlogged and barely able to speak, Baknov found himself spread out on the fishing boat fantail. A crewman hovered above him while another entered the cabin to get blankets. His joy over surviving his close brush with death soon succumbed to the intense hatred driving him to search for his father and LT Brent Maddock.

He believed his ability to make these assassinations rested in the hands of his rescuers. *My English is good enough, but there is no doubt my identity will be compromised. Who else could be floating alone out here other than Soviets?*

Baknov feigned unconsciousness until he could work out a plan to prevent being turned over to authorities upon reaching port as this would foil his goal to settle accounts with the two men he hated.

The crewmen wrapped the survivor in blankets, inflicting agony into Baknov's left arm, his injury unknown to them. Baknov gritted his teeth but continued to appear unconscious. They carried him below to the warmth in the cabin.

"We should get him out of these wet clothes," said one.

"Yeah," said the other. "Do you recognize him?"

"Nobody from around Grays Harbor."

"He's wearin' some kind of Navy uniform."

"Nah. I used to be in the Navy. He must be Coast Guard."

The men tucked Baknov into a bunk.

"Guess we better head in and get him some medical attention. How far out do you make us?"

"About five hours. Is it something we should break radio silence for? Maybe we could get a helo out here."

Baknov's spirits sank, and then elevated when he heard one of them say, "Nothing can be done for him ashore that we're not doing here. Last guy that broke silence got his license suspended for two months. I say let's head in. Fishing's been rotten anyway."

Then Baknov came to a grim conclusion. *This boat will reach shore under the cover of darkness and I will be the only passenger.*

He began to reflect on how to make this happen.

Beneath the Arctic Polar Ice Cap

Commanding Officer (CO) Jack Olsen, short and heavyset with premature loss of graying black hair, sat in the ship's wardroom behind a cup of coffee, alone. His nuclear-powered submarine USS *Sterlet*, a *Skipjack*-class, passed the final days of a long deployment and his crew yearned to be home. With the worst of the patrol over, tension among the crew had diminished to almost non-existent. Nonetheless, Olsen could barely manage his anxiety.

Their New London, Connecticut base, destroyed by a nuclear exchange between the United States and the Soviet Union, saw the loss of most dependents and friends of *Sterlet* crewmen. A war that Olsen considered pointless had wiped out every major naval base on both American coasts.

Fortunately, both sides realized the futility of a massive nuclear world-ending exchange, as something to win must remain for the war to have a purpose. Most wives and families fortunate enough to be out of the original targeted areas rejoined their husbands and fathers, relocating with them to temporary submarine bases. Others simply had enough and took up inland dwelling as far from both coasts as possible.

Sterlet would homeport with accommodations by Canada at the Bay of Fundy, located in the northeastern end of the Gulf of Maine between the provinces of Nova Scotia and New Brunswick.

Olsen envied his crew's resiliency. He thought, *Submariners know how to suck it up.* He was on a Pacific patrol in the 688-class USS *Denver* when the idiocy erupted.

On the heels of a regular overhaul in Bremerton, Washington, Olsen's wife with their two children flew to her parents' home in Illinois, unknowingly in time to escape the Pacific Coast attack, but they had returned to Fundy in time for Olsen's return.

He could only speculate on the feelings of his men not fortunate enough to have surviving families, but forced these thoughts from his head.

What's done is done; there's no turning back now. It's what lies ahead that counts. I gotta save my energy for that.

Executive Officer Brent Maddock's arrival stirred Olsen from his reverie.

"Looking pretty comfy, Captain. Must not be doing my job. I'm supposed to give you things to worry about."

The wardroom or officers' mess, like other spaces in the ship, served multiple purposes: meals, conferences, coffee breaks and recreation. Not well appointed, but it did have a large table topped with green billiard cloth and room enough for the entire complement of eight officers.

"I can find plenty of my own, thank you," said Olsen. "A big one is, we've wandered around here for six weeks on nothing but dead reckoning, and gyrocompasses don't work worth a damn at these high latitudes. Do we have any idea of where the hell we are?"

Maddock could afford to be glib. Both officers served together in *Denver,* Olsen as exec and Maddock as weapons officer.

Brent Maddock stood above his peers in command presence. Navy lean, bright blue eyes, five-eleven and tipping the scales at one hundred seventy pounds.

"Way I see it, Captain, all we have to do is head south."

Olsen asked, "How do we figure out which way that is?"

Grinning at his skipper, Maddock replied, "From the North Pole, there's only one direction … south. And isn't that the way we want to go? Just keep the BQS-fourteen running. When we're out of ice, surface and find out where we are with my sextant."

"Yeah, Brent. How do we know the south we're taking ends up in the Atlantic and not the Pacific?"

"I have a suggestion, Captain. How 'bout a game of cribbage to decide that? You're an east coaster and I'm from the other one. Whoever wins, that's where we'll be."

The words had scarcely left Maddock's mouth when a deafening explosion shook *Sterlet* to her very soul.

Lights flickered as the vital busses automatically transferred to the battery-powered Ship Service Motor Generators (SSMG) from steam-powered Ship Service Turbine Generators (SSTG). Downside of this, SSMGs place heavy demand on the main storage battery's limited capacity.

Both the skipper and exec sprang to their feet and raced to the attack center, where they saw crewmen in various states of disarray, but all recovering and still at their stations: helm, diving planes, ballast control panel, conning officer and chief of the watch, all in complete control. Stress is the enemy of good decision making and submariners survive by that axiom.

Olsen demanded, "What've we got?"

LTJG Wayne Dewars, conning officer, replied in a steady voice despite his churning stomach, "Probable torpedo strike, Captain, and whoever's shooting at us is damn close. The explosion came just seconds after sonar reported a torpedo inbound aft."

Aft told Olsen the torpedo approached directly astern and was masked by *Sterlet*'s rudders and propellers, in the *baffles*.

The 7MC interrupted. "Flooding in the engine room through the shaft seal! Everything is busted up back here. Unconscious troops were moved to the Auxiliary Machine Space (AMS). Better get Doc back here."

"Doc's on the way," Olsen replied … then added, "Nice job." He turned to Chief of the Boat, Al Smith and ordered, "COB, take a walk through the boat and tell the troops what we know. And add that we're working up a plan and will let everybody know soon as it's doped out."

Officially COB, Smith presently performed chief of the watch duty. "Aye, Captain. Soon as I can get a relief."

Olsen pressed the 7MC talk button. "Maneuvering. Lock the shaft and inflate the shaft boot seal. Report what you know when you know it. Check for flooding other than through the seal."

The captain didn't have to identify himself because everyone aboard recognized his voice.

"Aye, Captain."

Maddock jumped in. "Sounding!"

Dewars replied, "Hundred thirty feet beneath the keel and damn good thing it's that close 'cause that's where we're going."

With the main propeller shaft locked, speed could not be used to maintain depth.

Staring at his skipper's face, Dewars asked, "Blow all main ballast, Captain?"

The captain took an instant to assess this action then said, "No. Our chances are better on the bottom. We're more stable there."

At Prospective Commanding Officer School, Olsen learned that blowing ballast lowers the ship's center of buoyancy. *This likely will roll it sideways against the ice pack underside.* Opening ballast tank vents in that configuration would prevent air release, leaving the ship stuck there unable to re-submerge and recover. *Sterlet*'s stern settled first due to the partially flooded engine room.

Maddock seized the 1MC and said, "Stand by for collision with the bottom! All hands find something to hang on to." Sensing the crew's anxiety and wishing to better it, he added, "For now, we're under control."

Sterlet's descent accelerated toward the ocean floor. On impact, the 252-foot, 3,100-ton submarine shook more violently than she did from the torpedo strike. She rolled five degrees to starboard then came to rest.

Olsen took the 1MC and said, "We're good. All compartments report leaks to the attack center." He then shifted to the 7MC. "Maneuvering, Captain. Report engine room situation."

"Captain, shaft boot seal is holding. Two feet of water over lower level engine room (LLER) deck plates."

U.S. Temporary Submarine Base, Washington Coast

Rear Admiral Eric Danis and a recently promoted Lieutenant Woody Parnell huddled over coffees in Danis's palatial yacht turned submarine flotilla flagship. Moored in a temporary base on the northwest Washington coast, the yacht had been donated by a citizen who now had no use for it. The sudden and destructive war between the United States and the Soviet Union made recreational use of the Pacific inadvisable.

A tall slender man, Danis had premature gray hair and matching gray eyes that could bore through a person, yet show compassion. He commanded a combined flotilla of Attack and Trident ballistic missile submarines and their repair support facilities.

Danis said to the young officer, "I see the weight of that extra stripe on your cuff hasn't affected your cup-lifting ability, Woody."

Parnell grinned. "After selection, I did a lot of pushups to get ready, Admiral."

His early selection to full lieutenant did not diminish Woody's cherubic expression. He regarded his boss through baby-blue eyes that sat beneath a bush of reddish-blond hair.

Small talk always preceded the broach of main topics and this one had run its course so the admiral said, "Your tour on *Denver* has only started, but you've been promoted out of a job."

Parnell had received a Purple Heart and Navy Cross for bravery during a dangerous operation while assigned to *Denver* and skipped lieutenant junior grade in an accelerated promotion.

"I know it's early," Danis said, "but I'm nominating you for weapons officer of a fast attack."

Butterflies took flight in Parnell's stomach. He believed at least three years would pass before getting this assignment.

Woody exclaimed, "Wow!"

Nothing else escaped his lips.

"You're a hot tactics guy, Woody. Inventive, which you know is in short supply. There's been too many distractions over the past few years and we let war-fighting slip to a lesser priority."

The admiral admired the young officer and considered him a breath of fresh air in the submarine community.

Woody had heard the admiral go on about this before. Much had muddied the waters prior to this deadly conflict with the Russians. Inventive guys tended not to be among top class standers so were left arbitrarily by the wayside. Parnell, one of a few, also fulfilled selection criteria for nuclear propulsion training.

Danis believed that political correctness had also taken its toll. *Recently, red-hot skippers were fired on the spot for the manner in which they ran their ships, tactical excellence hardly even a priority. Not much good comes from war, but at least it forces attention back on the right track.* A good sailor, Danis chose not to share this particular feeling except on rare occasions with his wife Eve.

"There's now a new problem we gotta belly up to, Woody. Good intelligence tells us Soviet boomers hide under the Arctic ice cap. They find open water then *icepick* themselves close to overhead ice. Lying motionless against the ice makes it impossible for our ADCAP torpedoes to discern them from nearby ice ridges. Quiet as hell up there, the impulse from our launchers can be heard for a country mile. When they hear it, look for 'em to kick it in the ass and get outta Dodge. We gotta make them rethink that."

"What's the plan, Admiral?"

"Sea Lance … rocket-propelled long-range submarine-launched missiles that can air-drop Mark-fifty torpedoes into a target area."

"I'm listening, sir. But Mark-fifties are torpedoes and have the same problem … and even Sea Lance requires a launcher transit."

"Two things. We'll replace the Mark-fifty with a high explosive impact-detonated warhead that goes off when it hits the ice. It's not enough to sink a submarine, but more than likely send it home to get fixed. Maybe enough to make the Russians give up on *ice picking.*"

"But what about the launch noise?"

"I said two things. We have a new gimmick, a Turbine Pump Ejection System (TPES) developed by a Navy lab in New England. You're going there and figure out how to get it into a *Sturgeon*-class *Six-thirty-seven*."

"Begging the admiral's pardon, but how am I going to do that?"

"If I had an answer, I'd go myself. Besides, I hear the war hasn't hurt the New England lobster fishing any, so consider this a favor."

Beneath the Arctic Polar Ice Cap

Olsen ordered all officers and leading chief petty officers to the wardroom for a council of war.

Limited capacity of their hundred twenty-six cell battery drove Olsen to order the chief of the watch, "Secure all equipment not necessary at this time. That means just about everything."

Captain Olsen and the others went forward to the wardroom and seated themselves about the table behind cups of what remained of the day's coffee.

Silence prevailed for a brief moment in *Sterlet*'s wardroom. All waited for the captain's remarks.

"Gentlemen, we're between a rock and a hard place. None of us has been in this situation before, so don't hold back." He cast what he hoped to be a reassuring glance around the table and wished the churning in his stomach matched the calm demeanor with which he spoke. "Best place to start is at the beginning. There are no dumb ideas. For openers, we're sitting on the bottom at three hundred feet under thicker ice than we can punch through. Our only source of power is a limited capacity battery. For mobility, we have the Secondary Propulsion Motor (SPM) but can expect no more than two to three knots from it and only for an hour or so. I'm guessing we can re-ballast to compensate for whatever water we can't get out of the engine room. That right, Dave?"

The captain had addressed Dave Rubin, *Sterlet* engineer officer, a slender man whose uniform hung about him like a sack.

"Preliminary numbers say yes," Dave replied. Tired brown eyes and disheveled black hair painted the portrait of an exhausted man.

"Good," said Olsen. "Now comes the easy part. What's the best way to use what we have left to get the hell out of here? We'll need an SSMG on line to do that. What's the prognosis of having that?"

Rubin replied, "I don't have that answer right now, Captain. Give me about an hour."

Olsen grinned at Rubin. He recognized the great load borne by the officer at so young an age. The skipper then attempted levity to loosen the grip of everyone's circumstance.

"Make that half an hour. That's why you get the big bucks."

Brent Maddock said, "You nailed it, Captain. Limited endurance is the driver. To increase it, we need access to the atmosphere. I say pick ourselves off the bottom with variable and main ballast, rig out the *outboard* and look for the thinnest ice we can find. We could even find open water."

Rubin asked, "And what if we don't?"

Maddock replied, "Use half of our capacity to search. If no open water, use the remaining capacity to return to the thinnest ice we've encountered in our search. Then try to punch up through it."

The others present exchanged skeptical glances.

"*Skipjack*-class *Five-eighty-fives* are not configured to punch through ice," Rubin countered. "The sail isn't hardened and we can't point the sail planes straight up."

Maddock replied, "I agree, Dave. But look at it this way. We can improve our chances with the planes at full rise. Even if we beat up the topside and still punch through, we'll have air to run the diesel and recharge the battery. It's not necessary to get the planes above the ice. They'll come to rest against it."

"A problem here, Captain," said Dave. The bridge access hatch is below the sail-planes' level. If they stop under the ice, the hatch will be under water."

"But not the snorkel mast," Maddock explained. "This lets us recharge the battery and move on. Maybe find open water or ice thin enough for the sail planes to poke through."

Nodding tentative agreement, Rubin asked. "But how long can we keep this up?"

Olsen replied, "As long as we have to. Once above the ice, we'll stay there and radio for help via the most secure mode we have."

The captain looked about his officers and chief petty officers then asked, "Comments? Recommendations?"

Brent Maddock said, "Don't recall if I read this somewhere, or if somebody told me, but the whole ice pack is floating and ten percent is above water. This means if the surrounding pack is ten feet thick then one to two feet thick polynya ice should be above water and bulged upward. The sail planes still won't break through, but it might be enough to put the bridge access trunk just above water."

The captain responded, "Well, at least it's something to hang our hats on. Anything else?"

"Yes," Maddock replied. "How likely is it that whoever shot at us will do it again?"

Silent glances took place around the wardroom.

"If I can answer my own question … he sure'n hell can't find us while we sit on the bottom. And with any kind of luck at all, the ice pack will move him away from us." Seeing uneasy expressions on the others, Brent added, "Look, guys, it's no disgrace to be afraid. Anyone who's not scared as hell has something wrong with him. Big thing is … don't let it stampede us into doing something dumb."

Maddock believed his last remarks necessary though preferably from the captain who remained silent.

Olsen scanned the other faces and heard no further comments then turning, he addressed his leading radioman, "Chief, we'll likely need a new antenna, so put the big think on how you'll do that."

To his engineer officer, Olsen said, "Very well then, Dave, get us ready to lift off the bottom and let me know when that is. Power's running out, so sooner is better." Then to Maddock, "XO, explain our plan to the crew. Leave the impression our chances of getting out of here are good. I'm going aft to check on the injured troops."

Chapter 2

North Pacific off the Washington Coast

In one of the two bunks inside the cramped fishing boat's cabin, Vasiliy Baknov continued to feign unconsciousness, waiting for an opportunity to present itself. A short man with penetrating blue eyes and curly golden hair, his superb physical condition had sustained him through his recent ordeal in the ocean.

The vessel's crew, comprised of an older and a younger man, guided their boat across open sea toward what Vasiliy construed to be their home port. In a conversation he overheard, the older man estimated they would reach port in five hours. Baknov had to take action and soon.

Like an answered prayer, although the Russian believed in no deity, the older man came down into the cabin, climbed into an adjacent bunk and pulled a blanket over himself.

Soon heavy snoring convinced Baknov the man slept soundly, a cue for the Russian to commence action. Waiting five minutes until the man's snoring became regular, Baknov climbed from his bunk, removed a fire extinguisher from the bulkhead and crashed its butt down on the sleeping man's skull.

Blood trickled onto the pillow. Baknov sought the man's pulse at the carotid artery and found none. He looked about the cabin, found a large knife and went to the pilot deck where he found the younger man seated on a stool, monitoring the autopilot as the boat plied through moderate waves toward home.

The man exclaimed, "Well hello! It's good to see you up and about," the last words he would ever speak.

Baknov approached without saying anything and plunged the knife into the young man's heart. He then dragged both bodies aft and searched them. He'd need money and identification in order to travel in America, and found ample amounts of both in the pockets of his victims.

First, he removed the younger man's clothing then weighted the murdered crew with net anchors and dropped them into the sea.

He said, "I do regret sending my rescuers to their graves in this manner, but I have no choice. There is important work I must do."

Vasiliy went to the pilothouse and secured the engine. *I must not make landfall till after dark.* He looked at a worn sea chart and discerned the autopilot guided the ship toward Westport on the northwest Washington coast. He removed his uniform and donned the young man's clothing after cleaning the shirt of blood as best he could then weighted his uniform and dropped it into the sea as well.

Now to devise a plan. First, get safely ashore. Next, delay people from getting knowledge of my crime for as long as possible. Then blend in with the Americans.

When Vasiliy studied the chart, he saw a breakwater protruding westward from the town of Westport. *But how to find it after dark? Surely in this wartime situation aids to navigation lights and radio beacons are extinguished. I need to find the breakwater during the daylight hours and remain in sight of it till twilight. Then I have to proceed with caution to arrive precisely at dark.*

Then what? Yes. Load my clothes into a plastic bag, set the autopilot for due west, abandon ship and head for shore. It'll be days, possibly weeks before anyone becomes suspicious and by then I'll be long gone.

Baknov reckoned Westport to be south of his position based on what had been set into the autopilot. *But how long has this boat been at sea? Dead reckoning navigation deteriorates as a function of time. Head east and when land is sighted, run parallel to it in a southerly heading and look for the breakwater. Once sighted, use the remaining daylight to measure the effect of ocean current.*

An hour passed and a landfall appeared on the horizon. Baknov initiated his plan. After two hours, he began to wonder. *Nothing yet. Is it possible the breakwater is north of here?* Then a gap on the coast told him he had found the approach to Westport. Through binoculars, he spotted the breakwater that confirmed his assumption.

After nightfall and upon reaching the breakwater, he set the boat on a westerly heading, jumped into the sea with a plastic bag full of dry clothing and in a few moments, stood for his first time on American soil. Baknov had concluded the first part of his plan.

Now comes the easy part. Find Lieutenant Maddock and my father and see to them. He dried off, dressed and made his way over the rocky breakwater to the town of Westport.

Beneath the Arctic Polar Ice Cap

Jack Olsen spoke privately with Brent Maddock in the captain's stateroom. "Brent, I've pretty much got this all thought out, but want to run it by another set of eyes."

Olsen had not devised a plan but did not wish to reveal this to his exec. He hoped Maddock would have one.

Brent tried without success to lighten the mood. "Must be deep thoughts, Captain. But you always get it right the first time. I've seen you go all the way through a wooden pencil with absolutely no wear on the eraser."

Both men knew the situation had no precedent. No books written on the subject so everything had to come from between their ears.

Olsen said, "Dave Rubin paints a grim picture. Shafts of both SSMGs are bent and cannot be straightened. We can't turn the main propeller shaft so the reactor is useless to us. All of a sudden, we're a diesel-electric submarine."

Maddock nodded but continued in his attempt to get his skipper to stop worrying and start doing. "Diesel boats were around a lot longer than us nukes, and they worked. So why not us?"

"Has a diesel boat ever gone under the ice, much less bottomed under it?"

"Not that I know of, Captain. But they left us with one helluva legacy. Innovation."

"Why doesn't this make me feel all that good?"

"It shouldn't. I'm groping around for a solution."

"Are you implying I'm not?"

Maddock winced. For a while, he watched a gradual decline in Olsen's self-confidence and the troubling effects of his jangled nerves. They had once sailed together in *Denver* under a ruthless commanding officer, Captain Hal Bostwick, who observed but one priority: his own rapid climb up the ladder.

Serving as *Denver*'s executive officer, Olsen had been nearly harangued out of the Navy by Bostwick. However, Olsen's personal courage, an order of magnitude greater than his skipper's, enabled the exec to stand firm when it really mattered. Bostwick had wished to avoid a dangerous assignment given to *Denver* and demanded Olsen's assistance. After knuckling under to every prior command edict, Olsen got his back up and refused to assist Bostwick. Sensing a damaging post-action report by his exec upon return from patrol, Bostwick yielded, but not before accusing Olsen of being in cahoots with Brent Maddock.

Bostwick concluded, "Okay, you bastard, let me see the damn attack plan. But remember, and you pass this along to that arrogant running mate of yours, the Navy lasts a long time and if we survive this, I'll be well positioned to make you both damn sorry."

Delivering on his promise, Bostwick transferred ashore to the Bureau of Naval Personnel submarine detail desk and had his former adversaries assigned to the oldest submarine in the fleet. His alleged comment upon issuing the orders, 'Serves them right. The bastards deserve each other.'

Olsen, better cut out for engineering duty ashore, began showing accumulated stress from combined tours aboard *Denver* and *Sterlet*.

Maddock replied, "Not at all, Captain. I'm just trying to get our heads together and figure out how we get out of here. We owe it to the crew. Remember when you were a JG? The captain had all the right answers, so no one worried. That's where we are now. And we are doing things right. We don't let any panic drive us into making bad decisions."

The tone of their meeting reflected this.

A frequent question from people with no military experience on hearing of these events: *How can you be so calm with the whole world crashing down around you?* The question has a simple answer: *That's what we trained to do. And when you think about it, what other choice do we have?*

Olsen said, "We need a plan to save the ship, right? Should be pretty easy. Diesel boats sitting on the bottom under ten feet of ice with a near depleted battery always make it home."

The skipper recognized his unintended sarcasm and immediately regretted it.

Maddock fielded the remark carefully. "We'll get all we can out of what we got. Everything's been secured ... galley stoves, space heaters and hot-water heaters. Just now, no one's much worried about hot food and showers. Plenty of cold cuts for sandwiches."

Olsen read his exec's tone and body language and attempted to get a grip on himself. "Brent, do you have any idea how it feels to be skipper and about to lose your ship?"

"Yes, Captain. But given the option, getting the crew home safely makes the most sense. They come first. If we can save the ship too ... good. But priority goes to saving the crew."

Olsen regained his composure somewhat. "Save the crew. Of course. For theirs and the country's sake. *Sterlet*'s only months from the scrap yard. Experienced submariners are in greater demand than she is. If we have to lose *Sterlet*, so be it."

"Agree, Captain. If we can get enough of the ship above ice, figure out where we are and then get a few Chinook helicopters headed this way—"

Rubin's knock on the CO's door interrupted their conversation.

"Ready in all respects to lift off the bottom, Captain."

The three officers walked to the attack center, while yet another thought struck Olsen's solar plexus. *What if she doesn't lift?*

U.S. Temporary Submarine Base, Washington Coast

Lieutenant Woody Parnell gathered up his belongings and rode a jeep to a bus stop near the base.

A torpedoman driver, silver dolphins glistening from atop the breast pocket of his blue jumper, asked, "Where you headed, sir?"

Submariners referred to all officers as mister provided they knew his surname, otherwise, sir, except for their commanding officer. He alone earned the coveted title, Captain.

"To the other coast. Or what's left of it."

The driver knew of New London, Connecticut's appalling fate, so made no mention of it. Every U.S. Navy submariner received a significant amount of his training there; New London had become a de facto home port for every U.S. sailor who plies the undersea.

Despite being appalled by what happened there, memories recall the tired New England town which seemed not to have changed its personality since 13 October 1915, when the monitor USS *Ozark*, a submarine tender, and four submarines arrived in New London. The base eventually became a sort of submariner alma mater.

Some considered its destruction a deliberate Soviet measure to demoralize the U.S. Submarine Force. It did not—as the Russians recently learned in the Battle of the Bering Sea.

Parnell added, "Everything's ultra-secret these days, but you look like a safe enough bet. I'm headed for a Navy Laboratory in New England." The driver, a torpedoman logically interested in new launchers, Woody shared what he learned from RADM Danis, "I'm told it's quiet as a church mouse."

"That so?" the driver said. "Last I heard, the amount of energy required to accelerate a two-ton object to forty feet per second hasn't changed unless Newton's laws of motion have been repealed."

"What's your point?"

"How do you keep a burst of energy that big quiet?"

Parnell surmised, *This guy's mind tells me there's a lotta of good stuff ahead for him.* "Dunno. Guess that's why I'm being sent there … to find out."

When they reached the bus terminal, they saw several sailors milling about.

"Lucky guys," the driver said, and then added, "Going home, or to what's left of it. Will you be passing through Chicago, sir?"

"I haven't looked at the route yet, but it's highly probable."

The driver wrote a phone number on a piece of paper. "If you get a few minutes there, would you mind calling my mom and tell her I'm okay."

Parnell took it. "Be pleased to. What name shall I use?"

"Oh, yeah. Terry, sir … Terry Painter."

"Good to meet you, Painter. Parnell here. Keep on hitting the books. Based on what you've shown me in fifteen minutes, I think you can be much more useful to the Navy than stuffing torpedoes into launchers."

"Thank-you, Mister Parnell."

Had Painter's smile been any wider, it would have engulfed him.

Humbling to serve with such outstanding troops, Parnell mused.

The bus meandered south along the coast on U.S. Route 101, taking back roads to Portland, Oregon. The U.S. Army had seized Interstate 5, the west coast's main north-south artery, for exclusive military use.

A brief stop in Aberdeen permitted Parnell and several sailors an occasion to get coffee and a sandwich. When they re-boarded, a lone civilian joined them and sat inconspicuously in a rear seat.

Self-conscious, Parnell thought. *He's young enough for military service and likely doesn't want to explain why he's still a civilian.*

The bus departed Washington State via Astoria-Megler Bridge. From there it paralleled the Columbia River east on U.S. 30 through a host of sleepy farms that had been there over a hundred years.

That's what I'm going to do when this damn war is over. Farm. Maybe even here. Parnell recalled lines from a U.S. Civil War song, *"When brooks are overflowing, I'll be hooking up the plow,"* thus the hook had been set.

Their ancient bus wheezed to a stop before Portland's Union Pacific Station. Parnell picked up his bag and in sheep-flock style followed his fellow travelers to the ticket office. There, the clerk removed one copy from each transfer order stack and issued one-way tickets to each sailor's ordered destination.

A civilian passenger who had joined them in Aberdeen waited until last and paid for his ticket in cash. Parnell overheard him state Chicago as his destination. A sense told Parnell he had attracted the civilian's attention.

Seconds later, Woody found a seat and soon afterward, the man pointed to the adjacent one and asked, "Is this taken? If not, may I?"

"Of course." Parnell extended his hand. "I'm Woody Parnell."

The man took it. "I'm Warren Biddle. I noticed you were on the bus that brought me here from Aberdeen. I guess you're from the submarine base up north."

Parnell had developed a defensive attitude toward revealing what he didn't have to, especially to people he didn't know. But in this instance, in the purview of Biddle, where else could Parnell possibly have come from? Denying it would make him look stupid.

"Right, Warren. How 'bout you?" Then with just a trace of sarcasm, added, "Aberdeen. Right?"

"Actually, no. Westport. I work on a fishing boat. Or that is, I did until the damn war started. Dangerous out there. I don't know which scares me most, Russkis or the Coast Guard."

"Sorry about that, Warren. You don't get trouble from us Navy guys, do you?"

"So far, no. But I worry you might mistake us for someone else and start shooting or whatever it is you do these days."

Woody thought, *Seems like a good head*, then asked, "Where you headed, Warren?"

"Chicago. How 'bout you?"

"Don't think the Navy would be too happy with me for sharing that. Is east good enough?"

"I thought that when we pulled out of the station. And to answer your question, east is okay. Hey. I know this is kind of off the wall, but you being from the submarine base, thought I'd ask. Met a submariner coupla months ago in an Aberdeen bar. Ever come across an officer named Brent Maddock?"

Beneath the Arctic Polar Ice Cap

COB Al Smith, tall, slender and dark-haired, manned the ballast control panel, heart of the operation to lift *Sterlet* off the bottom. He earned this assignment by being steady and decisive.

The diving officer of the watch, Dave Rubin, began to counsel Smith, "Dammit, Chief, if I order you to do something that's not right, don't do it and tell me why. This is no time for protocol."

"Aye, sir," Smith replied in a tone that said that's what he would do whether Rubin had ordered it or not. They plowed new ground and Smith planned to leave nothing to chance.

Rubin ordered, "Start with auxiliaries. Pump both to sea. We'll find out pretty quick if we need fore and aft trim."

Smith responded, "Pumping auxiliaries to sea, sir."

"Very well. Report on the thousands."

"On the thousands, aye. One … two … three." Smith noted the depth gauge did not budge and said, "Recommend shifting the pump to negative, Mister Rubin. There's not enough left in the *auxes* to get us off the floor."

The skipper and exec stood quietly, signaling their approval for what happened.

Rubin said, "Make it so, COB. Keep reporting thousands."

"Thousands, aye sir." Smith began at one. When he reached eleven, worried frowns spread about the attack center, including on Olsen and Maddock.

"Fourteen ... fifteen ... we're moving! Secure pumping," Smith directed, not waiting for Rubin's order.

The sound level from the collective sighs of relief would have alerted any listening sonar within fifty miles.

Sterlet rose twenty feet off the bottom.

Rubin ordered, "Rig out SPM, train zero-zero-zero and activate."

Eyes shifted to the pitometer log measuring speed through the water in nautical miles per hour.

The needle flickered then moved, one knot, two and settled at two and a half.

A chorus of *yahoos* rose in the attack center and quickly spread throughout the ship by men bundled up in as much clothing as they could find. With electrical heaters secured, temperatures hovered near freezing.

"Make your depth one-zero-zero feet."

"We're rising by the bow, Mister Rubin. Recommend moving a thousand from after to forward trim," spoke the COB's steady voice.

"Make it so, Chief."

Olsen told Wayne Dewars to relieve Rubin. The skipper wished to know what endurance remained and how to best exploit it. He needed his chief engineer for that.

"Okay, Brent, take charge of the overhead ice survey."

Entering the sonar shack, Maddock found the operations going better than had he ordered it himself.

"We'll have a look every five minutes. Leaving the BQS-fourteen on continuously is a power drainer."

Maddock asked, "What's been the average?"

"Ten feet on top, Mister Maddock."

"How thick and what's the frequency of thin spots?"

"As low as two feet, sir, and almost an hour between them."

Maddock guessed they had forty-five minutes remaining battery at best. Moving water around with trim pumps burns a lot of can.

And we needed the drain pump to push the flooded engine room water out against a hundred forty pounds of sea pressure. He concluded, *If we get out of here, it'll be a miracle.* He recalled the series of miracles needed to bring *Denver* safely home from her first war patrol. *Maybe we're not out of 'em just yet.*

Upon reaching the wardroom, Maddock found his skipper and chief engineer wearing the grimmest expressions he'd ever seen.

Olsen said, "We've completed taking battery specific gravities. Fifteen minutes remaining. Twenty at most."

"Okay. I'm back to sonar. We'll take a look and hit the thinnest ice we find."

Speechless, Olsen nodded his assent.

Maddock reached sonar and with a trace of edge on his voice, demanded, "How thick?"

An anxious sonarman replied, "Ten feet."

"What's the thinnest you've seen?"

"Three feet, Mister Maddock. Five minutes ago. You said look for two feet."

Without responding, Maddock went to the attack center, ordered the conning officer to reverse course then returned to sonar.

A measure of steadiness returned to Maddock's voice. "Okay, guys, let's find the three-foot spot. We're headed back that way."

Joining them in the sonar shack, Olsen addressed Maddock. "I sent Dave on a walk through the boat to secure everything we don't need. First thing, lighting." The ship subsisted on battery-powered battle lanterns. "Then listening sonar."

This sounded more like an order than a statement to Maddock. *Skipper's back in the game.*

"Secure the BQR."

Four minutes crept by like an exhausted snail climbing a pole as four pairs of eyes glued themselves to the BQS-14 display.

His voice crackling with anxiety, a sonarman exclaimed, "I think I see it!"

"Recommend stop the ship, Captain. We can coast to it from here and it'll save us a few amps."

Olsen went to the darkened attack center and gave the order. "Reverse SPM position and stop motor."

"Aye, Captain."

Wayne Dewars carried out the order.

Sterlet coasted to a stop beneath a sizable overhead patch of three-foot ice.

Olsen conferred with his exec. "We gotta get this right first time, Brent. Had only one class in this at PCO School, but I paid attention. Buoy ourselves by pumping auxiliaries to sea. Stop pumping soon as we're moving upward. Don't want to have too much buoyancy when we make contact or we might roll over instead of punching through. Then increase pressure on the ice with short bursts of air in the ballast tanks. Okay, let's do it!"

Maddock thought, *Hot damn. The captain's the captain again.*

Chapter 3

Bureau of Naval Personnel, Washington, D.C.

Captain Hal Bostwick sat behind his LMD-4L (large mahogany desk-4 legs) at the Chief of Naval Personnel office. His passion to make flag rank (commodore) now rested on the verge of fulfillment. The selection board had reached its findings and would report out on Friday evening—this day by design to permit disappointed non-designees a weekend to drown their sorrows.

Hal Bostwick collected an owed favor from a board member who quietly let Hal's cat out of the bag. Bostwick's immediate concern: where to be posted. Plush jobs often proved blind alleys that also included splendid quarters, prestige, and early but nicely conducted retirement ceremonies. He felt he must avoid those like the plague and thought, *But what better springboard than the Bureau of Personnel.*

Most line officers climbed the promotion ladder on the strength of leadership and demonstrated abilities to hone their ship's combat efficiency to a fine edge. But no large organization is immune from politics, however lofty its mission statement. The famous German Chief of Staff Karl von Clausewitz recognized this and made provisions to abate it in his personal philosophy; *All soldiers fall into a matrix: ambitious, lazy, intelligent and stupid. The intelligent-lazies make excellent field officers. The lazy-stupids are perfect ground troops, but the intelligent-ambitious are destined to be generals. The ambitious-stupids, however, are dangerous and must be taken out and shot immediately.* But in Germany enough ambitious-stupids fell through the cracks to create chaos in that country's future.

The U.S. Navy is not immune to this syndrome.

Bostwick could not be termed as stupid. But with demonstrated weakness in submarine warfare knowledge, he chose to pursue a career in this field. Extremely ambitious—this combination could be argued to a degree as fitting Clausewitz's *ambitious-stupid* criteria.

Bostwick knew that organizations require political structure to function, regardless of any high-intended purpose and despite well-intentioned regulations human beings enforce, or in some cases fail to enforce. His uncanny talent to identify weaknesses among those positioned to advance his career enabled his rapid ascent of the promotion ladder. He found it easy to gain *owed favors* from senior officers if he had the *goods* on them. He had used this technique on members of his selection board with obvious success.

He also knew the most solid ladder rung for him would be a posting to a frontline operational billet. Lack of required skills did not deter him for Bostwick had become an expert in extorting these from subordinates. *I'll just pull the strings I need to get posted as commander of the submarine group newly assigned to the Canadian Bay of Fundy.*

Beneath the Arctic Polar Ice Cap

Though none of the crew had ever been a party to pushing 3500 tons of submarine through three feet of ice before, the attack center watch personnel sprang into action like a well-oiled machine. Basics upon which submariners survive kicked in—training, experience, and if that should fall short, inventiveness.

U.S. Navy surface forces travel in battle groups, and someone is always nearby to ask, or borrow things from. Not so beneath the waves where survival depends on supplies loaded prior to departure, including substance between the crew's ears. Thus, hopes elevated for success in getting out of this apparent impossible situation.

Chief Smith, aware the hull expands as a function of decreasing depth resulting in increased positive buoyancy, checked *Sterlet*'s rate of ascent by incremental reflooding of auxiliary tanks.

Olsen and Maddock admired his touch and seeing he needed no advice, neither gave any.

Smith ordered the sail planes to full dive.

The planesman questioned, "Full dive?"

Grateful their probable stupid question came from a crewman, both Olsen and Maddock wondered the same thing.

"Trailing edges are sharper than the leading," Smith replied. "Makes it easier for them to poke through."

Sterlet's rate of ascent slowed to a rate that made the upper fairwater ice contact barely noticeable. His perfect batting average made it obvious he should remain in charge.

Olsen said, "Nice job, Chief. What now?"

"Recommend hold here a few minutes to see if we record any roll. Barring that, empty variable tanks slow and even. That should push hard enough against the ice to where we begin to penetrate it."

Maddock added, "Good plan, Chief. We'll need main ballast to finish the job, though. But first, get us wedged in good and tight to reduce roll probability when we start the blow."

Olsen agreed. "We need to get a snorkel up soonest. Atmosphere in here getting so thick we can soon float in it." Power reduction effort included minimization of ventilation and heating equipment, making all feel as if wrapped in a cold, damp blanket. "How far we gotta go for that?"

Smith studied Maddock a second. The chief had no wish to tell the captain, *three feet of ice, three feet to go.*

Maddock fielded the captain's question diplomatically. "Keel depth four-seven feet should do it, Captain."

"Can we get there by just pumping variable ballast?"

"The sixty-four thousand dollar question."

"Let's get started then."

Chief Smith ordered pumping variables while every pair of eyes in the attack center stared at the depth gauge. For a while *Sterlet* remained motionless. Then a groaning sound from above signaled the ship had begun to punch her way through.

Blowing main ballast without inducing a roll moment became the tough part. Chief Smith ordered a series of five-second blows to all tanks simultaneously until more groans from above announced the ice pack began to yield. Smith nevertheless continued with short blows. *If it's working, stay with it.*

All eyes in the attack center stayed fixed upon the depth gauge to see if it would show any movement at all, severity of frowns in proportion. Even Smith's brow began to furrow as he reckoned the ballast tanks had been blown almost dry. Then prayers in the minds of all in *Sterlet* received a simultaneous answer. A resounding *crash* from above signaled the fairwater had broken through. Audible sighs of relief could be heard throughout the ship.

Olsen said, "Up number one periscope," sounding more like a question than order as he scanned Maddock's face.

Brent nodded and the huge Monel shaft hissed up from its well.

Lowering the handles, Olsen pressed an eye to the lower optics and looked into an Arctic twilight.

This time he sought Maddock's advice by asking, "Raise the snorkel mast, XO?"

"Do it, Captain."

Chief Smith opened the control valve and a smooth rumble signaled the operation proceeded normally. Once in the fully raised position with the head and engine induction valves opened, the crew felt ear popping as the air pressure equalized with the atmosphere throughout the ship.

"Commence snorkeling when ready, Chief. Recharge the battery fully, then let's get some heat in this *pipe* (reference to their ship).

Maddock studied the depth gauge. "Sail planes got us hung up, Chief. They're not gonna poke through, so raise them to zero. That should bring us up another foot or two."

Chief Smith carried out the order and as Maddock predicted, the ship rose eighteen inches.

Maddock said to the captain, "The bridge access hatch should be just about at the surface. I'll climb up the trunk and check. If I can push it up with the lugs partially retracted and no ocean comes in, it means we can access the bridge. Otherwise, I'll slam it shut and we'll try something else."

Whatever the hell that'll be.

Olsen knew it meant securing the lower hatch after Maddock passed through … if the trunk flooded, his exec would be drowned. The skipper wished Maddock had recommended the action rather than volunteer to do it himself, but Brent, already in motion, headed toward the trunk. Knowing Maddock to be essential to *Sterlet's* survival, Olsen had no wish to take this risk. Selecting an alternate would signal the designee of less importance than Maddock.

Against his better judgment, he replied, "Do it, Brent."

Minutes later, Maddock rigged out the crank handle and began to retract dogs to the bridge access hatch. Figuring he'd achieved a quarter inch clearance, he pushed … the hatch lifted easily. No water. Half an inch more, same result. *What the hell.* Brent retracted the lugs fully and flung the hatch wide open. No water. *Somebody up there must like the hell out of me.*

Maddock thrust his head through the opening. The frigid Arctic atmosphere nearly overwhelmed him. His nose hairs stiffened. *My God. Nobody down there better even hiccup.* The ocean surface reached to within an inch of the hatch coaming. Beneath the ice, no waves threatened to spill over and flood the trunk. *And we're positively buoyant, so it can only get better.*

Hard luck *Sterlet* finally got a break.

Maddock hurried to the bridge and looked out over an icy wilderness that disappeared below the horizon in every direction. Enough of *Sterlet*'s black fairwater protruded above the surface to make her easy to spot. Problem: undesired spotters likely existed in abundance here.

That would have to be fixed.

Cross Country Train Ride

Vasiliy Baknov under his Warren Biddle alias had to make his way across the United States from the Pacific Northwest to Chicago. It didn't take Baknov long to gauge unassuming, puppy-dog friendly Lieutenant (LT) Woody Parnell as not only no threat, but possibly even an ally. The train rumbled and swayed in a syncopated melody causing both men to sleep for the first hour. A conductor awakened them to inspect and punch tickets, an occasion to embark the two in a conversation.

In response to Baknov's question, Parnell declared he not only knew Brent Maddock, but they had served on the same submarine. He did not name *Denver* for security reasons and believed there was no need to.

Parnell said, "Warren, bet you had a great time with Brent. Doesn't his sense of humor just blow you away?"

The Russian employed remarkable psychological abilities. He let Parnell describe his friend until he understood Maddock enough to speak with intelligence about him. "You got that right, he had me laughing till I thought my sides would split."

Parnell's enthusiasm for talking about Maddock overruled his better judgment. He related several tales, most of them set in shore-side environments, but a few from sea experiences. He could do that without identifying *Denver* as the location.

Baknov said, "Tracks exactly with the Brent Maddock I met in Aberdeen. Is he still there? Would be nice to see him again."

"He's been transferred, but I'm not allowed to say where."

"I understand completely. Just hoped when I return to Aberdeen, I might see him again."

"Well, I can tell you he's no longer there."

Baknov got the important part of his answer. He would not have to travel back to the west coast. Logic kicked in. *If he's not at the only US west coast submarine base, he's in the Atlantic Fleet. They likely have only one there also which shouldn't be too hard to find.*

Vasiliy Baknov using his Warren Biddle alias had already gleaned more information from his naïve target Woody Parnell than he thought possible. And then another plum fell into *Biddle*'s lap.

"I have a favor to ask, Warren. I thought my trip east would take me through Chicago. But the conductor tells me I'm changing trains in Denver."

"Sure, Woody. Anything for a friend of Brent Maddock."

"I promised a sailor I'd call his folks when I passed through Chicago. That won't happen now. Would you mind making the call for me?"

"I'd be pleased to." *What a stroke of luck. I'll need some friends in Chicago if I don't want to stick out like a sore thumb.* "What's the fellow's name?"

"Terry Painter … here's the phone number. Tell his parents he's okay and look for him to be promoted soon. Knew him only a short time, but sure liked what I saw. Also, due to broken communications and limited coastal delivery, don't expect to hear from or be able to reach Terry for several months."

Parnell believed he had no need to explain Painter would be on an FBM (Fleet Ballistic Missile) deployment.

"Be happy to pass that along to his mom and dad. Should make them proud."

"Yeah ... and thanks, Warren."

"No problem, Woody."

Parnell then leaned back and fell into a deep sleep.

Biddle thought, *Not only will I tell them, Woody, but I'll deliver the message in person. How could I even hope for a better way to ingratiate people than this.* Parnell had said Painter's father was the second family generation to labor in Chicago's stockyards. *They'll be eating out of my hand in no time at all.*

Ice-picked to the Arctic Polar Ice Cap

No sweeter spring breeze ever smelled or felt as good as the one that blew through *Sterlet*. Space heaters were restarted as well as the galley ranges. Soon the crew would get a well-deserved hot meal.

Sterlet officers, less the officer of the watch, assembled in the wardroom for a council of war. Olsen wanted to identify the major issues and prioritize them.

Maddock said, "We stick out like a sore thumb, Captain. How 'bout we fasten a bunch of fart-sacks (mattress sheets) into a blanket big enough to cover the fairwater?"

Relief has a tendency to promote levity.

Rubin said, "From the smell of some of my snipes (engineer enlisteds), I'd say their *sacks* have to be blacker than the sail."

The remark drew a laugh, but Olsen persisted.

"What's the plan, Brent?"

"Like I said. Cover the fairwater with the whitest stuff we have. COB's already collecting the *sacks*."

Olsen nodded. "Big decision. Do we call for help or press on?"

Faces scanned each other; the skipper needed to hear the right answer, not merely what he wanted to hear.

Maddock took control. "Captain, we made it here by the greatest stroke of luck I've ever seen. The probability our luck will continue is far too low. And we know *Sterlet*'s next stop is the breaking yard. I say, leave her here."

Scanning the other faces, Olsen received no conflicting opinions. Nor did anyone's words reveal any advice.

He demanded, "Well?"

Maddock jumped in. "Let's make this easy. Gentlemen, do any of you disagree with what I recommended?"

Silence.

"Think you've got your answer, Captain."

Giving up his ship under any circumstance is a captain's worst nightmare. The skipper hesitated, then spoke, "It pains me to agree with you, Brent. Your position rests on fact, mine on emotion alone. We'll get someone out here to pick up the crew then scuttle her."

Olsen could barely let these words escape his lips.

Maddock sensed this. "It's the only option you have, Captain."

He gave a reassuring look at his exec, but Olsen said nothing.

Maddock took over the meeting. "First, we figure out where we are. No radio transmissions until we know that. The Russkis have more radio direction finding equipment trained this way than a swarm of hornets."

Opening guns of the war had destroyed GPS satellites. Prior to then, no one paid attention to cumbersome techniques that involved use of astrological data and sextants. Maddock, fascinated by the topic, developed an approach and became proficient on his own.

Prior to the war, one could not conceive of being without GPS. In *Sterlet*'s dire situation, Maddock's passion became a lifesaver. Moments later he stood on the bridge with a quartermaster seaman, who in addition to carrying a stopwatch and notepad, had several cups of hot coffee—not for either of them to drink, but to warm Maddock's hands between observations. Sextants are very delicate instruments and cannot be operated while wearing gloves.

Maddock noted COB had covered the entire superstructure with white sheets. He thought, *Spotting them visually would be tough. When the U.S. helicopters arrive, the camouflage would be dropped. Nothing men can't or won't do to stay alive.*

A deep twilight exposed the entire horizon and about all the navigational stars Maddock needed to fix their position. He would use Polaris, the North Star, to establish *Sterlet*'s exact latitude. Several observations coincided, assuring him he got it right. Though he knew why, Maddock found it remarkable how at high latitudes, summer and winter constellations could be viewed simultaneously.

Maddock triple-sighted a total of seven stars to ensure he had their position right. When finished, he and the quartermaster dropped into the control room to verify if they acquired enough information to establish their position perfectly.

"Okay, Sparks," Maddock addressed Radioman Chief Benito Bondini, "draft me the shortest possible message that says where we are and we need them to come get us."

"You got it, XO." Bondini disappeared into the radio shack.

Soon he emerged beaming and presented his exec with what Bondini considered the shortest and sweetest message he'd ever written, other than the one in which he proposed to his wife.

He wrote, 'USS *Sterlet* coordinates,' followed simply by, 'proceed immediately with three Chinook birds to rescue crew.'

"Bondini, how did we ever win World War Two without you?"

The chief's grin threatened to exceed the limits of his face.

Sterlet employed a broadcast system that could compress and transmit a message of that size in two seconds. It gave radio direction finders little more than a transient from which they could not adequately identify the signal and its true bearing.

Tempted to say, "Do it," Maddock ordered the chief to run it by the captain first. He had good cause to worry about his skipper. In his view, Olsen's behavior seemed to Maddock a bit bizarre. *This is not a good time to make him think he's being disregarded.*

With Olsen's approval, Maddock ordered Bondini, "Squirt it!"

A warm ship and hot meals lifted crew attitude significantly, almost enough to make it appear pushing further south might be a better option. Maddock reminded himself, *the skipper placed logic above emotion.* The decision would stand.

Maddock and Olsen sat for a time alone in the wardroom.

Olsen said, "Choppers will be here first light in a.m., XO. Are we ready for scuttle? We'll need to leave someone below to pull the vents. He'll have plenty of time to make it topside before the sail slips under."

"I'm happy to do that, Captain."

"And worst comes to worst, I'm confronted by dogfaces with no XO. We'll find someone else, Brent."

Chapter 4

Murena*-class Soviet Submarine *Lenin
Beneath the Arctic Polar Ice Cap

Captain 1st Rank Dmitri Borkowski, commanding officer of the Soviet *Murena*-class (NATO designated as a *Delta*-class) ballistic missile submarine *Lenin*, sat behind a cup of tea in the officers' mess and addressed *Zampolit* (political officer) Yuri Anikanov. "That was much closer than I care to come."

His ship sped north to seek refuge deeper in the Arctic.

"Ah, *Komrade Kapitan*. You worry too much. The protective device worked exactly as planned."

"The Navy pays me many rubles for worrying. We have lost too many submarines to the Americans in this war."

Borkowski refrained from using the term *stupid war*, a view he shared with a great many colleagues. *Zampolits*—tentacles of the Communist Party, sole orchestrator of current hostilities—liked nothing better than reporting disloyal acts. Discretion the better part of valor, Borkowski made it a point not to engage the *zampolit* in policy discussions with the vodka bottle opened. He'd learned *vino est veritas* (wine brings out the truth) and would take no chances.

"Yes, *Komrade*. But for us to gain the ultimate triumph, risks must be taken. Should we be ordered to launch a strike ... we're unable to do so."

"Worse, we could be broken up on the bottom and unable even to receive that order. The Americans are equipped with Mark-forty-eight torpedoes. Just one of them could end it for us."

Anikanov could never best Borkowski in tactical logic, so dropped the subject. "Do you think the American detected us?"

"We have no indication of this. Pressed up under the ice cap, we make hardly any noise at all, certainly less than background sounds. Ice floes grinding against each other tend to get quite loud. But that works for the Americans also."

"Did we detect him?"

Borkowski hated more than anything Anikanov's useless tactical discussions used only to satisfy a need to be knowledgeable in an area of which he knows nothing. "I believe so, but can't confirm it until we review sound tapes recorded after the torpedo detonation."

"Do we know the type of submarine encountered?"

The captain placated Anikanov. *Toss the bastard a crumb. Maybe it will shut his stupid mouth.* "I did not think of that. I'll have the *michman* (sonarman) check it immediately."

Wearing his overbearing smirk, Anikanov left the wardroom.

Borkowski took a long sip from his cup of tea and asked the stewardsman to pour another. Deep in thought where he often went, the captain reflected upon his considered view of the absurd world situation. *Wars are contrived by a privileged few who don't dirty their hands fighting them. This is done only by young men and women with absolutely nothing to gain, but confronted with duty to Mother Russia, carry out the idiocy forced upon them. It's a mystery to me how assholes like Anikanov are persuaded to spread their poison.* Borkowski knew the *zampolit* efforts focused on securing loyalty through fear. He wondered if the American counterpart submarine commanders underwent similar experiences onboard their ships. Experience gained while serving with the Soviet Embassy in Washington, DC, gave him to believe they did not.

North Chicago, Illinois

Warren Biddle (aka Vasiliy Baknov) stood on the front porch of a run-down turn of the century Victorian house that stood like a tired old man for a hundred or more years. Width couldn't be more than thirty feet, but stacked three stories high. This provided the large number of bedrooms consistent with a time when families averaged ten to twelve children. Large families helped to offset high infant mortality rates during those days and provided hands to help impoverished families survive.

Biddle mounted two concrete steps and twisted the ancient bell lever, probably the first and only one ever installed, waited two minutes and rang again. A middle-aged woman opened the door and regarded her visitor tentatively.

Sensing her apprehension, Biddle moved immediately to placate it. "If you are Mrs. Painter, I have news from your son Terry."

"Yes. I am Mrs. Painter," escaped her mouth guardedly. "Do you have bad news?"

"Not at all," said Biddle in perfect English. "Terry is well and happy. If I may, let me introduce myself. I'm Warren Biddle from Washington State. I've seen Terry there several times and he asked me to get in touch with you when I came to Illinois."

"Oh!" the woman said.

Her husband arrived and she explained the situation.

The senior Painter said in a loud, welcoming voice, "Come in. You've seen Terry? Wonderful. Have you had dinner? Mary Agnes and I were about to sit down. We have plenty of room at the table."

This was exactly what Biddle wanted.

He hesitated a second then said, "It's very kind of you, but—"

Biddle played the humility game to its hilt.

"No buts. Come on in. Do you like pork?"

"I love it, sir." Painter, a short balding man appeared to have eaten much pork in his lifetime and looked as though he didn't get addressed as *sir* too often, so Biddle would play it to the limit. "Thank you so much. Is this okay with you, Mrs. Painter?"

Mary Agnes, though graying, still bore traces of the attractive young woman she had once been. She regarded her husband through an unhappy expression then reluctantly parroted his invitation.

"I'm John Painter and this is Mary Agnes."

Biddle acknowledged but would stick with Mr. and Mrs.

The Painters led Biddle through a sparsely appointed parlor and dining room to the kitchen.

Half apologetically, John said, "We eat our meals here. Coziest room in the house. Right, Mary Agnes?"

Nodding agreement, she set another place and the three sat down to the best meal Biddle had eaten since arriving in America.

In response to their questions, he employed the same technique used with Woody Parnell to learn about Brent Maddock. He let them describe their son then played it back like it had come from his own recollection. "Though I saw him only a few times in the tavern, I learned so much about him. This house. I recognized it immediately, exactly as he described. He loved growing up here."

John Painter offered exactly what Biddle needed. "Four Painter generations lived in this house. Silas Painter, Terry's great-granddad built it in the late eighteen hundreds." John finished his second glass of wine with predictable results. Great family pride, particularly in offspring, abounded in his conversation. Then he said, "Tell me about yourself, Warren."

Biddle, grateful for having studied American history, invented a tale of how his forebears had traveled over the Oregon Trail and settled in what was then the Oregon Territory. Four generations later, they remained in their initial occupation: fishing.

While Mary Agnes set about clearing the table, Painter asked, "Well, what brings you to Illinois?"

"War has all but ended fishing in the northwest. I had to find something else."

"Why'd you pick Illinois?"

Biddle grinned then said, "I looked for the farthest place from the bombings. Illinois seemed a good bet."

Painter frowned, showing this fight clearly did not set well with him. "Well," he said, "let's hope they get it straightened out soon."

Biddle noted no anti-Soviet tones in his host's dialog. Not so among conversations held not all that long ago in Russia. The Communist Party had whipped Russians into their desired mindset. He quickly dismissed his recalling. *It is as we always believed. Americans have no stomach for combat. By this notion they will be defeated as Mother Russia triumphs.*

"So where do you stay, Warren?"

"Actually, nowhere yet. But I'll check into a hotel."

"Nonsense. Tonight you stay here. You've given us such happy news of Terry, it would be an honor for you to sleep in his room. And we have some brandies to put away. I'd say you'll be in no condition to walk, much less find your way to a hotel."

The remark drew its expected laughter from all except Mary Agnes Painter.

Biddle went through the motions of objecting, but cleverly caved to Painter's urging. *Thanks to Lieutenant Parnell, I know it will be several months before they can check me out with their son.*

Later, the imposter Baknov stretched out in Terry Painter's bed. Sleep did not come easily. *John and Mary Agnes Painter surely don't represent the American masses who must truly hate us for attacking them. This is all hogwash. I must not let myself be taken in. Perhaps this is a ruse and in the morning police will be here to take me away.* In his heart, Baknov did not believe this. His keen insight into human nature prevented it. After a time, he drifted into the most peaceful sleep he had known in perhaps years. True, he hated all things American, except maybe John and Mary Painter.

Mary Agnes turned in after her wine and brandy-laden husband slept soundly. She had remarkable intuition and wished to tell John, "There's just something about Warren Biddle."

But it would keep till morning.

USS *Sterlet* Partially Broached Through Arctic Polar Ice Cap

LTJG Wayne Dewars stood on the bridge, his arms continuously banging against his chest in rhythm with his stomping feet, both measures to encourage blood to circulate freely. He recalled plebe (freshman) year at the Naval Academy and the answer he recited to hazing upper-classmen's question—*How cold is it in Maryland, Mr. Dewars?*—*Sir, colder than the rim of a cocktail glass, colder than the tip of a polar bear's ass.*

Although, he thought, *not nearly cold as it is here.* Nothing in Dewars's recollection approached the chill he now felt as OOD in the Arctic. *This is truly the ass-freezin' season.*

Swilling hot coffee helped but had other drawbacks. Lowering a zipper at these temperatures introduced a whole set of problems.

The starboard lookout yelled, "Mr. Dewars! Choppers headed this way."

Theirs or ours ran through Wayne's mind.

He demanded, "Bearing!"

"Zero-nine-zero," came the reply.

He thought, *At least they're from the right direction.* He ordered over the 21MC, "Notify captain and exec, choppers in sight ... zero-nine-zero relative. Help verify they're ours with the type eight."

"Attack center aye, bridge. Mister Maddock on his way up. Scope on the choppers. Mr. Rubin says they're Chinooks."

Brent Maddock shouted, "Exec up," and climbed onto the bridge. "Drop all the camouflage, Wayne. Let's give 'em every possible chance to spot us."

Dewars wished another set of eyes would confirm the choppers were ours but carried out the order.

"Bridge, Captain. Confirm Chinooks. Then suit up the crew in anything they can find. When they reach the bridge, get 'em out on the ice soonest."

"Aye, Captain."

Before long, crewmen mounted the bridge wearing the strangest combinations ever seen on a U.S. submarine. Only common article: blankets from their bunks.

A seaman complained, "Skipper said we can only bring what fits in our pockets."

Maddock grinned and said to the seaman, "From the size of your pockets, you better be damn sure you don't fall through the ice, sailor ... it's only three feet thick."

Per naval tradition, the most junior left the ship first. Following the seamen came E-4s (3rd class petty officers), E-5s, E-6s, E-7s (CPOs) and finally the COB.

Maddock charged Smith, "Don't let those guys do anything dumb down there on the ice, COB."

"When have I ever been able to control *dumb*, Mr. Maddock?"

The officers filed topside, followed by the captain.

Three giant Chinooks settled onto the ice and *Sterlet* crewmen began piling aboard. Escorting Grumman F-18 jet fighters circled overhead, prepared to deal with anyone who might try to impede the rescue effort.

Dewars and the lookouts descended to the ice, leaving only Maddock and Olsen on the bridge.

"So, who gets to pull the plug, Captain?"

"Naval tradition says captain's the last man to leave the ship. I'll do it, Brent."

"No, Captain. We need you to help win this war. And you're able to do that better than anyone down there on the ice."

"What are you worried about, Brent? I'll pull those vents and be outta that hole like a scared jackrabbit."

Looking Olsen directly in the eye, Maddock said, "Captain?"

"Get your ass down on the ice and that's an order, Brent."

Reluctantly, Maddock complied and Olsen disappeared beneath the bridge access hatch.

When Brent reached the ice, all but a few of the crew had been loaded into the copters. He turned and fixed his eyes to the bridge.

Ice shook under his feet, signaling *Sterlet*'s main vents had been pulled. A minute passed and Olsen did not reappear on the bridge. The sail began to settle then disappeared beneath the ice.

Commander Jack Olsen had opted to go down with his ship.

Command passed to Maddock who climbed aboard the last chopper. They took off and headed toward the Bay of Fundy.

Maddock sickened over failing to do what he believed he should have done.

Bay of Fundy Submarine Base

Woody Parnell's ancient Canadian bus rattled over twenty miles of the roughest road he'd ever seen. Not allowed to enter the base, the bus dropped Woody at the main gate.

Though going through the motions of being a Marine sentry, submariners simply did not make the grade. Specialty demands of their ratings left no time to remain proficient in military procedure. Following a half-hearted military salute, the main gate petty officer dispatched Parnell to the BOQ (Bachelor Officers' Quarters), currently a tent with promise of improvement in the form of nearby Quonset huts under construction.

Weighing the heaviest on Parnell's mind—boat assignment. He harbored an outside hope of reconnecting with and perhaps working for former shipmate Brent Maddock. *Sterlet* being one of the last of the dinosaurs meant Maddock would soon be transferred. Due for command, Woody hoped Maddock would become CO of whatever SSN 637 got the TPES, Parnell's ultimate destination.

Parnell looked about the base and saw many similarities to the *Pitstop,* nickname given the base's Pacific Northwest counterpart. Sunken hulks formed an adequate breakwater, while moored barges provided docking space for two SSN 688 class and a 637. Several cranes and a floating dry dock rounded out the base. A number of nearby Quonset huts likely housed the machine shops, and like the *Pitstop,* a commandeered palatial yacht served as the commodore's flagship. Overall, the base appeared a beehive of activity.

Parnell's tent, shared by three other officers, stood vacant except for Woody. He dumped his belongings into an empty footlocker and secured it with a combination lock. Woody cleaned up at a nearby washroom, donned a khaki uniform and walked the mile and a quarter to the flagship. The yacht not in commission and Woody unsure of the boarding protocol, played it safe, following the only procedure he knew.

Woody snapped a salute to the colors, and then to a petty officer that stood watch while he said, "Lieutenant Woodruff H. Parnell reporting as ordered. Permission to come aboard."

"Come aboard, sir. I guess you want to see the commodore." Not waiting for an answer, the petty officer said to a seaman standing nearby, "Darby, take Mr. Parnell to the commodore's office."

Commodore Ken Omensen's office followed an old diesel-boat axiom: small, but it had room for everything but a mistake. Tall and wiry with piercing blue eyes, Omensen rose to greet Woody.

Introductions exchanged, traditional coffees ordered, the two sat down and observed the Navy custom of small talk prior to business.

Though Omensen could have been no more than fifty, Parnell noticed the past year of continuous stress had taken its toll.

"So tell me about that rascal Eric Danis."

"Admiral Danis, Commodore?"

"Yeah … admiral. Guess I gotta have it rubbed in. We're Naval Academy classmates and he's already got a rank on me. How's he doing? Heard lots about him but haven't seen him since basic sub-school. Married a real sweetheart from Conn College for Women across from the submarine base. Eve."

"Recently saw her in Washington, Commodore, and she's still a knockout."

"Only Eric could find a wife that ages like a good wine."

They went on like this a short while then got down to business.

"Woody, you've been to Newport and seen this Turbine Pump Ejection System. Dammit all, I hate acronyms. I'm supposed to call it a TPES. I'm sure you spotted the *Six-thirty-seven* moored across the loch. She's in process of having one installed. As you might suspect, that's where you're going."

"Learned a lot about it at Newport, Commodore."

"What do you think?"

"Loudest thing you won't hear is the big thump we get from ram launch systems. But the energy needed to get a big object from a launcher doesn't change. Some of that has to be converted to sound. Things being like they are on the open ocean, radiated noise data has to be collected at Narragansett Bay. Looks good there, but only open ocean will provide proof of the pudding."

The commodore answered with a concerned look. "Not exactly what I wanted to hear. Big problem in the Arctic is those damn Russian ice-pickers. They know what a US launcher transient sounds like and will get off and running at the git-go. We're counting big on the TPES."

Omensen immediately regretted his pessimistic tone in the presence of a junior officer. He groped for his next words. *This should be benign enough.* "What do you think of the east coast?"

"What's not to like about it, Commodore. But I have a question. Why are we up here instead of Narragansett Bay, a perfect spot for this operation?"

"Same reason the *Pitstop* sits on an isolated coast in Washington State. No telling what the Russians will do when they get their backs against the wall. If they resort to nuclear weapons again, better in a less populated place."

Parnell saw the logic and agreed. "Commodore, is it kosher for me to ask about USS *Sterlet*? Coupla my old *Denver* shipmates are aboard her. The skipper, Jack Olsen, and XO Brent Maddock. Is there a chance Brent will get command of your *Six-thirty-seven* with the TPES? It'd be a real pleasure to serve with him again."

Omensen's expression took on an even more tired look. "I'm afraid I have bad news for you, Woody." He went on to relate *Sterlet*'s recent saga and concluded with, "They were heloed to a railhead three hundred miles north. We expect them here tonight."

"I'm so sorry to hear this."

"Woody, the toughest job in my life was to tell Olsen's wife what happened. There's no need for her to think it was anything other than an attack and sinking and her husband's inability to get off the ship before it sank. You understand, she must never find out what really happened."

"I understand, Commodore." Parnell found it difficult to equate his exec on *Denver* with the same Jack Olsen that had taken his own life. "I've such fond memories of Jack. Any further details?"

"Afraid not. But Maddock assures me we'll get all the data incident to *Sterlet*'s sinking."

"Commodore, I assure you, you couldn't ask for a better officer than Brent to be involved with this. I'm confident he'll bring you a thorough analysis and damn good ideas to counter the problem."

"I've met Maddock several times and find him consistent with your description. What we have here is the hottest firecracker since this damn war started. If the Soviets know how to be invulnerable under the polar ice cap, we're in deep yogurt."

"Count on Brent, Commodore. He'll figure something out."

"You have no idea how much I hope you're right. But after all this, I do have a bit of good news for you, Woody. Another of your *Denver* shipmates is on his way here to relieve me: Commodore Selectee Hal Bostwick."

Woody Parnell felt it altogether possible his chin might fall all the way to the floor.

Chapter 5

Bay of Fundy

Woody Parnell uncapped a bottle of JD Black (Jack Daniel's Black Label Whiskey) and set two paper cups on a footlocker between the cots in Parnell's temporary quarters. Brent Maddock sat opposite. A look at his watch confirmed the lateness in the day for a long awaited meeting with his old shipmate.

Commanding officer's first priority: ensure safety and comfort of his crew. Their train arrived shortly after midnight and Maddock got his men situated in a sparsely furnished, but comfortable WWII-hangover personnel barge. Some men required medical attention, which Maddock arranged for immediately. All base personnel knew about *Sterlet*'s crew and quickly provided every resource available.

Seeing that the needs of his crew and officers had been attended to first, only then did Maddock see to his own needs. With this responsibility completed, Maddock could find time for his friend.

Apologizing for the paper cups, Woody said, "Black is meant to be drunk from glass and neat. Hope you like neat 'cause I don't have any ice either."

"No problem, Woody. Just uncork the bottle and give it to me. And by the way, what the hell's this with two full stripes? What happened to LTJG? Navy get rid of them too?"

Parnell explained.

"Well, you caught up with me."

He had yet to learn about his recent promotion to Lieutenant Commander (LCDR).

Woody poured heavy belts of Black into the paper cups and the old friends touched edges at his toast, "To world peace."

Maddock added, "Can't get here too soon for me. But in the meantime, we gotta kick a lot of Russki ass to make that happen."

The two sat on bunks since the quarters had no chairs.

Brent exclaimed, "Damn this is good, Woody! My first drink in eleven weeks. You sure know how to welcome a guy home."

"Just had a terrible thought, Brent. Suppose all the Russians did on opening day was destroy the JD distillery. It would've sunk US morale to such a low, we would've surrendered the first day."

"Perish the thought. Well, they didn't, so the war goes on. But more importantly, update me on what's happening at the *Pitstop*. Guess the place has gone to hell since I left."

"Actually, it took a while for everyone to even realize you were gone. As you might expect, that's when things began to improve."

"Yeah? How 'bout Captain Buchanan. He doin' okay?"

Maddock referred to *Denver*'s CO.

Woody replied, "He changed Bostwick's Hades into the Garden of Eden. You could see that comin' from a mile off before you left."

"They busted the mold after they made Buchanan."

"You gonna ask me about Den Mother?"

Parnell used the nickname of Maddock's love Bea Zane.

"Cat got an ass? I've been gone seventy-seven days, so I expect there'll be seventy-seven letters from her at the base PO when it opens in the morning."

"Look for only one … a *Dear John*. When you left, she couldn't glom on to me quick enough."

Maddock took a sip from his paper cup. "Nectar of the Gods, Woody, and if Bea was interested in you, look for the sun to rise in the west. Hope she and her dad do okay."

"Saw a lot of Dave at the *'Stop*. He and Admiral Danis are thick as fleas on a dog's back."

"They go way back. But Bea?"

"She'd come by to pick up her dad and chat if I happened to be topside. But only once, before I left, they had me with Admiral Danis out to the *Digs* (Zane's nickname for their nearby vacation home). Nice evening. And your gal's a great cook. Not bad lookin' either. She comin' out here?"

"I miss her a great deal. But she has a dad to look after. And maybe you noticed, family accommodations are not too hot here. Top it off with I'm gone well over half the time. All that considered, it'd be selfish to ask her to come here."

After several *pulls* of *Black,* Woody became understandably more lucid. Though barely twenty-five, under these circumstances he tended to become profound.

"Have you laid all this on Bea? Isn't she part of the equation?"

Maddock replied, "Give me a break, Woody. You're not old enough to talk like an adult."

North Chicago, Illinois

An infant when his father Yuri defected to America, Lieutenant Vasiliy Baknov, knew him only through photos and verbal accounts by Ekaterina Baknov, Vasiliy's mother. The eighty-six-year-old elder Baknov once dazzled audiences as a prima dancer with the Kirov Ballet. He last danced with Ekaterina in a production of Adolph Adam's *Giselle* fifty years earlier. During an infrequent Kirov visit to America, Yuri defected, pleading for asylum based on the Communist Party's suppression of artistic freedom. Claiming his life would be in danger, the U.S. State Department granted the world famous dancer asylum and in the process gained a significant political victory for the United States.

While a child, Vasiliy had only respect for his father, for all he knew of him came from his mother who, although abandoned, remained deeply in love with her husband.

However, the defection, widely known in the Soviet Union, later hung like a noose about young Vasiliy's neck. Schoolmates scorned him, but worse, security considerations threatened to prevent his entry into military service. A great hatred for his father emerged, as well as for the country that accepted his defection.

Fortunately, realizing Yuri Baknov would never return to her, Ekaterina took as her lover an influential state official who cleared obstacles from Vasiliy's path.

Hatred for his father continued to burn in Vasiliy's breast. He learned Yuri retired from the New York Ballet and became employed at a ballet school in Chicago. Tracking him down would be easy. *How many ballet schools could there be in Chicago?*

A remarkably skilled mechanic, Vasiliy, *aka* Warren Biddle, quickly found employment at a garage in North Chicago. He thought it ironic he serviced many cars owned by his avowed enemy: Navy men stationed at the nearby Great Lakes Naval Training Center.

He had rented a small apartment, but maintained contact with the Painter family. Despite dedication to his mission, he continued to make occasional visits. Though loath to admit it, dedication did not include immunity to loneliness. Even the suspicious Mary Agnes had become less wary and warmed to him.

Yes, I've got everything going exactly as planned: an established operation base, good job and naïve people to support me. What possibly could go wrong?

During the first night he spent at the Painters, Vasiliy searched Terry's room. In the night table beside the bed, he found a snub-nosed .38 caliber revolver and a box of cartridges. Mary Agnes treated her son's room like a shrine, determined to touch nothing until he returned home. After locating his father, Vasiliy could easily remove and return the weapon without fear of being detected.

Good. Find my worthless father and give him his just reward. Then to the east coast and attend to Lieutenant Maddock. Justice must truly be on my side for everything to fall in place so nicely.

Bay of Fundy

Commodore Ken Omensen, Brent Maddock and Woody Parnell sat about traditional coffees in the dining room of Omensen's palatial yacht flagship.

They had returned from seeing Jack Olsen's wife and children off for their sad return to Illinois.

The commodore spoke, "Did I do the right thing? Or should I have told her the truth? But how do you tell a woman her husband committed suicide? I can imagine nothing that would devastate her more than what she already is."

Brent answered, "You did the right thing, Commodore. You're right. The truth would only add to her misery."

"But how many of *Sterlet*'s crew know? It would be terrible for the news to reach her from someone else."

Brent sensed Omensen's anxiety and put it to immediate rest. "I was the only person positioned to know Jack made no attempt to get off the ship. Count on my silence, Commodore."

"Thank you, Brent. I'm putting Jack in for a Navy Cross and I'll need your help with the citation."

"Of course, Commodore."

Woody found himself glad they wore working uniforms that did not include decorations. He felt circumstances attendant to receiving his Navy Cross to fall well short of Olsen's, so wearing it would have felt awkward for Woody.

Omensen drew a sigh. "I hope I never have to do that again, lie to someone I know and care about. Particularly regarding the death of a spouse. Oh what a tangled web we weave ... when first we practice to deceive."

Parnell offered, "Believe Walter Scott meant that to apply only when the motive is ulterior, Commodore."

Brent thought, *Second time in twenty-four hours Woody has talked like an adult. Better start listening to him.*

Discussion about Jack Olsen continued, then trailed off to their meeting subject—What had happened to *Sterlet* and why.

Omensen asked Brent, "Do we have anything to go on?"

Brent explained, "Keeping crew minds occupied was essential in the hours between the attack and punching through the ice. Otherwise the pucker-factor might've reached a new all-time high. Among other things, sonar tapes ran continuously, so I had Chief Giambri review them in detail."

Omensen asked, "Find anything definitive?"

"No, nothing definitive. Much data, but no answer," said Brent. "We have evidence to show the torpedo did not come from the ice-picked BN."

The commodore's brow furrowed. "Well, from where, then?"

"Sixty-four thousand dollar question, Commodore. We know duration of the torpedo run was too short for it to have come from the boomer. And there was substantial bearing difference between the weapon and submarine."

"Any ideas? This is damn serious."

Parnell said nothing but scribbled on a notepad hard enough to put him at risk of writer's cramp.

"To the best of my knowledge, the Russians have no equivalent to the US CAPTOR (encapsulated torpedo capable of being moored as an anti-submarine warfare mine). And if they do, how can they make it determine the difference between us and them?"

"Nothing on this from earlier surveillance missions?"

Parnell replied, "Checked out all the germane stuff in the vault, Commodore. Nothing."

Omensen said, "Looks like we got our work cut out for us."

Maddock replied, "Maybe this new TPES plan provides a Band-Aid while we work this out."

"Glad you brought that up, Brent. One is being installed in *Steelhead* and Tom Bintliff's due for relief. That's where you're going, Brent. It's only a *Six-thirty-seven*, but Woody and you are the right team for that boat."

Without success, Parnell struggled to keep a happy expression from his face.

Chicago, Illinois

Vasiliy Baknov sat at a restaurant in the loop section of Chicago. Over a cup of tea and a sandwich, he studied the arts section in the Chicago Tribune. There he hoped to find a path leading to his aged father. In Baknov's perception, accounts needed to be settled.

Surely the old man teaches ballet now and if there are any leads, they have to be here.

Time converged on Vasiliy. His biggest concern, use of Warren Biddle's identification might soon be compromised. He frequently checked televised news reports for some word on the real Biddle's disappearance. So far, nothing. As he had expected, deaths of two fishermen off the Pacific Coast did not make the cut for national news. A bleeding-heart anchor might pick it up, but lack of any compelling circumstance made follow up unlikely. Bad news draws the most viewers which pleases advertisers no end.

A buxom waitress, having sized Baknov up as a bachelor and available, returned frequently to refresh his tea. Vasiliy paid her no mind. Involvements with women tended to lower one's guard, and things for Vasiliy currently went too well to take extracurricular risk. He'd pledged himself to quite another agenda.

Baknov's American experience thus far contradicted much of what he'd learned from the Communist Party. His pay at the garage surprised him. Enough to rent an apartment well above the cut of those he'd seen in Russia. Enough pay to eat well and maintain an uncommitted cash reserve that grew weekly. In addition, knowing Warren had no car, the garage owner let him use the loaner vehicle when not in use by a customer. The growing cash reserve would provide means to move about the country in his search of Brent Maddock after he disposed of his father.

Baknov knew getting paid in cash *under the table* accrued mutual benefit to payer and payee. Using Biddle's social security number might put Vasiliy at risk and surely raise conjecture that Biddle's death may not have been accidental. As far as Baknov's identity being compromised when Mary Agnes and John Painter's son Terry returns, Vasiliy reckoned he had at least two months before beginning to worry over that.

He copied several promising phone numbers from the *Tribune* and went to a phone booth with a pocketful of change and tried them one by one. After a few calls, pay-dirt.

A female voice at one ballet school responded, "Yuri Baknov? Oh yes, he's retired now, but he does come in once a week. He's such a dear man. Would you like him to get in touch with you?"

"Oh no. He would have no idea who I am. I'm just a fan who continues to admire him so much."

"Well, he does visit the studio every Wednesday morning about nine. Perhaps you can come by and meet him. I'm sure that would please him immensely. What is your name, please?"

Vasiliy Baknov quickly hung up. He had his information.

Bay of Fundy

Sterlet's crew assembled in a personnel barge for a most somber event. As senior surviving officer, Brent Maddock presided. The agenda consisted of three segments: memorializing the late skipper, CDR Jack Olsen; painful breaking up of the crew, most of whom had passed the last three years together; and then formally striking *Sterlet* from Navy records.

The men had shared harrowing experiences and survived in large part through abilities to depend each upon the other. Now, they would be cast upon vagaries of reassignment at the whim of some clerk and sheets of paper drafted at the Bureau of Naval Personnel.

With the crew and officers assembled, Maddock entered the room and COB called, "Attention on deck." Then snapping a salute, he announced, "Crew all present or accounted for, Captain."

Though not formally assigned as such, the senior officer aboard a submarine assumes the title of captain.

Brent returned the salute. "Have the crew stand easy, Chief of the Boat."

The term COB had its place in times of informality, but not for solemn ritual.

Maddock began, "Officers and men of *Sterlet*. This is a sad day for us. But we are submariners and we well know how to deal with tough times. The fact we are here attests to that allegation.

"It is proper we begin by honoring our late commanding officer. It has been a privilege to serve under Commander John Olsen, Jack to most of us who knew him well. Our very survivals are attributed to his great skill, selflessness and compassion for his crew. His final act reflected his belief that a commanding officer must not order a crewman to do anything the captain is unwilling to do himself. Sadly, it cost him his life. Quartermaster of the Watch John Howe rescued the national ensign and commissioning pennant prior to scuttling *Sterlet*. As most of you know, Mrs. Olsen has returned to her home in Illinois. These must be presented to Mrs. Olsen with proper ceremony. Several of you will go to Illinois on leave shortly so I'll call upon you to perform this ceremony. I am confident you will do *Sterlet* proud."

Maddock paused for a moment to let his words set in. Each man had personal views and Brent gave the crew time to reflect on them.

"Beginning today, we go our separate ways. Please know that serving with all of you has been an inspiration and an honor for me, and know that your skipper, Captain Olsen, often reflected to me this same esteem for his crew. I know how heavy your hearts are on this sad occasion of breaking up *Sterlet's* crew. I am reminded of words spoken by a daughter to her dad on the occasion of his relief as a submarine commanding officer. 'Don't be sorry it's over; just be glad it happened'."

Maddock paused again.

"Be glad it happened and bring to your new ships the values and sense of duty you helped formulate in *Sterlet*. This will serve you, your new shipmates, and our country well."

Brent dropped to an informal tone. He took a deep breath and said to his men, "I know it's hard for you to believe the old exec can get choked up." He forced a smile. "Especially after the personal head bangings I've had with some of you."

Laughter among *Sterlet*'s crew showed Maddock he'd succeeded in elevating spirits a bit.

Two flagpoles erected for the occasion bore *Sterlet*'s national ensign and commissioning pennant. Maddock read a letter from the U.S. Navy Bureau of Ships proclaiming *Sterlet* had been struck from the records.

Maddock nodded to COB, who ordered in the best military tones he could muster, "Crew, attention. Hand salute."

Brent directed Quartermaster Howe to lower the pennant and national ensign. This completed, Maddock invited the entire crew to reassemble in the base enlisted mess hall where they'd *splice the main brace* (old Navy expression meaning the crew is authorized to imbibe alcoholic beverages) and tell outrageous stories to each other just one more time.

Meanwhile, Commodore selectee Hal Bostwick arrived at the Submarine Group flagship with orders to relieve Commodore Ken Omensen. During their initial meeting, Bostwick went through his usual politeness and humility ritual to mask seeking out soft spots in his predecessor's tenure. Though Omensen had done a superb job of creating an effective submarine base from virtually nothing and scheduled to receive a Legion of Merit upon relief, Bostwick unobtrusively focused only on possible shortfalls.

He would invent a few if none could be found. Subsequent to relief, he would use these at Omensen's expense for rungs on the ladder of his own ambitious career.

Through a forced smile over their obligatory coffees, Bostwick asked, "So Ken, what do you see as the biggest problem?"

Omensen went over what passed between him, Brent Maddock and Woody Parnell about the attack on *Sterlet*. "That's a nut we must crack. Otherwise, the Russians emerge with absolute control of the ice pack."

"So what's the plan?"

Explaining the TPES experiment, Omensen then said, "Logic says some kind of defense parameter is set up around the Soviet ice-picked boomers. We're able to detect and locate them from a safe distance. But we have to close for torpedo attacks and that's where the trouble begins."

He went over the tentative plan to use the TPES-modified Sea Lance missile combination.

Bostwick busied himself identifying what Omensen should have done, but didn't. He hoped to later send subtle messages on how screwed up the command was before he arrived and straightened everything out.

"So what's the next move, Ken?"

The commodore told of how he'd assigned Maddock and Parnell to the TPES-equipped *Steelhead*. "Barring any new surprises, Hal, we hope to deploy them within the month. Maddock and Parnell were with you in *Denver*, weren't they?"

Replying in a voice fraught with faked praise, Bostwick said, "They were. You couldn't have picked finer officers for this job."

So, Maddock. What goes around comes around. This time your ass is mine. And the career ending I have planned for you will be the most disastrous in Navy history.

Chapter 6

Bay of Fundy

Newly assigned Weapons Officer LT Woody Parnell along with *Steelhead*'s chief of the boat (COB) supervised loading a Turbine Pump Ejection System (TPES) into the torpedo room. An unproven system, only the portside launcher had been reconfigured. The ram had been removed and replaced by an axial pump powered by an air-driven turbine. Air from a high-pressure bank would be released into the turbine at the instant of weapon launch. The pump would then flush a 246-inch long by 21-inch diameter, ton and a half weapon from the launcher at fifty feet per second.

Submariners often live by what they know. Installing an untried device always raises hackles of a crew; not only over whether it will work, but side effects of failure. A number of submarine near and actual catastrophes originated at the launchers. Skepticism evolved as the main tool for ameliorating this problem, and a great deal of it accompanied the TPES installation.

Despite rapid promotion to lieutenant, Parnell lacked experience and appreciated having COB Quartermaster Chief Jacques Henri by his side. Henri and Parnell served together in USS *Denver*. Then Quartermaster Second Class, Henri cut the figure of a handsome young black. He had been a party to Parnell's winning the Navy Cross and won a Silver Star for his own participation in boarding and capturing a Soviet minesweeper.

Henri's rapid rise to CPO and COB had its consequences. Though barely thirty, stress initiated gray streaks already began to appear in his hair. Likely humble origins in East St. Louis inspired Henri to excel in all undertakings, *excellent* falling short of the *outstanding* degree Henri demanded of himself. Being comparable to anyone else did not pass muster; he felt he had to be better.

A crane seated atop a barge lowered the ejection system toward *Steelhead*'s torpedo loading hatch, the weather cooperating nicely. Hardly a breeze stirred and the mid-afternoon sun shone down brightly. A foot above the deck, Henri's clenched fist signaled the crane operator to stop and lock the cable.

Henri's job as COB: make the new officers look good while at the same time never letting them feel they're not in charge.

"Mr. Parnell, do you think it might be better if I went below to be sure the ejection system is properly transferred from the crane to the torpedo room handling equipment?"

Woody regarded Henri with half a smile. "Took the words right out of my mouth, COB. Let me know when you want the crane to lower away."

In the torpedo room, Henri and two yard workers skillfully moved the equipment from chain fall to chain fall until it positioned directly above a newly prepared bed on the port launch cylinder. They carefully lowered the system until it fit into its new home.

One of the workers declared, "Perfect."

Henri would have it no other way. "Good. Now let's get this thing bolted down. I'm overdue for coffee and you guys are too."

North Chicago

Vasiliy Baknov, under his pseudonym Warren Biddle, climbed into his loaner car from the garage and drove to Mary Agnes and John Painter's home. He called John under some pretext knowing full well it would result in a dinner invitation. *Americans are so easy to manipulate. This leaves me to wonder why we have not defeated them by now.* Vasiliy needed the occasion to visit Terry Painter's room and procure the pistol stowed there.

On Baknov's arrival, John Painter welcomed his guest with a customary offer of something from the liquor cabinet. Vasiliy had often noted the nearly full bottle of Absolut Vodka with remorse.

Much as he longed to drink of it, something Agnes Painter asked during his initial visit cautioned that his true identity might already have been compromised. "Do I hear an accent, Warren?"

"An accent? Have you ever visited the Pacific Northwest?"

"No, but we always planned to."

Baknov managed not to reveal any relief in his expression. *This woman's intuition is uncanny. I must be on my guard.* He replied, "If you ever get out that way, you'll find everyone talks like me."

A master reader of expressions, Baknov looked for one but found none on Mary Agnes Painter.

Vasiliy took nothing for granted. But as his visits became more frequent, Mary Agnes warmed to him. Inwardly, an emotional angry young man dedicated to righting perceived grievous wrongs done him and Mother Russia, he had another dragon to slay; a man's heart beat in his breast, not immune to loneliness and a real need for compassion. Conquering this comprised Vasiliy's most immediate trial. He'd come too far and would not bend to the very weaknesses that ultimately he believed would topple the United States.

Aboard USS *Steelhead*

LCDR Brent Maddock, like all new COs, savored his first day at sea in that capacity. Coupling this with emerging from an intense maintenance period, could be likened to a day of cleaning bilges, followed by a hot shower and off for a night on the town. Brent's spirits soared proportionately.

Drifter, an oceanographic laboratory research ship from Woods Hole, Massachusetts, awaited *Steelhead* in the open ocean to test the new missile ejection system. Restricted waters of Fundy could not accommodate the test because of too much ambient noise. But the open ocean belonged to everyone, and Maddock counseled his officers and crew to keep their butts on the edges of their chairs.

He cautioned, "Ivan doesn't give a rip if we've just completed upkeep. So look for him to welcome us back into the war."

Maddock used every occasion to elevate the crew's confidence in him. He felt this was essential to their morale.

Brent took advantage of all the sea trial personnel and supplies while en route. The customary cadre of civilian workers rode the trials, eager to accommodate each crew *weep* (complaint)—identify the problem and correction needed to make repairs. By the time *Steelhead* reached the open ocean, little remained to be completed.

Over Maddock's objections, communications exchange with *Drifter*, the Woods Hole ship assigned for the ejection system evaluation, would be by underwater telephone (*Gertrude*). Brent knew this would be like a beacon to any Soviet submarine that might be patrolling nearby.

Civilian government employees, ones who wrote test specs for assessing the TPES performance at sea and formulated the operation plan, expected naval officers to accommodate the tactical situation at sea—easier to specify than carry out. However, Commodore-select Bostwick approved it as written and would tolerate no deviations except those approved by him.

Arguing the point to no avail, Maddock recognized Bostwick's old familiar technique; lay out a requirement which Maddock will likely violate and nail him when he does.

Maddock's principal concern: Bostwick, himself. *We continue to be at war and despite a vigorous sea-trial agenda, we're still fair game for anyone who wants a piece of us. What a rotten time for this ambitious jackass to show up. Topping that off, a new crew whose confidence I've yet to earn, plus what might have been the quickest command turnover ever.*

It did not occur to Maddock that his COB, Quartermaster Chief Jacques Henri, worked the crew vigorously on the topic of their new CO, who had earned Henri's esteem during a previous tour in *Denver*. A perceptive man, the Bostwick-Maddock conflict had not been lost on Henri.

Steelhead sped into a moonless night on the first seaward run under her new CO. Southwest winds kicked the surface up to a heavy state three. This mattered not, for Maddock ordered the ship submerged when passing between Grand Manan and Brier Islands.

Although a submariner, Maddock's passion for standing on the bridge while surfaced reflected a love all mariners share for the sea. Like a jealous lover, the briny deep lures men away from wives, family, hearth and home.

Damn, I love this, Brent thought then took a final look around into the black night and went below. His officer of the deck ordered a southerly heading toward the prearranged rendezvous with Woods Hole's *Drifter* and submerged the ship.

Maddock waited in the attack center with a double-edged plan in mind; make sound tactical decisions and leave no doubt among the crew as to who calls the shots.

He ordered the conning officer, "Make dead slow speed and run at ultra-quiet. Have sonar search three-sixty and clear baffles every five minutes. We've no idea what kind of reception committee awaits us out here. I want every sound reported immediately." Brent felt a need to inject some humor. "And that includes whale farts."

Addressing the conning officer, he said, "Bill, call me if you hear anything, but not for thirty minutes. I'm meeting XO in the wardroom to show him who's the best cribbage player in *Steelhead* and I need that much time."

After thirty minutes, Maddock returned to the attack center and addressed Conning Officer LT Bill Bryan, "Anything, Bill?"

"Quiet as a tomb, Captain." Then through a grin, he added, "XO straightened out on who's the best cribbage player?"

Maddock mustered a sheepish look. "Some things take a little while." Then said, "Don't sound the general alarm, but man battle stations torpedo. Make ready two tubes with ADCAPS (Advanced Capability MK 48 torpedoes) and open the outer doors."

Through a confused look, Bryan executed the order.

Picking up the sound-powered phone, Brent rang maneuvering and said, "In a few minutes, I'll order a flank bell (max speed) and follow with a stop order in thirty seconds."

"Aye, Captain."

He wondered, *Why'n hell doesn't someone ask what's going on?*

Executive Officer Tom Bentley came to the rescue. With a look of apprehension, he asked, "What's the plan, Captain?"

"Just this, Tom. If anyone's out there, he's likely sitting quiet and waiting to hear someone come out of the Bay. Unless our intel is wrong, no Russki can hear a *thirty-seven* at ultra-quiet."

"Yeah, but he damn sure can if we're at flank speed."

"Right. But I'm betting he'll figure we can't hear him at flank speed and he'll kick ass to catch up. We'll shut down and go back to ultra and catch 'im with his pants down."

"What about range?"

The new captain astounded his exec. "Active sonar."

Active sonar almost never used by U.S. submarines had main power fuses removed to prevent inadvertent activation.

"But that'll tell him right where we are."

"It'll only give him a bearing which he has already. If he's close enough, we'll bang 'im with a coupla ADCAPS."

Bentley's brow raised as if surprised then said. "Captain, that sounds crazy enough to work."

Battle stations manned, sonar fuses installed and two launchers fully ready, *Steelhead* waited, cocked like a two-dollar pistol.

Maddock ordered Weapons Officer LT Parnell, "Use the starboard bank, Woody. Let's not depend on the ejection system till it earns its wings."

"Starboard bank ready," Parnell confirmed.

The captain asked LT Bentley, "Sonar alerted?"

"Alerted and ready, Captain."

"Okay, Tom, let's do it."

"Aye, Captain." Bentley ordered the helmsman to ring up all ahead flank, then paralleled his order to maneuvering via the 7MC.

Steelhead lurched forward as the huge propeller bit into the sea. Hull vibration made everything not tied down in *Steelhead* rattle quite loud.

Thirty seconds later, Maddock directed Bentley to order all stop.

Vibrations abated as *Steelhead* dropped to dead slow speed and returned to ultra-quiet condition.

The captain ordered Parnell to open the torpedo tube outers and demanded over the 21MC, "Hear anything, Sonar?"

"High speed screws bearing one-six-zero."

"Bang away, Sonar."

"Aye, Captain."

Ten seconds passed though it felt like an hour to the attack center party.

"Range, five thousand yards, bearings drawing right."

"Good job, Sonar." Maddock addressed Parnell. "Fire one! Woody. Hold two till my order."

"One fired electrically, Captain. Standing by for two."

An excited voice came over the 21MC, "Target accelerating and turning away. He must hear the torpedo!"

The son of a bitch can do what he likes, but at five thousand yards, he's not getting away from an ADCAP. Maddock did a fast mental calculation. *Seven and a half minutes from now, he's toast.*

Three minutes later, Parnell looked anxiously at his skipper. Though he spoke not a word, his expression asked, "Fire two?"

Maddock demanded over the 21MC, "Update, Sonar."

"Torpedo and target merged to the same bearing. One-seven-eight, Captain."

"We got 'im!"

On Maddock's mentally deduced schedule, a distant explosion confirmed the balance of his thesis so he said, "This is the most dangerous time. Letdown always follows a tough navy yard session, especially after we take in lines and head for the open sea. Tendency is to relax and we can't afford that. I know we've been under a lot of strain, but this might not be the end of it. Tom, we'll remain at battle stations another half hour. If sonar finds nothing new, stand down."

The captain went to his stateroom and gratefully accepted a steaming cup of coffee from a smiling stewardsman who said, "We did good, Captain ... didn't we?"

"I guess you could say that," said Maddock as he smiled back.

Much had happened in Maddock's first day at sea, and the crew accepted their new boss quite happily. He reflected upon an axiom learned at the Naval Academy: *Morale of the crew reflects its confidence in the commanding officer.*

Steelhead crew morale reached a new high that day.

Chicago, Illinois

Vasiliy Baknov sat in his loaner car across the street from the ballet studio, hand fingering the .38 caliber revolver he had stolen from the Painter home. Anxious, he checked his watch ... 8:45 a.m. He hoped his father, Yuri Baknov, would be punctual. *That woman said he arrives at 9:00 a.m. Let's hope the old bastard is on time.*

He never met his father but had located enough recent photos to recognize him. The young man focused upon the endless stream of reasons for hating his father to overcome any compassion he might feel at the moment of truth.

In the rearview mirror, Baknov saw an old man walking toward the car, cane in hand and appearing physically impaired.

It's him. The traitor to Mother Russia.

Yuri Baknov's path would take him directly past the car, giving Vasiliy a clear shot at two yards. The moment of truth approached. Vasiliy removed the pistol from his pocket and cocked it.

Enjoy your final breaths, old man.

Suddenly, Vasiliy came to grips with the fact he laid eyes upon his father for the first time. *A moving moment, but I am undeterred.* As Yuri passed, young Baknov aligned the pistol for a headshot. His finger tightened on the trigger as he had been taught at cadet school. *Slowly. Easy, easy. Don't pull the trigger ... squeeze it.* Vasiliy's arm steadied as he tracked the elder Baknov's head with perfect sight alignment. First a side headshot, then a back headshot.

Ready in every way, yet Vasiliy could not let his trigger finger squeeze. The would-be assassin lowered his pistol and watched his father disappear into the dance studio. Vasiliy rationalized, *Just as well. Look at him. Old and decrepit. Putting the old bastard out of his misery would be a merciful act and traitors deserve no mercy.*

All this to no avail, for Mary Agnes Painter as mothers are prone to do, exerted a significant influence over Baknov. Mothers instinctively guide their children's thoughts and perception of the world. Although not related, Vasiliy found himself in the role of surrogate son in young Terry Painter's absence.

Try as he may, he found little to vindicate what he'd been taught of America by the Communist Party. He conceded that the quality of life in America exceeded what he experienced in Russia. Vasiliy thought, *Maybe it's what makes them so soft and gullible.*

Per his plan, Vasiliy drove the loaner due west and abandoned it. He hoped this would put pursuers off the track, making them believe *Warren Biddle* returned to his home in the Pacific Northwest. *Subsequent investigation will reveal the real Biddle had been lost at sea. And my using his identity will surely raise flags.*

Baknov planned to use the money he accumulated working as an auto mechanic to sustain him at least a month, plus cover the cost of a train ticket from Chicago to Philadelphia. Once there, he would locate America's new submarine base and find Brent Maddock. *By then, this newfound compassion will be purged from my system.*

USS *Steelhead*

Brent Maddock directed his Exec Tom Bentley to have the underwater telephone (Gertrude) fuses pulled.

"But how will we rendezvous with the Woods Hole ship?"

"*Drifter*'s on the surface, so it's also safe for us to be there. We got a big ocean, so why do anything that makes us easier to find?"

"But this means breaking radio silence to get Commodore Bostwick's permission to deviate from the operation plan."

Grinning, Maddock said, "Forgiveness is easier to get than permission. At least that's what I'm told. Maintain radio silence."

"I don't know, Captain. The commodore was very specific."

"This is not my first go around with Bostwick. I guarantee, if he were aboard he'd do it my way. Tom, a Roman Senator, Lucius Aemilius Paulus Macedonicus, once was commissioned to lead an invasion of Macedonia in One-sixty-four BC. He got many and conflicting directions from those who voted to send him off to fight but were unwilling to join him. So, in an address to the Senate, Paulus said he'd take advice only from those who would come with him to Macedonia."

Maddock continued, "The operation order for the Battle of the Bering Sea where we kicked so much Russian ass was code-named *Macedonian*. That's because Admiral Eric Danis came with us instead of directing from safety ashore. This is our Macedonia and Bostwick isn't here."

"Wow, Captain. I'm not sure I understand."

"I'll explain later. Here's the new plan. When we locate *Drifter*, surface nearby. Hopefully, they have someone who reads flashing light. If not, we'll come alongside and communicate by bullhorn."

Midmorning on the following day, *Steelhead* surfaced when she encountered *Drifter*. Interrogation by flashing light got no response. Maddock thought, *The damn technology age is letting too much good stuff fall through the cracks,* then conned his ship within hailing distance. A relatively smooth sea state two cooperated.

Maddock raised his bullhorn, "Brent Maddock here, Skipper."

From *Drifter*, "Morning, Captain. Jim Campbell. You scared the hell out us until we recognized you as a *Six-thirty-seven*."

"Sorry about that. We encountered a bad guy and had to dispatch him. Didn't know if any of his buddies lurk around, so not a good idea to signal our presence with Gertrude."

"Can't argue with that. How do you want to proceed?"

Maddock explained the plan called for ten different events. By spacing them exactly thirty minutes apart, *Steelhead* would be able to reach each test location and carry out her assignment without a Gertrude exchange.

"We'll synchronize our time and execute on that schedule. If something goes wrong, we'll surface and make contact."

"Good plan, Captain. What if something goes amiss at our end?"

"Do you have any explosive charges?"

"Yes."

"Drop one and we'll surface to rendezvous. I want to add an eleventh event. When we finish, transfer copies of all the data to us. We might need it sooner than you can get it to us through the mail."

"You ready to start?"

"Let's do it."

The TPES experiment consisted of *Steelhead* taking position 10,000 yards from *Drifter* and presenting various aspects at several key depths to permit recording the sound signature of each launch. The shipyard had provided weighted and balanced shapes to simulate weapons in *Steelhead*'s inventory.

Woody Parnell took charge of the TPES operations, being the only man aboard that knew anything about the ejection system. Having this responsibility spread his grin from ear to ear. However, very subtly, the COB looked over his shoulder to insure he would do his principal job: make Parnell look good.

Steelhead and *Drifter* rendezvoused after conducting Maddock's 11th event. Jim Campbell sounded the bullhorn, "A bit early to say, Skipper, but it looks like you have a better mousetrap."

"Thanks, Jim. Have a good trip back to the Hole." Then turning to Tom Bentley, "Now, the fun part. Go home and explain to the commodore why we didn't get his permission to not use Gertrude."

Chapter 7

Oval Office, White House

Rear Admiral (RADM) Eric Danis experienced uncomfortable moments in his life, but nothing approaching those of his current dilemma. He sat in the lobby, twiddling his thumbs, and wondering why he had been summoned to the White House. Danis thought perhaps President Andrew Dempsey used the prolonged *heel-chill* technique to soften up his visitors. If so, it worked quite well. After what seemed an eternity, though actually only twenty minutes, a secretary conducted Danis into the Oval Office.

President Dempsey rose, walked around his desk and extended a hand. "Admiral Danis. How good to finally meet you. I would have made this sooner, but I understand your hands are quite full out there on the west coast."

Danis took the offered hand. "Mr. President. This is indeed an honor. My wife is green with envy. Neither of us has ever been in the White House."

"Eve. Is that right?"

"It is, sir. How did you know that?"

"My spies, Eric. Before they let me talk to anyone, I've got to know all about them. I understand your son Patrick has had a few brushes with the law, but seems to be straightening out."

"Patrick's a good boy, but you're right. He's been in his share of hot water. For a while, he refused to speak with me, but that's over now. Actually, I'm quite proud of him."

The President invited Eric to sit. "You Navy people drink a lot of coffee. Can I get you some?" He had sensed Danis got his back up a bit at the mention of his son. "I guess Patrick will follow his dad into the Navy?"

"No, Mr. President. I'm not a proponent of the 'chip off the old block' syndrome. Patrick's his own man, and I prefer it that way."

"Well, I am sure he'll do fine. Apples have a habit of not falling far from their trees."

As Danis expected, the President did not have enough time for small talk and ended it abruptly by saying, "Eric, I've called you here for several reasons. Mostly to thank you."

"Thank me, sir?"

"Had it not been for the victory you gave us in the Bering Sea, I'd have been forced to capitulate by an SOB who shall remain nameless. We were getting our butts whopped until you came along. My worthy antagonist would've had us speaking Russian by now."

Danis smiled. "You are very kind, Mr. President, but I had a great deal of help with that. Contrary to popular rumor, had I been there by myself, I doubt we'd have won."

"Well, at any rate, you did."

A secretary brought their coffees. When she left, Dempsey got to his second point: summary of the world situation. "We're winning, Eric, but not fast enough. Big problem, the American public is not good with long wars. It could come down to all the Soviets have to do is outwait us. Here's the situation."

The President explained. "The Soviet Union, though controlling all of Europe except the British Isles, now have the same problems as did Hitler and Napoleon before them. Overly long supply lines and unrest in the occupied countries."

"What do you have in mind, Mr. President, and how can I help?"

"The Reds won't quit until we get boots on the ground in Europe and push them back into Russia. We must stage resources in Britain and invade the continent from there. Logistics … and lots of 'em are what is needed that can only get there by ship. World War Two all over again. Soviet interdiction of our logistics by air is not a problem, or at least not a big one. We have control there. The submarine threat is a different matter. Again, World War Two revisited. The Joint Chiefs seem dry on options to work the ASW (anti-submarine warfare) problem."

An interesting picture formed in Danis's mind. *He can't be thinking what I think he is, can he?*

President Dempsey confirmed the suspicion. "Eric, I know it jumps you a rank, but I'm appointing you Chief of Naval Operations (CNO). This is not just because I wanted to repay you. We need someone who understands ASW and your name tops the list."

Danis attempted to speak, but Dempsey interrupted him. "Yeah, I know. This'll irritate a lot of your Navy buddies, but it's cast in concrete. SECNAV (Secretary of the Navy) wants it, and so do I."

"Have you advised the incumbent?"

"I have. There's no problem. He admits he's burned out and even turned down an appointment to Joint Chiefs Chairman. His background is aviation and he knows it'll take a submariner to crack this nut."

"I don't know what to say, Mr. President."

"There's nothing to say. A neat perk of my job, I get the final call in these matters. Look at the bright side, Eric. Your wife wants to visit the White House. I'll arrange for Mildred to have her over for tea. Now, when can you start?"

"I'll have to check with my wife."

"No need. I spoke with Eve this morning and she's already packing. I think she was a bit surprised by my call, though. Have you got a good interim guy till we get a replacement?"

"A good man. Dave Zane. Retired Navy and will likely run the base better than I do."

Steelhead en route Bay of Fundy

LT Woody Parnell sat in the wardroom with the captain, exec and Sonarman Chief Phil Giambri, surrounding a good deal of the recently collected TPES data spread out before them.

Giambri's background in underwater acoustics delayed starting his leave following *Sterlet*'s incident. Needed to ride *Steelhead* for the ejection system evaluation, he simply bowed to the inevitable. It also made him the logical meeting lead.

He began, "Captain, far as radiated noise levels getting out into the ocean, TPES has the same requirement as every other launcher; eject a weapon into the ocean at fifty feet per second."

Maddock enjoyed mixing it up with his troops. "So, Chief, you're telling me we took all this risk just to validate the law of conservation of energy?"

"You could say that, Captain, but the law has an escape clause; energy changes its form and that's what we have here. The old launchers have a distinctive noise signature, the *thump* sound when a piston bottoms is a dead giveaway."

Parnell asked, "But can't a TPES pulse be heard from the same distance?"

Giambri replied, "Yeah. But them recognizing it is a whole new ballgame. From what I gleaned from the tapes, it's similar to a lot of natural ocean noises I've heard. I'm sure glad the *Pinkos* don't have one. Until they figure out what we've got here, we have one helluva leg up on 'em."

While scanning faces, Maddock said, "Speak now or forever hold your peace. Is this something everybody feels good about using for our next run under the ice?"

Tom Bentley replied, "With all due respect—"

Maddock interrupted, "When was that ever a problem?"

His comment drew the expected laughter. Maddock considered levity an equalizer for stress and used it often.

Bentley continued, "It's a no-brainer. Even if it gives us no real advantages, there's no apparent defect we know of."

Parnell added, "And according to the wire feedback from the shapes, we get fifty feet a second. Let's go for it."

"Okay," said Maddock. "We use it. Now, as long as we got you here, Chief, what's your assessment of where the torpedo came from that got *Sterlet*?"

Giambri replied, "Not a prayer, Captain. But I'm certain of where it didn't come from … the boomer or another submarine."

Bentley asked, "How do you know that, Chief?"

Maddock waved the exec's question away. Shipmate with Giambri for the better part of three years, he knew the chief would not have said that unless he knew it to be correct.

The meeting came to an abrupt close at the sound of the general alarm, followed by "Man battle stations torpedo!"

While everyone sprang into action, the collision alarm's piercing tones rang throughout the ship and struck the crew like a blow in the solar plexus. *Steelhead* executed torpedo evasion.

Racing to the attack center, thoughts ran through Maddock's mind. *You'd think the damn Russians would at least give us time for a wardroom meeting. Next, they'll interrupt our cribbage games.*

Murena-class Soviet Submarine *Lenin*
Severodvinsk Shipyard

Captain 1st Rank Dmitri Borkowski, commanding officer of the Soviet submarine *Lenin*, sat in the wardroom with an old navy colleague, Mikhail Turgenev, a direct descendant of Ivan Turgenev, the gifted Russian nineteenth century novelist. The genes of Ivan's father, a colonel in the Russian Cavalry apparently did not reach his great-great-grandson. But those of Ivan made up for it in spades.

Mikhail actually had an impressive military career, although clearly a fish out of water. He had been commanding officer of their submarine where Dmitri, a junior officer then, idolized his captain.

A strong friendship evolved and continued to flourish. Mikhail yielded to the inevitable upon relief of command. He retired from the service and took employment in the documentation department of the Severodvinsk shipyard. The fit proved a natural one for the great-great-grandson of a famous writer.

Both men, passionate about their homeland, shared many great concerns over the direction it now followed. As a consequence, when assured they could not be overheard, shared concern over the system by which absolute authority over their country was exercised by a select few.

As soon as the stewardsman provided teas, Borkowski roared, "So, how are you, old friend? Or should it be *Tovarish* (Comrade) old friend?"

"All depends on who's listening."

"Not to worry. That jackass *Zampolit* Anikanov went directly to headquarters, likely at this very moment reciting a litany of faults he uncovered during our last run."

"He can't be worse than the one I had. And by the bye, are we beating the Americans to the extent our leaders claim? Three years ago, it was to be only six months before our beloved premier would sit at the desk in the Oval Office."

Borkowski said, "I'm told the delay is accounted for by changes in strategy that brings greater advantage to Mother Russia. Our stunning victory in the Bering Sea has relegated the Americans to a watch and wait mode."

Mikhail shook his head. "Another such victory and expect NATO Headquarters to move to Moscow."

"Frankly, Mikhail, what have you learned of our true situation?"

Dmitri and Mikhail loved their country and wished it to exceed in its current effort. Both had put their lives in peril to this extent.

"Not unexpectedly, the length of our logistics lines drains us, as it did Hitler during his visit here forty-eight years ago. We feel it. Most of our repair parts come from surviving hulks of the *Bering Sea* victory. What are your feelings, Dmitri? How are things at sea?"

"*Ice Castle* works exceptionally well. Not one of our ballistic missile submarines has been attacked. I had to move recently when a *Safety Belt* unit successfully attacked and probably destroyed an American submarine, but we were never in danger."

"I wonder about that policy. Do we believe the Americans will initiate a preemptive strike and wipe out our land based missiles before we can respond? I frankly do not think that will happen. The Americans, like us, want something of value left to claim at the conclusion of this nonsense."

"Ah, Mikhail the poet. It must have a happy ending for the poem to sell."

"I would not look for that sort of logic among the authors of our current dilemma. The circumstance is dire. But the only way to overcome this is to admit it exists. Peace with America is the only solution and I believe this is possible, *if* we don't condition it with occupation of their country, an absurd concept."

"Mikhail, peace would likely permit the Soviet Union to annex almost the entire European continent. However, now we encounter resistance groups in every occupied country. They do not have the wherewithal to kick us out, but believe the Americans, as they did in Nineteen forty-four, will come to their aid. Though, without this hope, enough Europeans will yield to us to permit consolidation of what we have conquered."

"So what's to be done, old friend?"

Dmitri replied, "We could be taken to the wall just for having this conversation. Nothing. For now, anyway."

Clearly the old friends needed respite from all this complexity.

Mikhail said, "I'm sure all *Lenin*'s vodka is consumed after such a long voyage."

"There might just be one bottle left. Stewardsman!"

Steelhead underway Bay of Fundy

Maddock did not need to ask *What've we got?*

Conning officer Bill Bryan shouted, "Torpedo inbound, Captain! I'm increasing speed to flank and turning away!"

Seizing the 21MC mike, Maddock said, "Sonar, Captain. Is the weapon pinging?"

"No, Captain. Passive."

Taking charge, Maddock ordered, "All stop, rudder amidship. Bill, set condition ultra-quiet in a new world-record time."

Through an astounded look, Bryan replied, "But, Captain!"

Maddock replied, "The weapon's not pinging. And it can't listen to what it doesn't hear. Make ready tubes two and four. Let's give this new system a baptism in fire."

Sonar blurted out with clear edge on voice, "Close aboard and closing rapidly, Conn!"

"Report change of bearing soon as you hear it."

"Slight bearing change to right."

Everyone within earshot of the sonar transmission gritted their teeth in anticipation of an explosion.

Knowing the bearing change indicated no weapon contact with *Steelhead* and it would proceed to go on its way, Maddock said, "Sonar, your best recollection of initial bearing."

"Three-one-six, Captain. Weapon passed us and opening, sir."

Sighs of relief spread audibly throughout the attack center as crew confidence in its new skipper rose yet again. *He is a leader easy to follow* ran through the minds of many crewmen.

"Sonar, any contacts at the initial torpedo bearing?"

"Nothing, Captain."

"Good. Woody, set heading three-one-six into an ADCAP and shoot. No limits."

"Aye, Captain. With the TPES, don't expect target to know anything till he hears our inbound." Seconds later, "Torpedo on the way, fired electrically."

The precision with which the attack center crew performed did not reflect their nervous stomachs.

Maddock announced to the fire-control party. "He's gotta be well within range if he's been quiet since launching the torpedo. Look for him to crank it up when he hears our weapon. Woody, adjust torpedo heading to new target bearing from sonar."

ADCAP torpedoes remain connected by wire to the submarine after launch and can be redirected continuously.

"New bearings from sonar, aye, Captain."

Maddock ordered, "Sonar, keep an ear on that outbound and report any change." *Things going too well breeds complacency and we don't need that right now.*

"Conn, Sonar. New target three-two-two. Definite submarine cranking up, bearings drawing right." The unmistakable voice of Chief Giambri rang from the 21MC like a healing salve. "He hears our torpedo."

Maddock ordered Parnell, "Lead him twenty degrees."

Parnell responded, "Twenty degrees, Captain. New torpedo heading three-four-two."

"Sonar. Our fish running?"

"Perfectly."

Maddock nodded although he could not see the reporting sonarman. "Bill, ahead dead slow and make for periscope depth."

He thought it not a good time to state his reason. If the Soviet torpedo doubled back and struck the ship, he wanted to get as many of the crew out as possible.

Unable to hide the triumph from his voice, Chief Giambri stated, "ADCAP shifted to short-scale pinging, Captain. We got 'im!"

A distant explosion confirmed the chief's claim. Though it could be heard throughout the ship, no cheers erupted, only expressions of relief in that *they* lost, not *us*. Contrary to established stereotypes, warriors engaged in combat like it less than anyone. They well know risks and consequences and prefer to avoid it as often as possible.

The crew's thoughts went out to the defeated enemy, now undergoing a submariner's worst nightmare, that of water flowing into their ship with no way to stop it. These men have families and sweethearts they long to be with, but these submariners will forever remain at sea.

Years after the war has ended, veterans of both sides might meet, eat, drink too much and exchange outrageous tales. Why not now? But until this madness ends, the question is better left unasked. Dehumanize the enemy, gather up the pieces and live to fight another day.

Bay of Fundy

Commodore (COM) Hal Bostwick sat in his palatial yacht-housed SUBGRU headquarters and seethed over the information he received, RADM Eric Danis's selection to CNO.

Number fingerers (officers determined to reach the top at all costs, competence not a factor) formed a loose network. Though *fingerers* trusted no one, especially each other, mutual advantage accumulated from networking, and so they did. A fellow *fingerer* phoned Bostwick earlier in the day with the impending news.

On a bad note, Bostwick parted with Danis in Washington State at odds over Brent Maddock. Danis served notice that Bostwick would do better to find someone else to pick on. Hal felt upstaged by the young officer and Bostwick did what any *fingerer* would do. Plan to discredit him and get him out of the way.

Although he had actually nothing to do with it, Bostwick blamed Danis for failure to receive the Congressional Medal of Honor from President Dempsey. Simply put, America desperately needed a hero, and Bostwick reached Washington, D.C. a day too late.

Bostwick scheduled a meeting to berate Maddock for scrubbing Gertrude in communications between *Steelhead* and *Drifter* during the TPES test. He planned to use the incident to serve Maddock notice that he had put his command tenure in jeopardy. One more strike and out. Bostwick correctly suspected that Danis followed Maddock's status closely. *Fingerers* did not like the idea of getting across the CNO's breakers, so Bostwick would tread carefully.

Brent arrived on time and sat the customary fifteen minutes in the outer office before admittance to Bostwick's domain.

A master showman, Bostwick greeted *Steelhead*'s commander warmly. "Brent. So good to see you. How long's it been?"

Brent took the unexpected warm greeting in stride. "I don't rightly remember, Commodore. About a trillion gallons of water under the fantail?"

"Sounds about right. Sit down and tell me all about the TPES evaluation. And congratulations. A week in command and already two notches in your belt. Good decision not to use Gertrude. I had no idea the bad guys had us pinpointed, but getting good intelligence is a bit hard these days."

Neither Bostwick nor Maddock understood the true significance of the notches. A Soviet exchange of duty in the Bay of Fundy resulted in both Soviet reliever and relieved submarines being destroyed. This would raise no hackles in Severodvinsk until the relieved ship became overdue for return to port. The Bay of Fundy would be clear of Soviet opposition for at least three weeks. Worse, seriously diminished Soviet resources would be further decimated by the loss of these two ships.

"Thank you, Commodore." A bit disarmed, Brent believed he'd be taken to task about the Gertrude decision and had spent most the night formulating a compelling answer. But the meeting went well, much to Brent's surprise. The two retold old *Denver* tales until Bostwick pleaded a busy schedule.

They exchanged cordial salutations and parted. As Maddock left, Bostwick reckoned, *Enjoy it while you can, but you'll screw up. I'll see to that, and when you do, it'll be curtains.*

Southern Illinois

Jack Olsen's wife Rita sat serenely between her two sons as an American Legion Honor Guard performed a plaque-dedication ceremony at the local cemetery.

Four *Sterlet* Illinois resident submariners stood at attention. At its conclusion, the CPO presented their ship's last national ensign and commissioning pennant to the captain's wife and widow.

Afterward, as they proceeded to their car for the drive home, a young man overtook them. "My mom, Mrs. Olsen, would like you to drop by our home before you leave."

The CPO spoke for the group, "Certainly."

Later, in the parlor of what had once been a farmhouse, the four sat down, uncomfortable in that none had ever socialized with a captain's wife before."

The CPO began inelegantly to recite the crew's condolences he had presented at the ceremony. Though appreciative, Rita Olsen needed more. These are the men who last saw her husband and she wanted to know all.

"Like it or not, you must stay and have lunch with me."

Rita's mother and dad quickly emphasized the invitation.

The CPO began with an account of Jack Olsen's final heroic act, the others chiming in with bits and pieces omitted.

"The captain refused to order any member of the crew to perform a task he would not do himself."

All paused a moment to let that settle in.

Rita changed the mood. Who could possibly know her man better than fellow submariners that shared so tiny a space with him for so long?

She said, "Now, gentlemen, please tell me about my husband, the man."

At first, they spoke only of serious, respectful aspects of their captain. But with Rita's encouragement, they quickly got into the normal then funny, and then outrageous. The atmosphere softened accordingly with frequent laughter interruptions and would have gone on for hours if Rita's mom had not insisted they sit for lunch.

Later, when the men departed, Rita embraced each one, then blinked back a tear and forced a smile.

"Thank you for loving my husband."

Rita watched from the front porch as the auto carrying the four *Sterlet* sailors disappeared down the road. She felt as though a proper goodbye had finally been said to her beloved husband.

Chapter 8

Near Severodvinsk

Dmitri Borkowski sat with his friend in Mikhail Turgenev's well-appointed study. They used the eve of Borkowski's deployment back to the Arctic as an excuse for dinner together. Wives of both men busied themselves out of sight in the kitchen.

A fire crackled in the bed of a huge fireplace centered on a wall of Mikhail's study. Completely filled bookshelves covered the rest, including six Turgenev first editions.

Borkowski began paging through one of the books while he said, "Mikhail *Mikhailovitch*, this one alone must be worth a million rubles. Plus the other five makes your family solvent for at least the next three generations."

"You are correct, Dmitri, but then whenever are you not? But these are my great-great-grandfather's. And to redeem the rubles, they must be sold. Would this not be like selling your oldest son to the gypsies?"

"I suppose. But, right now I hunger for a little Rachmaninoff."

A signal Dmitri wished to talk and to overwhelm the NKVD bug placed *secretly* in Turgenev's home.

Mikhail had positioned his phonograph directly below the bug. A skilled engineer, he knew if they spoke a decibel lower than the blaring speakers, their conversation could not be recorded. Soon, the moving and powerful notes of *Rachmaninoff's Piano Concerto No. 2* filled the room and shielded their conversation.

"Ah, Dmitri. It is good we Russians like our music loud."

Borkowski nodded. "Mikhail, you should know the *K-seven-sixteen* submarine is two weeks overdue for its return from the Bay of Fundy."

"Has anything been heard from her?"

"Nothing. My guess is that she's gone. And this gives me great concern about *K-six-ninety-nine*. Might both have been sunk during the relief process? If so, the Americans have free ingress and egress to Fundy until we get something over there."

Turgenev pondered a second and said, "True. The northern fleet is spread thin as a single pad of butter over a full loaf of bread. We cannot bear more losses. And guarding approaches to Fundy is costly ... too much time passes in transit where we have no access to the enemy. This reduces the probability of sinking more of their submarines. This should be a top priority now instead of protecting ballistic missile submarines that will never fire a shot. That is unless the Party wishes to destroy the world."

"Our situation deteriorates, Mikhail. Much fortification is needed if we are to keep the Allies from getting a toehold in Europe. Perhaps we should take a lesson from the Nazis ... slave labor."

Borkowski's sarcastic voice signaled the absurdity of this proposal. Both knew it to fly in the face of true Russian heritage. Hence, finding enough troops to enforce it would be impossible and might even incite mutiny.

His voice returned to serious tones and Borkowski said, "Hiring non-Russians is not a solution. The occupied countries grow more restive and will not be party to impeding the arrival of Allied relief."

"You are right, Dmitri. The only solution is interdict supply lines between the United States and Britain. Logistics by air are token at best and not to be worried about. Merchant ships are needed. Right now, we have submarine assets to interdict this, but not if we continue to lose them like in the Fundy effort."

"The erstwhile von Clausewitz wrote that war cannot be won without full support of a nation's people. Lucky for us Hitler never read *On War* or he'd have known this. Despite the optimistic pronouncements from the Party, Russians are tiring of war and I sense support for it diminishes."

The Rachmaninoff Concerto entered the adagio movement with its signature series of slow, soft chords. The men had to lower their voices accordingly.

Turgenev added, "And did not Chinese General Sun Tzu toss a log on the Clausewitz fire? I recall from Naval School, Tzu said, 'If you know your enemies and know yourself, you can win a hundred battles without a single loss'."

"It was true for those times," Borkowski said. "Losing a war meant only occupation of the losing country. Now it can be the destruction of the entire planet, for there is risk of a nation with its back to the wall resorting to nuclear weapons."

"A bleak outlook indeed."

Borkowski continued, "I see waging of war forced into taking a different slant. Like corrupting the enemy government from within. No, Mikhail. Topple the government peacefully, then jump in to fill the power vacuum. This can be done in America. I learned that while working at our embassy in Washington, DC, before the war."

"You did? Tell me about—"

A summon to dinner from Turgenev's wife interrupted their discussion, followed by, "Mikhail, why must the phonograph be at full volume? Is old age affecting your hearing?"

Bay of Fundy

Brent Maddock, LT Parnell and the COB stood hands on hips on the ammunition-loading barge. A rainy, blustery day for weapons loading is bad enough then Henri sighted a new challenge chocked tightly onto the barge deck.

Head shaking, COB asked, "Pardon my French, Captain, but what in the hell is that and what're we supposed to do with it?"

"We're first to use it, so I guess we get to name it. Maybe another one of your contests. The winner gets a brew on me at the base canteen."

"But ya gotta tell me what it is first, Captain."

"It's a new weapon for attacking ice-picked Soviet boomers."

"Hmm."

COB's expression showed his annoyance at not having been previously informed.

The skipper liked this. A good COB questions everything. Only tight security prevented knowledge from being generally distributed, but now the cat had leapt from its bag.

"Probably the simplest device since the Second World War's Mark-fourteen torpedo. Just like the *fourteen*, it's got propulsion and guidance systems to push a warhead to the target. A little different though. It flies through the air, has twenty times the range of a Mark fourteen, is infinitely faster and has a heavier warhead. And the stuff in it will give a much louder bang."

Henri countered, "But even if we hit a new Soviet *Typhoon*, we won't hurt it. Biggest submarine in the world, Captain."

"You're right, COB. But I'm guessing it'll give him one helluva headache and get him moving. And when he does, his butt is ours."

Parnell's eyes widened. "So what's the game plan for finding and ranging the boomer?"

The skipper grinned at his first lieutenant (officer in charge of the deck force). "Woody, didn't they teach you in sub-school that skippers don't have all the answers? We toss out a ball and expect you young brilliants to kick it around."

COB asked, "Captain, how close can we get before encountering whatever it is that got *Sterlet*?"

"Chief Giambri's got all the data and went over it with a fine-tooth comb. His best guess is whatever they're using is probably eight thousand yards from the boomer."

While he nodded, COB said, "A Giambri guess is about as close to an exact measurement as you can get. And look up there."

A blue patch appeared among the blanket of gray clouds that hung over them and Parnell said, "It's in the southwest, COB, so don't get your hopes up."

Per an age-old seaman-thumb rule, a blue patch in the sky *big enough to patch a Dutchman's britches* foretold a favorable change in the weather. But it has to be in the northwest. A heavy rain-laden wind gust vindicated Parnell's assertion and the men moved to shelter under a deck-cover overhang.

Maddock had thought his attack plan through and knew the best way to implement it. He would ask questions of the troops, resulting in them arriving at his answer. Inspire them to take ownership. *US Naval Academy Plebe Leadership 101.*

Friday mornings found commanding officers of the submarines being refitted at the Bay, assembled for weekly *note exchanges*. COM Bostwick normally presided, but excused himself this day, likely because LCDR Brent Maddock's recent victories over Soviet submarines in the Bay would dominate the agenda. The commodore had no wish to hear it from the one he considered an adversary.

Maddock, newest and most junior commanding officer in the SUBGRU, had long been a burr under Bostwick's saddle. Brent rose rapidly through the ranks because of talent and leadership qualities. Bostwick took the political route, a fact that festered within his commodore bosom.

Eleven COs listened intently as Maddock went over each detail of his two recent enemy engagements, interrupted frequently with questions on why he had deviated from prescribed tactics.

He explained, "Simply because relying on them would have gotten us killed."

His statement caused eleven jaws to drop almost to the green billiard cloth table cover.

Then he added, "Answers to every situation are not covered in a manual. You've got to think out of the box. We're all nukes and share the same penchant to follow directions contained between the covers of a book to the letter. With the RPM (Reactor Plant Manual), compliance is not merely an option, but a career death sentence if we deviate the slightest iota. Tactics are far too dynamic to hang your hat on a single peg. No one has all the answers."

A CO annoyed at being talked down to by a subordinate asked, "You invented tactics on the spot? I find that impractical."

"Not in the least. In the main, I based decisions on published tactics then mentally analyzed their intent and improvised when guidance failed to scratch the itch."

Another exclaimed, "Wow! This is totally new ground for us."

"Ground you'll have to explore. You owe it to the country and your troops. Getting them home in one piece sets squarely on my front burner."

The first CO asked, "Will they let us get away with that?"

"Who are they?"

"Our bosses up the line."

Maddock grinned. "They won't be aboard so you won't have to tell 'em. Look. My dad started out as a troop in *forty-nine* aboard a Key West diesel boat. Told me he learned everything he needed to know about submarines from the COB the day he reported aboard. 'Keep the ocean outboard of the pressure hull. And remember, the only purpose of everything between the torpedo rooms is to get the launchers into attack position.' That includes what's between our ears. We've drifted away from what got us through the Second World War. We better get back to it if we expect to win this one."

Eleven senior COs to Brent resented the newcomer's *arrogance* but for lack of any convincing arguments, they made no comments.

The Oval Office

President Dempsey greeted his new CNO, Admiral Eric Danis. "You've had the job almost a week now, Eric. So tell me how you're going to get what we need to Britain and bring this damned donnybrook to a happy conclusion."

"Mr. President, I understand Mother Teresa once said, 'I know the Lord never burdens one with more than they can handle, but sometimes I wish he didn't have so much confidence in me'."

"A turner of phrases. I didn't know politics was in your future. You'll wait till I retire of course?"

"I dodge enough Navy political bullets, thank you. After this job, it's total retirement. The Mojave Desert. Eve and I decided that when the war took us there from San Diego to set up a submarine squadron headquarters. A lot of boats survived the initial strike and needed logistic support and direction. Awkward, but about the only place we could provide it from."

"Your base in Washington State. Isn't that where you pulled it all off?"

"I didn't pull a damn thing off, sir. It takes a village. And, Mr. President, when this is over, many back pats will be handed out. One has to go to Dave Zane. His was the strongest hand in the Bering Sea victory. Trust me. It couldn't have been pulled off without him."

"I'll keep that in mind, Eric. But first, we gotta win this damn war and that's what I hired you for."

"I've already told you the Mother Superior story, Mr. President. And rest assured, I've assembled some of the coolest heads in ASW (antisubmarine warfare)."

"No damn back climbers among them, I hope."

"No sir. Once heard getting this job required establishing a network of movers and shakers in all the warfare groups. Guys who tell you the way it is regardless of consequences. That is, if you want to get anything done. Got myself some pretty good boys."

"So, what can you say to make me feel good about this war?"

"We have an idea, but it'll take some fleshing out."

"Let's hear it."

Danis felt President Dempsey's attitude to be very similar to his own. "Here's the way we see it. Our *Burke*-class DDs (destroyers) have towed arrays."

"Towed arrays?"

"Yes. Listening hydrophones at the end of a long cable. If the ships go slow enough, they can detect and localize submarines out to the first convergence zone."

"Convergence zone?"

"Thirty-two miles, give or take. Problem is they have no weapon to access targets at that range."

"So what good does the—"

"Towed array."

"Towed array do?"

"It could do plenty. *Burke* class has vertical launchers. We have a small inventory of Sea Lance missiles that can reach that far and drop a Mark-fifty torpedo on the target."

Dempsey grimaced. "And you don't have enough, right?"

"Words right out of my mouth, Mr. President."

"Well, let me tell you a likely reason. There is a finite number of vertical launchers for contractors to fill. And these contractors reside in Congressional Districts. New mousetraps take up space in those launchers, which lowers production numbers for the incumbents. This makes contractors unhappy. And contractors reduce campaign contributions which in turn makes politicians unhappy."

"I sorta guessed that, Mr. President. I was project manager here in DC on the Sea Lance program. I didn't understand the resistance we got from the warfare groups. It's the bridge for everyone's ASW shortfalls, but shunned like the plague. Even by submariners, who more than anyone should have known better."

"This shouldn't come as a surprise to you, Eric, but even a few blue suiters are not always above reproach. Post retirement jobs are a factor along with bending to politicians in exchange for other considerations."

"Depressing. But I knew something about this. While at Sea Lance, I attended a meeting in Norfolk and heard a *Burke*-class skipper tell of tracking and localizing our quietest attack submarine at the first convergence zone, a *Six-eighty-eight*. He pleaded lack of a weapon that could reach that far. After the meeting, I heard an admiral tell the skipper his ship's performance was an anomaly and achievable only because of the young CO's exceptional crew and it would not do to outfit the entire *Burke*-class fleet on that basis. I suspected, but wondered what the admiral's true agenda was. Learned later he retired and took a job with a vertical launch weapon provider. Not Sea Lance."

Dempsey asked, "What are you converging on … a new tactic?"

"Basically, Mr. President, having *Burke* towed arrays backed by Sea Lance missiles in the vertical launchers. Have each convoy accompanied by appropriate numbers of *Burke*-class destroyers and attack submarines. If a Soviet nuke submarine has a Mark-fifty dropped on him, he'll have to crank it up. When he does, he's duck soup for our attack submarines. But we need a lot of Sea Lance missiles and damn quick."

Dempsey's grin spread from ear to ear. "You hold up your end of the stick and I'll hold up mine."

Bay of Fundy

USS *Steelhead* embarked upon her first war patrol under new skipper, LCDR Brent Maddock. Conducting an all-officers meeting in the wardroom, he said, "We'll take it slow and easy exiting the Bay. Maybe give it a brief kick in the butt once in a while to flush out any waiting Soviet submarine who wants to get on our track."

Parnell asked, "What if he's already on our track, Captain?"

The skipper, *king of wisecracks*, tolerated them from his officers and retorted, "We find out why the pay's so good." Following with, "No, Woody. The probability of that is sufficiently low to take the risk. And it's highly likely on TPES trials (turbine pump ejection system) we got both ships in the process of relieving. That should open the Bay for a few more weeks. Now, the purpose of our meeting. Chief Giambri's sonarmen will find the ice pickers, but how do we range?"

As young officers are prone to do, none wanted to embarrass themselves with a stupid response, so an exchange of grim faces passed over the table.

Maddock relieved the pressure. "None of us have that answer, so let's kick it around a little. For openers, Woody ... how do we normally range? Might be a good idea to start there."

"Lots of fancy names for the methods, but if we're just listening, they all boil down to triangulation."

Bill Bryan jumped in. "Problem is, the base leg of the triangle can be no greater than max ADCAP range. Actually, about half an ADCAP range. If we shoot at max range, the target will easily evade our fish."

Maddock thought, *Good. They're getting with it.* Then he asked, "What's the major difference between an ice picker and the situation you just described?"

Parnell replied, "A no-brainer, Captain. The picker is stopped and we risk getting shot at by whatever the hell he's planting to protect himself. That's what got *Sterlet*."

Bryan exclaimed, "That's it, Woody! The new weapon extends the available base leg to as long as we want. That'll put us well beyond effective range of their minefields, or whatever the hell they're using. No way can the target hear a Sea Lance coming ... and with the TPES, it's doubtful he'll hear our launch transit. If he does, he won't recognize it. We can have a second round on the way before the first one detonates. We've got some damn good tools."

Maddock said, "But you're the ones who figured out how to use them. Maybe call it the Bryan-Parnell tactic?"

Many military officers became famous by having their names associated with a tactic.

"I vote for *Steelhead* tactic," said Parnell. "There's too many guys involved to single anyone out."

Mission accomplished went through the captain's mind.

Steelhead cleared the Bay and made for the Arctic ice cap.

Severodvinsk

Submarine *Lenin* finished a hasty turn around and stood ready to depart for points north. Skipper Dmitri Borkowski stood on the main deck with his friend Mikhail Turgenev.

Borkowski said in a low voice, "Everything is aboard except the stupid *zampolit*. We delay departure for the least useful baggage of the deployment."

Turgenev replied, "Come now, Dmitri. What's not important about reassuring your sailors the Party is behind them all the way?"

"You really don't want to hear my answer, old friend. It's so full of venom, I wouldn't trust even you with it."

"I'm sorry our discussion of the other night was interrupted."

Dmitri said, "Yes, but interrupted by a magnificent dinner. And finishing the evening sitting by the fire with our good ladies. Surely nothing is better than that."

Turgenev replied, "About our pre-dinner topic. It's one we must pursue further. We may have stumbled onto something important."

"Regardless, what can two men do with it? Especially mavericks like ourselves."

"Plant the concept in the mind of someone who can. And make them believe it's his idea and that he has much to gain from it."

"Interrupted once again," Borkowski said, "but this time by the last person I'd expect something good from if given our idea."

The *zampolit* mounted the brow with a sailor following him carrying luggage. As usual, *Zampolit* Anikanov did not apologize for delaying the sailing, nor did he acknowledge the captain.

Four days later, *Lenin* reached the Arctic and uncovered a launch polynya (opening with thick ice nearby to ice pick).

Borkowski made plans to deploy the *Safety Belt* units circling the ice pick in an eight nautical mile radius and spacing them at three thousand yard intervals. This part of the mission considered dangerous, *Lenin* proceeded carefully.

Now comes the fun part, Borkowski pondered, *sit here for three months with absolutely nothing to do. But on the other hand, this is much preferable to abruptly being ordered to launch missiles, a prospect both my countrymen and the Americans abhor.*

Chapter 9

USS *Steelhead*

In prewar Puget Sound, Brent loved leaving port on the surface while breathtaking northwest vistas slipped by on both shorelines.

Bay of Fundy offered similar diversions, but the threat of enemy submarines deemed it prudent to submerge soon as sufficiently deep water became available. Maddock didn't get his vistas. *Steelhead* abided this axiom, submerging on crossing the hundred-fathom curve then departing on her first Arctic patrol under a new skipper.

Apart from occasional periscope glimpses at polynyas, the next sixty plus days would be passed with eyes feasting on little other than *Steelhead*'s impersonal interior. Movies helped, but most had been seen at least once by the crew. Current entertainment media did not rank high among preparations for patrol. Maddock and COB Henri huddled in the captain's stateroom to discuss this. Both knew boredom to be a condition avoided to the greatest extent possible.

"Had a talk with Giambri and a few of the older chiefs on this subject, Captain."

"I envy those guys, COB. I really would've liked to have served on a smokeboat (diesel-electric submarine)."

Henri asked, "Do you like the idea of one shower a week whether you need it or not?"

Maddock replied, "As long as we all got ripe together. But I sure wouldn't want to be first out of the shower and have to smell the guys who hadn't had theirs. Tell me, COB. And it's true 'cause I noticed it. The old *dieselers* seem to take things better in stride than the younger guys. Why do you think that is?"

"Hard to put a finger on it, Captain. We were every bit as serious as the nukes about our jobs and equipment, but we didn't carry it over into communal life aboard. I don't know. Sometimes it seems the nuke guys believe recreational time is time taken away from doing their job. Watching a movie seems to be a shameful thing, but not nearly as shameful as peers getting caught doing it. Gives 'em a guilt complex."

Maddock recalled a *Sterlet* auxiliary gang officer who took pride in bragging during the month-long refit prior to deployment. He left the ship only to visit overhaul sites where equipment under his purview underwent repair and maintenance. Brent wondered about that being a good thing but said nothing. Nuke officers seemed to have a need to prove who worked the hardest.

"Now you know why I'm glad I never had to be a COB. As skipper, all I gotta say is fix it, COB."

"I'll do that of course, Captain." Henri shared a smile with his old *Denver* shipmate. "Actually, our recent brushes with Ivan have refocused attention on non-engineering topics. Maybe if we can make everyone see the ship continues to run well in spite of this diversion, it can create other and happier breaks."

"I don't know how you'll do this, COB, but as I explained before, it's not my job to know. Let's keep our finger on the pulse of things and get back together every now and again to talk about how things go."

"We'll do that, Captain."

"Speaking of diversion, gotta go to the wardroom now for an all officers to talk about how we're going to approach the ice. You're right. The recent Ivan brushes have increased tactics interest by orders of magnitude. Ever notice how unwanted consequences can change priorities and have good effects?"

A short time later, Maddock sat at the head of the wardroom table and conducted his meeting. "You've had a night to sleep on it. I need some thoughts. Make that *we* need some thoughts."

Tom Bentley remained as XO to ensure a smooth transition of command and would do so for at least one patrol. "I have an itch but can't quite pinpoint it. We're missing something. I like the basic concept … take advantage of Sea Lance bombs' long-range for targeting. But target motion? We're used to leading the target and this one is dead in the water."

Parnell explained, "It's not really. Current moves us around. The surface winds push the ice pack in a different direction so target speed and direction over the ground are different from ours."

Maddock liked the way his meeting went.

He knew he sat among good minds that became more self-assured as fear of making mistakes diminished and said, "Let me throw a little more crap into the game. Until now, submarines, ASW weapons and targets have always operated in the same medium. All three are moved by the current at the same speed and direction. Makes fire control a lot simpler. When the Sea Lance bomb hits the atmosphere, all that goes by the board. Then what?"

Blank expressions around the table.

"I recall from a class at the Naval Academy," said Bill Bryan, "that when bombarding fixed targets ashore with dumb ammunition (no guidance systems and fly ballistic trajectories), we had to know where we were with respect to the target. Computers did the rest."

"Problem is our target moves over the ground," Maddock said.

Bryan looked embarrassed, but Maddock quickly picked him up. "There is application, Bill. No existing technique will work by itself, but combinations of them might. Keep tossing stuff out and we'll eliminate vagaries one by one."

Parnell, a student under Maddock when the skipper served as weapons officer in *Denver*, appeared to have given it the most thought. "We can use relative target position as long as we calculate what effect ice movement has on target motion. Actually, Chief Giambri is working on it. We have plenty of time, so why not make a complete circle around the target?"

Encouraging Parnell, Maddock asked, So Woody ... how do you see this helping?"

"If target motion over the ground is different from ours, plotting will show the circle to be not a true one. Oblong. From that, we can get target bearing, range, speed and direction. Coupled with missile time of flight and we got a good aim point."

"Sounds okay, Woody. But if we turn a circle, why won't it be a true circle?"

"Put the target on our beam. Each time the bearing changes, we adjust course to bring him back on the beam."

Bryan asked, "What about passive sonar bearing accuracy? It changes as a function of a whole bunch of things. Won't that screw things up?"

Parnell replied, "Chief Giambri says these errors are predictable and he's worked up an algorithm to fix that."

Silence a moment around the table.

Maddock said, "Okay, everyone, rethink this through and probe for holes. Don't forget, we thought we had the answer after the last meeting and learned we didn't. So keep pickin' at this strawman. Now, to more important things. Don't know about the rest of you, but the odor of burning wood is overwhelming in these tight spaces. Cribbage time, video games or whatever you guys do to relax when you're not on watch. Should you walk by my stateroom, be quiet."

Aboard Ice-picked *Lenin*

Captain 1st Rank Dmitri Borkowski sat in his stateroom and managed to keep his eyes open while *Zampolit* Yuri Anikanov rattled on for an hour about his usual nothing. One had to be careful, for at times, it almost seemed as if birds of the air would overhear an untoward word and pass it to the NKVD, identifying the speaker.

An unspoken consensus had developed among Borkowski's fellow commanding officers, none of them were happy with the *zampolit* assigned to their ship. They wondered if this could be a collective symptom of trouble within the government overall. Qualifications for the *zampolit* job are simple; be only smart enough to parrot the Party line and sufficiently ruthless to turn in even a family member should criticisms be made about the Party.

The Party made no effort to force Navy line officers into this mold, likely from realizing needs of the two positions mutually contradicted each other. Perhaps it had learned how Stalin's 1930s' purge of professional officers resulted in a massive army with leadership so weakened it could not defeat the infinitely smaller Finnish army in the *Winter War*.

Borkowski said, "Very enlightening, *Komrade Zampolit*. You must pass this on to the men."

The obese Anikanov construed this to mean he held Borkowski by the scruff of his neck then without further thought, he waddled contentedly along the passageway to his stateroom.

The captain stretched out on his bunk, relieved the hour-long headache had come to an end. He pondered his recent conversation with Mikhail Turgenev. Thoughts returned to his prewar tour of duty in the United States where he gained insight into life in America. He had plenty of time to acquire this as his family did not accompany him, likely a measure to ensure he did not defect.

The embassy strictly regulated media Borkowski got at his quarters, but from time to time, he watched television outside in public places. His outings consisted mostly of making pickups at dead drops (where spies dropped secret material for the embassy). Frequently, he arrived early and killed time inconspicuously at a bar or restaurant. Perfect English and without accent, he sustained his anonymity well, making Dmitri the best choice for this assignment. Dead drops in nearby rural Virginia, close to public facilities, provided him with these diversionary accesses. TV commercials fascinated him.

Exceptionally intelligent, Borkowski easily saw how presenters focused not on message content, but on manners of delivery, often made by celebrities with absolutely no knowledge of the product, or by cool, beautiful people in vernacular of the day. He also noticed attractive women presented products intended for male audiences and vice versa.

Borkowski simply could not understand how rational people could be persuaded to buy items based not on merit, but upon who told them to buy it, how and why. And these missives must work in order to earn extreme fees posted for them. *Could Mother Russia use these same techniques to manipulate Americans into espousing her cause?*

Back then as a young officer, he toyed only mentally with these ideas. *Marx was wrong. Media, not religion, is the opiate of at least a large percentage of American people.* Dmitri marveled at the ease with which audiences could be manipulated and made to cheer where it best served the show producer. And producers seemed able to make audiences ignore major issues throughout the world.

He ruminated the topic as a young zealot, mainly for self-entertainment, but abandoned it on return to the Soviet Union where other and more important tasks distracted him.

Subsequent disenchantment with the war and his interrupted conversation with Mikhail Turgenev, stimulated Borkowski and he began to think seriously of its potential as a non-destructive way in which to overpower the United States. *What a wonderful way to fight wars. No one gets hurt and nothing is blown up.*

Aboard *Steelhead* under the Arctic Ice Cap

Tom Bentley aroused Maddock from a deep sleep. "Sonar reports a faint fifty-hertz line (sound emanating from machinery rotating at 50 cycles per second, like Soviet submarines' ship's service power generators). No noticeable bearing drift, Captain, so we figure it's stopped."

"Any idea of range?"

"No. We're proceeding directly toward it at dead-slow speed. Chief Giambri says the rate of volume increase gives range clues. He's on it."

"Good. Give me a minute and I'll meet you in the sonar shack."

A host of submarine firsts lay in store for Maddock and he would have to *suck 'em up.* He knew that most successes or failures hinged on the crew's perception of the captain's level of confidence and determined he would not disappoint his troops.

Maddock entered the sonar shack and signaled his comfort level by injecting humor. "XO, is this the real thing or just another excuse to get even for your recent cribbage drubbing?"

Bentley took it in stride. "Dream on, Captain, dream on," then asked Giambri for an update.

"Good morning, Captain," Giambri greeted. "So far, signals are too intermittent for a range guess. But factoring in background noise and what we know of Russian submarines, I'm guessing twenty thousand yards plus."

"Chief, any chance we're in some sort of sound channel and might lose him?"

"Highly unlikely, sir."

"How 'bout bottom reflection?"

"No. That has a mushy sound. This is coming directly from the horse's mouth."

"Keep your guys on it, Chief. When we get a solid signal, put him on the beam for a range check. Call me before you turn."

"Aye, Captain."

"When's the last time you slept, Chief?"

"Been a while, but I'm okay."

"Don't want you poopin' out on us at a critical time."

"Promise not to, Captain." Giambri gestured toward a locker that doubled as a bench. "I catch a few *Z's* over there when things quiet down a bit."

Maddock shook his head and left.

He directed Bentley, "Get Woody up. "I want to go over his ranging scheme one more time."

When the skipper took his place at the wardroom table head, the duty stewardsman poured him a cup of black coffee and said, "Every time XO gets you up in the wee smalls, Captain, it turns out to be an *all-nighter.*"

"Thanks, Benson. You're probably right, but after I wrap myself around this it'll be just like midmorning."

A sleepy-eyed Parnell entered the room with Tom Bentley. "Mornin', Captain. I guess it's morning ... right?"

"Something like that, Woody." Maddock explained the tactical situation then asked, "Have you put any more thought into the ranging technique?"

"I did, Captain. Made a mistake about the intercept problem. There is none."

"None?"

"Sea Lance has an inertial guidance system and will conduct the payload to whatever location we enter. Either geographical or relative to us works."

"Good thinking, Woody. Keep this up and I'll be working for you at our next duty station."

The attack center messenger prevented Woody from getting his cup of coffee. "Sonar reports strong steady signal, Captain, and recommends you come to the shack."

Maddock swallowed his final coffee gulp. "Let's go, Woody."

The three officers walked to the attack center where Giambri reported he already requested a new heading to put the target on the starboard beam.

"Big concern, Chief. Keep farthest from him consistent with maintaining continuous contact. We got a good idea of where his defensive ring is and its effective range. But don't push our luck."

"Aye, Captain."

The depth-control party reported via the 21MC, "Sonar, Conn. Steady new course zero-one-five."

Giambri responded, "Sonar, Aye, Conn. Make it a steady one. Have the QMOW (quartermaster of the watch) maintain a careful DR (dead reckoning) plot. Give me a mark when we've traveled five nautical from this spot."

"Mark at five, Sonar. You got it. And we got the COB for QMOW."

Maddock, relieved at hearing the COB news, said, "This should be good enough for a safety margin, Woody. We still need to refine it with the big circle?"

"It's our best shot to find out how much the wind is moving the ice around relative to us. It's our first outing, so let's get it right."

Maddock grinned at his weapons officer. "I'm bettin' there's no Easter-egg effect and we get a perfect circle."

"Fifth of JD Black?"

"Are you old enough to drink?"

"Bet or no bet, Captain?"

"Bet."

"Good. I say our circle's going to be oblong enough to make an Easter egg jealous."

After a lengthy wait, "Mark!" came over the 21MC.

An hour later, Parnell determined preliminary triangulation range to the target: 9,700 yards.

He said, "This makes circumference of the circle about thirty nautical miles. Best we can do at ultra-quiet is three knots, so we got a twenty-hour ranging exercise on our hands, Chief."

Giambri responded, "What else have we got to do, Mr. Parnell?"

Parnell returned to the wardroom and briefed the captain.

When he finished, Maddock asked, "Sure we're far enough away from their defensive weapons' system?"

"Per Giambri, *Sterlet*'s attack initiated at twelve hundred yards. This gives us a safety factor of about three and we're a lot quieter than a *Five-eighty-five* class boat. From a green, newly promoted lieutenant's point of view, we should be good, Captain. That make you feel better?"

"Long as the lieutenant is parroting Chief Giambri's assessment, I'm okay with it. Now, tell me about the Sea Lance bomb theory."

Parnell barbed right back at the captain. "I taught Giambri everything he knows. Now, about the bomb. The warhead has eight hundred pounds of high explosive. The payload is configured to punch through seven feet of ice and detonate when it's clear. This focuses the energy in a channel directly under the ice ... exactly where the target is. Anything less than a direct hit will not sink the target, but it'll do such a number on his inertial equipment, he'll need to drive home and get it fixed."

"Is it fair to say the term direct hit is synonymous with miracle?"

"Actually, Captain, nothing like that's happened since three wise men rode into town on their camels. But we can always hope."

"Woody, scalps in the belt are nice, but by only wounding him, we add to his already overstretched logistics. Although the ship is of no use to them, it and its crew must be maintained."

"I see your point, Captain."

"Look, if things go according to plan, it should be pretty quiet around here for the next twenty hours. Use them to rest up. I'm going to sonar and order Giambri to the goat locker (CPO quarters) for some badly needed sack time."

"Captain, if he gives you grief, make him take the indispensable-man test."

"The what?"

"Have him stick his finger into a cup of water. If the hole stays there when he pulls it out, he's indispensable and can stay in the sonar shack."

"Get that sorry butt of yours in a bunk, Woody."

"Aye, Captain."

Maddock convinced Chief Henri he'd not be needed personally to draw the plot for a full twenty hours, so the COB got a little kip (rest) too.

Twenty Hours Later

A Cheshire-cat grin paled in comparison to the one worn by Parnell. A chart spread out over the wardroom table contained a plotted circle, clearly egg-shaped.

He asked, "Do you have any JD Black aboard, Captain? Sure could use a jolt, but about half the size of the one you'll need after this major defeat."

"What do you expect, Woody ... tears? I say show me a good loser and I'll show you a loser. Now, convince me we can get target course and speed from this."

"Mark the ten best circle center locations we have and draw a line through them. Should be straight as an arrow. That'll give heading and distance covered divided by time and speed."

"We need to keep an exact DR till the missiles are gone—"

The attack center messenger interrupted. "Sonar spotted a polynya big enough to shoot through, Captain!"

Maddock turned to Tom Bentley. "Show time, XO. Sound battle stations' alarm."

A muffled *gong-gong-gong* rang throughout the ship as its crew headed for their posts.

Chief Henri laid out a perfect diagram of the overhead open water. "Recommend fire here, Captain." He pointed to a spot near the edge of the polynya. "Target coordinates plotted from here, and here for a follow-on if you want to let a second round go. Got coordinates for that too."

"Okay, Chief. Nicely done. Immediately before shooting, take a final sonar bearing to be sure it tracks with what you got set in the *one seventeen* (MK 117 digital Fire Control Computer)."

"Match final sonar bearing, aye, Captain." And then thought, *You're not making this easy, are you, Captain*?

The moment of truth reached, a missile left, kicked out by the TPES. No shudder throughout the ship as with the conventional launcher. The weapon broached and sensed atmosphere, the missile ignited and headed down range toward the ice-picked Russian.

Every gut in *Steelhead* began to wrench as the crew wondered, *What did we forget that's gonna turn around and bite us on the ass?*

Chapter 10

Soviet Submarine *Lenin*

Captain 1st Rank Dmitri Borkowski sat in his stateroom and struggled through a copy of *Fathers and Sons*. He did this in deference to author Ivan Turgenev's great-grandson and longtime friend, Mikhail. Borkowski found more stimulation in the likes of Fyodor Dostoyevsky's novels, *The Brothers Karamazov* one of the captain's favorites. He'd read it four times with plans to do so again.

Dmitri closed his stateroom door to prevent the nosey *zampolit* from *noting with concern* the captain's reading included material other than party propaganda. This infrequently worked, for more often than not, the arrogant bastard entered without knocking. Borkowski learned early on, a *little person* given power handles it much in the manner of an alcoholic with a bottle of vodka.

Reading permitted Borkowski to set aside the world madness he abhorred, if only for a short while. In this instance, *short* meant exactly that.

An ear-shattering explosion from a pressure wave hit *Lenin*'s starboard side like the proverbial ton of bricks, rolling the ship to starboard as the hull pivoted on its ice pick away from the blast. With *Lenin* initially plunged into darkness, Borkowski felt his way to the diving station.

Emergency lighting kicked in concurrent with his arrival.

With blank faces, the diving party looked to Borkowski for explanation. Seeing no one had any answers, he went to the sonar operation room. There he found the *michman* quaking in his boots.

"My displays are all gone, Captain. The power—"

"It'll be back soon."

Dmitri knew if the main ship's generator could not be restarted, battery-powered static inverters would quickly kick in and provide the needed alternating current. He had not long to wait. After a few moments, the sonar displays came back to life.

Not so with the *michman* who had to be prompted into action.

"Settle down, son. I must return to the control station, but I need to know whatever you find."

Removed from its ice pick, *Lenin* floated back to the ice and began to roll. Borkowski ordered ballast tanks flooded to prevent positive buoyancy from capsizing the ship. He started to order the diving officer to repeat the initial ice-picking procedure when a second explosion interrupted, this one more distant than the first. Emergency lighting flickered but remained on.

Dmitri calmed his crewmen then directed the diving officer to call each compartment for a damage report and initiate recovery procedures. The crew knew carefully thought out action to be the principal ingredient in recovery and swung back into action as they had been trained to do.

Borkowski returned to sonar and found the *michman* composed.

"I have no contacts other than running torpedoes from our protective field. I am certain they were triggered by the explosion."

"Very well. They are far enough away to pose no threat to us; deactivate the field."

He knew *Lenin* would have to leave her station and took action to prevent being attacked by his own defensive weapon system.

The *michman* removed a key from the chain around his neck, unlocked a safety panel that covered a switch and activated it. Thirty seconds later, he reported deactivation signals received from all units except those that had been deployed by the unidentified blast.

Returning to the control station, Borkowski received grim news.

The control officer could hardly keep traces of elation from his voice, knowing that repair could only be possible at Severodvinsk. "The ballistic missile weapons' inertial systems are damaged beyond repair. There's better luck with the turbine ship's generator. Bearings are damaged, but we have replacement parts. Should take about five hours."

Next, Borkowski returned to his stateroom and found the ashen-faced *zampolit* in his chair. "What has happened, *Komrade Kapitan*? Are we in danger?"

The captain replied, "I have no idea of what happened, but the ship is in no immediate danger."

Anikanov's worried look yielded to a snarl and he demanded, "What are you doing about it?"

Borkowski maintained his composure though a trace of sarcasm resonated. "Determining what needs to be fixed, so we can fix it."

Steelhead

Brent Maddock came to the realization that he had not thought through a post-attack plan and did not do well at straw grasping.

Surrounded by pleading looks, it occurred to him the action plan is a no-brainer. *Figure out what happened and go from there.* "I'm going to sonar and start listening for clues on whether we inflicted any damage and find out anything else I can." *Good for the crew to occasionally get their minds around the fact their CO hasn't got all the answers.*

Chief Giambri's expression indicated that wheels spun fiercely between his ears.

"What do you know for sure, Chief?"

"Nothing, Captain. But a helluva lot of other stuff. Couple this with what we've heard, I'm guessing one of the bombs went off pretty close. The other, not so close. Too much bearing difference between explosions."

"What makes you think one hit close?"

"Lost the fifty-hertz line soon as it went off. It takes one big bang to knock out a ship's generator. Bad part of that is, until he brings it back on line, we have no contact."

Maddock took a moment to take this in as his own mental wheels shifted to overdrive. "Too dangerous to approach close enough to reestablish contact with the defensive weapons' belt he's got in place."

"Might've gotten a break there, Captain. Three of his weapons got activated by the blast. They didn't pick up anything, just circled. We got a good enough fix on 'em, it'll provide a path to go if that's what we wanna do."

"Anything else, Chief?"

"Yeah. Kinda strange. Heard a short frequency modulated signal from the target bearing. Next heard what appeared to be a response from one of his weapons. My guess is the target's getting ready to haul butt and shut down his field. I doubt the weapons' sensors can differentiate between one of theirs and one of ours."

"Will you hear him if he gets moving?"

"Make book on that, Captain. Average Soviet boomer sounds like a sea bag full of broken dishes. We goin' after him?"

"The sixty-four thousand dollar question. Haven't figured out the answer yet, but we'll do the best thing."

"Can I toss out an idea, Captain? How important would it be if we brought one of those Russian defensive weapons home with us?"

The Pentagon, CNO Office

Admiral Eric Danis looked up from a stack of papers that all but obscured him from view. His aide, CDR Leo Wade, entered the spacious office on the Pentagon E-ring, outermost offices of the building—only ones with an outside view. Danis sat at his desk, flanked by American and U.S. Navy flags. A northwest window provided a view of the Lee Mansion at Arlington cemetery. At midsummer, the final rays of sun in the office served as a cue: *Time to go home.*

The aide announced, "I got Mr. Zane on line two, Admiral."

"Thanks, Leo. Maybe you can find a wheelbarrow and haul this crap out of here."

"Fat chance, Admiral. Now you know how lucky the guys are that don't make CNO."

"Just hand me the phone, Leo." Danis punched the line-two button. "Dave. How you doin' old buddy?"

"Not bad for an old guy. What do I call you now ... *Your Grace?*"

"Just like at the digs (Zane's home on the Olympic Peninsula), anything but late for dinner."

Both men sat quiet a moment and basked in the good fortune of re-contacting.

Danis broke the silence, "Guess the *Pitstop* (nickname for the Pacific Northwest temporary submarine base) has gone all to hell since I left?"

"You've been gone? How come nobody told me?"

They poked back and forth for a time before Danis got down to the purpose of his call. "Dave, something recently came to my attention. You know no love is lost between COM Hal Bostwick and Brent Maddock. I'm sure you know Brent made lieutenant commander and has *Steelhead*."

"I am aware of both events, Eric. Bostwick wanted to bounce him out of the Navy and would have had you not intervened. So what's up now?"

"Bostwick is the commander of *Steelhead*'s sub-group and a backstabbing son of a bitch. He likely still has it in for Maddock."

"That would be my guess, Eric. Are there plans for nipping this in the bud?"

"Well, you know Bostwick's famous for end running. To go around me, he'd have to contact the Secretary of the Navy. I doubt even he has the nerve to do that, but I'd put nothing past him. My immediate plan is for a CNO visit to the Fundy base. Dave, I still can't get my mind wrapped around that title. Always believed CNO was a big deal. Oil paintings of an admiral with a stern look sitting in front of an American flag, but now I know better."

"Eric, with a wife like Eve to keep your feet solidly on the ground, there's no chance your head will ever grow bigger than your hat. How's she shakin' into those plush quarters at the Navy Yard? Probably misses the shack she dolled up out here."

Danis said, "Eve can turn a pup tent into a castle. She gets a lot of help. Sometimes I think a little too much. Lotta things she'd rather do herself, but we roll with the punches."

"Eric, I'm sure you didn't call just to chat. Is there anything I can do for you?"

"Matter of fact, yes ... the Bostwick thing. I plan to visit Fundy next week. CNO needs a presence there. Not to spy on Bostwick, mind you, although I would like to be kept informed. The Fundy operation is expanding with a workforce of Canadians and US shipyard workers that survived the initial attacks. It's all been hip shots so far, but now it has grown too big to continue in that vein. I need someone who understands administration. I have one of the Bremerton Shipyard survivors in mind. Are you sitting down?"

Steelhead

Brent Maddock sat with his officers and discussed, *Where do we go from here?* Earlier in the day, sonar reported the Soviet target had gotten underway and proceeded south. At issue: do we follow and sink, or let him go? Consensus: let him go.

Contrary to established media stereotypes, *scalps in the belt* do not drive submariner *modus operandi*. That honor went to winning the war. The advantages of sending the damaged boomer home exceeded the reasons to destroy her. It adds to already overstrained Soviet logistics, but most important, it carries back the message that something new and frightening has to be contended with. Maybe rethink the ice pick idea. That would greatly aid the Allied effort.

Maddock announced to his officers, "Chief Giambri made an interesting suggestion … find one of the devices that got *Sterlet* and bring it home."

By now, *Steelhead* officers had come to know their CO to be anything but conventional, hence none registered surprise.

Bentley's response contained no astonishment, only curiosity, "How can we find one? It makes no noise, so we can't hear it. The under-ice is too irregular for active sonar to pick it out."

Maddock grinned his special grin. "The Mark One eyeball." Disappointed the comment garnered not one surprised expression, he continued, "We got a good fix on the boomer's last position. Giambri's worked the distance from there to the defensive weapon circle. We start there and work inward, keel depth eighty feet with both scopes raised and search."

Parnell asked, "Any chance we'll activate it like *Sterlet* did?"

"Always a chance of that, Woody, but we think the boomer shut down the field in order to leave."

"Could it have been reactivated after the boomer left?" Bill Bryan asked.

"Yes, but unlikely. It would be a threat to wandering Soviets as well as our submarines."

Bentley asked, "What do we do when one is spotted, Captain?"

"That's where Woody comes in. The weapons department has two SCUBA (Self-Contained Underwater Breathing Apparatus) outfits. Looks like we're gonna get to use them. We get a good hover trim beneath the device, lock out two divers, stop by forward locker, remove a mooring line, tether it to a cleat and the device, then we'll pull the damn thing loose with ship's propulsion." (Forward locker: topside free-flooding line stowage in forward ballast tanks.)

Parnell asked, "Then what? We can't tow it because the line will get caught up in the propeller."

"Simple, Woody. When we put the line back in the locker, we also stow the device there."

Through a straight face, Woody replied, "Shoulda thought of that one myself."

"Yes, you shoulda. Work up a plan and we'll reconvene in an hour. I suspect the device includes a new Soviet USET-EightyK (air-dropped seventeen point five inch ASW torpedo with a biplanar active/passive homing system)."

He smiled at Woody. "And it'll fit in the line locker."

"Aye, Captain. Back in an hour with details."

"But you don't mind if we start searching now, do ya? Light's pretty good up there."

"Of course not, Captain."

"And Woody."

"Yes sir."

"You're not one of the two who'll be locking out with the SCUBAs. Important stuff for you to do around here and I don't want to take the risk."

"What happened to 'Never ask your men to do something you're not willing to do yourself'?"

The next day, Conning Officer Bill Bryan called out, "Device in sight. All stop."

Maddock entered the attack center and took over number one scope. "Well, doesn't that look pretty?" He observed a shaft that disappeared into the ice. Beneath it sat a control device atop a lightweight torpedo. Parnell stood at the captain's elbow. "Suit up, Woody, you're goin' in."

Before long, Woody and leading Torpedoman Andy Anderson in dry suits waited at the escape trunk lower hatch. Beside them, Chief

Henri stood giving his customary advice. He told Parnell the COB should be going and not the weapons officer, but Henri failed.

Woody's simple, straightforward test. "Chief, have you ever made a scuba dive?"

His answer, "No," ended the discussion about *who* goes.

Maddock shook his head and thought, *Way to go, you guys. The two men we can least likely do without are about to be locked out of the submarine.*

The captain clucked at them like a mother hen and did a poor job of masking his anxiety.

"We'll, be fine, Captain. Just don't leave without us."

The COB added, "Don't forget, Mr. Parnell, the last time you left the ship on a mission. You got yourself shot and I had to patch you up."

He referred to Parnell leading a raiding party from USS *Denver* to capture a Soviet minesweeper.

"I don't think there's anyone up there to shoot at me, COB."

"Respectfully, Mr. Parnell, you'll think of something."

The dry-suit duo disappeared into the escape chamber. Minutes later, Maddock watched them through number one periscope swim to the device trailing a mooring line.

The captain thought it unbelievable how well everything went, then cried out, "No! Dammit, Woody!"

The inventive weapons officer attempted to dislodge the device by himself. Placing flippers firmly against the ice and assuming the fetal position, he grasped the torpedo fins and attempted to pull the device free. However, his breathing hose snagged in a torpedo propeller blade. Applying more leg pressure than his gloved hands could handle, they slipped from the fins with obvious results. His body straightened and the ensnared breathing hose parted, quickly draining the remaining air in his tank in a cascade of bubbles.

Parnell's jerking body quickly caught Torpedoman Anderson's attention. He yanked the mouthpiece from Woody's mouth and inserted his own. Parnell quickly realized what had happened and the two exchanged Anderson's mouthpiece on their way back to the escape chamber.

When they dropped into the torpedo room, COB got in his, "I told you so, Mr. Parnell!"

After repairing the hose, a crewman with diving experience joined Andy and finished the job per plan with *Steelhead* propulsion dislodging the device.

Later Maddock confirmed his decision to the XO. "We've got to abort the patrol and get back. This'll probably save us a few boats."

Bentley remained silent but thought, *COM Bostwick wants your butt and this gives him the perfect opportunity.*

Office of the CNO

"Hello, Hal. Are you keeping everything well in Fundy?"

COM Bostwick considered each sentence from a senior officer to possibly represent another step on his ladder. "Well as can be expected, I suppose. No big problems come to mind."

"That's good, Hal. Knew I could count on you to do a good job."

"Well thank you, Admiral. Any concerns?"

"None from me, Hal. But the President has a few."

Danis could almost hear a gulp all the way from Fundy. He then let Bostwick in. "Nothing big. Mainly about postwar administrative repercussions of a joint Canadian-American civilian workforce. Everybody's on the same page now, but this fight's gonna end and we don't want to leave too many wrinkles to iron out."

Bostwick took his predictable defensive stance. "Do you have specifics, Admiral? I'll damn well scotch anything going on here that's not right."

"Not in the least, Hal. Your job is to turn around submarines and get them back in the fracas. And I can think of no one better than you for the job. I plan to visit in the near term and personally thank you. I have a civilian survivor of the Bremerton, Washington, Naval Shipyard attack I'll bring with me to take care of the administrative end, a CNO liaison officer to be left there. Not a spy, mind you. All communications between us are via the chain of command. I'd like to schedule my visit to coincide with *Steelhead*'s return. Understand our friend Maddock has a trophy for us. If okay with you, I'll hang a Legion of Merit on him."

"Of course, Admiral. That would be spectacular."

I'll just bet it will, went through Danis's mind.

Luckily, the CNO had tentacles everywhere. He needed them. Danis intercepted a Bostwick plan to sack Maddock for returning *Steelhead* early from her patrol. *God love the yeomen* (enlisted clerks that run Navy's administration) *for banding together. How would the Navy run without them?*

Steelhead Approaching Bay of Fundy Mooring

Ships in port at the Bay and commands ashore communicated by flashing light, reducing probability of signal interception. A mile and a half from the dock, *Steelhead*'s QMOW handed the captain a handwritten message they received only moments before.

Maddock exclaimed, "What! Have this verified."

"Already did, Captain. It's true."

Maddock handed the message to his XO with the order, "Get below and straighten things out the best you can."

The message read:

CNO TO BOARD IMMEDIATELY UPON ARRIVAL.

Maddock winced. "Knowing Danis, he'll want to walk through the ship and shake everyone's hand."

Ashore, Admiral Danis turned to the new CNO liaison officer at Fundy and handed off a set of keys. "Here. You take these. COM Bostwick gussied up a Quonset hut for my quarters. Been eons since I bunked on a submarine, so I'll hang out in *Steelhead*. And my guess, the food's a helluva lot better there than on the base."

Maddock looked down from the bridge to direct line handlers as *Steelhead* docked.

Maddock heard Woody Parnell yell out Bea Zane's nickname, "Den Mother!"

"It can't be," Brent said, not believing his eyes.

Yet there she stood beside the CNO. He had not seen Bea in eleven months, and as soon as the brow went over, Maddock raced up the dock to her, barely taking time to salute Admiral Danis and Commodore Bostwick. Brent and Bea locked into a tight embrace, interrupted sooner than they wished by applause from all who stood around them.

This has to be the most awkward circumstance of my life, he thought. *All I want is to just be there with my woman and here stands our boss and the CNO.*

Eric Danis defused the situation. "Brent, would you please drive Miss Zane to my quarters. She will bunk there. Thought I'd try *Steelhead* for tonight. It's been a long time since I slept in a pipe (vernacular for submarine)."

Brent drove Bea to the CNO quarters. Their conversations overlapped to the point they both wondered how anything got said.

Entering the Quonset hut, Brent could only say, "Wow!"

No surprise. Bostwick had pulled out all stops for the CNO.

Inside, they exchanged a long sensuous embrace. Bea looked at him through the happiest expression he had ever seen on her face.

She said, "Admiral Danis left a bottle of champagne and some caviar chilling in the fridge."

He smiled at her. "Do you really think we could get through it before—"

Her instant "No" interrupted further conversation.

Later, Woody Parnell fulfilled a longstanding wish. His favorite line in the film *Dr. Strangelove* occurred when the President could not reach the Soviet Premier at the usual phone number, so the Russian Ambassador gave him another.

The President asks, "Where is this?"

Replying, the ambassador said, "Our Premier is a man of the people, but he is also a man … if you follow my meaning."

Woody sought an occasion to use that line ever since he'd seen the film.

COM Bostwick provided the opportunity at a reception aboard his yacht an hour after *Steelhead* reached port.

He looked about and asked, "Where's the guest of honor?"

Woody drew upon his best basso Russian accent and said, "If I may, Commodore. Our captain is a Navy man, but he is also a man … if you follow my meaning."

Chapter 11

Soviet Submarine *Lenin*

Captain 1st Rank Dmitri Borkowski sat with his officers in a council of war. The agenda: Where do we go from here?

The chief engineer presented a material summary of the ship. "We've suffered no major watertight integrity breaches. The hull is intact, and though the ship's service generator got knocked off line, we have it operating. Damage to the inertial navigation systems is beyond our ability to repair at sea."

Zampolit Yuri Anikanov picked up on this. He believed it would require an early return, much to the disdain of his superiors who already fought an overwhelming shortfall problem of submarines on station. He would monitor the proceedings carefully and pounce upon any excuse to leave *Lenin* at sea. Nothing looked better on a *zampolit* dossier than advice rejected by a line officer that should at least, in the Party's view, have been taken.

Borkowski asked, "Any damage to the main propulsion shaft?"

"No, *Kapitan*," the chief engineer replied. "We have spun it several times and all seems good. Is there a probability the attack was initiated by a submarine?"

The *zampolit* eagerly jumped in with, "No chance at all. I have personally gone through the intelligence folders and find nothing in the American submarine weapons inventory that could have caused that explosion."

The captain said, "Thank you for that bit of wisdom, *Komrade Zampolit*. But you have to admit they are resourceful bastards. We'll proceed out of here quietly and with our cannons cocked."

"So, *Komrade Kapitan*, your decision is to abort the patrol nine weeks early without authority from ashore?"

"All of the documentation is available to our learned *Komrade Zampolit*. We will of course implement whatever advice you have for us. But, without the navigators, we cannot launch missiles, so we waste the Party's time by remaining on station."

The chief engineer explained the gyrocompass continues to work but could give no assurances that it had not been knocked out of alignment by the blast.

Borkowski said, "We see the sun well enough through the ice to get a bearing when it passes our meridian. Compare the sun's south bearing to the compass. Plenty good enough to get us out from under the ice canopy. Questions, gentlemen?"

The *zampolit* said nothing, nor did any of the others.

"Good. We get underway shortly after noon tomorrow."

Returning to his stateroom, Borkowski attempted to re-immerse himself into *Fathers and Sons*. He could not. His superb mind had its own agenda and would permit accommodation of nothing except Mother Russia's dilemma.

She chased a dream that evaded every would-be conqueror in history: world domination. Her paper-thin logistics train spread through countries that did not wish Russians to be there, countries that grew increasingly restive. Circumstances fast approached those faced by Nazi Germany at the turning point of World War II.

Then, it fell upon military leaders to do what had to be done in order to salvage whatever hope remained. But they failed and their country paid grievous consequences.

There would be serious talks with Mikhail Turgenev when *Lenin* returned to Severodvinsk.

Bay of Fundy

A host of top scientists flew in from various U.S. laboratories to inspect the Soviet defensive weapon recovered by *Steelhead*. Per Woody Parnell, *Never have so many counts and no-accounts assembled in one place since the signing of the Versailles Treaty. And you saw where that led.*

The device had been completely disassembled and analyzed by expert electrical, electronic, propulsion and structural engineers. Its key to success—simplicity. Typical of Russian technology. An overheard comment went, *If this were American, it would have five times the complexity, ten times the cost and likely perform ninety percent as well as the Soviet version.* And it would have to be

MILSPEC (Military specification). It's been said a MILSPEC mouse is an elephant.

COM Bostwick and his commanding officers assembled to hear the final outcome and learn of its effect on future operations.

The briefer opened with a summary statement. Knowing where he would go facilitated officer comprehension of the vast number of validating details. The old adage: tell 'em what you want done before telling 'em why and how to do it.

"This is a very simple device," the narrator began. "The USET-EightyK consists of an ASW torpedo supported by a sensor, activation-deactivation switches and an ice-pick shaft. The almost certain modus operandi: Soviet boomer finds open water then plants a defensive circle centered at the ship's planned ice-pick position. When ready, the defensive circle is activated by an acoustic signal from the submarine. The reverse happens when a ship departs the area. The circle is deactivated, also with an acoustic signal."

An officer asked, "Why deactivate? Leave it there as a trap."

Maddock fielded the question. "For them or us? I don't think the sensor gives a damn about whose submarine it hears. Don't forget … any direction you take from the circle center goes through the circumference where the mines are."

"You're absolutely right, Commander," the narrator confirmed. "That's why deactivation is a one-way switch."

A CO asked, "It can't be reactivated?"

"No. Soviet boomers never reuse an ice-pick location. They're paranoid about getting caught."

This drew a round of laughter from the submariners.

Maddock said, "An affliction we share with the Soviets. If its location is compromised, all the accumulating advantages to a submarine are nullified."

The narrator asked, "Is there an advantage for us to be able to activate and deactivate?"

Another CO shouted, "Hell, yes! If we catch the bastard planting a field, we can activate it and hoist him by his own petard."

Then a third CO added, "It opens another tactical option. If we find him and want to close for a point-blank ADCAP shot, how will we know the field is deactivated?"

"A small transducer responds."

"But can't he hear it too?"

"Only in the unlikely event his gear is on. My guess is it won't be … a measure to prevent deactivation. We've assembled some devices to work with your Gertrudes (underwater acoustic phones)."

"How soon can you have them in? My ship leaves tomorrow."

Looking at his watch, the narrator replied through a smug grin, "What time do you want it installed? We took the Russian approach … simple as possible."

St. Croix River, North of U.S. Bay of Fundy Base

A longtime swift-river fisherman, Woody Parnell liked nothing better than the feel of current pushing against his waders and the tug of a strong fish at the end of his line. While in Washington State, he had encountered a few wily steelhead trout and liked the idea of being assigned to the namesake of this noble fish.

A befriended yard worker told Woody of the St. Croix River where Atlantic salmon abound this time of year while making their way upstream to spawn.

On the eve of *Steelhead*'s return to the Arctic, Woody promised to grace the wardroom table with fresh salmon. He borrowed an eight-weight fly rod and a box of streamers (sinking salmon flies) and tackle from his worker friend and fashioned waders from a pair of heavy-duty garbage bags. Then Woody *borrowed* a jeep, strongly believing that under the circumstances, getting forgiveness is easier than getting permission, and drove to the wilderness north of the Bay. He found the St. Croix and a barely drivable road beside it. He passed two fishermen but continued to drive until he came upon a section of the river just below a set of rapids with a six-foot deep slot down the middle where the water flowed at a fast-walking pace.

Steelhead got a shortened refit because of her early return from patrol. Her crew used shore-based facilities to the greatest extent possible to ensure the ship's readiness for sea. This included many *round the clockers* from which Woody got no immunity.

Fatigued, Woody stretched out on the bank and shortly the St. Croix River's whispered lullaby, blended with the gentle breeze through nearby pine trees, quickly dropped Woody into the arms of Morpheus (Roman god of sleep and dreams).

After fifteen minutes that refreshed like several hours, the young angler arose and donned his *top-of-the-line* waders. He considered sneakers and bare legs but knew his body would be no match for the icy river.

Before long, engrossed in the great outdoor setting for his fishing passion, Woody prepared to fish. He selected one of his favorite streamer patterns from the box, *a gray ghost,* and tied it onto his tippet (various weight line between leader and fly). He stripped some line off the reel and began casting his streamer out towards the edge of the middle seam in the river. His line laid out flat on the water surface after a quick mend and his sinker tip took the streamer down to where the Atlantics were holding. Within minutes, an eight pounder took the gray ghost and gave a good account of itself, giving Woody a fight in the current for several minutes before he landed the silver beauty.

Woody carefully removed the hook, waded into the shallows and released the fish. He said aloud, "Just like the women in my life, love 'em and leave 'em."

Though a quality fish, Woody sought pounds in the high teens to low twenties. *How far would an eight-pound fish go with ten hungry officers?*

Fishers of the St. Croix, under a strictly enforced limit of one fish, tended to be picky.

Parnell indulged his ecstatic break from life aboard *Steelhead* with absolutely no guilt. He made a mental note, *When I retire and move to a farm, it'll have a trout stream running through it.*

He landed several more fish, one a twelve pounder he thought seriously of keeping. *Almost there, but still not big enough*, he rationalized. True reason: no wish to end such a great day.

Woody believed the larger fish were looking for a different presentation. He pulled out the streamer box and changed things a bit. He tied on a *Ballou Special* streamer, loaded the rod and laid a perfect cast across the middle of the river. A quick mend and he swung the streamer along the far side of the center seam.

The sudden jolt nearly tore the rod from Woody's hands. The rod doubled over as line stripped rapidly from the reel's spool creating Woody's favorite metallic melody. The fish stayed close to the bottom and shot downriver covering a hundred feet in a matter of seconds then exploded out of the water into a series of aerials, showing its size.

Omigod! Eighteen pounds if it's an ounce, raced through Woody's mind. A look at the spool showed not much line left. *Gotta move with him, or he's gone.* Parnell staggered along the slippery and uneven riverbed with appearances of a man who'd indulged far too many at a bar. Fifteen minutes into the fight, Parnell felt the fish tiring. *I'm tiring too, so we're even. Don't get cocky, Parnell, keep the line taut and gain on him.*

In twenty minutes, Woody had the fish reeled in to fifteen yards. Despite depleted energy, it continued to make a few strong pulls though clearly weakening. Before long, a twenty-pound Atlantic salmon lay on the stones, barely able to flap about.

An elated Woody Parnell turned to break down his rod, thinking of the fish stories he would tell his messmates as they feasted on the fresh salmon.

A sudden movement alerted him to a nearby presence.

He turned in time to see someone, his fish in their arms, walking toward the river. To his amazement and horror, Woody watched his prize trophy released back into the stream. The fish so tired it could barely move recovered enough to slowly swim toward midstream.

Woody raced to the river's edge and attempted to pounce on it, his own fatigue making the gesture not only futile but comedic.

Unable to recall ever being so angry, Woody rose to confront his antagonist. "What in hell do you think you're doing?"

A young woman snapped, "I don't *think* I'm doing anything. I *know* what I'm doing. I'm putting that fish back into the river where it belongs."

"Lady! I don't know where the hell you're coming from, but the law lets me take one salmon a day from this river. Now dammit! I released six already. That one was mine. And you got one helluva nerve doing what you did."

"Then why don't you call the police?"

"If there were any nearby, I would in a heartbeat … and happy as hell to press charges."

She began to lecture Woody, her voice harsh as any he had ever heard from a woman. "Do you know how many eggs there are in a fish that size? And you want to keep them from even being hatched. How can you be so damn selfish?"

"How many damn eggs are in that fish? I'll tell you how many … none! It's a male!"

"All the more reason to release him. Look at the size and strength of that fish. And now, thanks to me, he'll get to pass those genes to new salmon generations."

"What the hell are you, lady … the salmon nazi? Isn't a master race something right out of *Mein Kampf*? Do you get your orders straight from Hitler?"

"I'm a person very unlike you. I do what I think should be done; I don't wallow in my own narrow sightedness at the expense of others."

"Well dammit! Couldn't you have at least talked about it first?"

The woman shook her head. "I've learned closed minds cannot be reasoned with."

Not very attractive, Woody resisted the urge to say, *I can see why you don't get a lot of male attention, so maybe that's what you're really doing. Getting even.* Instead, he said, "Your mind isn't closed? Taking it upon yourself to decide what becomes of someone else's property … prosecuting attorney, jury and judge all rolled up in one?"

"I think there's no more to be said."

The woman turned and walked away.

Woody did not resist and said, "Thanks for giving me a look at the best side of you."

The woman paused an instant and started to turn around, but continued on her way.

Woody got in a final, "Screw you, lady, and the horse you rode in on."

Later that evening, Woody suffered the slings and arrows from his messmates.

Bill Bryan asked, "The salmon nazi let your fish go? Isn't that almost the same as the dog ate my homework?"

Tom Bentley got his oar in the pond. "Guys. Be fair. Has anyone ever known a fisherman who didn't catch a big one that got away?"

Woody fielded all the barbs he fully expected to receive but with an uncharacteristic lack of grace. He seemed unable to rid himself of the gnawing in his stomach brought on by that afternoon's event. His pet peeve: people with personal agendas who use them as an excuse to impinge on legitimate rights of others.

In the absence of Woody's hallmark comebacks, the *hard-ass* ribbing abated. Officers one by one left the wardroom to prepare for their final evening out. A line from the Navy song *Anchors Aweigh* goes ... *This our last night ashore, drink to the foam.* All planned to assemble in the base O-club and fulfill that admonition.

Brent Maddock stopped Parnell. "Sit down a minute, Woody. It's only a fish. Don't think I've ever seen anything bother you so much. You tell us everything?"

"Everything, Captain."

"Then why?"

"I hate to see people push others around and get away with it. That's all."

"Well, Woody, like it or not, you saw it today and I guarantee you'll see it again."

"Yeah, I know, Captain. And the frustrating thing is I can't do anything about it."

"Then, stow it, Woody. We're carrying enough baggage to sea and don't need more."

"I know, Captain. Surprised myself, even. Maybe I'm getting old and set in my ways."

"Yeah, maybe that's it. Now, let's get our asses over to the club and see who's first to be drunk under the table."

Woody regained his composure then asked, "Is Den Mother coming to drive us home in case we get tipsy?"

"If we're lucky. Now, out of the uniform and into some civvies."

Steelhead **back to the Arctic**

Bea Zane and Brent Maddock shared a final cup of coffee before departing the CNO quarters made domicile by the inventive woman. Raised the daughter of an active-duty naval officer, Bea had seen her mother do this countless times as they lived the Gypsy life.

They loaded Brent's bags into a Jeep issued to the new CNO liaison officer then Bea said, "Tell Woody the next time he needs a Jeep, please take mine. You would not believe the whining that went on in the office over him *borrowing* one. You should be warned, it made COM Bostwick furious. Actually, I don't think it really did, but he sure wanted it to look that way. Brent, I get a sense Bostwick doesn't like you."

"He's made a career of it, Bea. Don't sweat it. Guys like him always manage to fall into one of their own traps. And we don't have enough time to include him, so let's talk about happier things."

"Good. How long will you be out?"

"Military secret."

"I work for the Navy's top guy, you know."

"We all do ... after a fashion."

"Just as well I don't know. Time goes so much slower when you count days and that's what I'd do. What are you going to do after this? I mean, when there are no more wars to fight."

"I'd feel a helluva lot better if you had said *we*."

"I didn't say it deliberately. I don't want to make you feel like you're backed into a corner."

Brent reached up and placed a hand over hers on the steering wheel. "Can't think of a better one to be backed into. Let me say this ... I'm preoccupied with far too many things right now, so don't get a lot of time to think about it. But when I do, it always involves both of us."

"You don't know how happy that makes me, Brent."

"Can't be nearly as much as it makes me. After this mess is over, we'll make up for all the time it's taken from us."

They rode on in silence, each savoring the reassurances that passed between them. At the pier head, they stopped.

"Let's say goodbye here, Bea. I don't want to give the troops a bad impression."

"In one of my dad's favorite words, Brent ... *bullshit*!"

Arm in arm they walked the full pier length and stopped before the brow.

Tom Bentley yelled from the bridge, "Maneuvering watch set, ready in all respects to get underway, Captain."

Maddock acknowledged by touching his cap brim, then turned back to Bea. Taking her into a strong embrace, he gave her a kiss that would have to last two months, all to the accompaniment of yells, whistling, catcalls and cries of "Way to go, Captain" from the main deck.

Ottawa, Canada

Vasiliy Baknov sat across from the former Russian Embassy on Charlotte Street in Ottawa, Canada, where he studied comings and goings of the staff for over a month. Each day, he varied his clothing and observation point, and always prepared a plausible explanation for being at his chosen location if questioned.

The Dominion of Canada, a member of the Allied Forces, had broken ties with the Soviet Union, but as agreed by all, permitted a presence to be maintained there only as a means of communication between the warring parties.

Baknov had familiarized himself with faces and habits of all fourteen of the building's occupants. He had trailed them to their homes and through social patterns.

On one occasion, he had a *chance* meeting in the old city at a tavern one of the women frequented—Natasha Kirov. Russian enough and quite attractive to boot. For a time, Vasiliy stuck with his Warren Biddle cover. During their conversation, however, a *significant other* showed up. From all appearances, a Canadian from boots to hat.

This caused Vasiliy to wonder. A strict rule prohibited social contact between embassy personnel and foreign nationals.

Might the significant other be a Soviet plant? *If so, surely Canadian Intelligence, aware of this rule, would have checked out the man. Or could he be a Canadian plant? Oh, the stroke of good fortune that led me into the Navy instead of intelligence work. However, a lot of good that did. Look where I find myself.*

Funds Baknov accumulated as a mechanic in North Chicago began to run low, so he took a similar position in Ottawa. The job paid less than in America but enough to make ends meet.

He wished to serve Mother Russia, but could not if required to spend all his time simply sustaining himself. He believed contact with Soviets in Canada would solve his problem. The Maddock issue continued to burn within his breast.

One evening, while eating at a small restaurant near Baknov's flat, the *significant other* walked in, and without invitation, seated himself opposite Vasiliy.

With a voice tone that said he would take no nonsense, the man demanded, "Who are you, and what is your business here?"

Vasiliy, not one to be intimidated, replied, "I'm Warren Biddle, a fisherman from the American Pacific Northwest, displaced by the war and seeking a living."

"Then you can explain why a displaced fisherman conducts daily surveillance of the Russian Embassy and stalks its employees."

Proceeding cautiously, Vasiliy took the tough approach. "And why does a loyal Canadian citizen give a damn that I do this?"

The two men began to feel each other out. Earlier, the *significant other* identified himself as Thomas Baylor.

Answering Vasiliy's question, Baylor said, "Soviets are known to plant observers to ensure embassy employees toe the line." Then asked, "Are you one of those?"

"It's obvious neither of us trusts the other," Vasiliy replied. "I don't know which side you are on, nor do you know my allegiance. Until I know who you really are, I do not plan to give you rope enough to hang me. But I am willing to make the first move. You suspect I am not Warren Biddle but are unsure. I can provide proof that I am not. What do I get in return?"

Baylor asked, "Of what value are you to us? Perhaps this is a good place to start."

"If there are gaps in your knowledge about the Bay of Fundy American Submarine Base, I am the man to fill them."

Chapter 12

Steelhead's Return to the Arctic

Shrew Askew came by his name honestly, last name Askew and he closely resembled a shrew. Although its external appearance is that of a long-nosed mouse, the shrew is not a rodent but a closer relative of the mole. Shrews have sharp teeth, not the familiar gnawing front incisor teeth of true rodents. Maybe Askew didn't resemble a shrew all that much, but he came pretty damn close.

The human Shrew's mystique was not his physical appearance, although it did somewhat enhance his reputation of being the ship's oracle. In cahoots with the radiomen, Askew had convinced them to let him read the news received by radio a day earlier than when it would be run in the ship's newspaper, *The Stolen Head.*

The first commanding officer wished to call the paper *The Steelhead Morning News*, but the crew overrode him. Aboard ship, the *head* being a toilet and their limited number relative to crew size made *stolen* a natural.

Armed with his pre-published information, the Shrew held court in the crew's mess. With a blanket draped over his shoulders, head wrapped in a towel resembling a turban, and an audience of loyal followers, mostly the younger sailors, he astounded them with his accurate predictions of world events. They clung to his pearls of wisdom, amazed even more when *verified* the following day.

Maddock, like any rational skipper, grew apprehensive as his ship drew near the enemy's lair. Too frequently, he wandered into and out of the sonar shack and attack center. An intelligent skipper, Maddock reined himself in. *No need to make folks think I'm worried and upset them too.*

Tom Bentley bore the brunt of his captain's anxiety, being challenged to altogether too many cribbage games. Maddock used them as covers for more conversation.

Seated alone in the wardroom, Maddock and Bentley conversed. "So, here's the way I see it, Tom. We've doped out the Soviet game plan and come up with a sound retaliatory course of action. I know us warriors are supposed to just chuck spears and not think, but tell me what you think of this. Sending damaged ships back for repair puts a greater strain on their logistics than if we sink 'em."

Maddock regarded his executive officer through a frown.

"You're right, Captain. We're not supposed to think, especially on this subject. That's why we got top of the heap guys to do this."

Shifting to a cynical expression, Maddock said, "Guys at the top of the heap? They have admirals testify before Congress on how many ships we need when all their experience is in driving them. Aviators want more planes and carriers; surface warfare guys, cruisers; and our boss, submarines. So why even bother to call them in? Would you have a bus driver go to the company president and tell him how many and what kind of buses he needs?"

"Look at it this way, Captain. Are the guys they're testifying to any more capable of making the right call? Their main function is equitable distribution of the defense budget among their districts." Bentley paused to get the captain's reaction but got none. "I know this is going someplace, Captain, but like always, you're a foot or two over my head."

Maddock beat the sides of his hands on the table in frustration. "We need a strategy, Tom. The book says find the enemy, attack and destroy him. But the way I see it, the key word here is destroy. That means the total enemy. Sometimes I think the best way to do this is make him invest so many resources in infrastructure that he doesn't have enough left to conduct military campaigns."

Bentley replied, "That makes sense ... I think."

"Here's more on the way I see it, Tom. We hit ice-picked Soviet BNs with Sea Lance bombs, and if we catch a guy planting his defensive circle, we activate it and destroy the bastard with his own weapon. I see no advantage to putting our troops in more harm's way than necessary."

Bentley grimaced. "If I may, Captain, you know COM Bostwick wants your butt. I guarantee he'll get it if we do this."

Maddock looked like a man who'd just set down a great burden. "What's more important, my butt or getting these kids home in one piece? Especially when more advantage accrues to minimizing their exposure. That's a no-brainer in my book."

Pentagon

Eric Danis sat down to digest all he had heard at a recent JCS (Joint Chiefs of Staff) meeting. In his view, the massive Soviet loss of submarines during the Battle of the Barents Sea had hurt their war effort much more than the United States originally assessed.

Apparently, the Russian strategy had been to first destroy major U.S. Navy bases, buildings and repair facilities. Then with their huge Soviet submarine fleet, take out the major combat fleet and deny use of the sea by surface units. This would prevent any serious Allied seaborne threat while the Soviets firmed their hold on territorial conquests in Europe.

The Battle of the Barents Sea seriously diminished the Soviet capability to continue with this strategy. Knowing he had played a key role in the operation made Danis feel good about himself, but his conscience nudged him, *Time to get busy here. Meter's running and lots of folks out there are still getting shot at.*

Danis summoned his aide, CDR Wade. "Leo, round up the usual suspects." The CNO referred to his DCNOs, one for each warfare group (Deputy Chiefs of Naval Operations, Surface, Submarine and Air). "We might as well get this donnybrook started."

He knew each DCNO would have competing plans, the lead, of course, going to the drafter. He would patiently hear each one then diplomatically get his deputies to converge on the best overall plan.

"Tell each deputy the meeting purpose and they can bring along two assistants. Meet here at fifteen hundred and expect to be up till the wee smalls."

He knew thoughts of a long day always streamlined the process.

Before long, a dozen stars glistened from the uniforms of his DCNOs and their assistants as they sat about the CNO conference table. All rose when Danis entered, but he quickly asked them to be reseated and detailed the meeting purpose.

"Soviets are on the ropes but will consolidate their winnings if we give them enough time. Getting them out of Europe is essential, and the only way to do that is get the goods to Britain ... World War

Two revisited. I know all of you have given thought to this and I'd like a brief summary from each."

DCNO Air spoke first. "I have only two carriers left. Best way to use them is in support of what Surface and Submarine come up with. Air defense is a requirement for any plan. Major problem is Soviet submarines. My assumption is you'll need merchant ships to carry the goods. They'll need ASW defense. If it can be provided for them, there's no reason why my bird farms can't help out. Actually, they're not doing a helluva lot of good sealed up in port. My boys are hankering for some action."

It went back and forth like this until all concluded Eric's plan—convoys of merchant ships protected by *Burke*-class destroyers, *Los Angeles*-class submarines, and bird farms as available—to be the best overall plan and a workable solution.

Danis's threat of long hours achieved its purpose.

Ottawa, Canada

Thomas Baylor sat on a park bench and looked frequently at his watch. *I must stop doing this. It'll be quite obvious to anyone tailing me that I expect to make contact. I wonder if Biddle's real name is worth the risk.*

The half-life of a Canadian sympathizer to the Soviet cause is slightly more than two years. Baylor had been on the job nineteen months so he knew his tenure neared its end. But like others before him, the Reds recruited Baylor with promises of vast wealth when the Soviet Union won the war. For a time, this eventuality seemed *in the bag* but now not so certain.

Maybe I should bolt and run before Canadian Intelligence finds me out. But what kind of reward can I expect if Ivan finds me out. Baylor stood between a rock and hard place.

A derelict approached pushing a grocery cart filled with what few belongings the man had. Parking his cart near a bench, he took a seat. Tattered clothes, unshaven and hunched over, Biddle gave an exceptional impression of an old man who had fallen on bad times.

Baylor did eye-corner scans to ensure no one sat near enough to notice he and Biddle conversed.

He waited a moment, a newspaper blocking his face, before he acknowledged Biddle's presence and whispered, "Go ahead."

Biddle feigned sleep, his head bent forward, obscuring the fact he conversed. "No. You go ahead. I provided you with the first information. What did you learn of Warren Biddle?"

Baylor cast his eyes about cautiously, taking great care not to move his head.

He noted nothing of concern but spoke loud enough for only Baknov to hear. "Only that he is lost at sea, his body not recovered."

Confident Baylor already had enough information to turn him over to Canadian authorities and would have by now, he asked, "Then you are convinced I am not Biddle, but someone else?"

Barely audible, Baylor uttered, "Yes."

Now confident in Baylor's legitimacy, Vasiliy went on to explain the macabre tale of how he'd obtained Biddle's identity. "I am an officer of the Soviet Navy, Lieutenant Vasiliy Baknov."

Baknov then related the astonishing tale of his escape from *Zhukov* and being picked up by a fishing boat.

In conclusion, he revealed his navy identification number. "If you still have doubts, get my service record from the embassy and I'll validate each segment for you."

"That will not be necessary. Let's stick with Biddle for a time. Only risk is if the story of his disappearance reaches here. What is the chance of that?"

"Very unlikely, *Komrade*."

"It is good for us to avoid the term *komrade*."

"Now, I must be put in touch with whoever it is that can fund the mission and provide specifics on intelligence needed from the American base at Fundy."

"I shall get you that information, Warren."

"Soon?"

"Very soon."

Aboard *Steelhead*

A month into the patrol and so far no contact with the enemy. Maddock debated the issue with himself and decided not to involve his officers and crew in his decision to *wound, but not kill*. He decided a rumor might spread that he had lost his nerve. *Just like bringing the crew back alive ranks above saving my own butt, no other personal consideration can be a factor.*

Maddock had settled down and managed his own apprehensions much better than at the start of the patrol.

Even Bentley noticed. "Captain, last week we played cribbage to settle your nerves. Now it's just to beat my ass."

"Whatever you say, XO. I'm told COs are not supposed to have a nerve in their body. Ever figure we put too much effort into the demagogue factor? We have this underlying need for our leaders to be superheroes. What a bunch of crap! There are no demagogues ... just a bunch of guys who put their pants on one leg at a time."

Bentley replied, "Who in his right mind would disagree with the skipper, but you have a point. Vice Admiral Epworth ripped me a new one, like he does everyone else, and left me wondering why in hell would anyone who truly wanted to know anything about someone, put them through such stupid antics. Know why I believe no one stands up to him?"

"No, why?" asked Maddock.

"Because it's Epworth's way or the highway. Reason everyone says he's so damn great is because it's the only way to justify taking the abuse he dishes out. Otherwise, they'd look awfully stupid."

"So why did you stick?"

"If it weren't for this damn war, I wouldn't have."

Maddock replied, "Number me among the guys who caved in. I want a career in submarines, and what you say is true ... Epworth's way or the highway."

Chief Giambri interrupted their conversation. "Distant contact, Captain. Can't figure out what the hell he's doing. Suggest you come to the shack."

Maddock, Bentley and Chief Giambri went quickly to the sonar shack where the watch had the sound reproduced on loud speakers.

Giambri said, "He's Soviet. I can tell from the fifty-hertz line, but listen to this."

A *clanging* sound could be heard coming from the target.

"Dammit," Maddock said, "we had every scenario thought out and Ivan hits us with a new one. What do you make of it, Chief?"

"My guess, it's an ice-picked boomer making some sort of repairs on the outside hull. Sounds are too crisp to be from inside."

"So far I've taken your guesses to the bank. Let's do the circle range thing. Let me know as soon as the external noises stop and when you've got a good fix on him."

Giambri indulged a brief bask in the captain's confidence then returned to work. "Keep scanning the frequency band," he said to the sonar watch. "Listen for any clue. In particular, do the sounds have a pattern or are they random."

The sonarman replied, "You got it, Chief. But nothing to hang our hats on so far."

Maddock and Bentley returned to the wardroom. Taking seats, a stewardsman poured the mandatory coffees. They alone sat about the table, Bentley into his nervous habit of checking progress of his receding hairline.

"Don't worry, Tom. I'm told grass doesn't grow on a busy street."

Bentley replied, "Am I getting that obvious? Have to work on that," then got to their meeting reason. "What's the plan, Captain?"

"Damn, I wish I had that answer." Maddock rubbed his own head as if trying to clear cobwebs. "That's why you get the big bucks, Tom. Telling me what to think."

"Yeah, right, Captain."

Taking a long pull on his coffee, Bentley attempted a mask of deep thought, but came up empty.

The skipper went on, "Maybe get a good range on him. When the outside work stops, drop a Sea Lance bomb on him."

"Why when the outside work's finished?"

"Enough people already died in this war. From here on in, we'll kill only the ones we have to."

Knowing his captain softened on the idea of destroying the enemy, Bentley wondered for a moment, if Maddock had worn down under too much stress. He hesitated to offer his thought but did anyway. "Another eventuality, Captain. Suppose our bombs don't hurt him enough to make him return to port ... what then?"

"Off the top of my head, more Sea Lance bombs. We'll have to think about that one."

Bentley thought, *So much for the stereotype know-it-all warrior submarine skipper.* This vision swept over Bentley on the realization his next assignment would be command. *Maybe I'm not as unprepared as I think.*

"We only have six Sea Lance, Captain."

Concept to production of the bombs took only nine weeks due to the war. Peacetime, this would require at least two and a half years. But production had yet to meet demand.

Then Bentley added, "Balance of loadout is eighteen ADCAPs."

Maddock said, "We must be within counterattack range to use ADCAPs. Not so with Sea Lance bombs, why take the risk? And at the rate of one contact per month, we'll be headed back home about the time we run out of bombs. In the meantime, maybe poke around to see if we can find out what this guy is up to. This could be an important intelligence find."

"You mean penetrate his defensive ring? After what happened to *Sterlet*?"

"Don't forget, we know how to disable it."

"Bet your hat, coat and ass it'll work?"

"What other choice we got?"

Severodvinsk

Captain 1st Rank Dmitri Borkowski walked beside his friend Mikhail Turgenev through a local cemetery, considered a safe place to speak freely.

Mikhail said, "We must do what the German military attempted on twenty July forty-four, but be successful."

"Easier said than done, Mikhail. The Nazis had only one man to deal with and failed in what should have been a simple task. How much more complicated is ours? In addition to Premier Rostov, we have fifty or so thugs that would jump into his shoes in a heartbeat. How do we get them all to the same place at the same time? Most of them don't even like each other."

"A masterpiece of understatement, Dmitri. Despise is a more proper term. Maybe we can use this hatred and get the bastards to knock each other off, beginning with Rostov."

Winter would not visit for two more months but had already made its presence known in the leaf-bare cemetery. The men turned a corner, putting the wind to their backs, neither scarcely noticing. Being Russian meant oblivious to cold.

"Have you maintained contact with your colleagues who are sympathetic to our views?"

The men paused and appeared to focus on a headstone.

"Yes. But we are constantly on guard to ensure we have no plant among us. That would result in a record-size firing squad. Our numbers are set at twenty-one. Checking out new members grows more difficult with high inherent risks."

Dmitri's expression showed he did not expect this. "Twenty-one is hardly enough to begin a revolution."

"My friend, revolution is not a consideration. Our group believes the best course of action is to get the enemy to sue for peace."

Grinning, Borkowski shook his head. "Why should they do that when they are clearly winning?"

Looking at his friend, Turgenev responded, "The Americans were winning in Vietnam until a respected news correspondent reported the war to be unwinnable. You saw the result."

Borkowski donned a sage expression. "Chinese master warrior, Sun Tzu, tells us, 'The Moral Law causes people to be in complete accord with their ruler, so that they will follow him regardless of their lives, undismayed by any danger.' Without that, victory is impossible. This should be our point of focus."

The men turned and walked away from the headstone.

"We may have an American ally, Dimiti … a significant one."

Through a startled look, Dmitri asked, "We do?"

"Yes. The United States has a presidential hopeful. We know for a fact his plan is to turn the American public against the war, then campaign for election by advocating a negotiated settlement. A negotiated settlement, Dmitri. That would let us keep what we have now then consolidate and emerge as the greatest world force since the Roman Empire."

Dmitri thought, but did not share with his friend, *Haven't we learned from America what a stupid concept that is*? "Enlighten me, please. Who is our powerful ally within the enemy camp?"

Chapter 13

White House, Oval Office

Eric Danis defended himself. "Why didn't you warn me, Mr. President? I would've worn a hardhat, asbestos britches and hard-toed shoes for this session."

Having vented his wrath on the Navy's apparent lack of a plan to get combat gear to England, President Dempsey interjected a bit of humor. "That's what worries me about you, Danis. You don't even know asbestos has been illegal in the Navy for at least ten years."

"A bad ruling, sir. Had we known the level of your ass chewing, we'd have written a presidential exception. In this office, I wouldn't trust anything else, sir. Maybe we should change the rules."

Danis had not had that much time with the President, but felt he'd judged him sufficiently to know what he could get away with.

"Can I make a wild guess on the main problem, Mr. President?"

"Every damn guess I get from the Navy is wild. So why should I mind now?"

"I'm guessing you have a situation that hinges on getting this done. If so, what arrows can you give me for my quiver?"

Dempsey's grin betrayed his Irish descent. "That's what being President is all about, Eric. You know how it goes. If the damn Congress needed an answer next week, they'd wait till then to ask the question."

"I don't think Congress is the big rub, sir. The whole country admires the way you snap it into line."

Dempsey rose and looked for a time into the rose garden. "I need a miracle and damn quick. My unworthy opponent, and son of a bitch in the bargain, wants to prove we can't win this war and uses that as his main platform plank in the upcoming election to convince everyone we should give up. Dammit, Eric, I won't let that happen."

"You need an Atlanta, Mr. President."

"An Atlanta?"

President Dempsey walked back and forth behind his desk with obvious diminishing patience.

"Yes sir. Your opponent's tactic has been tried before and fell flat on its sword. In Eighteen sixty-four, Lincoln's opponent tried to convince everyone we didn't have enough at stake in the south to warrant continuing the war. Grant fueled the argument at Cold Harbor in August of sixty-four ... lost so many men the north saw logic in a negotiated settlement."

Dempsey tossed up his arms in exasperation. "Eric, I brought you in to complain about the Navy's lack of progress in getting done what I hired you for, and all you do is lecture me on the Civil War."

Accustomed to how President Dempsey used body language to overwhelm an audience, Danis stood with his fingers splayed and waved his hands up and down in the universal *be calm* gesture.

"Hear me out, sir. Lotta good lessons in history. Sherman took Atlanta, ringing a death knell for the south and the strategy of Lincoln's opponent. Think I got an Atlanta for you."

Danis went over the results of the last meeting with his DCNOs. "We can get this ball rolling but have a few loose ends to tuck in."

"How soon?"

"A month."

"A week will do nicely. When can I expect convincing results?"

"A month like I said, Mr. President ... and if you slice a minute out of that, I'll have my resignation on the chairman's desk first thing tomorrow morning."

"You're a hard-ass, Danis."

"I know, sir. I learned it from you. Now, have one of your flunkies tear into the Atlanta story and dope out specifics on how it killed the negotiated settlement argument. Might be some good fodder there. By the way, who is this erstwhile opponent of yours?"

The snarl on Dempsey's face would activate smoke alarms. "Senator Darrel Manning."

Aboard *Steelhead*

Brent Maddock, Tom Bentley and Sonarman Chief Giambri huddled about the myriad of digital displays in the sonar shack.

Maddock said, "Moment of truth, Chief."

"On your command, Captain."

They stood ready to test the disarming concept on a Soviet defensive minefield.

"Do it, Chief," Maddock said as he crossed his fingers.

Giambri's stone face masked his anxiety perfectly as he closed the activating key on the modified Gertrude (underwater telephone) transmitter. "Let's hope their sonar crew is bored to tears with being ice picked and don't listen so closely anymore. Also, the banging around they're doing makes it hard for them to hear us."

Agonizing seconds passed by like hours. Then deactivation signals from each weapon flowed in through a loudspeaker, drawing a chorus of relief sighs from the listeners.

"Now the target." Giambri had maximized the gain on each receiver and listened to every crumb of sound emanating from the Russian. After two anxious minutes, the chief concluded, "Nothing."

Maddock nodded his satisfaction. "Okay, we head in."

A bright late fall sun beamed down on the ice cap, illuminating the adjacent ocean, providing the best possible circumstances for *Steelhead*'s venture: pass beneath the target with number one periscope raised for visual surveillance of the Soviet boomer.

The ship's *best* ears had assembled in the sonar shack, each pair monitoring for the slightest sound that would indicate *Steelhead* had been counter detected. Two ADCAP torpedoes stood ready in flooded tubes with outer doors opened.

Maddock manned the scope, trained mainly on sonar bearings to the target, but occasionally swung about to insure nothing new had slipped into the mix. The ship at ultra-quiet condition proceeded toward the target. He marveled at the apparition. Filtered green-blue light funneled down making the skipper feel as though they entered the sanctity of a cathedral. *What a serene and beautiful place. Now man elects to invade and shatter its peaceful solitude.*

A dark shape appeared on the target sonar bearing and slowly took the shape of an ice-picked submarine.

"Everyone not on watch, into their bunks," Maddock ordered. "Pass the word verbally, compartment to compartment. We can't afford to make the slightest sound. Have maneuvering shift to the SPM and make minimum turns."

Slowly, the shape took on a Soviet *Delta*-class appearance.

"Wow! XO, take a look and confirm we see the same thing."

Taking the scope, Bentley echoed the skipper as he exclaimed another "Wow!"

"What do you estimate the range, Tom?"

"Ballpark guess … two thousand, Captain, based on high-power divisions keel to sail top."

"My guess too." Maddock wanted Bentley to have a vote of confidence. "Stay on the scope and take us directly under her and see what you can spot." The strong noise coming from outside the hull of the Soviet ice-picked boomer penetrated *Steelhead*. "See if you can figure out what's happening up there."

"Aye, Captain." Bentley recognized and accepted this expression of confidence. "Can see no apparent hull repair in progress."

Anxious faces instinctively turned upward, despite seeing only *Steelhead*'s dull overhead as she passed beneath the Soviet *Delta*, starboard to port.

Bentley announced, "Range opening, Captain."

"Make a Williamson," Maddock ordered.

This maneuver requires initiating a turn at full rudder for sixty degrees then shifting to full rudder opposite direction, swinging the ship two hundred forty degrees before steadying on the original course reciprocal. The tactic—developed by a diesel-electric submariner to recover out of sight men overboard at night or in restricted visibility—returns the ship to exactly where the man fell overboard. This maneuver continues to prove itself essential to a variety of emerging tactical needs.

Bentley implemented the order.

Circling beneath the Soviet submarine, every sailor in the attack center gritted his teeth. If detected, they could expect an immediate heavyweight torpedo strike sending *Steelhead* to the bottom. This placed great demands on crew confidence in their captain.

Maddock ordered, "This time, study the ice above the pick for any sign of activity."

"Aye, Captain."

The Williamson did the job. With only slight course adjustment, Bentley brought *Steelhead* directly beneath the Russian.

Bentley exclaimed, "Well I'll be damned!" Then he jumped back from the scope and said, "Take a look, Captain."

Manning the scope, Maddock saw outlines of men moving about above the ice and announced this to everyone in the attack center.

"What do you think they're doing, Captain?"

"I don't know, Tom. But we gotta find out."

Maddock winced at the plan that ran through his quick mind.

Ottawa, Canada

Vasiliy Baknov's type-A personality conflicted with jumping through *cloak and dagger* hoops of Thomas Baylor to accommodate his espionage business and tired of them. Baknov had been directed to take a cab after dark to a location six blocks away from his destination and walk the remaining distance. He arrived at the designated address and knocked on the door of a darkened building.

Soon, the unmistakable voice of Baylor asked, "Who's there?"

Vasiliy resisted an urge to reply *the Royal Canadian Mounted Police come to haul your ass off to jail*, but settled for "Warren Biddle," the name agreed upon earlier.

He entered and they walked to a dimly lit room where Baylor introduced a man seated behind a table as Dick. The man gave a stern look to Baylor, an obvious order to leave the room, and then invited Baknov to sit.

Dick frowned a minute then said, "You say you're Lieutenant Vasiliy Baknov of the Soviet Navy. Do you really expect me to believe that and the ridiculous story of how you got here?"

Vasiliy betrayed no emotion. "You believe it or we wouldn't be having this conversation."

"I wouldn't be so sure about that," Dick replied. "In this line of work, we survive by mistrusting everyone."

"That applies to me also," Vasiliy said, "and since I did not volunteer to be here, apparently you summoned me. So I suggest we set aside the preliminaries and get right to the subject."

Dick did not give up. "You should be aware that people … shall we say, who even fell under suspicion … well, we're not sure what became of them."

Through a stern look, Baknov replied, "I've overcome too much to be deterred by a simple threat and feel sorry for anyone who gets assigned to assassinate me. And if you give them the true story, I doubt you'll get many volunteers."

His expression did not change and the two stared each other down for several heartbeats.

Dick asked through a far less drastic tone, "There are a few things I must know for your story to make sense, most importantly, why did you make your way here from the west coast?"

Baknov related the story accurately.

Dick asked, "What made you decide not to kill your father?"

Vasiliy did not wish to admit being softened by Painter's parents and forced a snarl, "Killing him would be too merciful. He is a pitiful, decrepit old man waiting to die, remorseful over what he has done. I decided it best not to relieve him of that burden."

"What about your Lieutenant Commander Maddock vendetta? Will that interfere with work we might assign you?"

He wondered about the *we* specific identity and thought out his answer carefully. "My duty to Mother Russia and the Communist Party have priority over everything else in my life."

"Very well, then. Are you aware the turning point in this war has been reached and the Soviet Union is now on the defensive?"

He could not disguise his anger over Dick's remark. "I know of no such thing."

Immediately, Vasiliy regretted saying this as he came to realize Dick assessed his every mood and reaction. "Can you explain why you believe this?"

Dick went over each detail and made Baknov's gut wrench when he identified the key cause: seriously diminished submarine warfare capability, with blame laid mainly on communist defeat in the Bering Sea battle.

Baknov knew an expression of anger would not help his cause. They spoke English and Dick's accent made him not Canadian, nor any other foreigner with English as a second language. *American*, Vasiliy thought. Dick's next remark confirmed this suspicion.

"Allied victory is contingent upon American industry which was not significantly touched in the war's opening exchange of nuclear weapons. It again runs at near full capacity. The main problem is getting their products to the battle scene. Soviet submarines to date have posed the greatest interdiction threat, but their number has diminished enough to allow sea transport of munitions to begin."

Baknov wondered how he could possibly do anything to affect this. He had not long to get an answer.

"Despite the momentum change, our best opportunity lies in lessening the Americans' will to continue the war."

He wondered about Dick's use of the word *our* and said, "I am willing to help, but it's not clear how."

"There is an American politician that holds great sway over American opinion. He is convinced a negotiated settlement should be sought."

"Yes, but I still don't see—"

Dick cut him off. "Give him data to make America believe the Soviet submarine threat remains strong and Allied use of the seas to transport war materials is futile."

Aboard *Steelhead*

Brent Maddock, COB Jacques Henri, Tom Bentley and three seamen stood on the main deck after *Steelhead* surfaced in a polynya and moored to the ice.

Maddock spoke, "COB, I know we've been over this enough, but one more time."

Henri recapped everything, making sure his three seamen heard and understood the plan.

The party of four would make their way to the ice-picked Russian submarine to determine what was going on above the ice and outside the hull.

Each man, bundled in warm clothing with rifles slung over their shoulders, carried rations, and marker devices to assist in finding the Russian. Henri did not like the idea of arming his seamen, but Bentley insisted. Henri thought, *Give these kids rifles and you know damn well they'll shoot them. Then everybody will know where we are.* They topped all the materials with white sheets fashioned into camouflage covers.

With no natural points of reference on ice, human beings tend to walk in circles. Henri had thought it through. A series of stakes would be driven into the ice, the first after being vectored along the Soviet line of bearing until the ship began to fall below Henri's horizon. Thereafter, another aligned with the first, in line with *Steelhead* before she disappeared below the horizon. This would be repeated until they reached the object of their search.

Henri's seamen, excited over the prospects of doing something new and dangerous, had no idea of their peril.

"The distance from here is very close to eight miles on the nose, or damn close to that," said Maddock. "I'll leave you to judge the distance. As COB and a quartermaster to boot, this mission should be a piece of cake for you."

Henri grinned. "Didn't you say something like that when you sent me off *Denver* on a similar trip?"

"Yeah, come to think of it. That's why you can't take Mr. Parnell along. You got him shot the last time."

The men exchanged glances that harbored so much mutual respect, no words needed to be spoken.

He had a portable radio to use only if Henri required assistance in finding *Steelhead* on return from the mission.

It all began well. Henri had earlier calculated the distance where the top of *Steelhead*'s sail would fall below the horizon. He would time how long it took to cover that distance and use it to estimate the rate of closure on the target area. He would use the markers but back them up with pre-computed angular change rate of his shadow as the sun moved across the horizon. He considered this would aid him in walking a straight line better than a row of stakes.

Henri left nothing to chance. *One for one can be called pure luck, so I'm upping my record to two for two.*

When the sun slipped below the horizon, Henri estimated his position slightly less than six miles from *Steelhead*. He had the seamen build a windbreak of ice and spread their white camouflage into a combined overhead weather cover. Rations passed out, the young seamen ate ravenously.

For an instant, he toyed with limiting them, but dismissed the notion. In any circumstance, they could last unprotected on the ice no longer than three days.

Henri reached into his backpack for a logbook into which he'd pen a summary of the day's events. *What the hell is this?* His hand wrapped around the unmistakable shape of a whiskey bottle. It bore a note in the distinctive hand of Brent Maddock. *Bring some of this back, COB. I haven't tasted it yet.*

Henri asked if the men had brought cups.

"No, COB. When we get thirsty, we just pick up a little ice."

Arctic ice is frozen saltwater but the snow provides enough fresh water to quench thirst.

"Huddle around guys. We're gonna sleep soundly tonight." He showed them the bottle. "Now, anyone mentions this aboard ship, their asses are mine. Got it?"

"Got it, COB," chorused the three seamen.

Henri passed the bottle around. Each man enjoyed a welcome swig of the finest bourbon any of them had ever imbibed."

I knew the captain had good taste in women, but bourbon. How can you beat this?

The following morning, Henri woke to a *clanking* sound coming from the direction of their target area. He turned and found the three seamen cuddled up and sleeping, so decided to investigate alone.

He affixed a note to the underside of their cover. 'Don't you guys move a damn inch. I'll be right back.'

Henri removed a sheet from the cover and donned it, then moved with caution in the direction of the noise. A series of pressure ridges provided cover as he approached what had to be the ice-picked *Delta*. Scanning ahead with his binoculars, an hour passed before he could make out men moving about the ice, obviously performing a task of some sort. He stopped behind a pressure ridge a hundred yards from the activity.

Upon discerning the nature of their work, he thought, *Damn it all, we should've been able to figure this out.*

A working party of seven men busied themselves in an obvious effort to remove ice from above the ice-picked *Delta*'s missile launchers. This would make it unnecessary to find open water in the event the Soviet government initiated a launch order.

Henri wondered whether value of the intelligence find warranted risks taken by his party of four. He had not long to reflect on this. A sound behind him caused Henri to whirl about and draw his service pistol. He saw a terrified young Russian sailor, his hands raised into the air. Henri's immediate concern became that of being spotted by the other Russians. He mustered his fiercest expression and gestured with his pistol for the Russian sailor to get down.

The Russian fell to his knees, but that would not be enough. Henri gestured for the man to drop the top half of his body to the crawling position. *This poor guy picked the wrong time to go off and take a crap.* Henri's snarl faded to a grin. *At least he had enough sense to take it downwind of his shipmates.*

He made the sailor understand he would not be rejoining his mates. The Russian's fear of being executed for being out of his crew's earshot left him terrified beyond reason. Pulling the white cover over them, they began to creep away.

Henri attempted to reassure the lad of his safety with repeated smiles, but they had no effect at all. *He likely believes I'm happy about killing him.*

COB used wind direction as a device to navigate back to where he had left the seamen. Happy to see Henri, they didn't know what to make of the prisoner and immediately gathered up and cocked their rifles. Henri ordered his men to uncock them and hang them back on their shoulders.

Then he said, "Now, let's get a move on. It won't be long before this guy's buddies come looking for him."

They found the first stake, picked it up and began the long walk back to *Steelhead.*

Having heard nothing from Henri's radio, the captain and exec grew anxious. They scanned the horizon for any sign of the ice party. Two lookouts stood on the bridge to watch for aircraft and took many *peeks* in the direction their shipmates had disappeared.

One of them made contact and yelled out, "I think I see them, Captain! Two-four-zero relative!"

Maddock scanned the bearing with his binoculars. "Uh-oh, Tom. Might not be them. I see five men."

"I doubt five people on the ice can do us much harm, Captain. Let's wait and see who they are."

Maddock had no intention of doing anything else.

Half an hour later, the five boarded *Steelhead*, Henri grinning from ear to ear said, "Brought you a souvenir, Captain."

Henri had made it *two for two*.

Chapter 14

Aboard *Steelhead*

The terrified Russian seaman soon felt like anything but a prisoner. The crew determined their new messcook's name to be Ivan and overwhelmed him with attention and better food than the young Russian sailor had ever eaten. An intelligent, bright young man, he absorbed English quickly and had no problem with being assigned messcook duties.

Tom Bentley spoke of this to the captain. "A stop back in the crew's mess to watch our troops with this guy makes you wonder why the hell we fight one another."

"It's always been like that, Tom. The troops don't wanna slug it out. They prefer to stay at home, but the top of the heapers plan the wars and send them off to fight. Maybe their attitudes would change if they had to man a rifle and climb into the trenches."

"I have a plan, Captain. So help me, it will end war forever."

"What's that, Tom?"

"Get every government to agree to eighty as the minimum age required for military service. You know those old guys would never shoot at each other. I can hear it now ... an American yelling across the lines, 'How 'bout we meet halfway and swap you JD Black for some vodka?'."

"Problem with that concept is it'd work but the world will never settle for that."

"Captain, what are we planning to do to Ivan's ship?"

"Same as last time, but we'll wait for the noise to stop so it gives enough time for the crew to re-board then we hit 'em with a Sea Lance bomb."

"Then what?"

"Carry out the Patrol Order. Look for more ice-picked boomers and dispatch 'em."

"Dispatch 'em, Captain? Doesn't that mean sink 'em?"

"Now man battle stations … torpedo!" boomed over the 1MC, interrupting their conversation.

Upon reaching the attack center, they learned a submarine roared by with such a high bearing rate, collision had been avoided by a matter of yards.

Irate, Maddock entered the sonar shack and found Chief Giambri hovering over the operators. "How did we let him get this close? How far out did you make initial contact?"

If anything ever upset Giambri, he did a hell of a job covering it. "Working on that now, Captain. A few minutes ago, we had a quiet, distant contact that all of a sudden exploded on us. My guess … it came right at us, his hull shielding the propulsion noise."

"Any chance he heard us?"

"Not likely, Captain. Sonar is almost deaf at those high speeds."

"Boomer or attack?"

"Definitely attack, Captain. Preliminary classification: Victor III (NATO designation for Soviet *Shchuka*-class) attack submarine."

"Range opening, bearings steady?"

"Yes, Captain."

Returning to the attack center, Maddock, ordered, "Secure from battle stations and go into trail. He might lead us to more boomers. Keep our radiated noise level below his, but don't lose him."

The conning officer acknowledged.

"Alert sonar to be on guard for a *Crazy Ivan* (common Soviet tactic: abruptly reverse course to ensure they're not being trailed)."

Maddock headed to the wardroom and summoned the COB.

When Henri arrived, the skipper cautioned him about the POW. "Regardless of how laid-back he seems, watch him."

"Captain, how can anyone be involved with this crew and not be laid-back? It's a condition for survival."

"Yeah, COB, but play it safe. Particularly when we go to battle stations. Assign someone to keep him in the crew's mess."

Henri grinned and asked, "Would you like me to get a reading from the Shrew?"

"Would you like me to give you a swift boot in the ass?"

"A lot of damage can be done with a wooden mixing spoon, Captain. I'll get the biggest, meanest SOB aboard to monitor the messcook ... oops, I mean Russian."

No one else on board could get away with talking to the captain in that manner, and Henri only in private.

Maddock grinned at him. "You're not thinking of the Shrew, are you?" *The smallest man aboard.*

"Took the words right outta my mouth."

"You're incorrigible, COB. If you weren't two-for-two, I'd fire your ass."

"And deny me a three-for-three opportunity?"

"Get outta here, COB."

The men shared a laugh and Chief Henri walked aft.

Thank God for Henri, Maddock thought. *He's all that keeps me from going over the edge.*

Tom Bentley returned and asked Maddock, "What do you make of the Victor III near miss, Captain?"

"I'm thinking the boomer's wondering what happened to their guy and smell a rat, so they called in the heavy guns."

"Uh-oh."

"Look at the bright side. The more resources they send up here to find us, the less they'll have to interdict getting logistics across the Atlantic."

Woody Parnell entered the wardroom.

The skipper announced, his voice now jovial, "Here's Woody. On to better and brighter things. Maybe we can get him to tell us how that twenty-pound salmon got away."

Woody shook his head. "You work hard, do good and say your prayers, but they still beat up on ya."

Severodvinsk

Dmitri Borkowski glanced at his watch. *Turgenev is fifteen minutes late. Not like him.* A waitress approached for the second time to take Borkowski's order. At lunch hour the restaurant filled and empty tables did not put rubles into the owner's pocket.

"My friend will be along soon." Dmitri looked out the window then announced, "There he is now. Bring us two vodkas and we'll order when you return."

Borkowski rose to shake his friend's hand. "Ah, Mikhail. I don't know what's happening to me. Fifteen minutes late and I fret like an old woman."

"I believe you had good reason to. Maybe it is me who suffers from paranoia. Someone appeared to be following me, so I ducked into a tavern and watched him from the window. Just as I suspected, he stopped outside and waited for what I believed was me. But seconds later, a beautiful young woman approached. I watched them embrace and walk off together. The delight in their faces was too genuine to have been feigned. Ah to be young again, my friend. What did we do with all that youth, Dmitri?"

"Spent it boring holes in the ocean, Mikhail. We must encourage future generations not to do that."

They exchanged pleasantries for a time, then got down to the purpose of their meeting.

Dmitri said, "A number of officers are with us. Most are friends I have known long enough to be assured of their loyalty."

The skeptical Turgenev replied, "To whom?"

"My friend, two men do not comprise a revolution. People are what's needed."

"Revolution? Not a consideration as I recall, but then what else can be implied?"

Borkowski continued, "I know of no other way to bring this madness to its knees. The biggest threat is getting compromised. This comes with expanding our numbers, but risks must be taken."

"Are you up for it?"

"How can I call myself a man and not be?"

Turgenev reminded, "We began this only with the intention of getting the Americans to give up."

"Both of us know full well the ultimate consequences if the Soviet Union continues on its current plan. Signs of our exhaustion are flagrant. This whole thing started as a communist defensive measure. It's clear the Soviet Union is crumbling and would have by now if it were not for that disastrous plan they launched. America's agreement to a negotiated settlement remains key."

Turgenev, the consummate radical, a quality no doubt inherited from his grandfather, said, "You are right, my friend. Unconditional surrender is an overused stipulation by greedy enemies. It normally gains nothing more for the victor than would a negotiated peace and takes far more lives on both sides. What would have been the consequences of offering Germany and Japan the opportunity for a negotiated settlement when we had them on their knees?"

"Little would have changed, Mikhail, other than sparing millions of lives ... most of them Russian."

"Good. We are of the same mind. A network of intellectuals is already established in Russia. I am in daily contact. As a military officer, it is well that you remain outside this organization for now. But your help is invaluable. For openers, do you know anything about a Lieutenant Vasiliy Baknov who allegedly died in the Soviet submarine *Zhukov* on the northwest American coast? Per my contacts, he didn't die."

"Only that he served under my old friend, *Kapitan* 1st Rank Igor Sherensky, a good man and superb naval officer. Anyone who sailed with Igor had to have some good rubbed off on him."

Aboard *Steelhead*

Steelhead passed on the Victor III but slammed a Sea Lance bomb onto Ivan's *Delta*. Subsequently, Giambri heard her limp off, no doubt to Severodvinsk to lick her wounds.

Two weeks elapsed before they encountered an ice-picked *Delta*. Per plan, using the same tactic, a Sea Lance bomb surprised the *Delta,* likely causing similar or worse damage. Sonar reported a slight hiccup in the distinctive distant sound of her screws.

They patrolled two more weeks and found nothing. *Steelhead* departed station on her appointed time to rendezvous with her relief then headed south for Fundy, prisoner of war Ivan to an unknown future. Maddock toyed with the idea of saying nothing and inducting the young Russian into his crew, but then he dismissed the idea.

Problem with submariners, they're all the same. It would be tough packing Ivan off to heaven knows where, but *c'est la guerre* ('it's the war'; generally means 'cannot be helped').

Bentley and Maddock pored over the preliminary patrol report to be radio transmitted home.

"Captain, I agree completely with everything we've done and your reason for doing them. But our mission is to seek out and destroy Soviet assets. Even though two bomb hits answers the mail, saying why we passed on kill opportunities changes nothing and gives COM Bostwick his long-awaited chance to nail you."

"What are you suggesting, Tom?"

"Simply report the actions and omit the strategy part. That's not our job."

"I'll argue with you on that, Tom. Submarine COs by nature of the job must invent. We don't have the luxury of being in daily contact. When something not covered by our orders comes up, we act in the best interest of the country and Navy."

"But isn't that something you can submit as a recommendation and do just as well?"

"Tom, you are a loyal and competent exec. Your concern over what becomes of me does not go unnoticed. But look at it this way. How do we explain Ivan without admitting we passed close enough to the *Delta* to take him out in a heartbeat and did not?"

"Plead the importance of determining what they were up to on top of the ice."

"Then why couldn't we have gotten that intelligence, returned and finished the job? Tom, I appreciate what you're trying to do. But there's another point of view. Can you think of any job better than a submarine command? The way I see it, everything subsequent to that is academic. I'll be honest. Marrying Bea Zane and going off to do whatever we please has greater appeal to me than anything else after command."

Bentley disagreed. He believed Maddock to rank high among submarine force assets. He had so much to offer as a teacher on the submarine Prospective Commanding Officer staff or Division and Squadron commands. Tom also knew his boss made decisions only after deep reflection. And once made, trying to overturn one of those decisions is tantamount to overturning an Egyptian pyramid.

"Send the message, Captain?"

Bentley knew well what the answer would be.

Maddock wrote his name in the release box. "Send it."

Pentagon, Office of the CNO

CDR Leo Wade poked his head into Admiral Eric Danis's office. "A Miss Zane on the phone for you, Admiral. I tried to put her off, but she's quite insistent. Do you want to take the call?"

"Bea Zane? Yes, of course. Thank you, Leo. Should've added her to the cleared list."

Several hundred calls a day are received at the CNO office and require a filtering system.

Wade left and shut the door.

"Hello, Bea! What's happening up there?"

"Admiral Danis. I'm so glad I got through to you. There for a while, I didn't think I'd make it. That's quite a wall you've got around that ivory tower."

"Not to worry, Bea. All fixed for next time. Getting old and simply forgot to put you on the good-guy list. Call me anytime."

"Thank you, Admiral Danis."

"Can you call me Eric? Beautiful young women calling me admiral makes the old guy feel even older." Having detected an edge on her voice, he promptly asked, "Everything okay, Bea?"

"Not exactly. I need to call you on the scrambler phone, but the only one available is on COM Bostwick's yacht and he always has someone hovering over it."

"Believe I understand completely. Look for someone to contact you in person this evening. Now, on to more important things. How's that old rascal and former shipmate doing? Only intelligent thing he ever did in his life was marry your mother and have you."

They chatted for a bit longer, but Danis sensed Bea's anxiety and cut the call short.

After hanging up, he summoned his aide. "Leo, you look a little peaked and could use a one-day vacation in Canada. Order up a plane at Andrews and be on your way ASAP."

The CNO instructed Wade on how to contact his liaison officer. "Sorry, Leo, but I've already told you all I know. Bea's a good head and if she needs this, it's damn important."

Hours later, CDR Wade found an anxious Bea Zane standing before him on the Fundy tarmac.

He exclaimed, "Wow! The admiral warned me about your competence, but how did you know where to find me?"

Bea forced a smile, then hustled Wade off to a quiet place in the terminal where they could talk. She explained the substance of *Steelhead's* radioed preliminary report of patrol and went on to describe COM Bostwick's reaction then presented a copy of the report to Wade.

"I don't understand. This looks like a fairly decent report to me."

"What about the part on strategy?"

"LCDR Maddock is senior officer on the scene with no one to consult. He must make these kinds of decisions."

Bea made it a point to be especially friendly with Bostwick's entire administrative staff and found it easy to get whatever she needed from them. In this instance, a copy of a document to convene a general court-martial with the defendant as LCDR Brent Maddock for cowardice in the face of the enemy.

Bea made no effort to rein in her anger and spoke in tones so harsh they exceeded even what she believed herself capable. "The son of a bitch doesn't only want to destroy Brent's career but put him in prison for a long time."

"Bea, I get the feeling there's more to this than simply injustice. Is there something between you and Maddock?"

"Only if you consider giving birth to his baby six and a half months from now something."

Wade's jaw fell. "Oh my! Yes, I'd say that is something. When's the lucky guy due home?"

"In about a week. You look like you're too loyal a guy not to tell Admiral Danis. But let me tell Brent. He doesn't know and I want to see his face when he first hears about it."

Wade smiled. "My prediction ... you'll see the happiest camper of all time. Thanks for getting this stuff to me. I guarantee you, Admiral Danis will quash this in record time."

Wade went immediately to Bostwick's secure room, tossed out the watch petty officer, fired up the scrambler phone and dictated a message for immediate delivery to the CNO in the a.m.

By noon the following day, a top secret CNO FLASH precedent message reached the desks of operational commanders throughout the Navy, directing cessation of destroying Soviet assets in the Arctic except in self-defense. Cited reason: Critically damaging enemy submarines strains Soviet logistics to a far greater extent than destroying their assets. Use of Sea Lance high explosive bombs will continue as weapons of choice.

Bostwick seethed. Alone in his office, he balled up the message and slammed it to the deck.

A week later, first to cross *Steelhead*'s brow, a forced smile on his face, he shook Brent Maddock's hand warmly, congratulated him on a successful patrol and hung a Navy Cross on his nemesis. Bostwick's ability to contain his true emotions brought the definition of remarkable to a new level.

Brent spotted Bea on the dock and struggled to remain patient during the impromptu ceremony. The moment formalities ended, he ran to Bea and wrapped her in a tight embrace.

"Marry me, Bea," he pleaded.

Bea held his face in clear view. "I guess I'd better."

"Better?"

"People usually do that before they have a baby and we only have six and a half months to go."

Bea beheld Leo Wade's predicted happiest of all campers.

St. Croix River

Nothing quite wore a diligent officer down more than getting his ship prepared to go into harm's way. Woody Parnell understandably took a needed break. He confronted the stress of his past three weeks with a Jeep trip to the St. Croix. First time since an aggressive environmentalist released his prized twenty-pound Atlantic salmon.

This day, not even a strike, but it made no difference. Woody enjoyed more serenity just standing in the river swinging his fly rod than he could find anywhere else. Frequent naps on the river bank brought Woody to terms with exactly how tired he had become during *Steelhead*'s refit. Each shuteye began with a swig of scotch whiskey from the silver flask he carried in a reserved pocket of his fishing vest.

Born late in his father's life, Woody nonetheless shared many hours with his dad trying to snag the wily cutthroat trout from rivers near his Montana home. Shortly before his death, Woody's dad gave him the silver flask and vest he had worn for more than thirty years.

The senior Parnell laid on a condition: 'Son, every time you bring it home, the flask must be refilled with at least eighteen-year-old single-malt scotch whiskey. Your grandfather gave me the flask under the same conditions. Think of us each time you raise it.'

And Woody did, saying each time he removed the cap, "Thanks Pop and Granddad."

With daylight fading, he returned to his Jeep, this time borrowed legally from Bea Zane, climbed out of his waders, loaded his tackle and pondered a final couple of swigs to drain the silver flask. *Nope. Feeling light-headed enough and don't want to get across the breakers with Den Mother for breaking her Jeep.*

Feeling better than he felt in weeks, Woody drove off.

A mile down the road, he saw an old model Volkswagen that appeared partially off the road, its driver kneeling beside it.

Woody stopped, stepped from the Jeep and asked, "Can I help you? Looks like your Bug could use a tow." As he approached, the driver looked up. Astounded, Woody exclaimed, "Well I'll be damned … it's the salmon nazi! What the hell did you do? Run off the road chasing a fisherman?"

The woman looked at him through an angry stare. "I got a flat and pulled over to fix it. When I yanked the wheel off, the car's rear end rolled into the ditch."

"Well tell me, lady. How does someone who knows everything do something that dumb?"

"Just give me a hand. I'll pay you."

"What would I do with money? In this place, there's not enough to do to spend what I already make."

Woody knelt beside the woman. "Think I can jack it up enough to get the spare on. There's a tow chain in the Jeep and I can haul you back onto the road."

A barely audible "Thanks" could be heard from the woman.

Woody read a pained expression on her face and noted she held her right arm. "Are you all right? What's wrong with that arm?"

"Nothing. The car hit it when it fell off the jack."

"Let me look at it."

"No. Just get me back on the road and I'll be on my way."

"Lady, give me a look at that damn arm," Woody said in his best command voice.

She seemed to waver, but held her ground. "If you get me up and running, I can make it home."

"It's getting dark, lady. Unless you want to pass the night here waiting for the next guy to come along, give me a look at that arm."

She grudgingly extended it.

"Pull back your sleeve."

She complied.

"Lady, a tenderfoot boy scout with no first-aid merit badge could see it's broken. Get in the Jeep. We're going to the dispensary." Woody now understood why the woman could not erase the pained expression. "Here. Finish this off." He handed her the silver flask. "It won't fix your arm, but it'll make you feel a helluva lot better."

"But what about my car?"

"I'm in the Navy. Tomorrow, I'll bring one of my sailors out here. We'll fix it and bring it home. Give me the keys."

Her grimace melted ever so slightly. "Here," she relinquished her car keys then drained the flask easily. "Thanks."

She could look halfway decent if she put her mind to it. Too bad it'd shatter her salmon-nazi image. "I'm Woody Parnell. Unless you want me to keep calling you *lady*, what's your name?"

"Erica Hussey," barely escaped her lips, the bumpy ride clearly exacerbating her pain despite the whiskey.

Chapter 15

NAVSEA, Crystal City, Arlington, VA

One of the many perks a CNO has, is he can call meetings anytime he wishes. The meeting he convened on a cold November Friday morning was at the U.S. Naval Sea Systems Command in Crystal City, Arlington, VA. Attendees: CAPT Dave Zane, USN (Ret) and LCDR Dan Patrick from the Pacific Northwest *Pitstop*, Bea Zane, CNO liaison officer at Bay of Fundy, and from USS *Steelhead,* a submarine undergoing refit there, CO LCDR Brent Maddock, XO LCDR Tom Bentley and LT Woody Parnell.

Some years back, Dan Patrick along with Brent and Woody Parnell—in no condition to drive after having over-imbibed a touch too much ashore in Poulsbo, WA—had to be rescued and driven back to the BOQ by Bea Zane, thereafter dubbed *Den Mother.*

The meeting agenda was a simple one—refitting submarines at temporary facilities—it adjourned early Friday afternoon to the Gangplank restaurant. *The place to dine* in Washington, D.C. The restaurant sits upon a barge moored on the east side of the Potomac River, south of the 14th Street Bridge.

A handsome maître d', tall with graying hair, greeted them; his dusky skin tones offset by an immaculate white jacket enhanced his appearance. Politeness did not mask his absolute control over the staff and everything that happened in the smooth-running restaurant.

Even super-busy CNO, Admiral Eric Danis, managed to slip out of his office for two hours to join them. Since return transportation had been arranged for Monday morning, what better way to spend the weekend than to drive to Annapolis for Bea Zane and Brent Maddock's wedding?

Scheduling the event with such short notice would make for a sparse crowd in the 2,500 capacity chapel, so Maddock contacted Will Croom, webmaster for the class site, and asked that word of their wedding be passed to area classmates.

Admiral Danis also worked the problem by directing his aide to notify the Commandant of Midshipmen that CNO planned to attend. This would bring out a host of people. The commandant offered another benefit, hold a reception at the Naval Academy O-club.

On the eve of their big day, Bea admitted to Brent that in another month her bridal dress could no longer contain both their baby and her. Nevertheless, she stole the show.

USNA Chapel, Annapolis, MD

A picture of elegance, Dave Zane walked his daughter Bea down the aisle of a nearly filled to capacity chapel. She wore an A-line white-lace, tea-length dress with empire waist and capped sleeves. A single strand of pearls graced her neck and a rosebud tie encircled her waist. A pearl-encrusted headband held a short white veil in place. White open-toe slingback pumps completed the ensemble.

Maddock, Patrick and Parnell stood at the altar in blue service uniforms and ear-to-ear grins.

After Dave Zane placed his daughter's hand in Brent's, she whispered, "See? I told you guys nothing good would come of this."

The laugh among the bridal party did not go unnoticed by the congregation.

Vagaries of war being what they are, everything ended too soon. Monday, except for the bride and groom, each participant headed back to their jobs with happy, but fleeting, memories of the event.

November, cold as usual, Bea and Brent headed south for a brief honeymoon, but they made the most of it. CNO had a Navy driver that took Danis just about every place he needed to go, so the admiral loaned his personal car to the happy couple.

Pentagon, Office of the CNO

Upon return, Brent and the CNO tidied up business.

"Admiral, I'm indebted to you for taking pressure off of my Arctic decision."

"Brent, I'll be honest. I did it only because you were right. If you weren't, I could not and would not interfere in COM Bostwick's affairs. I suspect you know this."

"I do, Admiral, but I'm appreciative you made that call."

"I didn't make it alone. The chairman and joint chiefs were involved. But I spared them from hearing a Navy LCDR did their thinking for them. Doubt they'd have liked that. We made the decision because it's the right one. The urgency surrounding the matter just moved it up a bit."

The admiral smiled then asked, "Have you given thought to getting behind Bostwick? In *The Caine Mutiny*, the villain wasn't Queeg, the officers who failed to support him were the villains."

"Thank you, Admiral. I'll definitely give it some thought."

"There's really no thought to give. Bostwick is your boss and you owe him that."

Maddock thought the Queeg analogy a bad one. Bostwick did not suffer from lack of confidence, but ruthlessness in his obsession to reach the top.

"I'm sorry, Admiral. I'll change my attitude."

Danis correctly believed Maddock had given him a non-answer. "Another thing, Brent. Bea's assignment as CNO liaison officer is temporary and I believe now's the time to end it. Imagine the pressure on a boss with one of his officers married to a woman who reports directly to the CNO."

"Agree, Admiral. And in another six months, her hands will be too full for a day job anyway."

Maddock, eager to know what comes next, shifted the discussion back to their earlier topic. "If I may, sir, where do we go from here now the Arctic campaign is on a back burner?"

"Priority one shifts to defending logistic support between the States and Britain. It won't be easy. Remember what the Germans achieved with only twelve operational diesel U-boats on station. As far as we know, the Soviets can field at least twenty nuke attacks and fifteen more diesels. As I said, it won't be easy."

"When has it ever been?"

"You're right, Brent. You need to be briefed in detail. Someone will come to Fundy in the near term. He'll need affirmation from you operational types that we're on the right path. You might keep in mind, COM Bostwick will lead the charge. Fundy has best access to Atlantic sea routes. He'll need lots of help, so please keep in mind what I suggested."

"I will, Admiral."

"Another thing you might already know, Brent. Wars are lost politically as well as through the test of arms."

"USNA world history one-o-one. I am well familiar with that theory, Admiral."

"Frankly, I believe this country is ripe for something like that. The twentieth century has given us Americans a bellyful of war. There are people among us who would use that as a tool to make us give up."

Brent responded with a grim look and nod. For Bea's and his child, he wished for better than the probable consequence of surrender to the Soviets.

Danis continued, "As a consequence, top priority goes to Operation Clear Seas."

Washington, D.C.

Vasiliy Baknov had no idea he'd passed within yards of his nemesis Brent Maddock. This happened on the Arland D. Williams Junior Memorial Bridge over the Potomac River. Maddock and Bea en route D.C. to return Danis's personal auto to CNO quarters in the D.C. Navy Yard while Baknov motored to Middleburg, Virginia.

Under a forged passport, he arrived at Baltimore International Airport. A driver picked him up there and took him to a remote, ancient and restored farmhouse in historic Middleburg. The driver had apparently been directed to say nothing. After half an hour of yes sir, no sir, Vasiliy gave up and enjoyed the scenery drifting by. It shifted when they turned off the seemingly endless freeways and onto U.S. Route 50 near Fairfax, Virginia.

The landscape gave way to the Appalachian Mountains' rolling foothills, dotted with many new dwellings that had been given reasonably good effort to make them part of the early eighteenth century decor of the area's original colonization.

On the outskirts of Middleburg, the auto turned into an opening in a fieldstone fence that had obviously stood there for centuries. Soon, Vasiliy found himself mounting stairs to a veranda that wrapped around what once had been an austere farmhouse. It literally cried out the owner's wealth. A host of additions blended with the original structure to accommodate needs that vastly exceeded those of its original owner.

A man who called himself Harold greeted Vasiliy. He wore the livery of a servant and carried Baknov's bag to a well-appointed bedroom. Harold, likely anything but a domestic, paused a moment to explain the history and significance of the room's elegant furnishings. He then excused himself saying the others would be along in a few hours and that Baknov could rest if he cared to.

Vasiliy heard what sounded like a key being turned in the lock. A check of the door confirmed his suspicion, so he spread out atop a four-poster canopied bed and fell into a deep sleep.

Bay of Fundy

Brent's respect for Eric Danis caused him to reflect deeply on the CNO's admonition given in regard to COM Hal Bostwick. Maddock wondered about the right approach. Several scenarios raced through his mind but nothing quite jelled.

Maddock did not fancy himself a psychiatrist, so resorted to what sustained him best; think the problem through, identify its specifics and let logic do the rest. *Bostwick is ambitious to a fault. This is likely bigger than his need for vengeance against me. Might it be possible the best approach is get him to believe my goal is to make him look good? It actually would not irk me if it proved to be a tool to get the right things done.*

Maddock cooled his heels, the mandatory fifteen minutes before a yeoman conducted him in to see Bostwick.

"Brent!" Bostwick stood and extended his hand. "The old married man. 'Bout time! Most of us were married by the time we made exec."

Dammit! He doesn't pay much attention to detail. Maddock's first marriage ended in a messy divorce while a junior officer under Bostwick aboard *Denver*.

Brent found smiling easier than he expected. He took the COM's hand. "Some of us are feet-draggers, I guess."

"You got yourself a beauty ... and works for the CNO to boot."

Maddock related the CNO account of why she will no longer hold that job.

Bostwick, happy with this response, opened the right door. "I guess you had a lot of time with Admiral Danis?"

"Not as much as I would have liked, Commodore. His main concern is how we are at Fundy. Told him things took a noticeable upswing when you took over. Suggested you exploited all you had absorbed at the *Pitstop* and he seemed to like that."

He wished not to betray his agenda, so he avoided studying Bostwick's face for reaction.

"Very nice of you to say that, Brent."

"You know me, sir. Call 'em the way I see 'em. Jack Olsen, rest his soul, said if I hadn't joined the Navy I'd have made a helluva major league umpire. I did get a sense Admiral Danis looks for you to take the lead in Operation Clear Seas."

"I don't know about that, Brent," said Bostwick unable to mask delight in his voice. "That more properly falls under the purview of a DCNO."

"The admiral has this thing about point men."

"Point men?"

"Yes, Commodore. Guys who are actually there and turn the crank. The plan is one thing, but making it happen is where rubber meets the road. From his seat, and mine too for what it's worth, that guy is you. Fundy is home base for all our submarine assets in the operation. If they can't get turned around on time, they can't go to sea on schedule."

"Of course. But that's not new."

"There's more, sir. Returning COs need to be debriefed and the information quickly digested for COs about to be deployed. That has to happen here."

"I always thought that job went to the *spooks* in Washington."

"It does and will continue. But we can't afford for valuable nuggets not to go direct to the immediate needs." Maddock slowly reeled his boss in. "Fundy will get the backslaps for *Clear Seas'* success, and of course the butt kicks in the unlikely event there are failures. Tom Bentley is such a good XO, he leaves me with a lot of time on my hands. Would be happy to put my shoulder to that wheel, if you wish, Commodore."

"Exactly what I had in mind, Brent. Maybe we can get you even more time. In your view, is Tom Bentley ready for command?"

"He is, but if I may … Admiral Danis is big on Roman Senator Marcus Aurelius Paulus."

"Who was he?"

It took not long for Bostwick's impatience to show through.

"He was sent in One-sixty-three BC to lead Roman Armies in the fight against Macedonia. As I recall, the admiral's favorite words by Paulus went something along the lines of this. He'd take advice only from those who went with him to Macedonia."

Bostwick's brow furrowed. "What should I get from that?"

"Assembling a palace guard not actually in the fight would not set well with Admiral Danis. I suggest making it a rotating job distributed among COs recently returned from patrol. That way you'll always have quick insight to emerging problems and their solutions. CNO will want to hear about that."

"I like that idea, Brent. And appreciate your offer to help. I accept, of course."

Bingo, thought Brent. But he would watch Bostwick closely. The commodore had a habit of changing with the wind.

Brent returned to *Steelhead* for a council of war with his officers. He opened by summarizing his meeting with COM Bostwick. "This will not be easy. We have a much tougher job than in World War Two."

Woody Parnell offered, "Yes, we have a better equipped foe, but also better tools to deal with him. Allied submarines didn't have the mobility to keep up with a convoy, but they do now."

Maddock agreed. "But the trick is we gotta use them right. Fundamentals. Let's start now. Tom, you be the opposition. Position Soviet assets where they can do us the most harm and we'll develop a counter."

Bentley quickly stated, "Get the diesels out on station first by whatever means I can, sit quiet and wait for the convoys. Once they get out there, nobody's gonna find 'em till they start shootin'. Then it's too late. Position nukes to cover both flanks. When the diesels scatter the convoy, the nukes come in and mop up."

Maddock scanned his officers' faces as he asked, "So how do we counter that?"

Blank stares looked back at him from around the table.

"Nobody can think of anything?"

Silence.

Maddock had noticed a recent lack of tactical interest on the part of his wardroom officers, likely the lion's share of the fault accumulating to him. The skipper and XO normally worked these problems, without soliciting input. Consequently, junior officers busied themselves with the mechanics of running their respective departments. The advent of nuclear power had also taken its toll. Prewar careers in nukes swung mainly on engineering excellence, a distant and distinctly lower priority than war-fighting ability in the real world.

Maddock found this alarming. With the country at war and an increasing demand for commanding officers, he felt he had let the most important part of his job slip through the cracks.

"Gentlemen, it's clear to me, attitude adjustment time has come. Whether you like it or not most of you will be sitting in my seat much sooner than you think. XO and I won't be there to hold your hands and your ships will sink or swim based on how well you fight them. This meeting is adjourned and will reconvene in five hours. And you guys better come up with something a lot better than what you've shown me so far."

He got up and left the wardroom.

All sat silent a moment then an officer spoke up, "I hear when he was weapons officer as a lieutenant in USS *Denver* they called him Mad Maddock. I'm beginning to see why!"

Woody Parnell jumped in. "Let's start at the beginning. XO, our designated Russian would open with, and I quote, 'Get the diesels out on station first by whatever means I can.' How 'bout we figure out how he plans to do that and break it up? I'm sure the skipper would like that."

Everyone nodded assent.

Woody continued. "They did call him Mad Maddock in *Denver*. I was his shipmate. You think he's pissed now. Wait until you see him in five hours if we show up with no new ideas."

Sochi, Soviet Union

No assembly point in the world accommodated a conspiracy meeting among military officers better than Sochi. Favorite watering hole for Russian officers taking leave, meetings there raised no NKVD suspicions at all.

Several Soviet Army officers, concerned with the inevitable impending disaster confronting their armies deployed in Europe, eagerly enrolled in the Borkowski-Turgenev plot.

However, no one advocated surrender to the Allies. They preferred a negotiated settlement based on maintaining the status quo for both sides. Everyone would keep what they had. The Soviets, strong in the belief communism is the answer to world woes, would remain in control of Europe and in a generation or two, convince occupied countries of this system's merits. After that, just a question of time before the rest of the world would fall into line.

Dmitri Borkowski and Mikhail Turgenev summarized results of a recently adjourned meeting.

"I must be honest, Dmitri, I believe any long-term goal of world domination is impractical. It is a dream that evaded every leader who attempted it throughout history."

"What of the Pax Romanus? It lasted nearly a millennium," Borkowski countered.

"Dmitri, Pax existed only in the interior. There was constant fighting at the borders. And the footprint is only a fraction of what we contemplate. If you recall history, the biggest celebrations in Rome were to mark a victory at the borders. Generals paraded with their war spoils, including slaves."

"Mikhail, you have the soul of a poet. Small wonder your Navy career was cut short. We have a fear of thinkers. Maybe this reflects poorly on me."

"Not in the least, old friend. You are much wiser than me. You had the good sense to keep your light under a basket. Tell me. What have you learned of young Baknov?"

"I believe he is more liability than asset. He is opinionated, fiercely loyal to the Party and openly speaks of a vendetta in which he plans to assassinate his father. You know ... the dancer."

"Saw Yuri Baknov dance once. A magnificent artist. But anyone who would leave his wife, the beautiful Ekaterina, simply to defect, well, I just don't know."

"I am told our American contacts are quite excited about young Baknov and attempted to recruit him. I think it's a bad move."

"Then we must find a way to keep this from happening. We cannot permit the young zealot to nullify all our good work."

Pitstop, **Northwest Washington Coast**

Dave Zane and Captain Jim Buchanan celebrated with dinner together on the eve of Buchanan's deployment, likely his last as CO USS *Denver*, a 688-class attack submarine.

"I do believe this is a first, Jim, a Pacific Fleet submarine being dispatched for duty in the Atlantic. What do you make of it?"

"Can I make a wild guess? You know I can't open our orders till I'm underway, but here's what I think. Since the Bering Strait fight, the Pacific hasn't been very target rich. Could be simple as Six-eighty-eights are more useful in the other pond."

"Then why only you?"

"Do you like to yank everyone around, Dave ... or just me?"

"Gotta admit you're awfully damn easy."

Dave looked around the Grays Harbor restaurant and saw nothing but homesick submariners hoping to hook up with a girl.

"Look, Dave, that one over there looks enough like Mata Hari to be her great-granddaughter."

"Okay, smartass. I know for a fact these orders originated at CNO."

"Wouldn't be you had some one-on-ones with the chief when you were back there for your daughter's wedding?"

"Could be."

"Out with it, Dave."

"Okay, Jim. Something big is cooking but we're not exactly sure what. Eric, that is the admiral—"

"When I last saw him, Dave, it was Eric. I doubt anything has changed since then."

"He's up to his neck in politics. This is between you and me."

"I understand. Go on."

"Eric believes there are politicians who want to sell us out."

Buchanan frowned. "We got the Reds on the ropes, Dave. Why would they want to do that?"

"Why do they want to do half the things they do? I only know this. Something big is about to break and Eric needs you for it."

The next morning, Captain Jim Buchanan embarked on a patrol that would test his courage, wisdom and tactical skills to their limits.

Chapter 16

Middleburg, VA

Tires crunching on a gravel driveway awakened Vasiliy Baknov from a light, restless sleep. Soon, a knock on his door then quickly opened by Harold.

"You have a guest," he announced.

Irritated with being locked inside his room, Baknov made no response and only followed. He took a seat in the living room where a newly laid fire crackled in a huge fireplace of field stones similar to the ones he had seen in the surrounding property wall.

What happens next? Vasiliy began to have misgivings about being talked into taking this assignment. *I should have stayed with my original plan, hunt down and assassinate US Navy Lieutenant Brent Maddock. The idea is a sound one, but best of all, it's mine. Who knows what sort of idiots I've gotten involved with?*

His thoughts interrupted by a feminine voice behind him, Vasiliy rose and saw what could well be the most beautiful woman he had ever seen.

She spoke Russian. "I am Tania, Lieutenant Baknov. It is good to find time with someone who speaks my language."

Vasiliy reacted with one of his best smiles while his instincts reminded him, *Beware of those who appear least threatening.* He thought it best to open with a valid appraisal of his circumstance. "I see you know my name, Tania," he replied in Russian. "Or is it *Komrade* Tania? Please tell me your mission is not another boring attempt at proving I am not who I say."

"On the contrary, Vasiliy. May I call you that?"

He resisted an urge to say, *A woman as beautiful as you can call me anything she likes,* but instead replied, "I am relieved to know that and you may. I'm completely in the dark ... so why am I here?"

"In good time, Vasiliy." She went to the liquor cabinet and poured each of them generous shots of vodka. Then clinking her glass with his, she said, "*Za vas* (here's to you)" and seated herself.

He sat opposite and savored Tania's beauty. Tall, raven tresses with apparently every muscle perfectly proportioned and exactly where it's intended to be. He thought, *With a passion, Americans believe all men are created equal. But what of women? What a paradise for men were all women created as Tania's equal.*

"You should know, Tania, there is not enough vodka in the world to loosen a Soviet Naval Officer's tongue. If that's your goal, it's a losing proposition."

She ignored the remark. "I served at the Soviet Embassy in Washington before the war and was among several of the staff ordered to request political asylum. It was just a question of time before the FBI accepted our stories and removed us from their suspicion list. All this of course with a little help from our operative within the FBI itself. His job was scheduling random surprise follow-on checks, so we were prepared when those came."

"Do you suppose it's the same in the NKVD?"

"Not likely. Only here in the land of the free." Tania went on to reveal the plan, "To exploit American reticence and bring an end to the war ... temporary end of course. We need time to consolidate our gains and get on with finishing the job."

"I am told we have an ally in a high American place."

"We do, Vasiliy. Candidate for the next presidential election, Darrel Manning."

"Is he likely to win? What have we done to entice him over to our side?"

"Highly likely. American public is fed up with war and would elect the Devil himself if he promised peace. About the time Manning's second term ends, the Soviet Union will begin to absorb the rest of the world. He's been promised an elite position, Czar of all the Americas."

Vasiliy shook his head in disbelief. "How can someone that naïve rise so high in American politics? He'll be czar all right, of a prisoner barracks in the gulag."

Tania smiled then said, "How right you are, *Komrade*."

"But I remain curious, Tania. Why am I here and what is expected of me?"

Tania said, "How can you be so naïve and rise to the grade of lieutenant in the Soviet Navy? You will aid Manning in developing arguments to convince America she fights a futile fight. And you will reassure Manning the party's offer to him is genuine and that he *will* become Czar of all the Americas."

Aboard USS *Denver*

Captain Jim Buchanan sat in his stateroom with his Executive Officer, Lieutenant Commander Bob Douglass to open and review their patrol order. Delaying this event until after deployment all but eliminates a compromise possibility.

"What's your bet, Bob?"

"It's a sucker-bet, Captain. Nothing would surprise me."

Buchanan opened the smaller of two envelopes which contained an overview of *Denver*'s assignment. It read:

> WHEN READY FOR SEA ON/ABOUT 01 NOVEMBER, PROCEED SUBMERGED NORTH VIA BERING STRAIT TO ARCTIC ICE CAP. THERE, PROCEED OVER SPECIFIED TRACK TO ATLANTIC. PROCEED TO POINT ALFA. FROM THERE CONDUCT SURVEILLANCE OVER SHIPPING LANES U.S. TO GREAT BRITAIN. GATHER INTELLIGENCE ON POSSIBLE SOVIET PLANS TO INTERDICT AND DISPOSITION OF RESOURCES. RENDEZVOUS WITH USS STEELHEAD OFF BAY OF FUNDY COAST; LOCATION/DATE/TIME TBD AND TRANSMITTED VLF BROADCAST. CAPT BUCHANAN DESIGNATED TASK ELEMENT COMMANDER. CONDUCT LEAPFROG SEARCH; OBJECTIVE AS STATED ABOVE. REPORT SUBGRU HQTRS FUNDY ON/ABOUT 31 DECEMBER. REPORT ENEMY DISPOSITION. AVOID ENGAGEMENT WITH ENEMY. COUNTERATTACK ONLY AS LAST RESORT. REMAIN UNDETECTED RPT UNDETECTED.

Douglass reacted. "Makes me sorta hope we don't encounter anyone. Was always told nobody wins a fight by defending himself. Ya win by making the other guy defend himself. Maybe they should clarify how much *last* is in *last resort*."

Buchanan assumed his favorite role: teacher. "Remember the old John Wayne westerns? When he sneaked around to learn what the bad guys were doing, he never shot anybody. Finding out what they were up to was more important than knocking them off."

"Love him. Don't recall the movie, but in one I'm sure he killed the same Indian four times."

"Bob, have you had any *leapfrog* experience?"

Buchanan referred to a tactic wherein submarines interchanged decoy and hunter roles. The decoy, hoping to make a foe reveal his position would increase speed to full, making him easily detectible. The hunter laid low until the enemy ship revealed its position then increased speed to intercept the decoy.

"Not a bit, Captain."

"Well, read up on it. We'll be using the tactic."

"I will, sir."

"You already know attacks under the ice are off the table and reasons therefore. When we pass under the ice, we'll record what we see and tie it off there."

"We're equipped with the torpedo mine deactivators. Will we use them?"

"It's clear to me, we don't do anything but tiptoe through the tulips." Buchanan sensed Douglass's concern over being thrown into a meat grinder and being told to remain passive. "Frankly, Bob, I think we've been put on the leading edge of something big. The Soviets will not leave Europe unless we kick their asses out. This is the opening gun."

Douglass grimaced. *This'll make three times in this century we send human beings into the madness of a European land war.* Three of Bob's ancestors died in the trenches of *the war to end all wars* (World War I) with the British Expeditionary Force as infantrymen of the Argyle and Sutherland Highland Division. Douglass's family immigrated to America in 1920, two of them to die in World War II, one on Omaha Beach and the other holding off a final Nazi gasp at the *Battle of the Bulge*. Like many other Americans, Bob Douglass had been touched by enough war to last a lifetime. But like this one, circumstances thrust upon him, he felt no other option but to aid victory to the side most likely to establish a fortunate reality the world has never known.

"I'll break out the other envelope, Captain. The thick part and get with the guys. We'll have a game plan for you in the morning."

Buchanan well understood his XO's need for a statement of affirmation given his expressed reservations. "Bob. These guys are jaded." Final days of a submarine refit are intense twenty-four seven operations, each with everyone head down and tail up. "No rush. We're a good three days from the ice pack ... and anybody we pick up on the way, we'll make a big hole in him. Let the guys rest, we need keen minds."

"Aye. And thanks, Captain."

Buchanan smiled. "For what?"

Bay of Fundy

The final day before deployment, Woody Parnell and COB wrestled with low priority tasks traditionally put off until then. Because they are easy, tendency is to accumulate far too many.

Woody fretted, but COB's steady hand maintained perspective. "Mr. Parnell, the ones that get done will and those that don't won't. You established the right priority, so all the vital ones will."

Actually, Henri established the priorities, but made sure Parnell believed he did. Every successful submarine officer's career is traceable to at least one CPO.

Attempting to appear sage, Woody used the old philosophy gimmick by reciting a nautical standard. "Yep, COB, if you're not there when the tide goes out, the tide goes out without you."

Henri actually taught Parnell that truism, but went through the motions of being impressed.

Messenger of the watch interrupted. "Phone call for you, Mr. Parnell ... from Miss Erica Hussey. I told her you were unavailable, so she asked that you call her back."

Crap. Another straw for the camel's back. I just don't have time. Maybe when we get back. "Thank you, Severs."

Parnell pocketed the slip of paper with Erica's phone number.

The strenuous day ended. Woody, dog-tired, toyed with the idea of skipping the traditional 'This our last night on shore, drink to the *foe* (from the Navy song *Anchors Aweigh*)' party with fellow officers. *Always too many foe to drink to. I have the first watch tomorrow and don't need a hangover.*

He reached into his pocket and felt the paper slip. *This'll keep a coupla months. But what if she's gone by then? Ignoring her would be impolite and he did not wish to part on a bad note. Getting to know her during the broken arm incident revealed Erica not totally without redeeming qualities. Calling her can't hurt none.*

Woody used the ship's office phone. "Hello. Erica? Woody here. You called?"

"Thanks for calling back. Sorry for the late notice, but I'm giving a dinner party tonight and thought it would be nice if you came. After all, I owe you."

He wondered how she could have a dinner party with one arm in a sling, but nonetheless began fumbling for an excuse. He could not say he's exhausted and *Steelhead* would be underway in the morning because ship movements are secret. A night out with the guys is hardly a courteous dodge.

Let me see. Then he said, "I'd love to, but managed to bang up my ankle today. Doc says to stay off it a while. Another time?"

"Oh, bummer."

Dammit, why in hell do women do this? They know guys can handle anything but being responsible for making them sad. Even Woody's mom used it on him. The disappointment in Erica's voice rang like a loud bell in his ear.

He said, "Well, I guess I could hobble over to your place." *Damn, I can't believe I said that.*

Pentagon

"Leo. Come in here please," Eric Danis asked over the intercom.

In an instant, the hard-working CNO aide entered the office. "Yes, Admiral?"

"Are you good at conspiracies?"

"Convinced Rita to marry me, didn't I?"

"Guess that's good enough. Look. This is the third time I'm being called to the Oval Office without benefit of the Joint Chief joining me. Dammit, Leo, you're supposed to keep me out of this kind of trouble."

"All I gotta do, Admiral, is figure out how to get the President and the chief to knuckle under to a commander, USN."

"Well hell, that shouldn't take long. Look, Leo. This puts me in a tough spot. Don't want to get across the chief's breakers, but even less, the President's. You got an easy job. Get me back and forth between the Pentagon and Oval Office with nobody noticing." He grinned at his aide. "That oughta be pretty easy."

Wade shook his head. "Piece of cake, Admiral."

With some difficulty, CDR Wade convinced the White House Secret Service guard to pass his private car and the CNO through.

Wade parked. "I'll wait here for you, Admiral."

"No you won't. I'm told part of my position description is to train you. Must've been you who told me that 'cause I never read the damn thing. So, take notes or whatever the hell else you do at my meetings."

Wade knew full well that any note he took in the Oval Office would be confiscated before he left. But he had a good memory and would recall most of what he wrote.

Nevertheless, he responded, "Aye, Admiral."

Wade had never met the President, who they found to be in the foulest of moods.

Pacing about the office, there were no jovial preliminaries. "Admiral Danis, I need good news and damn quick. That idiot Manning is on a roll. Have you seen the latest polls? Forty-seven percent of the public wants to end the war … now. And it's growing. A month ago, it was forty-five percent. That's far too big a jump. Is there any way you can give me a club and soon?"

"There is, Mr. President. But it'll be a major breach of security."

"Eric, if we hand this country over to the Soviets … what difference will that make? If I can't convince everyone we have a solid plan that leads us to victory, we might as well start learning to speak Russian."

Danis explained *Denver*'s and *Steelhead*'s current mission. "I think as a result of their mission, we could make it clear that moving material to Britain is imminent."

"How soon?"

"Two months. A month and a half at best. And don't make me promise something I can't deliver by asking for it sooner. Can't be done. The North Atlantic is big and our ships are not all that fast."

"You don't say that when you ask for appropriations."

Danis did a lousy job of pretending to wince. "Neither does anyone else, Mr. President."

"I told you before, you're a politician, Eric."

"Mr. President. I know you're on a hot burner. I'll have Commander Wade grease the skids so we can get the latest to you as soon as we have it."

"Thank you. Knew I could count on you, Admiral."

When Danis and Wade walked out, Wade said, "If I had stayed at the Pentagon and you came back and told me what just happened in there, I wouldn't have believed you."

"Leo, every man puts his trousers on one leg at a time ... even the President."

Bay of Fundy

Woody Parnell stood before Erica Hussey's apartment door clad in his blue service uniform in the belief she might want to impress her guests with having a U.S. naval officer friend. He carried a bottle of vintage wine and reflected, *Hope salmon nazi's friends don't drink. Maybe I can take it back with me.* He rang the bell. In a moment, Erica opened the door.

"Evening, Erica." *Wow! I didn't think she owned a dress.*

Exactly Woody's height, dark-brown eyes from beneath equally dark bangs reaching almost to her brows, looked directly into his.

"Here," he said as he presented the bottle of wine.

"Thank you, Woody, and for coming."

She linked her good arm with his.

Giving a well-practiced limp, Woody correctly suspected neither fooled the other. He had never seen Erica in anything but her *salmon nazi outfit. Not bad.*

They sat and nursed healthy jolts of Canadian Club on the rocks. Conversation flowed easy much to Woody's surprise. He learned his hostess grew up in Oregon where she had acquired her passion for protecting salmon. Knowing they sat on opposite sides of that fence, the topic received only a light brushing. She has two brothers and a sister and graduated from University of Washington with a degree in environmental sciences. Engaged in energetic conversation, half an hour had passed before either realized it.

"Guess I'm early. Where are the others?"

"Others? Who said anything about others? I said dinner party. Not lots of people will be here."

"Then just two can be a dinner party?"

"Have you ever gone to a restaurant and told the receptionist a party of two?"

"Ya got me, Erica."

"Well, what about you? I told you my story."

Fumbling for words, Woody could offer only the traditional opening, "There's not much to know about me."

He hesitated at first, but with a degree of coaxing, he began to spill all his beans. He found Erica interesting and an easy person to converse with. Fight it he may, but soon he found himself having a pleasant evening.

After their second Canadian loosened him, he said, "After our bumpy start, Erica, I must admit I'm surprised you invited me."

"Do you recall the crude *guy* remark you made at the end of our first conversation?"

Woody reflected on his words. She turned her back on him and he'd said, 'Thanks for giving me a look at the best side of you.' Woody felt his apologetic expression needed no amplifying words.

"I get that often, and it never bothers me. But for whatever reason, hearing it from you pissed me off, and I gotta find out why."

"Are you?"

"I think so."

Though local chefs had nothing to fear, they sat down to a fairly nice meal that Erica had prepared. Best part of it, Woody's bottle of wine quickly found itself empty.

So much for getting to take it back with me.

The meal over, table cleared, they returned to the living room.

Erica interrupted their marathon conversation. "Do you dance?"

"I'm told I'm pretty good at the stumble."

Erica put a DVD into a player. Notes of the song *Always* made popular by singers of Atlantic Starr's R&B band floated about the otherwise silent room.

Woody remained seated.

"Well?"

He rose, they fell into each other's arms and swayed gently to the music, all traces of Woody's faked limp gone.

When the piece ended, Erica said, "Sleep with me, Woody."

"No."

Erica released him, stood back with hands on hips and asked through an astonished expression, "No?"

"I'll go to bed with you, but if either one of us gets any sleep, it'd reflect poorly on me."

At four-thirty a.m. they finally did fall into a sleep, deepened by mutual fulfillment.

Aboard *Denver*

Denver passed beneath the ice cap without incident. Jim Buchanan *bent* the rules a bit and deactivated a *picked* Soviet boomer's protective minefield. He would claim intelligence find in the patrol report.

Upon field deactivation, the boomer, apparently listening, immediately got underway. This indicated they had come to grips with the U.S. compromise of the Soviet boomer security system.

Buchanan and Douglass hovered around the sonar throughout the process.

Douglass said, "Captain, you've got an ornery streak. That poor guy was fat, dumb and happy till we came along."

Through a grin, the skipper replied, "Been told that before."

The sonar operator asked, "We goin' after him, Captain?"

"No, son. We've got bigger fish to fry." Buchanan never missed an opportunity to hone his crew to a sharper fighting edge. "But from here on out, finding our bigger fish depends on sonar."

The lad's chest swelled a bit. "We won't let you down, Captain."

Denver cleared the ice and proceeded south, reaching Atlantic shipping lanes a day ahead of schedule. Buchanan sat with the other officers in the wardroom for a council of war. He had previously read them the Patrol Order overview and now got down to specifics.

"Gentlemen, we complete the highest priority job first. Are there diesel boats waiting? If so, where and how do they get to and from undetected? Get that answer first and then find the nukes. But in the meantime, be damn sure they don't find us."

One of the officers asked, "Aren't our radiated noise levels well below theirs?"

"You're right, Tom. If we don't get careless. Long periods with no action promotes that. I want everyone, especially watch officers, to develop gimmicks."

Douglass asked, "Gimmicks, Captain?"

"Right. Devices to keep watchstanders alert. With nothing to do, minds wander and increase opportunity for error."

An officer asked, "Can you give us a few—"

The officer's request was interrupted by a demanding voice over the 21MC. "Captain to the attack center!"

Buchanan and his officers raced off.

The conning officer announced in an excited voice, "Take a look through the scope, Captain. You're not going to believe this."

Chapter 17

Bay of Fundy

Erica Hussey awoke to Woody shaking her.

"Wake up, Erica, and get dressed. Quick!"

She did not think it possible for laid-back Woody to be so upset. "What's wrong?"

"We overslept. Ship sails in forty minutes and I'm in big trouble if I'm not aboard!"

"I'll make some coffee."

Woody instinctively wanted to snap back and emphasize his stress over the possibility of missing the ship. *But I can't blame her. This is of my making.* He somewhat liked the start they had gotten off to and had no wish to rock the boat.

He said in a calm voice, "No thanks, Erica. It's really a big-time bad if I'm not there when the ship leaves. Please get ready as quick as you can and fire up the VW."

She did not fully understand, but complied. Erica's lead foot caused her Bug to reach the base with minutes to spare.

Woody successfully managed to look calm on the outside but figured he had ground at least a millimeter from his teeth surfaces.

They sped down the dock and came to a screeching halt before the gangway.

Brent Maddock, surprised his reliable first lieutenant would be late, had already tossed in a few last minute items to delay the departure. Pleased he didn't need them, Maddock did a double take when Woody arrived. *Why does that Bug ring a bell?*

Seaman Severs blew away the cobwebs.

Accompanied by vigorous arm waving, Severs yelled out, "Hi, Miss Hussey!"

The skipper indulged a laugh. Parnell told Maddock that Severs had accompanied him on the Volkswagen rescue mission. Clearly, Woody had passed the night with his alleged nemesis. Then frosting on the cake.

Erica emerged from the *Bug* with Woody, threw her arms about his neck and said loudly, "Goodbye, dear. Hurry back to me."

Damn, Woody thought. *She did that just to get even.* He had learned that behind the hard-assed environmentalist exterior lived a true comedian. *This lady's gonna take some sorting out.*

He could muster but only in a low, sheepish voice, "I will."

Erica planted a big wet one on him and Woody disappeared into the sail, climbed the ladder and mounted the bridge. A look at his skipper's ear to ear grin said explanation for being late unnecessary.

"Did I just see the salmon nazi, Woody?"

Parnell managed a sullen look. "I stand on my Fifth-Amendment rights, Captain."

Aboard *Denver*

Captain Jim Buchanan took the scope and agreed with his conning officer. He didn't believe it. The skipper needed no more than a three-second look.

The scope lowered, Buchanan could not believe his eyes. The biggest submarine he had ever seen snuggled up beside a Soviet *Tango*-class diesel submarine. Quiet seas permitted free movement about the main deck and for a gangway to span between the two ships. Like a column of ants, troops moved from ship to ship carrying provisions. Buchanan spotted what appeared to be a six-inch hose. *No doubt refueling the Tango.*

The conning officer said, "Talk about good luck. We stumbled on them. Sonar can barely hear 'em even though we know right where they are."

Buchanan replied, "Ever noticed the harder you work, the luckier you get?" The CO gave his conning officer a verbal pat on the back. "So that's how they keep their diesels on station so long. We should have figured that out. The Germans used the same technique in World War Two, called 'em *milch-cows* (milk cows). But these guys have to be damn confident. It's barely twilight and they're already hard at it."

LCDR Bob Douglass, XO, arrived in the attack center and heard the captain's assessment. "Allies are not using the surface now and figure no aerial surveillance because a submerged submarine cannot be spotted visually. So why bother looking?" Douglass went on, "The milk-cow submarine, Captain? Does it compare with anything we have in the NATO book?"

"Nothing I've seen, Bob. But spooks talk of a huge new boomer projected to be biggest in the world. My guess is they figured this is a more urgent near-term use for it."

"Captain, we're in a heap of trouble if the Soviets can leave diesels along shipping lanes. We can't find 'em till they launch torpedoes, then it's too damn late."

"Let's go to my stateroom, Bob."

They entered and closed the door.

"We got two fish in a barrel. Do we let 'em go or pop 'em off?"

"That's a tough one, Captain. I'm thinking if the milk cow is a prototype it may be the only one they have. Dispatching her shuts down a big piece of the operation."

The 21MC erupted, "Torpedo in the water, close aboard!"

Buchanan and Douglass bolted back to the attack center and found a frightened conning officer sufficiently composed to have ordered flank speed and put the inbound on the beam. Beaming torpedo inbounds at ships on high speed, confronts the weapon with low Doppler which significantly diminishes torpedo performance. Submarines at flank speed cavitate heavily. This forces the torpedo into a tail chase, requiring it to search through heavy turbulence. At that point, the conning officer ran out of ideas.

The calmness of Buchanan's voice in no way reflected his upset stomach. "Release ADC (Acoustic Device Countermeasure)."

Fourteen 6.25 inch by 108-inch ADCs are carried outside the pressure hull in two launchers, one on each side between the stern plane and lower rudder. Each launcher holds seven countermeasures for quick launch. The device returns *pings* from active torpedo sonars and with any kind of luck diverts the weapon away from its intended target.

Buchanan ordered, "Remain at periscope depth."

Operating at shallow depth presents the least optimal conditions for an ASW torpedo.

A scent of sheer terror permeated the attack center. Nothing left to do but the scariest thing a submariner confronts—wait.

A million thoughts race through the crew's minds, impossible to remember when and if the crisis passes. Buchanan remembered good things he had said to his wife and a few he regretted.

"Weapon range gating," a shaky voice from sonar declared.

Torpedo initiates a new *ping* after each valid return *ping* from the target.

He's got us, Buchanan thought. "Chief of the watch, conduct a thirty-second normal blow!" *That'll put us on the surface and give some of the crew a chance to get out for the Russians to pick up.*

As *Denver* broached the surface, a deafening explosion shook the ship from stem to stern. "Chief of the watch, secure the blow!"

Something sounded wrong to Buchanan. *It exploded close aboard, but apparently didn't strike the hull.* A quick check of the ship revealed no flooding.

The captain immediately ordered, "Open the main ballast tank vents and make your depth two-zero-zero feet."

At the ordered depth, Buchanan explained, "I believe the torpedo passed near the ADC and activated a proximity fuse. Gentlemen, count your blessings!

"Bob, go to the crew's mess. Have the cook load up a weighted garbage bag with lightbulbs and kick it out the GDU (garbage disposal unit) ASAP!"

Buchanan answered the exec's curious look. "The bad guys expect to hear breaking-up noises as we sink. Let's not disappoint them. As the bag sinks, sea pressure will start the bulbs popping."

"Aye, Captain."

"Man battle stations, torpedo," Buchanan announced to a greatly relieved attack center watch. "Now, let's go get that son of a bitch!"

Aboard *Steelhead*

Still smarting under the captain's recent *butt-chewing,* each officer arrived at a called council of war meeting with plenty of ideas. None of them particularly useful, but Maddock achieved his goal: get his officers thinking and set combat readiness top among their priorities. He'd previously read them the patrol order overview. It essentially ordered the rendezvous with *Denver* and laid out a general plan to join her in a survey of Soviet submarine assets deployed along North Atlantic shipping lanes.

Maddock got down to the specifics. Operation orders are written in a manner that streamline delegating segments to department heads. He passed these out, summarizing aspects of each that pertained to some or all of the other departments. Maddock had an aversion to *drag-on* meetings. He liked sharp agendas with only those specifically affected in attendance. He considered officer time too valuable to waste listening to material that did not affect them.

"We're gonna be working with Woody's and my old ship and former CO. So make us look good!" Perfunctory laughter followed, so Maddock gave them more. "Before we adjourn, Woody, tell us one more time how the salmon nazi released your twenty-pounder."

Parnell said nothing. Raised arms over a shaking head, he sauntered from the wardroom.

The attack center watch wound themselves up drum-tight. Refit is totally different from patrolling and they strove to ensure they made the transition. Sonarmen, butts literally at seat edge, listened and monitored displays intently. The exit from Bay of Fundy went without incident much to everyone's relief, Maddock in particular.

Brent and his exec sat in the wardroom and speculated over what they both understood to be urgency implied in the op-order.

Tom Bentley's dad, a retired U.S. Senator, Tom correctly assumed political pressure. "My take is the military carries out assignments and politicos worry about how quick."

Both men sensed a fading American appetite for continuing the war with the Russians.

"There has to be a connection," Maddock replied. "My granddad once told me every American during World War Two had a shoulder to the wheel of common good. Otherwise, we'd never have pulled it off."

"I have a theory on that, Captain."

"Shoot."

"World War Two warriors and the folks left behind emerged from the Great Depression. Hard times toughened 'em. They didn't have much but sure as hell they'd not let anyone take away what little they had. Like it or not, material possessions have this way of softening people. Today's folk have too much to give up and are increasingly reluctant to do so."

"Believe it's been with us from the onset, Tom. Everyone knows Patrick Henry's *Give me liberty or give me death* words. But apparently even he had reservations. Few today know a line that preceded it. *Is life so dear, or peace so sweet, as to be purchased at the price of chains and slavery?* Perhaps a growing number of Americans would now answer yes."

"In a sense, Captain, I agree. But Americans have the initiative gene. We all came from someplace else because our forebears believed they could do better. Imagine picking up, leaving family and going to a new land because you're unhappy where you are. Those are the kind of people I like and will ultimately sustain us."

"Your point?"

"Before Pearl Harbor, America was anything but agreeable to what we should do. Pearl Harbor got us all in lockstep. The initiative gene I referred to kicked in. Maybe that's what they want us to do. Give 'em another Pearl Harbor."

"Not all that sure, Tom. We had our Pearl Harbor a short while back and it wore off. My guess is they need another Battle of the Bering to give them something to cheer about."

Middleburg, VA

Vasiliy Baknov reflected upon all he had heard throughout the day, as he lay stretched out on his bed having been returned and locked in by Harold.

What have I gotten myself into? He had no training, nor any experience in the espionage business. Worst of all, none of the people with whom he had contact revealed their affiliations. *I can't even be sure they aren't equally uninformed about what's going on. Like ants drifting across a pond on a log and each one thinks it's driving.*

He lay back, hands behind head and thought of the exquisite Tania. *Perfect fit for the American pick-up line; what's a beautiful girl like you doing in a place like this?* Pleasant thoughts saw him off on a two-hour nap, later to be interrupted by a hand shaking his shoulder. Before opening his eyes, Vasiliy hoped it would be Tania.

No such luck.

Standing over him the inscrutable Harold said brusquely, "Get up and come downstairs."

That creep Harold doesn't get any nods for congeniality. Doesn't knock and hasn't spoken a cordial word to me since we met.

Arriving in the living room, he met three men who identified themselves only as Tom, Dave and Ron. Baknov correctly guessed them to be covers. *I wonder if they still know their real names.* It didn't take long for Vasiliy to determine their immediate purpose ... determine his true agenda.

He quickly recognized the good-cop, bad-cop technique. Bad cops, Tom and Ron, opened by saying in no uncertain terms they didn't believe a word of Vasiliy's story of being a stranded Russian Naval Officer. Anger in their voices inferred he should abandon his lie now, or confront dire consequences.

"Gentlemen, I'm certain there's good cause for you to ascertain this, and I suggest you are wasting time if your cause is urgent. You have the truth and you should get me started on whatever it is you want me to do."

Ron snarled, "Don't you just wish we'd do that? Are you a plant? If so, tell us and you're free to walk out of here safely. If we find out later. Well—"

Tom demanded, "What the hell more do we need? I say let's do what we have to do to get this bastard to talk."

Ron added, "And tell what he knows about our operation. And who else is aware."

Good-cop Dave jumped in. "But what if he is who he says he is? Then what? We can't afford to lose that kind of asset. Look. Give me a few moments alone with him."

Tom and Ron went through motions of complying with Dave's request but under protest.

Dave began with conciliatory tones, but Vasiliy interrupted. "Enough of this nonsense. You know the situation as well as I do. We both take risks. Don't think for a moment I believe confessing to be someone else would get me out of here in anything other than a weighted plastic bag."

Studying him a moment, Dave then said, "Wait here."

Though only fifteen minutes passed, it seemed to Vasiliy he'd sat in the room for an hour.

A tall, slender, late-fiftyish man entered the room. Handsome, not a single strand of hair out of place, he appeared to Vasiliy like a walking well-sculpted statue. *Nobody's as good as this guy looks.*

The man approached and extended a hand and said, "I'm pleased to meet you, Lieutenant Baknov. I am Senator Darrel Manning."

Aboard *Denver*

The troops needed a shot in the arm. All knew how close they'd come to *buying the farm*, each reacting in his own way. The skipper needed to get everyone back on track. The Russian remained a threat and during the torpedo evasion maneuvers, sonar had lost contact.

Buchanan opted not to hover over his sonar watch. The crew might consider it apprehensive on the skipper's part, a bad time for this to happen. However, he told Bob Douglass to do exactly that.

Confiding to his exec, Buchanan said, "It's okay for you to look scared. XOs are expected to be flaky."

The skipper correctly assessed the situation. Both the Soviet and American had to play the waiting game. It would not be good for the first one who blinked. The Soviet, previously identified as an *Alfa*-class attack submarine, had the advantage and probably knew the proximity of *Denver*'s location and classification as an American *688*-class that has considerable radiated noise advantage.

He thought about making a dead-slow run down the torpedo track, but realized he had entered a chess game with the opposing skipper. *That's the logical thing to do and he'll expect it unless he bought the lightbulb breaking-up noises. If he did, that improves our odds. It's time to make a move.*

After summoning Douglass, the skipper overviewed his plan. The exec could find no fault with it, so they proceeded. This time, Buchanan joined Douglass in the sonar shack, the explosion some thirty minutes past with attendant untangling of nerves.

Douglass had already assembled the best sonar *ears*, each focusing listening devices and digital driven displays.

The chief sonarman announced, "We're so much quieter, we can pass right over him without being heard."

Buchanan liked confidence and believed the chief had it right. "But right on top him, if someone drops a coffee cup, it's all over."

"He only makes twelve knots submerged. He can't run from us."

"Agree," said Buchanan. "I'm betting he knows that too, so he'll sit quiet and wait for us to come to him."

Douglass illuminated another worry. "He carries twenty VA-one-eleven *Shkval* torpedoes. No acoustic homing but it's rumored to make up to two hundred knots."

"Guidance?"

"Autonomous inertial and a four hundred sixty pound warhead."

"No acoustic homing?"

"At two hundred knots, all it will hear is itself."

"Needs damn near perfect TMA (Target Motion Analysis) solution to hit us with one of those." The captain continued, "My guess, he'll use the same weapon as last time. An ET Eighty."

All looked at the captain but said nothing.

"Listen. This is no time for making me happy by not saying what's on your mind."

"Captain, you think a helluva lot faster than the rest of us. Give us a minute to digest what you just said." The chief added, "He carries twenty *Shkvals*. He could fire five or so to cover his bet."

"Good, Chief. What's best to listen for to regain contact?"

"The fifty-hertz line from his ship's generator. From what I hear, they're not too good at keeping its noise inside the hull."

The sonar operator announced, "Got it! A fifty-hertz line."

Buchanan then said, "Passive ranging is difficult with a stopped target. Head in until we pass under or over him. Dead reckon range outbound and when we reach ADCAP minimum range … shoot."

Douglass cautioned, "We better be damn quiet, Captain."

"Good. Take a walk through the boat and make sure everyone knows that."

Douglass wanted to ask, *What if we're at the same depth and collide?* Then he thought, *I better not. I would just get another of his smart answers.*

They proceeded to close on the *Alfa*.

A moment later, the AN/BQQ-five (listening sonar) operator reported, "Abrupt increase in volume, Captain. We're getting close."

"Mark on top when we reach there."

The operator grinned, "Or on bottom."

Buchanan kept his fingers crossed in hopes the Soviet skipper bought the lightbulb breaking-up noises, cut a notch in his belt and returned the *Alfa* to station. Throughout, the Soviet gave no indication he believed anything else.

"The bastards likely celebrated with a bottle of vodka."

When the range opened sufficiently, Buchanan ordered an ADCAP launched. Before the Soviet had time to react, a distant explosion could be heard clearly through *Denver*'s hull. This time, authentic breaking-up noises followed the attack.

Aboard *Steelhead*

Maddock said to his exec Tom Bentley, "Remember what I told you about making Woody and me look good to *Denver*'s skipper? How far to the rendezvous? ETA?"

"Navigator has us about six miles out. And we got our best ears, Chief Giambri on the Q-five."

"Even though *Denver*'s supposed to be quieter than us, tell the chief there's a fifth of JD Black for him if we make contact first."

"That makes two, Captain. Think Woody's offered him one."

The 21MC blurted, "Sonar contact!"

Brent and Tom raced to the sonar shack. There they found Giambri looking happier than anyone could remember. Giambri recalled a line in a Civil War movie he'd watched as a kid and always wanted to use.

Through the best southern accent possible from growing up in a South Philadelphia Italian neighborhood, he declared, "Hold ya fire, Cap'n. They's ah boys!"

Chapter 18

Denver-Steelhead Rendezvous

Courage is having the wherewithal to do what needs to be done regardless of how terrifying the prospects of doing it. Too much combat makes courage evasive and Captain Jim Buchanan had been *shot at* in both the Pacific and Atlantic Oceans. The mathematical prospects of survival diminishes as a function of encounter numbers, and this last one represented Buchanan's fifth.

He did not have the luxury of reflecting on this because his responsibility included both *Steelhead* and *Denver*. He considered life to be precious and would select the least hazardous alternative consistent with reasonable prospects of success.

Buchanan decided their initial CO to CO conference would be on the surface. A moonless night sky hovered over a reasonably calm sea to make verbal exchange possible. Though highly unlikely, Soviet assets would be in position to intercept flashing-light (can be read out to five miles), Buchanan hedged his bet. They would come alongside and exchange via bullhorn.

Buchanan had composed a number of prepositioned orders to be passed from *Denver* to *Steelhead* by highline. A line-throwing gun fired a tiny nylon cable across *Steelhead*'s bridge enabling transfer of lightweight materials between the ships.

Drawing alongside, Maddock raised his bullhorn. "Everything nice and quiet out there, Captain?" Formality yielded in verbal conversations between COs to the use of first names. However, Buchanan was once Maddock's captain in *Denver*, and to Brent, he would always be the captain.

"Quiet is a perception, Brent. Tell me how quiet you want it and I'll tell you how quiet it is. There appears to be a lot of bad guys out there. But they're quiet 'cause they got nothing to shoot at."

Maddock responded, "I get the feeling the President wants to change that, but not if he has to lose a bunch of men and ships."

Buchanan said, "The wish of every President since Washington. I believe we can get a convoy to Britain with acceptable losses if we manage ASW properly. You and I gotta figure out how to do that."

Taking a stab at humor, Maddock said. "That's why they sent out their best two guys."

"Hope you're right, Brent. Now we gotta prove it. Take a good look at the stuff I sent over. Should be good, but we'll yak again tomorrow night if it isn't."

Maddock knew if Buchanan had put it together, there'd be no glitches. "We'll do that, Captain."

"Overall plan is to search out the best shipping lanes and identify hard spots. A bunch of diesel boats waiting out there. They don't need to move around much, so they'll stay pretty much where we find 'em." Buchanan included the *milk-cow* operation in material high-lined to *Steelhead*.

"Do you plan for us to spread out or work in tandem?"

"Tandem. We'll cover a lot more ground quicker that way, and CNO is in a hurry."

"Agree, Captain."

"One more thing. We felt a close aboard explosion recently. The NLM (noise level monitor) shows little change, but when we drive by, tell us if you hear anything unusual."

"You got it, sir."

Out of things to say, Buchanan concluded, "It's safe here, but let's not push our luck. Dive and we'll check out our Gertrudes."

This was neither the time nor place to inform Buchanan of his marriage to Bea Zane and having *one in the oven*.

"Got it … pulling the plug." Maddock turned and said to the OOD, "Submerge the ship."

Paris, France

Mikhail Turgenev listened carefully to the Russian field marshal commanding Soviet troops charged with the occupation of Western Europe. Turgenev traveled to Soviet Army Headquarters in Paris, but met on a Seine River tour boat, both in civilian clothes.

The field marshal spoke first, "My men are disillusioned and demoralized. Like me, they see no value in remaining where they are for neither Mother Russia nor themselves."

Borkowski's and Turgenev's initial test of the waters showed much more discontent with Premier Rostov's regime than they initially anticipated. They concluded a coup attempt to be in the cards. They also encountered reluctance based on knowledge of what awaited participants if the coup failed.

Turgenev asked, "Do you think Rostov suspects our efforts?"

"Not likely. Complainers unearthed by *zampolits* are usually no longer around to complain further. And to my knowledge none of our people have suffered this fate."

An early November sun looked down through clear skies as the boat slipped by Ile de la Cite and the magnificent Notre Dame Cathedral. Turgenev thought, *How remarkable this city has lived through so much hostility, yet remains pristine.*

"What is it about our Russian people, Field Marshal? They have all the qualities needed, particularly courage and determination, to wrest their country from hands that do not wish it well then turn it over to ones that wish it worse."

"We are slow learners, Mikhail. Perhaps this time."

"I hope you are right. Much can be gained if major world powers unite for the common good. The way things are, developing countries are free to run amuck simply by aligning with one major power or another."

"You come by your poet's heart honestly, Turgenev. Problem with poets is they give us hope. World peace has always and will continue to evade man. Even our own efforts will do no more than amend effects for a time."

Turgenev said, "I am reminded of a quote by an Irish political philosopher Edmund Burke, 'The only thing necessary for the triumph of evil is for good men to do nothing.' We must persevere."

The field marshal acquiesced then added, "Problem Mikhail is all men consider themselves and their cause good."

"War requires young men to fight them. This diminishes our gene pool and costs us the means of making a better Russia."

"There you go again, Mr. Poet. Young men consider us old men to have lost our perspective and can't possibly understand the need to fight."

"You are wrong, Field Marshal. Young people deny counsel from older ones because it almost always contradicts young wishes. I am told an old head cannot be made to fit upon young shoulders."

They sailed past the Eiffel Tower, the most famous landmark in the world. Both men watched in the sort of awe felt by most who see it. It provides one a feeling of permanence for humanity despite humanity's apparent determination to destroy itself.

"Turgenev, at each meeting, we have this bad habit of wallowing in philosophy at the expense of completing our agenda. I understand we have managed to slip our spy into the mix of Party sanctioned operations in America."

Leaning back with a smug and pleased expression on his face, Turgenev said, "Better than that. The agent charged with filtering and disseminating information from America is on our payroll."

"That so? How do we find these defectors?"

"Preposterous as this might sound, Field Marshal, I believe the true reason is intelligent men able to read handwriting on the wall. Despite the Party's pompous talk, these men know we are over-extended and worse, unable to improve this dire situation. When all this is past, they wish for a soft place to land. Everyone knows we play a bluffing game the Allies are not likely to buy. Preventing America from getting a convoy to England is essential to the Party's hope of success, yet prospects of this are indeed grim."

The field marshal added, "Turgenev, we find ourselves in an awkward situation. The Party slips clues to the Allies that paths between America and Britain bristle with frontline nuclear attack submarines salivating over prospects of destroying convoys, but we have only a few remaining diesel submarines that survive because they were too fragile to participate in the Bering Sea battle."

"Why is this awkward? Seems to me it strengthens our hand."

"These diesels are manned by Russian seamen. And for us to succeed, we virtually sign their death warrants."

Mikhail Turgenev lowered his voice. "That is a risk only if they choose to fight. My colleague Dmitri Borkowski is a submariner who finds many of his colleagues also disenchanted with Rostov. We shall play every card we have."

The White House

CNO Admiral Eric Danis did not sit through the mandatory Oval Office twenty-minute waiting period.

President Andrew Dempsey greeted him at the door on arrival. "Come in, Eric. Sit down, please." The President gave no effort to mask his anxiety. "Please lay some good news on me."

"All depends on your definition of good, Mr. President. A helluva lot better than we've had."

Danis summarized a report on *Steelhead*'s effort to unscramble details relating to Soviet defense of the North Atlantic.

"How does that equate to something big happening and soon?"

"If you want my best guess, sir, in a month we can embark a convoy. That is if results of our current efforts justify this."

"What percent will make it across?"

"That would be hard to say. Two of my boats are pinning down expected enemy locations even as we speak. We'll know better when these results are in."

"And then what?"

"The better our search, the higher probability of success."

"Expected casualties?"

"Moderate, Mr. President."

"Light would be better. You caused me a big problem, Eric."

"Me?"

"The Lincoln analogy. 'If there is a straw to be grasped, I'll find it.' So I researched every crumb I could find on that subject."

"I'd like to hear what you found, Mr. President."

"That analogy is so much akin to our situation it frightens me. Everyone loves to quote Santayana's 'Those who do not read history are doomed to repeat it.' It's a bunch of crap, Eric. We read it and still repeat it. I'm stuck in the same position as Lincoln. It's fair to say the country wants to lose no more of its daughters and sons in war. Yet, if we back out, you know the Soviets will keep pushing."

"I tend to agree, sir. The thing that goes through every American mind is what the hell difference does it make? Another couple years and we'll be right back at it. So why bother?"

Dempsey released a sigh that came deep from within. "Lincoln knew how many men would be lost to capture Atlanta. If prior to the campaign, he shared that with the public, there's no doubt they would have demanded a negotiated settlement."

"But he didn't, sir."

Dempsey had developed a sense of confidence in Danis. "No, but morally, should he have? Presidents are not God. Lincoln went ahead because he believed it essential the Union be reunited. But did he have the right to buy victory with more lives than his public was willing to pay? There's where I find myself."

"Mr. President, you are showing me the advantages of a military career over politics. But despite all, Lincoln authorized the Atlanta campaign and was still reelected."

"Yes. Only because the public felt obligated to gain something for all the lives expended. With victory all but a given, they agreed to continue the war."

"I see your point. Mr. President. Limit casualties to the greatest extent possible consistent with getting convoys to Britain. This is an automatic consideration in all military plans. Eisenhower was devastated knowing he sent so many men to their deaths on six June forty-four. But it had to be done and fortunately we had a man like Ike to do it."

"But he had the nation solidly behind him. That's where the real decision 'it had to be done' came from. I don't have that."

"Mr. President, if this is any comfort, we have the Navy's best two submarine officers working this problem even as we speak."

"Exactly what I expect of you, Eric. Otherwise, you wouldn't be CNO. Move out as quickly as you can. I hate to think of it in these terms, but before the first convoy sails, you must give me an estimate of projected casualties."

"You'll have it, Mr. President."

Dempsey rapidly shifted to a lighter mood. "I always wanted to hear a Navy guy say, 'Aye, aye, sir' to me."

"Aye, aye, Mr. President."

"Humor me, Eric. Aye, aye, sir."

Danis grinned, raised his right hand in salute and said, "Aye, aye, sir."

Aboard *Denver*

Skipper Jim Buchanan combined exceptional submarine tactics' skills and keen intuition to produce his operation plan. He knew communications between *Denver* and *Steelhead* pivotal. Navy protocol called for clarity and brevity. In their circumstance, brevity could mean the difference between life and death. Submarines survive by being quiet and communications between submerged submarines required radiated noise.

For brevity, the dominant factor, he devised a method wherein all probable directions could be depicted in combinations of four alphabetical letters and selected a, e, n and t. Each required two or less keystrokes of the Gertrude transmitter key. This significantly lowered probability of enemy counter-detection.

Meanwhile on *Steelhead*, hard-assing Woody Parnell over the salmon nazi replaced cribbage as the main wardroom diversion. Though Woody stood firmly on his Fifth-Amendment rights, fellow officers saw what they saw. So the relentless beat went on.

One junior officer said, "Now we know what really happened to Woody's twenty-pound salmon. He and the nazi ate it!"

Another said, "Yeah, Woody. Did the nazi boil, grill, bake … or did you guys eat it raw like sushi? I hear that way has the same effect as raw oysters."

Woody had heard enough to know rebuttal inconsequential and only promoted more comments, so he didn't respond.

He jumped on diversion. "Sushi! Had we known about that, we'd never have fought Japan in World War Two and worked out something better."

Chief Giambri came to the rescue, deflecting further officers' slings and arrows like an avenging guardian angel.

"Signal received, Captain."

Everyone hustled to the sonar shack, Tom Bentley bringing up the rear with the code book tucked under his arm.

"Tango Echo, Captain," reported the sonar watch.

Maddock knew it was a test, but let the process work itself out.

Bentley said, "That means Test. Acknowledge with Tango Echo at time of receipt plus twenty minutes. Verify, Captain."

"Verified. I know it's a short signal nobody's likely to intercept, but keep your ears on. I'll be in the shack a minute before our acknowledgment transmission to see if we have any unwelcome company. Transmit only on my order. Everybody understand?"

A chorus followed, "Yes, Captain."

"Good," the skipper said then departed.

The response consisted of a *dash* (Tango) followed immediately by a *dot* (Echo) the entire signal requiring less than a second.

Maddock would take no chances. The prospects of returning home to a new son or daughter increased his already cautious nature.

Middleburg, VA

Darrel Manning confirmed the impression of an American politician Vasiliy had formed while in Cadet School. Impeccably dressed and groomed, engaging smile, calming voice, his overall demeanor literally cried out, *I'm a good man and you can really trust me.*

Manning, oblivious to the fact well-trained Baknov knew each of these to be warning flags, continued to lay it on.

"I understand your voyage here has been quite intriguing. I would like to hear about it when we have more time."

Is this man aware he could have made a fortune on the stage? Baknov could play the game also. "I would like very much to share that story but know of the great demands on your time. Perhaps our futures hold some mutual recreation time."

Manning thought, *This guy is remarkable. Not a trace of Russian in his accent and he phrases like a verbal athlete.*

"I hope so too, Vasiliy. May I address you by that name?"

"Of course you may, Senator."

Manning, though determined to enlist the young man to his agenda, still felt the need to establish who was boss, so did not offer use of his first name.

It did not pass unnoticed by Vasiliy, who likened their meeting to a pair of brigands, each phrasing platitudes while they picked each other's pockets.

"Vasiliy, World War Two, likely the greatest injustice inflicted on mankind, resulted in sixty-five million deaths. That's deaths, Vasiliy. Not wounded and missing. Add in those numbers and the sum becomes astronomical."

Baknov resisted an urge to correct Manning. *The Great Patriotic War is what we call it.* "I understand that, Senator."

"I'm quite certain you are also aware totals accumulated in this war are merely a fraction of those of the last war. At least to date."

"I am, sir."

"Vasiliy, I am a patriotic American, but more than that, a citizen of the world. My greater duty is to the planet."

Can this jackass think I believe all this crap? "Of course you are, Senator, as am I."

"Good. I am told you are of that persuasion. It is incumbent upon people like us to ensure World War Two is not again inflicted upon mankind as it is almost certain to be under our current leadership, both Soviet and American."

This guy is full of it. "I agree, Senator. What do you suggest?"

"There is no doubt in my mind, if the Allies are able to safely get a convoy to Britain, we shall plunge ourselves into a prolonged conflict like the world has never seen."

Vasiliy thought, *Also end whatever chances you have of being elected President to say nothing of being Czar of the Americas.*

"I had not thought of it in those terms, sir." *This son of a bitch is painting a picture of himself as a man who wishes to save the world and take nothing for doing so.* "What role do you see for me, sir?"

"I am told your reputation as a submarine warfare tactician is second to none in the Soviet Navy."

"An exaggeration, sir. But please go on."

Manning continued to present himself as a competent man who would succeed in anything he put his mind to. "If Allied convoys are to be interdicted, it will be by submarines. I will provide you with information to get your assessment and advice. An intelligent man like you must surmise communications are already established with cognizant Soviet intelligence activities. Through my seat on the Senate Intelligence Committee, I have access to US counterparts and can provide important intelligence. Your job is to assess its worth so we can make best use of our limited communication window with your people."

Right. Sort it out so you can provide the Soviets with only what you want them to know. You're a crooked bastard, Senator, but then aren't we all? He surely does not believe he's getting this for free.

"Forgive me, Senator, but I currently have no means and must sustain myself. And then when all this is past, where, when and how can I expect to come down?"

"For now, all your needs will be filled right here. You're safe in Middleburg. Moving out and about is too risky and you are far too valuable for us to take that chance."

Right, I will remain your prisoner. I wonder if that includes the favors of Tania. I could do much worse. And when you're finished with me, it'll be a pair of concrete boots and a swim in the Atlantic.

"Lieutenant Baknov, be assured that whomever's hand helps wrest the world from the ghastly dilemma it now confronts will know its gratitude."

Baknov decided it a good time to be humble. *But soon as the opportunity presents itself, I'll put considerable distance between me and this damn place.*

Manning handed a document to Baknov. "I would like your assessment earliest." He rose and extended his hand. "So good to meet you, Lieutenant Baknov."

He exited in a manner that would make Caesar envious.

Vasiliy spread the document over the table before him.

TOP-SECRET REPORT, USS DENVER
PRELIMINARY ASSESSMENT OF SOVIET
SUBMARINE ASSETS ON NORTH ATLANTIC
CONVOY ROUTES.

Baknov read the entire report transmitted from *Denver* to the Chief of Naval Operations, his anger toward and hatred of all things American refueled by the account of a Soviet submarine sinking.

These swine must be made to pay.

Chapter 19

Aboard *Denver*

Skipper Jim Buchanan and Exec Bob Douglass forced down what had to be at least their eighth cup of coffee in as many hours.

"We dance on a precarious tightrope, Bob. Nuclear power has revolutionized submarine warfare. Before, we ran mainly on the surface and submerged for only short periods. Now, it's turned completely around. But you don't get something for nothing."

Buchanan grinned, his expression resembling the *Grinch who stole Christmas*.

"You lost me, Captain. But what else is new?"

Buchanan explained his theory that U.S. submariners performed so well in World War II because they always stayed alert and on edge. "The basic MO made everyone continuously cognizant of risk. Surfaced and bouncing around in enemy-controlled waters to recharge batteries evoked quite a pucker factor. They got only weekly showers 'cause making fresh water from saltwater took more electrical power than they could afford."

"All this has a point, right Captain?"

"Surprised you can't see it. Our source of power, independent of the atmosphere, is infinite. We don't worry about anything. Heat, free use of galley stoves, everybody looks and smells squeaky clean from daily showers ... awfully easy for our guys to lose their feel for our perilous situation and let their guards down."

Douglass replied, "Okay, I see where you're going, Captain. We gotta nip this in the bud without unduly alarming the crew."

"Bingo! How do you propose to do this, Bob?"

"I don't have the slightest, Captain, but I suspect you do."

"Work them too hard. Unnecessary drills and anything else you can think of to piss 'em off. Best way to fend off complacency. And you gotta be the fall guy."

"Me?"

"Yeah, you. It's a submarine fact of life. Captains are good guys and execs are the *pains-in-the-ass*. So run 'em into the ground and I'll lick the wounds of troops that take it too hard. Make 'em angry, Bob. Complacency and anger are mutually exclusive terms."

Buchanan tossed out another further agenda. He had aversion to permitting written directions to rule over sound logic. But everyone needed counsel. Though need for rigid chain of command had been well established over two thousand years of naval operations, it did not excuse an exec for letting his boss make a bad decision.

The skipper's technique for getting the most from Douglass; bounce things off him. *Present options like a decision already made. Good training for an officer due for a near command of his own.*

The technique is a good way to invoke discussion and it also prepares an officer to act decisively, but not bullheaded if a junior officer presented a valid contradictive view. Buchanan had educated Douglass that way during the past year. Double-bladed advantage resided in the technique: reduced probability of Buchanan calling it wrong, and prepared Douglass for command.

"Bob, I know what the orders are, but aren't we spotting diesels so someone can come along later and take them out. Why not now?"

Douglass saw merit in the concept, for he had also considered it. However, he would play his expected devil's-advocate roll. Every decision has pluses and minuses.

"Can think of several reasons, Captain. Won't this tip our hand that we're softening up a passage to get convoys through?"

"Good point, Bob, but what can they do if they know that?"

"Not a helluva lot. But I'm taught forewarned is forearmed. I'm not really sure. All I can think of is … if they have another rabbit to pull out of their hat, this'll alert them to do so."

Buchanan liked the way their discussion went. "Otto Lilienthal was a German aviation pioneer killed in a glider flight. He's alleged to have said just before he died, 'Risks must be taken.' Everything's a crapshoot, Bob. Additionally, there's apparent urgency at the White House. So let's get this donnybrook started. We can likely kill off enough opposition to risk sending a convoy much sooner than later and my gut tells me this is important."

Douglass smiled. "Was with you from the first page, Captain, but figured you wanted some flack and obliged. But here's some real crap to toss in the game though. We only have five Sea Lance missiles. To attack quiet, sitting diesel boats with ADCAPs, we gotta close within counterattack range and we need to lower that risk. How do you plan to do that, Captain?"

Buchanan gave his exec the famous *Grinch grin*. "I dunno. You'll figure out something. Maybe double-teaming with *Steelhead*. Write this up and we'll pass it to Brent Maddock. He's got a good tactical head."

The skipper could not resist an opportunity to delve into his favorite pastime: thinking through and creating new tactics. "While you're mulling it over, here are a few pointers on close-in attack."

Douglass recorded the captain's points in a notebook.

"Both ships in a close-in situation are going slow.

"Quiet is paramount. Take every measure to maintain it.

"Do not use electronic-announcing systems.

"Pass all routine words via messengers throughout the ship.

"Make no plane or rudder movements.

"Pass all urgent communications via sound-powered phone.

"Tell maneuvering to slowly shut the throttles.

"Get good target solution (range, course and speed) as we pass."

Buchanan added, "More than likely, the target will be at bare steerageway or hovering. We'll likely lose contact at around two thousand yards as the range opens. The Fire Control System will continue to generate a solution without sonar contact, using our previous solution.

"Open torpedo tube outer door by hand pumping.

"Secure *return to battery* air to Torpedo Ejection Pump to reduce telltale acoustic transient from firing the launcher.

"Select appropriate tube bank to allow torpedo to make a big turn to the ordered course without shutting down due to anti-circular run safety feature.

"By the time generated target range reaches six-k yards, have target twenty to thirty degrees aft the beam on ready launcher side, then shoot on generated bearing.

"After the torpedo launch, move immediately away from firing point. An enemy counterfired weapon will be down the bearing of the incoming torpedo.

"Put distance between our launch position and enemy ASAP without cavitating (overspeeding propeller).

"Oh, and have countermeasures ready to launch if necessary.

"He'll also speed up and you'll regain sonar contact, so refine your solution and get another attack off if first weapon misses and he's still in range.

"Got all that, XO?"

Bob replied, "Yep and writer's cramp to boot."

"Include that in the stuff we send to Maddock."

"Aye, Captain."

Aboard *Steelhead*

"Conn, Sonar, notify the captain *Denver*'s a mile out and will pass overhead in five minutes." Giambri directed the sonar watch to ensure all listening devices at full gain and recorders loaded and ready with fresh tape.

A moment later, CO Brent Maddock and XO Tom Bentley entered the sonar shack.

Maddock asked the traditional, "What've we got, Chief?"

"*Denver* inbound, Captain."

"How does she sound?"

"Heard a lotta quieter eighty-eights, but nothing worth sending her home over."

Listening as *Denver* passed overhead, Maddock said. "Even with her *ding*, she's quieter than us."

Bentley added, "Per Captain Buchanan's instruction, no need to surface for an info exchange."

"Tom, put on your skipper's hat which you'll be wearing soon enough. If you suspected damage to your ship, how reassured would you be by a *no* response?"

"I'm a slow learner, Captain, but getting there. Chief, key the midnight surface rendezvous signal."

On the surface some time later, Maddock figured that too much good luck made him nervous. Another inky-black night and calm seas for the info transfer, but *Steelhead*'s skipper would take it.

After the highline transfer and per sonar data recorded when *Denver* passed over *Steelhead*, Maddock bullhorned, "You're quiet as a church mouse, Captain."

Buchanan said, "I'm sending over some mission revision stuff. Getting tired of this watch and wait crap so let's go and kick some Russki ass."

"Sounds like a plan to me. I say do it, Captain."

Middleburg, VA

The instant Senator Manning departed, Vasiliy Baknov dove into the purloined USS *Denver* patrol report. He had been out of touch with the Soviet Navy for four months. Even then, his knowledge remained limited by what the Party chose to release to his ill-fated Soviet submarine *Zhukov*. Not wishing to demoralize the submarine force, information on the massive scope of Soviet losses in the Bering Sea Battle had not been passed along to individual fleet units. So when he completed reading *Denver*'s report, he puzzled over why ancient diesel-electric and not front-line nuclear-powered submarines patrolled the critical Atlantic shipping lanes.

I couldn't care less about what Czar Manning expects. My main concern is how to get this before the right eyes in the Soviet Navy to best exploit it. Damn, I hate this intelligence business. Who do I trust? In all our cadet training, they never taught how to sort out the good from rotten apples.

A knock on his door interrupted his rumination. *Well, here is something new. So far all I've had is that bastard Howard poking his nose in without knocking.* To the best of Vasiliy's knowledge, the door had been locked and he could not open the door for a guest.

He took a chance. "Come in."

No sound of a key turned in the lock, but the door opened and there in all her glory stood Tania.

Vasiliy low-keyed his pleasure with this pleasant turn of events. *The Czar must wish to discourage any plans I may have for escape.*

Maybe he's not as dumb as I think. There's no more compelling reason I can think of to make me want to stay.

"Ah, Tania. To what do I owe this honor?"

The Russian beauty caught Vasiliy's tone and twinkle in his eye and doused them as with a bucket of cold water.

"Not to what you think. But I do wish you a pleasant evening and night for that is all the time you have to get a report ready. It must be prepared by early morning. One of our operatives will be by at seven a.m. I suggest you make it good. You should not permit yourself to be fooled by Darrel's exterior gentle manner."

"Darrel? Not Senator? Tell me, Tania, you're not in line to become Czarina of all the Americas, are you?"

"Perhaps in Manning's view, but you should not be surprised, Vasiliy. I, like you, find no sacrifice for the sake of Mother Russia too great."

To say nothing of 'for the sake of Tania,' Vasiliy thought, but under the circumstances believed this best to remain unspoken. He knew Manning was an expendable asset. *What happens to Tania when this comes to pass? Clearly cut from the same stock, we'd sleep well together in the same bed. And she is not hard on the eyes.*

He recalled being the only survivor from *Zhukov*'s complement of seventy-two. Perhaps his luck would hold, but for now he felt it unwise to push. Besides, a nightlong effort lay before him.

Aboard *Steelhead*

Brent Maddock pored over the new material on Buchanan's revised plan. He took no issue with the decision to swim against the tide, though ramifications from shore would surely follow.

He knew CNO Eric Danis more than likely would be pleased. Though not written into regulations, there had always been a submariner axiom allowing that upon arrival on a scene, if written instructions are found inconsistent with observed circumstances—improvise. But another unwritten rule said don't push your luck and cause for deviation from instruction had better not be a leaky pail.

Maddock's concern did not run deep, for he harbored no notion of a brilliant naval career. Let the chips fall where they may. The reality of a new son or daughter seemed to dominate his thoughts.

On the weekend before Brent's Pacific deployment from Bremerton, Washington, in USS *Denver*, Bea and he drove to Cannon Beach on the Oregon Coast. The serenity and beauty of its landscape captivated him. He found thoughts of living there with Bea after retirement delightful. But since then, the war had given him appreciation of life's uncertainties and fragilities.

A line from a favorite musical, *The Music Man*, now revisited Brent often. *If you keep putting things off till tomorrow, you'll be left with a lot of empty yesterdays.*

What if we have a son?

The combination of this and memories of Cannon Beach brought to mind another recollection. While still quite young, Brent heard a World War II story that touched him deeply. A young boy's soldier father surprised his son with an unexpected visit home from the war and met him on a beach. They walked in the sand together and discussed many things, mostly advice and overdue expressions of love by his dad. After a time, the boy paused, looked out to sea and saw a passing ship. He turned to point it out and found his father gone. The boy looked back along the beach where they had walked but saw only one set of footprints: his own. Brent would make certain when he walked the beach beside his child there'd be two sets of footprints in the sand.

However, Maddock knew constant diligence was his ticket home as well as for everyone in *Steelhead*. He could afford reflecting on these considerations in the few and fleeting moments available. But he would not let his wife and unborn child down by losing sight of his grave circumstances.

Severodvinsk

"It is good we have watched so many spy movies, Dmitri. How else could we have become so efficient at it?"

Mikhail Turgenev and Captain 1st Rank Dmitri Borkowski met each time *by accident* with Borkowski never in uniform. They represented to everyone, as only two old friends delighted with unexpectedly running into each other, this time at a street café where they stopped for tea.

"You must tell me all about gay Paris, Mikhail. I mean only the parts you want to talk about," Borkowski teased. "I'm certain a man of letters like yourself finds many, shall we say, manly diversions in the City of Light."

To emphasize his point, a delightful, buxom young woman came to the table and took their orders so Borkowski continued, "It is hard for me to conceive of traveling all the way to Paris in hopes of finding better prospects."

"Too many years behind us, Dmitri. Most of them with you knowing more and much better than you imply."

"But I am told, old friend that a light bulb grows brightest just before it burns out."

Turgenev shifted gears. "My field marshal contact confirmed all we expect. Soviet conquest of the world has hit the same breaking point of all the others who mounted this futile effort. Widespread disenchantment with continuing the war is rampant."

"You are the writer, Mikhail. Do we have a plan and schedule for activating a coup?"

"We have more than enough key people in place and apparently all the right ones for no one has reported our activities to the Party."

Dmitri wore a grim expression and said, "What a bloodbath that would make."

Mikhail added, "Perhaps not. Most of the *bloodletter*s work with us. Our main challenge is coordination. This is extremely difficult. Our esteemed Party recognizes it essential to maintaining control."

They fell silent when their waitress brought teas, followed by both sharing prolonged glances as she walked off.

"Ah to be young again, Mikhail."

Turgenev returned to their agenda. "A bloodbath followed the twenty July nineteen forty-four attempt on Adolf Hitler, despite the military being solidly behind it. I have a theory about the major contributing factor."

"You keep me in suspense."

Turgenev took pride in not letting enthusiasm override good judgment. "It should have been conducted concurrently with a major military setback against Germany, one the public was forewarned of as portending ultimate disaster. We must do the same thing."

"We have it, Mikhail. If an Allied convoy makes it from the US to Britain, look for a reenactment of the Great Patriotic War, but this time in the opposite direction. The concept of losing eleven million Russian souls in a futile cause is a powerful persuader."

Turgenev agreed. "A second, and possibly a more deadly issue is reignition of nuclear war. When our half-assed leaders recognize their backs are against the wall, look for them to think only of themselves and not the Russian people."

"Those very thoughts are the ones that terrify me most, Mikhail. Our coup must be so swift no time is allowed for that."

Dmitri continued, "When the Allies succeed with their convoy, seizing power can quickly follow. First item of business, get control of the nuclear weapons. We have many friends in that corps. Problem is the Party is closely intertwined with the release process. But ordering their release is a far cry from pulling the trigger. All the trigger pullers are with us. So, Mikhail ... what do you see as our greatest liability?"

Borkowski then studied his friend for a reaction.

Mikhail replied, "The Soviet operative in America, Lieutenant Vasiliy Baknov. From what we are able to discern, he is allied with an influential American who wishes to climb the political ladder by convincing his public the war is lost and no more lives should be expended. Baknov's job is to provide supporting rationale for this. If America is first to request a negotiated settlement, then our efforts come to nothing."

"I agree, Mikhail. Is there a chance he could get onto us. I know his communications are filtered by our NKVD plant, but I am told Baknov is quite resourceful and will find a way."

"A risk we must take, old friend. But the main issue is quite simple; Russia must request a negotiated settlement before the Allies do. The best way to make that happen is for the Allies to get a convoy to Britain. I am certain Baknov's main function is to provide the politician with sound arguments to show this is impossible."

Borkowski replied, "But his father is in America and quite happy there. Might his influence be of use?"

"That's certainly a rock worth looking under, though an unlikely one. Vasiliy Baknov operates under an alias that makes him all but impossible to uncover."

Feeling the conversation had run its course, Turgenev said, "For now, Dmitri, there are more important things. Let us summon our delightful waitress and order another tea so two old men can bask yet one more time in magnificent memories of being young."

Aboard *Denver*

"Captain to Conn," came over the 21MC. "Snorkeler contacted."

Buchanan and Douglass walked to the attack center. Rushing would likely incite crew anxiety, so they sauntered.

Buchanan looked at Douglass through his usual *I want to second-guess* expression. "He won't be up long enough for us to get a range, so we won't get a chance to drop a Sea Lance on him from here. We'll have to close and find him on passive sonar."

Diesel-electric submarines had occasional need to recharge batteries, but low movement practiced by the Soviets drastically reduced snorkel time and significantly increased interval duration.

"A little dangerous, Captain. When he finishes, look for him to drop down and put his *long ears* on."

"What do you suggest, Bob?"

"Get the best estimate of range based on noise levels we're receiving. Proceed inbound cautiously, shutting down everything we don't need as we approach where we think he is."

Buchanan felt good about what he heard, mainly because he saw results from how he'd trained his exec. "What kind of attack?"

"Sea Lance is lowest risk. Come close enough to get a good range. Then open to where he can't hear or identify our launcher transient noise."

"Good thinking, Bob."

"Thanks, Captain. On the way in, I'll alert sonar to recover target bearing by listening for unusual sounds. These guys have been out here a long time and are likely to get careless."

"What the hell do we need me for?"

"To provide an ass for me to whip in cribbage. Let's go to the wardroom and get started."

Douglass felt an instant of great pride in himself. He'd just received the greatest affirmation he'd gotten since he began fourteen years of naval service.

An hour later, *Denver* passed beneath her hapless target. Per Douglass's prediction, transients from the target provided frequent bearing updates.

"Okay, Bob. This is your call. You make the attack."

Douglass grinned at his boss. "At least an hour before we call away battle stations. Enough time to whip you two out of three, if not three."

A messenger call to battle stations interrupted their third game, Buchanan salivating over the probabilities of a sweep.

Upon reaching the attack center, Buchanan announced, "Mr. Douglass has the conn."

The exec responded, "Aye, Captain. Make ready tubes one and two. We'll fire a Sea Lance and listen for detonation. If none, we'll let the second one go. Sonar, do you have contact?"

"That's negative, Conn. Last transient a minute ago matched with generated target bearing."

Douglass addressed the Fire Control Panel Operator. "Match generated bearing and shoot. Sonar, report missile impact and torpedo start up."

The Sea Lance borne MK 50 torpedo made a distinctive sound.

A slight shudder throughout the ship indicated a missile launch. Forty seconds later, sonar reported to the conn, "Missile impact. Torpedo running."

Soon, a distant detonation could be heard through *Denver*'s hull.

Sonar reported. "Guess you heard that?"

Douglass confirmed, "Aye, sonar," then said, "Listen for breaking up noises."

"Aye, conn." A minute later, "No breaking up sounds."

Douglass looked at the skipper. "Give him the second barrel?"

Being so far into the war, Buchanan had developed an aversion to taking life unnecessarily and so he said, "He's had enough grief for one day, and no longer a liability. Let him go. He's the Soviets' problem now."

Chapter 20

Washington Examiner Lead Article

MIDTOWN, IA — Sounding very much like a presidential candidate, Senator Darrel Manning lashed out against the administration's continuation of the war to an audience of three thousand, most sympathetic to his views.

"*America has never surrendered* is a myth. Our excuse for leaving Vietnam was simply a cover to keep from saying the s-word. We find ourselves in a similar situation now and have a President who chooses to burden the American people with only more pointless deprivations than to belly up to the inevitable."

Manning went on to present grim prospects of an Allied victory, stating outrage over sacrificing young American men and women in futile combat.

"When does the President plan to abandon his hopes for a legacy and come to terms with his expending lives of sons, fathers, mothers and cherished family members for no other reason than to gain one?"

A lone dissenter wearing an American Legion hat cried out, "Manning, you traitor!" The troublemaker received a quick shout down and unceremonious removal from the rally.

Manning fielded the taunt graciously then complained further about inactivity of the administration.

"Have they no compassion for our traditional ally, Great Britain? Isolated, the English people suffer deprivations that exceed the worst of World War Two while we sit idle. Our British Allies need relief, but Soviet submarines lace every conceivable North Atlantic convoy route and will lay waste Allied attempts to breach it."

The crowd applauded and took up the chant, "Manning, Manning, he's our man. If he can't do it no one can."

The senator abided a moment then said through his famous smile, "I have not decided to run, but President Dempsey seems determined to force my hand," gaining him a standing ovation.

The Oval Office

Admiral Eric Danis had encountered anger in his time, but none approaching that shown by President Andrew Dempsey. A copy of the *Examiner* lay on his desk, which seemed only to further aggravate Dempsey each time he looked at it.

"That arrogant son of a bitch," the President roared. "Have you seen this, Eric?"

"I did, sir, and watched the senator on TV last evening. The article comes close but misses a few points. The Legionnaire was shouted down by only a few, and those were likely plants. The rest remained silent and appeared not in agreement with evicting the man. But by carefully selecting sound bytes, they gave a much different impression in the morning news from what I got watching the event live."

"The damn media manipulates America to any position it chooses. They give an impression of how America stands on an issue and the country falls into line. Not because they believe it but don't want to appear stupid for not. Peer pressure, just like in high school, but its baggage altogether too many Americans can't dump. We must stop this or the Soviets will clean our clock. But we're not gonna fix it here. That's for my stupid press secretary to handle, though I don't look for much to happen. That's the downside of taking big campaign contributions."

"I didn't hear that, Mr. President."

"You're not supposed to. So when am I getting a convoy to Britain and put egg all over Manning's handsome face?" Dempsey grinned at the mental picture of this literally happening.

"Acting on our latest info, Mr. President, a massive convoy is loading out as we speak. Before triggering the green light to embark, we need a little more good news from *Denver* and *Steelhead*."

"How soon, Eric, and what are the expected casualties?"

"My best estimate in two weeks and Soviet attacks should be minimal."

"Minimal?"

"Minimal, Mr. President. I am unable to provide numbers at this time. There are many Soviet submarines out there, but contrary to what the senator implies, they are diesel-electrics of severely limited endurance and capability, not nuclear-powered ships. This signals Russia scrapes the bottom of her resource barrel."

"How sure are you?"

"Mr. President, we can only surmise based on intelligence in hand, but there is good reason to believe this intelligence is sound."

"Eric, what you say might be indicative of wider problems among our ferocious foe."

"Mr. President, that's a political assessment. You know us warriors are not good at that. But if you want a humble opinion, I say very likely."

"You wouldn't say that just to cheer up an old man, would you?"

"Not in the least, sir. But there is a problem. Senator Manning. It's not good to tell the enemy what we know. He should not be announcing we are aware of their submarines interdicting vital convoy routes, and speculating on the debilitating effect it has on Allied determination to continue the war. We can't serve that kind of intel to the enemy on a silver platter."

"Good point, Eric. But the Fourth Amendment is all he needs to justify that."

"The Fourth gives no authority to release classified information. Or are senators above the law?"

"Hmm."

Severodvinsk

Captain 1st Rank Dmitri Borkowski sat opposite Vice Admiral Viktor Viktorovich Kirov in the latter's office. Knowing the NKVD had bugged his office, Kirov greeted Borkowski with innocuous conversation while holding a finger to his lips in the universal gesture showing it's unsafe to speak freely. They rattled on as Kirov scribbled on a piece of paper, *Invite me to visit your ship for lunch.*

"Admiral Kirov, I've come to tell you my crew would be delighted if you could join us for lunch today."

"How kind of you. This likely is our last day of good weather. Do you mind if we walk? At our age, constitutionals grow increasingly important."

Borkowski agreed, knowing the admiral wished to carve out safe conversation time.

Interrupted by salutes from every sailor passing their way, Admiral Kirov explained the North Atlantic current situation. "We hang on by a thread, Dmitri." He described the pattern of diesel submarines spread across North Atlantic shipping lanes. "They are difficult to maintain. Two of the new Project nine-four-one submarines (NATO designation *Typhoon*) are modified for logistic support and remain on station; otherwise, we could not sustain an adequate presence. Recalling our submarines is a risky option. The NKVD controls our communication system."

Dmitri replied, "We have much support, but if the coup fails, this support will melt like termites into the woodwork. It is as the American President Kennedy said following his invasion of Cuba disaster, 'Victory has a hundred fathers; defeat is an orphan'."

"I suspect there are many more heads in danger of rolling than there are axmen. What do you believe is our greatest risk?"

Borkowski answered, "We juggle three balls. First, consolidate our coup taking great care to keep the NKVD in the dark. Second, the Allies must get a convoy safely to Britain. This will be the signal event to permit pulling off the coup. And third, a loose cannon, a Soviet Naval Officer, Vasiliy Baknov. I am sure you know of him."

"I do."

"Baknov poses two problems. The first, his efforts will provide an American senator ammunition to make America request a negotiated settlement. If this happens, all bets on the coup are off. So timing is critical."

"And the second?"

"He gets wind of the planned coup and gets information of it to the NKVD."

"How could Baknov possibly learn of this?"

"An immobile northern fleet, a *Tango*, torpedoed in American waters sets helplessly on the surface. The captain has been instructed to surrender. His orders are to get the crew on deck and scuttle the ship when a rescue vessel arrives on scene. It is not known whether any of the officers are aware of the planned coup, but one likely is. Commanding Officer Andrei Sherensky, son of *Kapitan* 1st Rank Igor Sherensky, the Russian patriot lost in the submarine *Zhukov*."

"But how can Baknov get access to the *Tango* crew?"

"Senator Manning can move mountains and is positioned to do so in his quest to gain rationale for the Americans to quit. Baknov is sure to be involved."

The admiral winced. "But even if he finds out, how can Baknov possibly get this information to the Kremlin? There's no contact with America."

"Quite simply, Admiral. Release it to the American press. By doing this, he both fuels Manning's cause and defeats ours."

"The clock ticks rapidly, Dmitri, and our best option is to clear the way for an Allied convoy."

"Do you have a plan to do this, Admiral, and how will the Americans know our submarines have left the shipping lanes?"

The admiral smiled. "I have a plan for both. But right now there are more pressing things at hand. I am told the chef aboard your submarine *Lenin* makes the finest borscht in all the Russias."

North Atlantic near Bay of Fundy

An *Iroquois*-class Canadian destroyer carefully approached the object of her search, a Soviet *Tango*-class diesel submarine listing heavily to port with a white bed sheet flying from a raised periscope. Their ship down by its stern, the *Tango* crew assembled on deck as lifeboats from the Canadian warship approach their disabled vessel.

With no assurance the lame and surfaced *Tango* will not launch torpedoes and suspecting a trap, the destroyer stands off on the submarine's beam presenting a narrow bow-first aspect vastly reducing hit probability should the *Tango* launch weapons. This did not happen. Victim of *Denver*'s recent attack, the stricken ship had no fight left in her. The Russian skipper judiciously decided to save all his crew not killed by the MK 50 torpedo strike.

The commanding officer, last to leave his ship, set twenty minutes in the scuttling charge activators before departing. Climbing onto the main deck, he promptly settled into a waiting lifeboat. With fifty-nine of a seventy-four man crew well clear, the scuttling explosions *boomed* sending their *Tango* forever into the deep.

Last of his crew to board the rescue ship, Captain Sherensky crisply saluted the Canadian National ensign. In broken English, he formally surrenders his crew and expresses appreciation for their rescue to the destroyer CO then presents the skipper with a silver sugar bowl carried from the now sunken submarine. He smiled. "We no longer wear swords in the Soviet Navy. I hope this will do."

A Canadian translator interposing, the Soviet CO bade the Canadian warship lie to for a brief memorial service for the fifteen shipmates who now rest in the Atlantic depths. Following the sorrowful moment, the destroyer CO set their course for Halifax, Nova Scotia where the Russian crew will be detained along with the prisoner captured on the Arctic ice by USS *Steelhead*. Though unstated, the Soviet skipper knows he and his crew will be isolated until completion of a thorough interrogation.

Middleburg, VA

Lieutenant Vasiliy Baknov's head spun. *So many pieces to this puzzle, but I must not let it detract from my focus. My goal in the beginning was to give my life if necessary in the service of Mother Russia's efforts to stabilize the world.*

He pondered over his current situation, a prisoner given no initiative whatsoever. *Does this Manning really intend to get his country to sue for peace? Or, am I being used simply as an intelligence-gathering device for the Americans? Stop this, dammit. So far all I have is conjecture.*

He learned in cadet school this planted only seeds of panic. *I must sort out what I know for sure ... which is not a lot. Even more importantly what more do I need to know and how to contrive a means for acquiring it.*

A good judge of character, he mentally reviewed the people with whom he had contact.

He wrote off Harold immediately. *The bastard keeps his job only because he is big enough to enforce my captivity here. Escaping requires only outwitting the witless. But before I do that, determine whether I am better able to carry out my work within or outside of these premises.*

Tania is an open book. She will fall in the direction of the best opportunity for her. She is likely easiest to make an ally of, so I must convince her my prospects are likely the ones to be fulfilled. Next comes Tom, Dave and Ron. The Americans have a term: the three stooges. But they certainly knew how to get what they wanted from me, so beware. How were they selected? One or all of them could be informants for the President who merely permits Manning to gather enough rope to hang himself. I must develop a technique for smoking them out. Perhaps planting a false concern to see whether it reaches Manning and makes its way back to me.

But the toughest one is Manning himself. Is he really a blowhard politician? He shows evidence of this, or is he a loyal American who wants only to save his country from the agony of continuing this futile war? In this case, I am behind him. But I must be careful. Saving his country clearly does not set atop his priorities for he seems sincere about his Czar of the Americas prospects. But the conclusion here is regardless of his true intention, his means of attaining it is consistent with interests of the Soviet Union.

Okay, Vasiliy. Take this straw and spin it into a plan of gold.

Aboard *Steelhead*

Brent Maddock bullhorned to Jim Buchanan on the heels of the latter's victory over the Soviet *Tango*. "A nice scalp under *Denver*'s belt, Captain. Up for a bet? *Steelhead* ends up bagging more wins than *Denver*. Let's say a fifth of Johnnie Walker Black."

Both ships lie to in a sea state three, having to stand closer than previous rendezvous in order to be heard over the sea noise. Above them hangs a sliver of moon, raising concern over the increased probability of being spotted.

"Like taking candy ... no, make that scotch from a baby."

Maddock replied, "That mean we're on?"

"You got it, Brent. Have you spotted any more?"

"Couple of possibles, Captain, though nothing we could put a weapon on. But that's bound to change."

"Do you get the feeling there's not as many out here as expected? We covered a lot of ocean and so far only three between us. What are your thoughts? Possible to get a convoy through with acceptable losses?"

Maddock thought, *Acceptable losses? Whatever the hell that means.* "In my view, yes, Captain. But I make no guarantee our politicos share this view."

"Agree, but it's all we got to go on now. Taking a chance, but I'm transmitting a report to CINC-LANT-FLEET (Commander in Chief US Atlantic Fleet) and advising a screen of SSNs should fan out ahead of the convoy to clear the path of any bad guys."

"That requires a low SOA (speed of advance) so our nukes can spot hovering diesels. They don't make a helluva lot of noise."

"Right, Brent. But just getting a convoy moving toward Britain with minor losses accrues a lot of political advantage."

At that moment, a radioman mounted *Steelhead*'s bridge. Taking care to assure Maddock that no one had read the message, he passed a covered clipboard to the skipper.

Using a red-lensed flashlight, Brent read the order and whistled. Passing the light and board to Tom Bentley.

The XO's response came back in a whisper, "Holy smoke!"

CO EYES ONLY
TOP SECRET
FROM: CINCLANTFLT
TO: STEELHEAD
INFO: DENVER

    STEELHEAD CEASE CURRENT OPERATIONS. PROCEED AT BEST SPEED TO THE BARENTS SEA CONSISTENT WITH REMAINING UNDETECTED. ENTER SOVIET INLAND WATERS AND PROCEED TO SEVERODVINSK APPROACHES. ORDERS TO FOLLOW.

Maddock called to USS *Denver*. "CINC-LANT-FLEET message from the last broadcast … you should have and read immediately."

"Have it and did, Brent."

"By your leave, Captain?"

"Carry on, Brent. And don't forget … you owe me a fifth of Walker Black."

"I won't, Captain."

Following a moment of silence, the voice of Jim Buchanan floated across the space between ships, "Go with God, *Steelhead*."

The two ships slipped beneath the waves.

Chapter 21

Aboard *Steelhead*

One must be cleared at the level of classified information in order to access it. But there is another equally significant rule. A person must have *need to know*, i.e. requires the information in order to perform his function. An officer cleared at the highest levels may not access low-level classified material if he has no *need to know*.

However, inherently intelligent, submariners are hard to keep in the dark. Though few crewmen have a *need to know* of *Steelhead*'s revised assignment, a helmsman from the seamen gang knows the ship's heading and speed and can put two and two together.

Engineers will notice the decrease in seawater temperatures and easily guess where they have to be for that to happen, many having been there before.

Skipper Brent Maddock and XO Tom Bentley struggled with this dilemma and bounced ideas to manage it off each other. The CO's stateroom provided privacy for their meeting.

The skipper said, "We need to find a way around this, Tom. I know what the book says, but we're flinging these guys into who knows what. They deserve more than just a blank stare."

Bentley wondered, *Is the skipper showing signs of wearing down? No one has a better right than he does. Some humor should loosen him up.* "We could take the Shrew route, Captain. Have him go into a trance and tell the guys we're feeding 'em a bunch of bum dope and we're really heading south to some tropical liberty port."

Maddock didn't react as expected and clearly, their circumstance troubled him greatly. "Need to know, Tom. Give me your best assessment. Wouldn't we get better performance from the crew if they're aware of the magnitude of what confronts us?"

"Captain, these troops will follow you into hell without batting an eyelash."

"Not a time for platitudes, Tom. But thanks anyway. If what you say is true, doesn't it grow out of their confidence that I always level with them? Time to cut the crew in. What do we have to tell them other than we're heading north? We don't even know why."

Bentley thought a moment how COM Bostwick would exploit this to slake his perpetual anger toward Maddock. "You want to tell them, or me?"

"You, Tom. Like I always say, COs give out good news, XOs the bad."

A week later, *Steelhead* entered the Barents Sea off Russia's northwest coast. In the interim, an amplifying message instructed them to take station at specified coordinates at stipulated date and time. It contained no instructions on what to do upon arrival.

"What we're up to has to be more sensitive than anything I've ever encountered. What about you, Captain?"

"Agree, Tom. But I also believe conjecture is inaccurate at least ninety-five percent of the time. So let's focus on what we know."

Maddock and Bentley huddled with coffees in the CO stateroom.

"Which isn't much," Bentley ventured.

"More than you might think. We didn't encounter a single threat over the entire transit. Did you ever make a Spec Op to gather intelligence here before the war?"

"Two, Captain."

"Bet you averaged three to five encounters by the time you reached here. And the same on the way back, right?"

"As I recall, very close to those numbers."

"There has to be a reason," Maddock said. "I come up with only two. The Russians no longer have sufficient resources or we're being fished in."

"Fished in? Our instructions come encrypted directly from CINC-LANT-FLEET."

"Right. Experience has shown all codes are breakable. The Japs and Germans learned that the hard way during World War Two and suffered big time losses. I know what I just said about conjecture. But even if we're wrong on both counts, the first one poses no problem. The second could be fatal. I know Chief Giambri's troops are on the ball, but maybe have him tighten up a bit."

Bentley said, "But if we tell the troops this, won't it suggest to them what to look for? Consequence of that is a lot of well-intended but false information."

"Agree," said Maddock. "We'll use the Giambri filter. He'll instruct his troops on what to look for and how to find it, but not why. Findings will be reported to him. He'll make sure only the significant info is passed to us."

"Captain, you're beginning to discourage me. I'm ready for command, but you keep opening doors to new rat holes."

"Tom, let me put it this way. You're a helluva lot more ready than when I came to *Steelhead*."

The unmistakable voice of Woody Parnell floated over the captain's 21MC. "Captain to the Conn!"

Though impertinent to order the skipper *on the double* when summoning him to the attack center, the edge on Woody's voice clearly implied it.

Maddock wondered how many times he had demanded *what've we got*, but did so anyway.

"A submarine, Captain. But it indicates no one expects us to be here. He's making more noise than a sea bag full of broken dishes."

Maddock and Bentley entered the sonar shack not surprised to find Chief Giambri hovering over his sonarmen.

"Been listening to this guy for an hour. Initially we thought he was a civilian surface craft, but some other clues clearly show him definitely a submarine."

"Anything changing?"

"Running straight as an arrow and steady as a rock, Captain. Maybe we should stop him and ask if he knows there's a war on."

"My guess, it's a logistic ship headed out to service diesel submarines in the shipping lanes."

Giambri suggested, "We could strike a mighty blow here."

He clearly fished for insight into *Steelhead*'s current mission.

Maddock saw through the chief's comment and said, "Can't take that chance, Chief. He'd probably shoot back and piss off our messcooks who're setting up for the evening meal."

The captain knew an attack would reveal their presence in the White Sea and could not take that chance. He had much bigger fish to fry. Or so it would appear.

The exchange of grins showed neither man believed what the other said, but they would live with it.

Maddock and Bentley retreated to the wardroom for a nerve settling cribbage game, but immediately interrupted by a messenger with another CO EYES ONLY, shifting their destination back to the CO stateroom. Maddock spread the message out on his desk.

CO EYES ONLY
FROM: CINCLANTFLT
TO: STEELHEAD

UPON REACHING STATION, MONITOR ALL
SENSORS. UPON RECEIPT OF SIGNAL W-W-W
REPEATED THREE TIMES AT THIRTY SECOND
INTERVALS, KEY R-R-R ON GERTRUDE. REPEAT
THREE TIMES AT THIRTY SECOND INTERVALS.
SURFACE AND RDVU WITH SOVIET AKULA
SUBMARINE. RECEIVE ONE PASSENGER.
RETURN CONUS AT BEST SPEED CONSISTENT
WITH REMAINING UNDETECTED.

Both remained silent for a moment to let the magnitude of this instruction set in.

Commenting first, Maddock asked, "Are we getting paid enough to do this kind of thing?"

Oval Office

Eric Danis arrived only to be rushed as usual into the office for his meeting with the President.

Danis thought, *Nice to be too important for the normal twenty minute heal-cooling wait.* "Good morning, Mr. President. We've got to stop meeting like this. People are beginning to talk. Especially the Joint Chiefs Chairman. He feels bad about being left out."

Dempsey had already ordered their coffees. "If he doesn't like it, I can always replace him. With you, maybe? Think he'd like that?"

Danis replied, "Don't do me any favors, sir. Eve and I bought a lot in a small Mojave Desert village and we want to build on it before I reach my dotage."

"You don't get any sympathy from me, Eric. Despite all you've heard, this is not exactly our dream house. Mildred and I target for anything with a golf course on the ocean."

"Atlantic or Pacific?"

"Either." Dempsey ended small talk abruptly. "Look, I know *Steelhead* can't transmit, but what does your gut tell you?"

"Just this. If anything bad happens to Brent Maddock, you'll have one tough and angry wife to deal with."

Dempsey caved in on the small talk. *We need to loosen up.* "Well, she won't have to crack White House security. I expect my good friend Darrel Manning will have me impeached by then."

"Mr. President, if it makes you feel better, we've got the best possible man to pull this off. So my gut tells me it will work. Radio silence is imposed on *Steelhead* so we won't have that answer till she reaches Fundy."

"Any feeling for when that might be?"

"My best guess, a week after the rendezvous which is today and depending on what she encounters en route home."

"In the meantime, what about the convoy?"

"Ready to go, Mr. President."

"Good. Dispatch it."

Danis shook his head. "Recommend we hold off till *Steelhead* gets back, sir. I strongly suspect the person they pick up will give us a good estimate of probable casualty rates."

"Eric, we're on the horns of a dilemma. Manning heads the Senate Intelligence Committee. It's nothing short of a miracle we've kept him in the dark so far. Experience shows someone's bound to spill the beans and it's just a question of time before that happens. Getting a convoy to Britain is our only hope to keep from bowing to the Soviets. Once it's on the way, Manning will be unable to recall it, especially if we don't experience high losses up front."

Eric broached what they discussed at their last meeting. "Have you given thought to placing Senator Manning under surveillance? Information published in Iowa's Midtown paper makes him look awfully suspicious. Although I doubt we could make anything stick, bringing him up on charges would as a minimum put him on the defensive long enough to buy the time we need."

Danis got one of Dempsey's famous combined elated and sneaky grins as the President said, "It sure would be good to watch that sleazy bastard squirm. But he won't do that. He'll figure some way to turn it around and bite me on the ass. Much as I hate to admit it, Manning's the best politician I've ever met. Remember the chant we had as kids? 'I'm rubber, you're glue. Everything bounces off me and sticks to you.' That's Manning."

"Is that a yes or no, Mr. President?"

"Yes. Politicking takes time, and it might just get us enough. But don't look for Manning to get knocked out of the saddle. That's not gonna happen."

Aboard *Steelhead*

Maddock assembled his exec and several key officers to reveal and discuss his plan. Feeling he'd done right by telling his crew they patrolled the Barents Sea approaches to the White Sea, he had no need to tell them more.

The skipper liked softening the mood when he had weighty topics to discuss. "Okay, we've beat up on Woody and the salmon nazi enough. I don't want another word spoken in this wardroom on it ... that is, unless any of you hear something new."

Shaking his head, Parnell tossed up his hands and said, "You confess your sins, make a good act of contrition, do penance and still get no absolution."

Nervous grins from Engineer Officer Bill Bryan and the XO signaled time for Maddock to shift gears.

He described the content of CINCLANTFLT's latest message. "We've very little to go on because the identity of whomever we're picking up needs to be protected. Although it's transmitted in the most secure system we have, there remains a miniscule probability it could fall into the wrong hands. We can't take that chance. Our immediate problem ... rules of engagement. The way I see it, we gotta let them shoot first."

Woody exclaimed, "First, Captain! Doesn't that run against General Patton's advice? 'No *sunnuvabitch* ever won a war by dying for his country. You win by making the other *sunnuvabitch* die for his country.' I don't know the exact math, but odds of coming out on top when you concede the first shot are dismal."

Maddock said, "I know that, Woody. So we need an alternative that boosts our escape odds. I need the exec, you and Bill to work that up for me. We need it quick. We're already in the White Sea and must expect they have defensive assets in the area."

Bentley chimed in, "Captain, letting the bad guys shoot first is like putting a gun to our head."

"I know that, Tom. Clearly, CINC-LANT-FLEET implies the importance of our task and the high value accruing to carrying it off. That says to me, we must take risks and prevent anyone from knowing we're here."

Parnell whistled. "With all due respect, Captain, if we pursue that policy and encounter a bad guy, we almost guarantee we'll fail the mission."

Bentley added, "I recommend this, Captain. Be first to shoot until we have something worked up."

"I can go along with that."

Before falling off to sleep for whatever time Maddock could be spared from the attack center, a warm feeling crept over him. He'd gotten the answer he wanted. His officers will stand up to him if they believe he embarks along the wrong path. This is the substance of submarine survival in combat. Maddock had trained them well. *Now comes the easy part, get to the rendezvous point undetected, sort the good Akula out from the bad ones, pick up our passenger and get the hell out of here.*

Middleburg, VA

Vasiliy Baknov sat with Darrel Manning's underlings, Tom, Dave and Ron, in the immense living room of the senator's country estate. In true *spook* fashion, they gave only their first names, even those questionable in Vasiliy's mind.

Baknov thought, *Maybe I suffer from acute paranoia, but I distrust everyone.* Therefore, he became extremely cautious. *Is my cooperation consistent with needs of the Soviet cause? Or are these idiots intentionally or otherwise a detriment to it?*

Ron, the apparent leader, said, "I have important news. A Soviet submarine crew has been captured and interned in Canada. The senator wishes to know if this can be of value to us."

With his head spinning, Baknov thought, *How can this be? An entire crew? One or more survivors, maybe, but not all of them.*

He compared the event to his own escape from the stricken *Zhukov.* "How certain are you?"

Through a sneer, Ron said, "Absolutely, no question!" At the same time, he thought, *Do you believe we are idiots?* Ron had no way of knowing Baknov registered a similar thought. Ron then asked, "My question for you is, how to make the best use of this?"

"We must have access to them. Is this possible?"

"I cannot answer that precisely, but Senator Manning is capable of opening a great many doors. The polls show fifty-five percent of Americans support the senator's efforts for a negotiated settlement. That gives him a lot of political clout."

Baknov seethed. *Then dammit, I can't tell you precisely whether this is of any value.* But he wisely chose a honey route. "Of course. But sooner the better. Expect the Allied military to compartment these submariners until every possible crumb of intelligence is squeezed from them. How soon can we make contact?"

"The senator works on that even as we speak. But there's another problem. Your Warren Biddle cover is blown. The CIA knows who you are and looks for you."

Ron related the story.

"That Pacific Coast submariner, Terry Painter, returned from the Pacific Northwest to his home in Chicago and his parents told him of his friend, a Warren Biddle, who had stayed with them for a time. Painter quickly denied knowing anyone by that name and told the authorities the man had to be an imposter.

"His father protested and said you had identification and lived in Westport, Washington. He said you told them that you met Terry at a tavern in Grays Harbor. We know the kid don't drink and doesn't frequent taverns in Grays Harbor or anywhere else so we believe what he said when he told the authorities that he doesn't know you."

"Old man Painter turned over to the local authorities a photo and everything else they had about you. The police then found out about a Warren Biddle of Westport, Washington, who disappeared while on a commercial fishing trip with his partner. They believe the man with Biddle's identification had a hand in his disappearance and any associated crimes. A young detective researched major events at or about the time of Biddle's disappearance and found out about the sinking of a Soviet submarine in the vicinity of the fishing grounds. They believed Biddle might have picked up a survivor and paid the ultimate price for his compassion.

"The detective faxed the imposter's photo to the CIA, and got a positive ID on you ... Russian Navy Lieutenant Vasiliy Baknov. And furthermore," said Ron with a trace of glee in his voice, "you've been traced to the East Coast through that stolen ID. So we must keep you under wraps now."

Baknov thought, *Likely story. These bastards probably set all this up to keep a tighter hold on me. But whether they did it or it's as they say, results are the same. Some powerful people in the United States are now looking for Lieutenant Vasiliy Baknov of the Soviet Navy—me. Regardless of who incited it, the consequences to me are the same.*

Aboard *Steelhead*

Daylight hours had grown short by the time *Steelhead* reached her station off Severodvinsk. At twilight, skipper Brent Maddock ordered the ship to six-three feet and took cautious looks through the attack periscope. The attack scope has a small profile at its top, lowering probability of detection visually or by radar. A downside, smaller optics permit less light down the shaft, making it difficult to spot objects after dark.

An electronic countermeasure (ECM) scan detected no radar strengths capable of returning echoes from the larger Type 8 scope, so he shifted. A small continuously monitored ECM antenna sat atop the 8, broadening Maddock's comfort zone. However, he continued to restrict his observations to three-second peeks. He had no hope of spotting a periscope, but felt the need to insure no nearby shipping could spot *Steelhead* when she surfaced for her rendezvous with the Soviet *Akula*.

The question raced through Maddock's mind, *Who'd have ever thought?* Ever steady, known to have ice water running through his veins, Brent found himself taking deep breaths to suppress fluttering butterflies in his stomach.

"Down scope," Maddock ordered. "Make your depth one-five-zero feet."

"One-five-zero feet," replied the chief of the watch. Then he said, "Planesmen, you heard the captain. Ten degrees down bubble."

"One-five-zero, ten down," the planesmen acknowledged.

Steelhead dropped her nose and headed to a safer depth, quieting the skipper's butterflies for a time.

He turned and addressed his exec. "Nothing to do now but wait. The easy part, right?"

"Right, Captain"

Bentley's tone indicated he believed otherwise.

Three hours crept by like an exhausted tortoise. Maddock, wearing out the floor covering between the wardroom and sonar, finally announced to his exec, "You got it, XO. I'm hitting the sack for a few."

As though Maddock had flipped a switch, the excited voice of Chief Giambri called out, "We're getting the signal."

Maddock responded, "Here we go. A new first. Two belligerent combat units meet without a flag of truce. Let's do it, XO."

Half an hour later, *Steelhead* made bare steerageway at periscope depth. Maddock decided if they had to run into something, the hit would not be a hard one.

Sonar reported the target closing from astern, bearings drawing left. "Should come up a few hundred yards on the starboard beam."

They seem to know right where we are and our heading, Maddock thought. *These guys are better at targeting than we give 'em credit for.* "Sonar, report soon as you hear tanks blowing."

"You got it, Captain," Giambri bellowed through the sonar shack door, loud enough not to need the 21MC.

A moment later, "Thar she blows!" Giambri yelled, followed by, "I've wanted to use that line ever since I read *Moby Dick*."

"Chief of the Watch, surface the ship," Maddock ordered.

Soon, Maddock and the OOD stood on the bridge. They looked to starboard and could barely make out the *Akula*. Illuminated by flashlights on the main deck, they saw a rubber raft with a life-jacketed passenger seated in it. Abruptly as she emerged, the *Akula* slowly slipped beneath the waves leaving the raft and its passenger adrift in the White Sea.

Maddock ordered the bow turned toward the raft and Woody Parnell, COB and three seamen to the main deck. In minutes that seemed like eons, the deck force hauled raft and passenger aboard and disappeared below decks with both.

Turning to Tom Bentley, Maddock ordered, "Okay, submerge the ship and let's get the hell out of here."

This completed, Maddock went to the wardroom and found a rather pleasant appearing man enjoying a cup of tea.

Looking up, the man said in broken but perfect English, "Good evening, Captain, permit me to introduce myself. Mikhail Turgenev. And I'll save you the trouble of inquiring. *Fathers and Sons,* but five generations later."

Chapter 22

Aboard *Steelhead*

Maddock's job as CO is to suspect everything, so he had normal misgivings about the Russian who boarded *Steelhead* for a ride to the States. *Is he truly the person he claims to be?* Maddock considered the risk low, for the *Akula* arrived at the exact time and coordinates specified in the CINCLANTFLT order. Nonetheless, Brent began at arm's length and held their opening conversation privately in the captain's stateroom. Additionally, this would permit discussion of CO EYES ONLY material if needed, but he mainly wished to take stock of Turgenev.

The good-natured Russian soon had a skeptical Maddock at ease. Brent found him engaging, happy and optimistic about everything, not unlike a grandfather comforting a grandson.

The deal-closer came when Turgenev said, "Russians are good people but have a penchant for permitting the wrong people to govern them."

"Mr. Turgenev, it seems most countries suffer that condition, even my own."

"Mikhail, please. And, yes, Captain, but your country gets an opportunity to change that every four years. I envy your country's system. Democracy is by far the least efficient form of government, but despite all, it shows itself to be the best. Regardless of problems and time attendant to getting consensus from four hundred thirty-five representatives, issues are ultimately resolved with no one taken out and being shot."

"Mr. Turgenev—"

"Mikhail, please. Indulge an old man."

Maddock thought, *Who'd have ever thought I'd one day be on a first-name basis with the great-great-grandson of the magnificent Ivan Turgenev. This would indeed impress my Bull (English, history and government professor) at the Naval Academy.*

"Mikhail ... you know much about our country. More than I know of yours, I fear."

Smiling, Mikhail said, "You are a young man, yet to come to grips with what you are told to think might not necessarily be what you should think. I too was once young, though what you behold might contradict that. I assure you, a delightful journey awaits."

Maddock liked how the man's name rolled from his tongue and thought, *And to be fortunate enough to have a mentor like you showing the way.*

The Russian continued, "People of the world vote with their feet. Consider the lopsided ratio of those who wish to live in your country to those who wish to leave. That says a great deal, my friend."

Feeling like he had attended a lecture incident to receiving a philosophy PhD, and as much as Maddock enjoyed their meaningful banter, he needed the conversation to get back to the here and now. As a subject changer, he fought the urge to say, *So you're really a great-grandson of the famous author?* But Turgenev probably had more of that in his life than he wished.

Instead, Brent said, "The means of your arrival astound me, Mr. Turgenev. Soviet submarine operational control must be far less rigid than I'm led to believe."

"Mikhail, if you would. I am not certain of what you mean."

"Mr ... Mikhail," Brent corrected. "Doesn't every Soviet ship have a political officer to scrutinize each move?" Maddock probed, but thought it wise to frame his questions in a manner that made them easy to ignore if Turgenev so wished. "Surely he is aware of your transfer to my ship."

Mikhail thumped the desk with a huge balled fist, a Russian tradition to illustrate being amused. When his massive laugh abated, he said, "Our learned and inspired *zampolit* normally performs what he does best ... nothing. And when not doing that, he either stuffs his face or sleeps. A full revolution could go on right beneath his pointed nose, and he would miss it."

"That surprises me."

"He had no idea I was even on board. I wore a rating's uniform. Though I'm three times the median crew age and likely twice the size, our *zampolit* did not notice. I attended one of his lectures and have not been so entertained since last watching a ballet."

"But when the ship surfaced. Surely he knew."

"Ritually, he takes an evening nap and never wakes up in less than two hours. Our *zampolit* is a sound sleeper."

"It's good that he is, Mikhail. Now, is there anything you can tell me to improve the safety of our trip home?"

"The submarine command has ordered our Atlantic submarine assets, such as they are, to stand down. Problem is, a few mavericks will disobey and others might simply not receive the message."

"I see. What you tell me does little for my comfort zone."

"Comfort zone?"

He explained and promised not to use any more American slang.

"Please don't stop that, Captain. How else can I learn?"

"What you said about the stand down is important. I sense our President is under great pressure to offer a negotiated settlement to the war. Getting a convoy to Britain might be what is needed to get the American public to hang on."

"Now that is astounding! Much more so than deceiving our stupid *zampolit* to let me escape. As you might suspect, Russians are disenchanted with the war. We are spread thin as a noodle and our people suffer deprivations of just about everything. Landing a convoy in Britain will signal the beginning of another Great Patriotic War, but this time against us instead of the Nazis. All we can look forward to are eight and a half million Russian combat deaths. I am complicit in an impending coup against the Soviet leadership. We believe the right time to strike is when an Allied convoy reaches Britain. This is essential to our success."

"You're right. This is astounding! Is timing that important?"

"Very. The organization in place is flimsy at best. As I said, Russians have a penchant for allowing the wrong people to come to power, but once it's done, these same Russians are understandably intimidated. The only chance for the coup to succeed is if a convoy reaches Britain. The Soviet leadership will be aware, but helpless to stop it. My purpose for coming to America is to report these facts and to represent the new government following the coup."

"Mikhail, there is a problem. My instructions are to maintain radio silence until reaching America. Four days at best."

"Four critical days, Captain. And remember what I told you. What you are told to think might not necessarily be what you should think. Perhaps this is the opportunity for you to embark on your delightful journey."

For an instant, Maddock considered, *Is this a ruse to get us to embark a convoy and have it shot to pieces? What could be better for the Soviets? No. I'm too good a judge of character. Turgenev is genuine.* He said, "Let me bounce this off my Executive Officer."

When summoned, Bentley arrived on the double and Maddock briefed him on all that transpired then said, "Draft a message, Tom. But let's continue to think on this."

Maddock considered reciprocating by inviting Mikhail to address him as Brent, but wondered what effect it might have on *Steelhead* crewmen so he did not.

Mikhail said, "It's a long trip ahead. Perhaps there is something I can do to earn my keep."

"Now look who's using American slang."

"You are wrong, my friend," Mikhail responded with what Brent would later term *the Turgenev academic smile.* "The phrase *earn your keep* is much older than your country."

"Perhaps you can share some sage advice as we make our way to port," said Maddock.

"I once commanded a Russian submarine, but *Steelhead* is well-appointed in that regard. And I am a terrible advisor, so I better stick to something I can do well."

"Who am I to argue literature with a descendant of the great Ivan Turgenev? I'm sure we'll find a niche ... no, make that a place for you. And, I agree. Nothing is more boring than sitting and drinking coffee for four days."

"Tea, Captain. I'm told I spin a good yarn. Do you think that might entertain the crew?"

"You said you were a submariner. I'm sure you know how unpredictable they can be. We'll only find out if we try."

The Oval Office

ADM Eric Danis reached the halfway point between the Pentagon and the White House when he received a summons on the car telephone to report immediately to the President. Expecting the call, Danis left his office fifteen minutes earlier, hoping to walk into the Oval Office with Dempsey still on the phone.

Dempsey knew Danis had anticipated the meeting topic, so jumped right into it without even ordering coffee. "What do you make of it, Eric?"

"One, it's authentic. Lieutenant Commander Maddock's a good head, but I guess that point's already been made. I guarantee he would not breach a strict radio silence order unless he's confident the intel is hot and valid."

"I thought along the same lines. Maybe you and I spend too much time together. A planned coup within the Soviet Union! Doesn't that take just about all the wind out of Manning's sails?"

"Only if we release it. I strongly recommend against that, Mr. President. I can think of no better way to get the planners to pull in their horns than alerting the Soviet Premier that this is in the cards."

"Interesting, Eric. Would you be offended if I sought a second opinion from someone else?"

"Not in the least, sir. But be careful with this information. A leak could turn the whole thing into a fiasco."

"Dammit, Eric, you make my life miserable. This thing is too big to insulate ourselves from the best advice we can get."

"I understand, sir, but look at it this way. A massive convoy has been at sea two days. That puts them five days from Britain. We've had remarkably few attacks. One ship lost, another damaged and being towed back to port."

Dempsey paced back and forth, assuming his harshest voice and toughest political demeanor. "Eric, the public is champing at the bit to end this blasted war. Two days out, you say? In the five remaining days casualty rates will increase. Maybe even enough for Turgenev's people to call off the coup. In this case, *gonna* is a bird in the hand; *might* is a bird in the bush."

"That's true, Mr. President. But Turgenev says the Russian submarine force has been directed to stand down. And Maddock is highly confident he is the real thing. So I'm not sure the low rate experienced to date is luck of the draw."

The President said, "But if they've been directed to stand down, why any losses at all?"

"There are lots of Soviet submarines out there. It's impossible that every one of them got the stand-down message."

Dempsey fumed, his technique for intimidating advisors as to how much he wanted to go with the *bird in the hand* fizzled. Informality dropped. "Admiral Danis, just two men, you and I, will make what might be the most critical decision in our country's history. You are that confident?"

"Mr. President, I have given you my best assessment of the situation. I believe sitting on the coup information to be the best option available to our country. But you are the Commander in Chief, sir, and I'll stand solidly behind whatever you decide."

Dempsey abated. "Why in hell did that damn Truman have to establish 'the buck stops here'?"

"Because it does, sir. President Truman just happened to be first to wrap words around it."

"I'm taking your advice. If it's wrong, the fault is all mine."

Searching for a comeback, Danis found none, so remained silent.

The subject exhausted, Dempsey changed it. "Tonight's the night, Eric. The CIA's been watching Manning's country home in Virginia. Several former Soviet Embassy staff have been spotted coming and going, and that's enough to warrant springing the trap."

Middleburg, VA

His face pale, Darrel Manning read the message from *Steelhead,* then read it again. "This … this can be a fatal blow to all my efforts. If the American public gets wind of it, I will plunge in the polls. I'm amazed the President has not released this information by now."

He addressed mainly Dave, but concurrently spoke to the others, Tom, Ron, Vasiliy and Tania.

The senator regained his impeccable demeanor. "What can we do about this?"

Vasiliy Baknov offered a suggestion. Although they didn't know each other, the argument Baknov presented to Manning stood exactly opposite to advice given the President by Eric Danis.

Baknov explained, "The reason for the President not releasing this information is precisely why you should. If you do, I assure you there will be no coup. But many traitorous heads will roll in the Soviet Union. Unfortunately, not Turgenev's. I don't know the bastard personally, but know of him. He had a controversial Navy career which ended with his early relief as a submarine commanding officer. He is affected by being a descendant of the Russian novelist Ivan Turgenev, which is likely why no other action was taken against him; it does not surprise me he is complicit in all this."

Dave asked, "You say we should release this information. How can we do this without compromising ourselves and the senator?"

Tania and the others followed along, sensing that something unpleasant could abruptly end the delightful circumstance they had fallen into.

Manning had not considered this and showed his discomfort.

"I don't understand your concern," said Baknov. "The best way is to release this to the press. What a bombshell, and you know the prestige associated with releasing a story. Our government monitors the American press diligently. I assure you, the coup will be crushed mercilessly, strengthening your position for Allied Forces to initiate a request to negotiate a settlement."

Dave replied, "You are only partially right, Baknov; it is the kiss of death for a media agency to release a sensational story only to have it overturned. We have the message from *Steelhead*, yes. But how do we validate it without revealing our illegal access to top-secret intel and release information critical to American security?"

While Baknov searched for an answer, Harold entered the room, approached Manning and whispered something. The senator's face gave only a slight trace of falling.

After Howard left, Manning asked, "Would you excuse me? I would like a private word with Lieutenant Baknov."

The others rose to leave, but Manning stopped them. "No. Please continue to enjoy the fire and another drink. We shall not be long."

Though all remained silent, a feeling of discomfort overcame each one.

"Of course," Dave agreed.

Harold met Manning and Baknov in the hall and the senator demanded. "What do you know?"

"The house is surrounded," Harold replied. "Look for a knock on the door almost any time. I have activated the tunnel fans. You have three minutes at the most."

Being caught amongst Soviet defectors turned American citizens violated no laws but could raise suspicions an ambitious politician could do without. The paranoid Manning had previously ordered construction of an escape route as a precaution in the event he needed a quick escape from untoward circumstances.

Manning found himself in that situation. Caught associating with an escaped Soviet Naval officer would inflict irreparable damage, especially an officer in civilian clothes. That would make him an enemy spy.

Getting the tunnel dug posed no problem. Contractors abounded who would take on any project with no questions asked providing they got paid well enough and promptly.

Manning and Baknov entered the tunnel through a kitchen corner cabinet rolled back and forth for access. They proceeded to an outbuilding a hundred and fifty yards from the main house. Satisfied the surrounding ring of agents stood at least a hundred yards behind them, Manning gestured to a golf cart and they climbed in. The electrically powered vehicle, under a black cover to make it invisible in the dark, made not a sound as they traversed two miles over an old dirt road that ended at a golf course. Parking the cart beside a row of identical vehicles, Manning removed the cover then directed Baknov to a car parked in the unlighted lot.

After climbing in, they drove off.

Back at the house, Harold's predicted knock on the door occurred exactly on schedule. Initially, officers with flak jackets and drawn pistols burst into the study, directing everyone to raise their hands. Dave inched his way toward the fireplace to toss in and destroy the crumbled copy of *Steelhead*'s top-secret message.

An officer ordered, "Freeze!"

Plain clothed CIA agents entered after the room had been secured. They directed two of the officers to search the rest of the house and then began to pat down each person for weapons. The officer patting down Tania particularly enjoyed his job.

Dave's turn came. An officer ordered him to open his clenched fist; the message fell to the floor.

Instantly, an agent retrieved it. "Well, look what we have here."

The following morning, per direction of the President, the CIA chief reported findings of the raid.

A clear edge on his voice, Dempsey asked, "Those arrested ... where are they now?"

"They're being held, pending a hearing."

"Listen, and listen carefully," Dempsey growled. "Keep them locked up with access to no one ... and that includes attorneys. Who other than you knows the content of this message?"

"The officer who retrieved it."

"Lock him up too; it's vital to US security this information be distributed no further. Do you understand?"

President Dempsey's tone clearly emphasized the seriousness of the situation.

"I do, sir," came the chief's nervous reply.

After directing his secretary to get the Attorney General on the phone, the President said to the AG, "Pay attention. The CIA chief will be in your office in ten minutes. He's taken four people into custody and I want them isolated until further notice from me personally. That includes NO attorneys."

The Attorney General tried to respond, but Dempsey interrupted. "I don't give a damn about their civil rights. This is a matter of national security. I expect you to work that out."

The call ended and Dempsey said to the CIA chief, "Interrogate everyone, and I mean everyone who has had contact with the prisoners. If they're aware of any part of the message content, lock them up too. From now on, I want only the smallest cadre of your most trusted agents seeing to the prisoners' needs. And I want them interrogated daily."

"I understand, sir."

Excused, the chief walked away from the biggest hornet's nest he had ever stumbled into.

Aboard *Steelhead*

Mikhail found a way to earn his keep as the ship made her way back to Fundy. He lectured the crew on classic Russian literature, which took some doing. Initially, he spoke to an audience of one, but the sailor quickly spread the word. Audiences began to increase until only standing room remained in the crew's mess for his lectures. He discussed Russian tales in the crew's vernacular, contradicting notions of classic literature being boring. He cleverly eliminated narrative marginally needed to advance the plot, delivering only *meat* which the crew savored.

Among *Steelhead's* crew, Turgenev transitioned from *Who the hell is this Russian* to *What a neat guy.*

Brent Maddock alone knew the true reason for Turgenev's trip to America: following the coup, represent the new government to the United States. Never had so young an officer presided over such a significant mission.

Steelhead approached the continental shelf after a remarkably uneventful passage that emphasized validity of Turgenev's stand down message. *But things went too well* in Maddock's mind. When he sailed with CO Eric Danis in *Denver*, the skipper once advised him, "If things seem to go too well, they aren't," so Brent did not abandon his *always on the edge* seat.

It happened midway through Turgenev's lecture on *The Brothers Karamazov*. An earsplitting explosion shook *Steelhead* so hard it rendered most of the crew unconscious. The ship sank rapidly and jolted again when she came to rest on the bottom. By the grace of God, they barely crossed the continental shelf before this disaster, otherwise the ship would have been crushed in the deep sea.

They sat on the bottom under twelve hundred feet of ocean with no one aware of their plight or location.

Chapter 23

Aboard *Denver*

Executive Officer Bob Douglass woke skipper Jim Buchanan. "Captain. Sonar thinks they have contact on *Steelhead*, a *Six-thirty-seven* heading for Fundy."

Buchanan, dog-tired as his ship made its way to port, had not slept a continuous five hours in the past two weeks. "Good, Bob. I'm not surprised. No idea where she's coming home from, but guess it should be about now. We'll know in a few days ... or, then again, maybe we won't. Need me up for this?"

"No, Captain, but taking no chance on getting my butt chewed out at breakfast for not waking you with the good news."

Giving Douglass a *Grinch* grin, Buchanan ordered. "Get the hell out of here!"

The captain's head had not quite hit the pillow when the piercing yell of Lieutenant Wayne Dewars boomed over the 21MC, "Captain to the attack center!"

Urgent tones in the young officer's voice hoisted Buchanan from his bunk. In skivvies and barefoot he raced to the attack center.

On arrival, Dewars said, "I think *Steelhead* just got torpedoed."

Both Buchanan and Douglass proceeded immediately to the sonar shack where they found Sonarman Chief Coker with back-up earphones donned.

"What can you tell me, Chief?"

"We were tracking a *Six-thirty-seven*-class moving toward Fundy, Captain. Heard an explosion immediately following what sounded like twenty seconds of torpedo run. I wasn't here, but checked the tapes. Fairly certain."

Buchanan's heart sank.

He bit his lip then asked, "Breaking up noises?"

"Didn't hear any, Captain. Loud thump at what I guess was the ship hitting bottom."

"Get a sounding, Bob. Chief, give me your best estimate of the explosion coordinates. We'll head over there, but slow and quiet. Whatever got the *thirty-seven* is still there and I don't want to be another scalp in her belt."

"Aye, Captain."

Douglass returned to the sonar shack and reported, "Sounding twelve hundred feet, Captain."

"Good. Hopefully some of the compartments are still dry."

Denver headed for the sinking coordinates without event. Perhaps the attacker had no wish to push his luck and departed the area. Whatever the reason, Buchanan took the good luck.

"Okay. Turn the receiver gain to full and listen for any sounds."

Coker didn't require an order for he had this operation ongoing. But giving the order made the skipper feel better.

Near Middleburg, VA

Senator Darrel Manning had driven through a myriad of darkened roads after departing the golf course, causing his passenger Vasiliy Baknov to be totally disoriented.

"That was a close one, Vasiliy," said Manning.

"I'm not certain what happened, Senator."

Manning explained, concluding with, "You are very vulnerable, Vasiliy. That's why I removed you from the house. You're charged with murder and espionage. Should you be captured there, it would raise a veil of suspicion all but impossible for us to overcome."

What does this bastard really mean? I'm obviously no longer of any use to him. Actually a liability.

Vasiliy expected the worst. Adding to Baknov's concerns, Manning had said nothing about their destination. Vasiliy didn't have long to wait before Manning confirmed his suspicions. The senator stopped beside a copse of trees with no nearby street light.

He said, "We'll be coming to some towns soon. It's been a while since I drove this vehicle, Vasiliy. Would you mind walking around the car to see if all the lights are on? I'll test the brake lights when you're in back. This is important. The police make lots of money ticketing cars for faulty lights. And it's not a good time for you to be recognized. Your picture is plastered all over the country."

The son of a bitch must think I'm stupid. He's going to kill me.
"Not at all, sir."

Pretending to have a problem, Vasiliy fumbled with his seat belt.
"Here, let me help."

When Manning reached over, Baknov seized the senator's arm
and put it in a painful hammerlock. Using his other arm, Vasiliy
thrust a hand into Manning's inside pocket and removed a nickel-
plated Smith & Wesson small frame .38-caliber revolver.

The need for courtesy had vanished and Baknov demanded,
"And what did you plan to do with this, you buffoon?"

Startled, the classic Manning majestic countenance melted into
one of sheer terror and a quaking voice contradicted the words he
spoke. "Nothing. I ... I carry this for protection. You never know
when someone might try to assassinate me."

Seeing through the claim, Baknov guessed Manning planned to
use his gun to insure news of the impending Russian coup did not
reach the media.

"Maybe someone's about to," Baknov threatened, but he had no
intention of following through.

An intelligent man, Baknov considered it made no sense and
represented more liability than asset. But it would unnerve the
senator, further lessening his immediate threat.

He unfastened Manning's seat belt and opened the driver side
door then said, "Get out and put up your hands."

A trembling Manning complied.

"Now, walk forward where I can see you in the headlights. Keep
walking till I tell you to stop."

"Please don't kill me, sir. Look. I can do a great deal for you."

"Give me your wallet and start walking."

Manning complied and moved ahead of the car, hands in the air
exhibiting none of his trademark cool composure.

Shifting to the driver's seat, Baknov fastened his seat belt. He
started the engine and sped toward a terrified Manning, swerving to
miss him at the last second.

What do I do now? Baknov needed food and a place to sleep. He
came upon a MacDonald's fast food restaurant and used the drive-
through. Parking in the drive-in lot, he devoured a hamburger, fries,

a drink and ice cream. He paid for them with a twenty dollar bill, the only cash he found in Manning's wallet.

Now to find a place to sleep. I can't use the Warren Biddle alias. Initially, he thought of hiding out in an austere roadside motel. *But how will I pay? I can't use Manning's credit card. He is too well-known for me to use his name.* Then it came to him. The senator's name would be a perfect alias. And he wouldn't have to stay in roadside fleabags, but four-star accommodations instead.

Baknov pulled up before a top-of-the-line motel near Manassas, Virginia and moments later, a night clerk registered him.

When he offered his credit card, the clerk said, "Welcome, Mr. Manning. I notice your first name is Darrel. Are you related to the senator by any chance?"

Smiling, Baknov replied, "I get that question often. No, but maybe a distant poor cousin."

False laughs by both men. "How long will you be with us, sir?"

"I'll be leaving in the morning."

"Be sure to have our breakfast buffet. It goes with the room."

"I will and thank you." *How perfect. And no need to hide the car. Manning won't report it stolen. He'd have to explain how the notorious Lieutenant Vasiliy Baknov of the Soviet Navy took it from him. Fat chance of that. And he won't report fraudulent use of his credit card for the same reason. Now I need to find a newsman and tell my story.*

Aboard *Steelhead*

Brent Maddock recovered from the shock, his head spinning, but with presence of mind to know he had to lead and immediately. Men nearby began to recover, among them Tom Bentley. The attack center watch picked themselves up and began systematic checks for anyone injured.

Maddock used his best command voice. "Everyone okay?"

Knowing that their captain remained in command had a calming effect. Responses came back indicating no serious injuries.

Waiting a moment, the captain ordered an appraisal of the ship's condition. He saw the attack center showed only emergency lighting and that caused him to believe the worst. An initial report confirmed no communication with anyone aft of the operations compartment. The hull had been breached ending any hope *Steelhead* could raise herself to the surface. Worse, all hands in the ship's after end had probably not survived.

Plenty of time remained to grieve losses. Maddock now needed to isolate any possible means of escape. He knew personal swim-ups not an option from twelve hundred feet indicated by the depth gauge. His men could be removed only with the aid of outside assistance. It could be done only with a DSRV (Deep Submergence Rescue Vehicle) that can dive to five thousand feet, find its object with sonar and affix itself to the hatch of a submarine. Using two pilots and two crew, it's capable of removing twenty-four crewmen with each descent.

Fortunately, a DSRV had been stashed at Woods Hole for loan to the Oceanographic Institute on nearby Cape Cod.

Steelhead's plight had to be known and her hull located before rescue could be attempted. Thinking forward, Maddock had issued a standing order to keep the battery zero-floated—continuously charged at low amperage to ensure it would be at full capacity in an event of ship's main power generator failure.

Maddock spoke to his exec in a calm, low voice. "Secure all electrical power to non-essential equipment. We need to drag this can (battery) out long as we can." Then he thought, *Now comes the easy part, figuring out how to let someone know we're here.*

A check with sonar found the Gertrude (underwater telephone) hydrophone seriously damaged. Chief Giambri reported, "Captain, it's all but gone. Can get a weak CW (continuous wave) signal out, but make no promises."

"What about the active sonar?"

"Looks okay, but haven't tested it. Problem is it uses a lot of power and all we have now is the main battery."

Active sonar is the least used equipment in a *Six-thirty-seven* inventory, so much so, the fuses are normally removed.

"Should we try it, Captain?"

Maddock pondered the idea. "I'll let you know, Chief. The son of a bitch that got us might hear it and figure he needs to come back and finish the job."

The captain had no way of knowing the attacking Soviet missed the first transmission of the stand-down message, being too deep to receive the signal, but had since recovered the order and no longer posed a threat.

Maddock returned to the attack center and found Bill Bryan inventorying surviving ship's systems and determining their status.

He anticipated the skipper's next order perfectly and fielded it. "I ordered all men who don't have to be up and about to hit the bunks. We'll use less oxygen and they'll be up and ready when we need 'em, Captain."

"Good thinking, Bill."

Satisfied all necessary activities being carried out, Maddock sought his passenger, Mikhail Turgenev. He found him in the wardroom not all that perturbed.

"Seems you are constantly put to the test, Captain."

"You could say that." Maddock knew panic to be the enemy of good judgment and maintained a low key. "Was told by an old CO, 'the most disappointed people in the world are those who get what they deserve'."

"A wise man, your CO. Is there anything you can, or are able to tell me about our circumstance?"

Maddock knew Turgenev did not concern himself about his own skin. His recent fearless activities in Russia attested this. His main concern: the performance of his critical assignment in America following the coup against the Soviet government. Without him, a serious power gap would develop and be filled by only God knows who. The captain briefed Turgenev on all that had transpired.

"Wish I had experience to draw upon. My command occurred when the Cold War was still cold. But now, Captain, the moment of truth. How do you see our chances?"

"In the US Navy, captains always look at the bright side."

"I understand that. But in a remarkably short period, we've become remarkably good friends. Maybe you can tell me, not as between naval officers, but as friend to friend."

"All depends on if we're found. If so, my guess is fifty percent." Maddock then explained function and availability of a DSRV.

Turgenev smiled, although forcibly. "My intuition says it will end well. Why do I say this? There is no alternative. I know there is grief to be felt for your lost men. You are wise not to dwell on this now, but you are a compassionate man and it will come later to you and painfully."

Maddock nodded. He felt himself slip a bit, but forced recovery. Of all incentives to survive, Brent found the greatest to be fervent determination to see and hold his unborn child.

The Pentagon, CNO Office

Admiral Eric Danis could not believe his good luck. A hundred-ship relief convoy stood only two days out of Britain and with only minor losses, most of these from air attack. The Allies maintained air superiority over the North Atlantic and inflicted far more damage to Soviet air assets than had been done to Allied merchant ships.

Addressing his aide, CDR Leo Wade, Danis asked, "Ain't this the damnedest war you ever heard of?" Then added, "They had the world believing we were on the ropes, and now appear unable to interdict a relatively defenseless convoy."

"I think we achieved much more in the Bering Sea battle than the Russians admitted." Wade knew his boss quarter-backed that operation and took this opportunity to suck-up. "They need submarines to control the Atlantic, and thanks to you, they just about ran out of them in the Bering."

Danis did not want to take all the credit so low-keyed. His main wish: build that dream house in the desert with wife Eve at his side, and pull in his horns.

"Okay to say that in here, Leo, but keep it under your hat. I look forward to you young guys picking up the slack. You don't want a bunch of old fogies muddying the water. I actually believe our current success originates in the hearts of the Russian people."

"You have a point, Admiral. My guess is they're a little more tired of war than we are. Makes it easier to set up a coup."

"Wash your mouth out with soap, Leo. Even I'm not allowed to say the c-word. At least not in polite company. But seeing you brought it up, chances of it succeeding are a lot better now that they made us complicit. Nothing short of brilliant how Turgenev set the whole thing up."

"True, Admiral. Don't you believe that a lot of lives would have been saved had the Allies been invited to weigh in on the World War Two, twenty July forty-four plot to get Hitler?"

Danis nodded his agreement. "In that regard, Turgenev's being here is essential to the coup's success. Otherwise, all that's achieved is creating a power vacuum. And whoever fills it in might screw us worse than we're already being screwed. Keep in mind, the coup will cause temporary loss of control over enough nuclear weapons to turn this planet to cinders."

"How do you see Turgenev preventing that?"

"His presence here will signal major world powers he is temporary leader of a new order in Russia. That's intimidating, especially in view of Russia's war-weary status."

Wade added, "Seems like we're on the downhill side with only two days to go for the convoy to reach Britain and Turgenev almost arriving here."

"You spoke the critical words, Leo. Two days to go and almost. Many a slip between the cup and the lip."

"Well, it sure looks good."

Danis jumped on his aide again. "Looks good is not necessarily good. Now add one more variable. The Soviets must not get wind of the coup before the convoy arrives."

"Is there reason to be concerned, Admiral?"

"Only in my gut, Leo. Democracy is great, but it's like a sieve. I know the President has this under the tightest possible wraps and we hope that's enough."

"I don't want a slip either, Admiral."

"Leo, you, better than most aides I've known, understand the importance of sitting on sensitive material. And a fringe benefit of interrupting your career to help out an old guy is education. So I feel obliged to share this. There's a coup being plotted in this country."

"There is!"

Wade made no attempt to conceal his surprise.

Danis explained what he knew about Darrel Manning's plan to seize power and the extent the senator would go to in order to succeed. "A bloodless coup, but it would have the same effect as the one Turgenev leads: capitulation. So it's vital the Russians initiate theirs first."

Wade, much younger than Danis, found this hard to get his mind around, but a brief exposure to politics aided his understanding.

As if from a paranormal cue, Danis's secretary buzzed the intercom. "Courier here, Admiral. Shall I send him in?"

"Please."

A bright polished young lieutenant entered, a side arm strapped to his right side and a locked pouch chained to his left wrist. The lieutenant performed the ritual of delivering a sealed envelope and prepared to leave.

Delivering a crisp salute, he asked, "By your leave, Admiral?"

Danis acknowledged the salute with a nod and said, "Carry on, Lieutenant," and the young officer left.

He read the message and gave Wade the grimmest expression the aide had ever seen as he said, "*Steelhead* is down and Turgenev with her. So much for *sure looks good*."

Aboard *Denver*

Captain Jim Buchanan's well-oiled machine sprang into action. Many among his competent crew did what needed to be done without orders. The skipper wanted two sonarmen on the phones focusing solely on searching for the enemy. Specifically, not involved with the downed *Six-thirty-seven*. Chief Coker had already established this when Buchanan entered the sonar shack.

"What's the latest, Chief?"

"Good news, Captain. We're picking up faint noise that sounds like machinery running. This means the entire ship is not flooded. Bad news is there's nothing to indicate presence of survivors."

"How far are we from the estimated coordinates?"

"Five thousand yards, give or take."

"How do you plan to fix the location?"

"We'll home in on what we're hearing. When the bearing shifts one-eighty degrees, we're there."

Buchanan recalled the words of his instructor at Prospective Commanding Officer School. "When you get the feeling you're no longer needed, you've done a good job."

Buchanan found his exec also running with the right balls. He anticipated the need to be able to recover the *thirty-seven*'s exact position when *Denver* returned to the scene. Everyone in *Denver* knew the wreck to be *Steelhead*, but none bellied up until positive identification established this. The U.S. Navy had become far too dependent on GPS (Global Positioning System) before the Soviet war. Now, with all satellites shot from orbit, it's back to square one.

Douglass said, "When we pass over the wreck, I'll log the coordinates shown on SINS (Ship's Inertial Navigation System), then surface and recover position the best I can and use the navigational fix to reset SINS."

"SINS? In my early BN (boomer) days we used to say if you can tell SINS where it is, it will tell you where you are. Are we still on that page, Bob?"

"Only game in town, Captain."

Buchanan's famous Grinch grin spread over his face. "Do we still have a sextant in the allowance? Let's surface and I'll put us within a quarter mile of where we are. The DSRV can do the job from there." *Hot damn. They still need me.*

"Captain to sonar!" bellowed the unmistakable voice of Chief Coker. "Positive ID on *Steelhead*."

When Buchanan arrived, Coker reported, "Faint Gertrude CW key, Captain. Seems like on the hour and half hour. Permission to transmit, Captain."

"Do it, Chief. Make 'em happier campers despite their plight."

Minutes later, Buchanan shot a round of evening twilight stars and went below. They plotted perfectly.

"Tell SINS where it is, XO," Buchanan quipped.

Configured to mount a DSRV atop her hull, *Denver* proceeded to Woods Hole, MA. As she reached the *Hole* approaches, *Denver* received a message directing her to do what she had undertaken on her own two hours earlier.

Buchanan reflected, *Maybe CINCLANTFLT has done so well, he too is no longer needed.*

Restaurant in Old Town, Alexandria, VA

Vasiliy enjoyed the bottomless budget with Darrel Manning's credit card. He dined and slept well, always cautious to relocate immediately after using the card. He knew Manning could track him down this way. Hotels posed no problem. They posted no charges until after checkout, with Baknov long gone by then. So he lived the good life, but had an agenda. He knew not for certain, but figured the clock ticked. This likely accounted for the recent CIA raid at Manning's Middleburg country home.

He wished to get news of the impending coup to the Soviet Premier. His best chance of doing this: the U.S. media. He banked on hunger first, a passion among American newsmen. However, those high in the pecking order despised retractions. This spelled delay, something Baknov could not afford. So he elected a small town newspaper reporter who had nothing to lose, and therefore no fear of losing it.

An overweight young man entered, looking to be in his mid-thirties, with thinning brown hair and obviously out of his comfort zone in the upscale restaurant.

Baknov caught his eye and beckoned.

"How do you do, sir? I'm Harry Hibbs. And you are?"

"It really makes no difference who I am, but if you need a name, call me Victor. Look. Let's not stand on ceremony. The menu is superb and the bar stocked with fine libation, so let's indulge. My treat." Baknov hoped alcohol might soften Harry's demeanor. It did. He later said to Harry, "How would you like to be first with the greatest scoop of the century?"

Chapter 24

Aboard *Denver* moored at Woods Hole, MA

CO Jim Buchanan and XO Bob Douglass stood on the bridge and watched the painstakingly slow loading of a DSRV on *Denver*'s after deck. Once in place, looking for all the world like a thirty-seven ton cigar atop the auxiliary space access hatch, its forty-nine foot overall length covered most of the after deck.

Wayne Dewars took over the same job he'd held on *Sterlet*: weapons officer and first lieutenant. In the latter capacity, he and COB supervised the loading operation.

Buchanan pushed Douglass to prepare him for his next assignment: command. "Give me your thoughts on running back to Fundy surfaced."

The skipper had already made up his mind.

"I like our chances, Captain. Diesel boats are the only opposition and likely unable to reach our track while we make flank speed. Submerged with the DSRV in place slows us down and it'll take forever and a day to reach *Steelhead*. She doesn't have forever and a day. It's a no-brainer, Captain. Priority goes to getting the DSRV to station ASAP."

Buchanan made a mental note: *Recommend Bob for command soon as we hit Fundy.*

Dewars and COB presiding over the loading operation, but having never done this, took a great number of recommendations from Woods Hole longshoremen. Guts churning over the delay, Buchanan and Douglass bit the bullet.

The exec recalled an admonition once received from a Navy yard rigger while Bob still wore LTJG stripes, *Why is there never enough time to do it right, but always enough time to do it over?*

He shared this with the captain.

"I think I ran into that guy during my first overhaul. The best repository for our energy is to insure *Denver* is ready to go off like a two-dollar half-cocked pistol when the DSRV is secured."

"Agree, Captain. Think there's enough time before that for me to whip your butt in cribbage?"

"Dream on, Bob."

The two officers disappeared into the bridge access trunk and headed for the wardroom.

"Good for the crew to see us relaxed, Bob. Makes 'em think they got nothing to worry about."

"Little do they know."

An hour later, *Denver* rounded Nobska Point, leaving it well to port as she sped on the surface for *Steelhead*'s coordinates.

Nothing quite like standing on the open bridge of a warship racing along at top speed into crisp weather. Buchanan and Douglass stood there, not because they had to but wanted to. Bill Bryan, an experienced senior watch officer, stood the OOD watch and needed no oversight.

The captain had a built-in excuse. Claiming not to trust SINS, he shot a series of sun lines and early evening twilight sightings to bring the ship precisely back to where they had found *Steelhead*.

Douglass sat in the wardroom with two DSRV pilots and two rescue personnel. There, the exec learned electric motors driven by silver-zinc batteries deliver fifteen horsepower to a single shaft. The vehicle has a thirty-hour endurance at four knots. She navigates and searches with sonar and can home on a signal from the stricken hull. Once there, she fastens herself to any deck hatch and can remove twenty-four personnel per mooring. Maddock reported eighty-three of *Steelhead*'s hundred-nine complement survived. Four dockings are required to move them to a Canadian destroyer standing by.

At the conclusion, Douglass said, "Sounds straightforward," and then thought, *Those damn straightforward things are the ones that worry me most.*

He had indeed reached readiness for command.

Restaurant in Old Town, Alexandria, VA

Harry Hibbs proved to be Vasiliy Baknov's *light at the end of the tunnel*. Ambitious and full of himself with no conscience whatsoever, left little doubt he would run with the story. Hibbs cared about Hibbs and not much more. Only problem, Baknov could not stress the importance of getting it out quickly without raising the reporter's antenna.

He had no idea of the planned coup's timing, only that he must get his information to the Kremlin before the fact, in order to quash it. Gently he probed Hibbs on when the story would appear in print.

Hibbs asked, "Why? Is that important?"

"My share of your bonus for breaking this. I got a deal cooking and need the bucks." Baknov thought it wise to further cultivate the greedy reporter. "And there will be more where that comes from."

Hibbs replied, "Strikes me you can't be too hard up. Top menu items in the city's number one restaurant?"

"I have a silent partner who's much better heeled than me letting me use his credit card. But, it'll soon stop if I can't fill my piece of the deal. Sooner is better than later."

"Victor, we haven't covered one little detail. What's your source for this story?"

Baknov would take the chance. What had he to lose? He would suck Hibbs in by stroking his arrogant ego. *This dumb bastard's transparent as a midwinter day in Novaya Zemlya.* "You are quite brilliant, Harry Hibbs. You know exactly who I am, but string me along. I was certain you recognized the notorious Vasiliy Baknov when you entered the restaurant but didn't turn me in. I wondered why and now believe I have my answer. This is all a game to you."

Hibbs could not believe his luck. He immediately recognized the name and saw the resemblance to photos distributed nationwide.

"I was ninety-nine percent certain," he bluffed. "But I'm a newsman. Finding out what you are up to is more important than claiming a reward, and my bonus will exceed the government offer by orders of magnitude. Citing you as the source of this tip opens doors. And, as a newsman, I am under no obligation to report you to the authorities."

He read Hibbs's startled expression like a book. *In a pig's ass you were*, he thought. Then he lied, "I am relieved. I doubt you'll believe this, but I wish to put the war behind me and take up a new life here."

Hibbs took it hook, line and sinker, then demonstrated how poorly he could lie. "Look, Victor. I think it's best I continue to call you that."

Baknov agreed.

Hibbs went on. "I need to validate my source to the editor." Hibbs removed a Pen Rapid EE.D variant of a miniature camera designed to accept an Agfa Rapid cassette. "Do you mind?"

"Of course not."

After snapping a few quick photos, Hibbs pocketed the camera. "With normal luck, the story goes out at midnight. Now let's squeeze your colleague's credit card a bit more. Bear in mind, the tab will be only a fraction of your bonus share."

My share? This idiot thinks I believe him. When he shows up with 'my cut,' he'll have authorities in tow and collect the reward on top of his bonus. If Manning picks up the tab, why not indulge? And in the near future, Hibbs will learn I've exploited him, in his own words, 'orders of magnitude' over the use he got from me.

Aboard *Steelhead*

Brent Maddock assessed conditions aboard and found them relatively good considering the ferocity of the attack on his ship. He did not share his concerns about sea depth pressure on the operations compartment after bulkhead. If it failed, everyone would be lost instantly, so fretting over it netted nothing.

Designed to withstand seven hundred feet maximum buoyant escape depth pressure, Maddock knew where they sat exceeded that. He also knew submarine designers hedged their bets and applied a hundred-fifty percent of required values. They sat a hundred-fifty feet below this safety measure. Fortunately, *Steelhead*'s designer apparently slipped a decimal point in the right direction.

Maddock comforted himself, theorizing the bulkhead held and would likely continue to do so. Others probably conducted the same mental exercise but remained silent. Discussion would only exacerbate an already grim mood.

The skipper, accustomed to assessing a situation, formulating a plan and enacting it, found himself frustrated over being able to do nothing but sit and wait. He tried not to reflect on the lost sailors aft of the operations compartment, but could not. Though all this weighed heavily on him, Maddock moved among his troops as if their perilous circumstance did not exist.

Mikhail Turgenev stopped by Maddock's stateroom for a chat. He had assumed a father-like status over the skipper. Turgenev broke the somber mood with humor. "Captain, I guess this is not a good time to ask you for another cribbage lesson?"

Maddock smiled. "You could say that, Mikhail."

"I admire the manner by which you sustain troop morale. In the Soviet Navy, commanding officers are older. You demonstrate remarkable wisdom for so young a man."

"I'm glad I come off that way. The feeling in my gut contradicts that. You wouldn't be just trying to make a scared CO feel better?"

"Not at all." Turgenev wished to use Brent's first name, but felt it best to await invitation. "The men admire your leadership and this will increase in the years ahead. Just the mention of Captain Maddock's name will bring smiles to their faces regardless of what you now feel in your gut."

"Thank you, Mikhail. Our top priority is to get you out of here and to Washington. We have more than just hope. As we speak, a colleague and former CO, Captain Jim Buchanan likely approaches us with a DSRV, the rescue vehicle I described."

"Your Navy is far more compassionate than ours. We have no such escape devices."

Maddock knew DSRVs are multi-purposed and had been used with great success to gather critical data on the Soviet Navy. He opted not to share this, knowing whatever fell out of Turgenev's coup, the U.S. would continue to monitor Russian naval activity. And vice versa.

"Thank you, Mikhail. The knowledge that we have them has a good impact on troop morale. Far as I know, this is our first actual attempt to rescue a downed submarine crew."

"How will we know when the attempt begins?"

Unsure, Maddock said, "We'll either get a signal from USS *Denver* or hear a loud *clank* when the DSRV moors to the escape trunk. To stretch out our battery, all major sonar listening equipment is secured and we only activate Gertrude hourly, starting at five minutes before and after. *Denver* is aware of the procedure."

"So then all we can do is just wait."

"Don't know if you're a praying man, Mikhail, but whatever happens, it better be soon. We have five hours left in the battery."

"Then what?"

"Better you not know."

The Pentagon, CNO Office

Admiral Eric Danis, a busy schedule keeping him at work well into the evening, reined in his elation. Two bits of good news. One, the convoy had reached Britain. *Two, no, call it one and a half down with one and half to go. Steelhead* had been located and a DSRV reached the area, but Turgenev had yet to be rescued.

Piecing together all he knew of *Steelhead*'s plight, Danis concluded the operations compartment remained unflooded and Mikhail Turgenev likely survived. Getting him out should be easy, but how does a *Six-thirty-seven* pressure bulkhead hold up at twelve-hundred feet? *Optimism is what lost the Battle of Midway for Japan.* Don't go there an inner voice warned.

But what to tell President Dempsey? *He'll be damn sure of wanting an answer when he gets this. I can give him all the pros and cons, but his bottom line will be what do I think. What do I think? The combination of Brent Maddock and Jim Buchanan working the problem makes me feel good about the chances.*

Danis buzzed for Leo Wade and presented what he'd just ruminated.

"Want to hear what a lowly CDR thinks, Admiral?"

"Exactly."

"Paint the bright picture. The way I see it, whether you're right or wrong, the end result is unchanged. So why not let the President feel good in the interim?"

"That simple?"

"That simple, sir. I'll call your car. It must be done in person."

"Good, Leo. Check to see if the President can fit me in."

"He can, Admiral. This is the hottest tamale on his plate."

Aboard *Steelhead*

A loud *clank* emanated from the torpedo-loading hatch, the only indication the Deep Submergence Rescue Vehicle had found the hull and prepared to fasten itself.

Not a minute too soon, Brent Maddock thought. The battery expired two hours earlier and except for an occasional flashlight, the crew sat in total darkness. Breaths grew short as the men sucked at what little oxygen remained in the unventilated compartment.

Maddock stood beneath the escape trunk as noises from the DSRV continued for what seemed an interminable period. He watched the dog wheel spin and an instant later, the hatch popped open. A pilot dropped into the compartment, extended his hand to Maddock and got immediately down to business.

"How many survivors, Captain?"

The skipper preferred not to give numbers. "We'll need four lifts. But oxygen is all but gone. Did you bring any?"

"Forty portable tanks, Captain. I'll have my crew bring them down. It's all we have, but change users every five minutes and you should be fine till the next trip. I'll bring more. Can we start loading?"

"Of course. Mikhail, you first."

"I'd prefer to remain and leave with you, Captain."

"Mikhail, we must be practical. If only you survive, our mission is a success. Without you, despite how many of the rest of us do, it's a failure."

"I see your logic, Captain. I'll reluctantly carry out your orders."

They shook hands and Turgenev disappeared into the DSRV, followed by twenty-three crewmen, Maddock calling each by name and patting them on the back as they ascended the ladder."

The hatch resecured, sounds of the rescue vehicle could be heard as it left.

Maddock knew what ran through everyone's mind. *Will they be able to find us again?* "Pilot said he got a good fix on us and should return within the hour."

The skipper did not share his greatest concern and thought, *How much longer will the operations compartment bulkhead hold?*

Maddock followed the protocol of evacuation by rank, lowest to the highest, but allowed Mikhail to go with the first group. Those trapped in a doomed submarine, watching the hatch close on the only pathway out played on nerves of those who awaited a later ride. The skipper sensed rising confidence each time the DSRV returned.

The vehicle arrived for the fourth and final load.

Before following Bob Douglass up the ladder, Maddock turned toward the operations compartment bulkhead and shouted, "Thanks, sweetheart ... and whatever engineer slipped the decimal point in the right direction."

White House, Oval Office

CNO Admiral Eric Danis entered the office and saw the President happier than a four-year-old on Christmas morning. His wide grin revealed wrinkles Danis had not seen before.

"Eric. We have Turgenev! Got the news while you were driving over." President Dempsey held up two fingers then said, "Two out of three. Now if we can only beat Manning's thugs to press. It's the signal to commence the coup. Turgenev wants to run an ad in all the big papers ... First Edition of *Fathers and Sons* to be auctioned by owner. That's all he gave us. My staff is working a back-up story. Problem is this won't stop the presses. It'll go out with the morning papers and I'm not sure how long it will take Turgenev's people to get the signal."

"Mr. President, what is the likelihood news of the impending coup falls through the cracks and we get scooped?"

"That's the tough question. It'll likely kill the coup. When the CIA pieces together what they got from people they picked up from Manning's Middleburg place, a high probability emerges that the Soviet spy, Vasiliy Baknov, was there, but escaped. He knows about Turgenev's plan. Expect him to release the info to the first newsie who'll listen to him."

Danis said, "I'm sure there's no point in declaring it a national security issue."

The President nodded that he agreed and said, "The best way to get famous is to be a bell ringer. And of course there's always 'the public has a right to know' dodge."

"No way to stop that?"

Dempsey's mood lost all the joy it had when Danis first walked in. "Only if we catch Baknov and soon."

Danis said, "I feel like a wet blanket for having broached this, Mr. President."

"Don't, Eric. Wet blankets are the only kind that come in here."

Restaurant in Old Town, Alexandria, VA

Vasiliy Baknov, confident his warning to the Kremlin would arrive in time to prevent the coup, enjoyed the rest of his glorious repast. He of course had no knowledge of what transpired in the White House a scant forty-five minutes earlier. Though he had come to detest the overbearing and arrogant reporter Harry Hibbs, Vasiliy, a true Russian, believed his impending triumph in need of celebration. He went along with Hibbs, permitting his normal diligence to be distracted and failed to notice a teenage girl several tables away paying close attention to him.

The girl nudged her father. "It's him, I tell you. I carry his picture in my purse. Look." Young girls tend to march to their own drums often in defiance of convention. She considered Vasiliy Baknov accused unjustly and wished to rise to his defense, and in the process developed a crush on the handsome young Russian. "I want to go meet him, Daddy."

Her dad surveyed the photo and agreed to his daughter's assessment. "No, you don't want to do that. It'll focus attention and someone else might recognize him. That would make you very unhappy."

She reluctantly agreed.

"Don't stare at him when you leave, it's sure to make him suspicious."

He passed the photo back to his daughter and hastily wrote on his check. *Call police. Man two tables away facing me is wanted. Soviet spy.*

The waiter, also serving Baknov's table, picked up the check and immediately noticed the scribble and thought, *I can't believe it. No wonder I recognized him.*

Moments later, as two uniformed police entered the restaurant, pistols drawn, background noise diminished to a whisper as clientele caught site of the impending arrest.

"Vasiliy Baknov," said the larger officer, "I arrest you for the murder of Warren Biddle."

A thought to draw his weapon ran through his mind but quickly dissolved. The fast thinking Vasiliy saw nothing to be gained. His major concern, quick release of the story he had given Hibbs.

"You got me," and turning to Hibbs, he said, "I'm sorry, sir ... what did you say your name is?"

Hibbs looked on, astounded, but said nothing.

Baknov said to the arresting officer. "We were both waiting for a table. When one became available, we agreed to share it."

Hibbs looked up. "That's right, officer."

A CIA requirement had been attached to the all-points bulletin. *Detain Baknov and all in his company. Incarcerate separately. Permit no outside contact till arrival of CIA personnel.*

The officer said, "I apologize, but you too must come with us."

Indignant, Hibbs stood. "Officer, I am a reporter and see no reason for my arrest."

"I'm sorry, sir, but you'll have to take that up with the desk sergeant. Come along, please."

Hibbs stood his ground. "I insist on calling my attorney."

He bluffed. He had no attorney.

"Please, sir. This is a national security matter. Not now, but you'll be able to contact him in due time."

The arrogant Hibbs would not yield. "Officer, do you know how many charges I can bring against you? Arrest without cause and denying me access to legal representation are just two."

Exasperated with arrogant Hibbs's pointless rhetoric, the officer said, "If you don't come along with us, I'll arrange for you to add police brutality to that charge list."

The officers patted both men down, removed Baknov's pistol, handcuffed them and left the restaurant. They entered a police car as the background noise levels in the restaurant quickly rose.

Chapter 25

Georgetown, Washington, D.C.

Senator Darrel Manning, a past master of selecting the perfect demeanor for bending audiences to his will, chose outrage for this session. He addressed members of his staff complicit in the Soviet negotiated settlement plot not among those arrested in Middleburg.

Though they became aware of the crisis for the first time, Manning nonetheless *chewed butt* as he attributed the entire fiasco to their incompetence. Well compensated, none objected. They all had grown too comfortable with lives accruing to fat paychecks and had no wish to bring this to an end. In full knowledge they plotted against the country, none seemed affected by this.

He knew how to find bright people untroubled by conscience.

The senator's voice resounded through his plush townhouse. "Damn it, I expect this to be fixed, and now! No one goes anywhere till we have a fix in place!"

He ranted on, then suddenly became aware his audience focused not on Manning, but who stood behind him. He turned and saw what proved to be a CIA Agent, arms folded with a pleased expression. Behind him stood half a dozen District of Columbia policemen, weapons drawn.

"Looks like we got us another nest of snakes," said the agent. Then to the senator, he declared, "Mr. Manning, I arrest you for committing acts of treason against the United States Government."

Manning snarled, "Do you know who you're talking to?"

"I do, and save your breath, Manning." The agent took obvious delight in omitting the senator title. "You know damn well we wouldn't be here unless we stood on solid ground."

The agent directed an officer to handcuff *the subject*.

A few moments later, Manning found himself in a patrol car with the agent who said, "Don't worry, Mr. Manning. We have everything you'll need, including an orange jump suit to replace that two thousand dollar Brooks Brothers outfit. I'm guessing by the time you'll be allowed to wear these clothes again, they won't fit. Would you like me to make you an offer?"

The White House, Washington, D.C.

Entering the Oval Office, Admiral Danis found President Dempsey ecstatic. Despite its low news value, Turgenev's signal made it to the international stage and his supporters picked it up. Immediately afterward, news of the Soviet coup and requested cease-fire dominated the world's tabloids.

"Mr. President, I don't recall ever seeing a happier camper than now. Congratulations, sir. This is a great day for you and the world."

"It is, Eric, much to the credit of your submariners. We should give that guy, Captain Maddock, the Medal of Honor. What do you think?"

"Let the dust settle a bit. Maddock's hurting over his lost troops, as are we all. Best thing we can do for him now is cut him a little slack. Plenty of time to hand out kudos later. Let's wait so we don't miss anyone. That said, I'm guessing you have more on the agenda than celebrating success."

"Told you before, Eric, get into politics. You've got a nose for it and would do one helluva job."

"Please, no favors, sir. Now how 'bout that agenda? We keep meeting without him and the Chairman's beginning to feel like the Lone Ranger."

"Told you before, the job's yours if you want it."

"And I replied, please don't do me any favors. Again, about that agenda?"

"Real treat for you, Eric. The new Russian Ambassador's presenting credentials to State and will make an office call when he's done. That should be in about fifteen minutes. Heard he has some pretty good things to say about your submariners. How they evacuated him from right under the Soviet Navy's nose and then picked him off the ocean bottom."

"Thank you, sir. It will indeed be an honor."

"Frankly, Eric, there is no one more deserving of being here for this than you."

Danis recognized a clear *got an itch* tone in the President's voice. "Anything you need from me, sir?"

"This, Turgenev is a great-grandson of the Russian who wrote *Fathers and Sons*. Ever read it?"

"No. Didn't have to. At Annapolis, we just had to remember titles and authors, nothing about what was in the books."

Dempsey's secretary interrupted, "Ambassador Turgenev has arrived, Mr. President."

"Good. Show him in please."

Dempsey rose from his chair wearing an ear-to-ear grin and strutted to the office door in a manner that would turn the proudest peacock green with envy.

Canadian Naval Base, Deep Brook, Nova Scotia
The Previous Day

Skipper Brent Maddock had never seen so big an assembly of counts and no-accounts waiting on a dock. COM Bostwick in full dress-blue uniform resplendent with medals and sword stood in the middle. All focused on the arrival of Russian Ambassador Turgenev, for each wished to be part of this historic event.

Maddock had other concerns: *Steelhead* dependents. He spotted them behind the crowd. In the middle stood Bea, gathering *Steelhead* families about her like a mallard hen with ducklings. Brent knew next of kin had been provided a casualty list and hoped Bea's flock included only those dependents belonging to survivors. Severely depleted energy would make it difficult for him to console families of lost crewmen. To do right by them, he needed more time than he presently had and a clear head. Brent's first order of business, greet his wife, and then look about to see if any dependents stand alone, a most discomforting prospect. But he would do what he had to do.

Moments before the brow went over, Maddock faced Turgenev for probably their last encounter.

He extended a hand and said, "An honor and a pleasure, sir."

Turgenev took it firmly, then covered it with his left hand. "This shall not be our last meeting, Captain. I promise you."

Smiling, Maddock added, "My guess, you're about to become a very busy bee, Mikhail."

"Never too busy for the man who twice saved my life. Now go, Brent. I shall address you by that name hereafter for you are more friend than captain to me. I envy your father for having so magnificent a son."

"You are kind, Mikhail."

"And now we must part. I see families standing behind the welcomers. Go to them. I do not envy your sorrowful task."

Jim Buchanan intercepted Brent when he stepped from the gangway. "I know you gotta do what you gotta do, Brent. Not sure whether this'll make you feel better or worse. Exactly thirty-three minutes after the fourth DSRV lift, *Steelhead*'s last bulkhead collapsed."

Brent looked his friend in the eye and said, "I'm here. So it makes me feel better."

"Welcome back, friend."

"Jim, it was you who punched the ticket and I'll be forever in your debt."

"Watch what you say, Brent. Last guy with that debt sends a monthly fifth of JD Black."

The expression shared between them said more than a million words.

Brent went to Bea and engulfed her in a long embrace.

She made no attempt to brush away tears. "I have never worried so much in my life."

"Sweetheart, you'll never have to worry that much again."

"Are you telling me what I think you are?"

"Yes."

Woody Parnell scanned faces in the crowd but did not see Erica Hussey. *I understand. She's not a dependent, so how could she know?* He saw Jim Buchanan sitting in a jeep, low profiling, as COM Bostwick and the others vied for the position of being the principal Mikhail Turgenev greeter, a futile effort. As soon as his foot touched Canadian soil, a host of the President's plainclothes secret service converged on the ambassador and drove him to a Learjet then flew him to Washington.

Approaching Buchanan, Woody asked, "Captain, are you driving back to Fundy?"

"I am, Woody."

"Can you drop me off in town?"

"You in a hurry? You don't have much baggage," Buchanan grinned his Grinch grin. Parnell escaped from *Steelhead* with barely his skin. The Canadians provided him a grungy foul-weather jacket, but an otherwise empty-handed Parnell traveled light. "Where can I drop you off, sailor?"

Minutes later, Woody knocked on Erica Hussey's apartment door. Beholding the caller, the young woman stood stunned but only seconds before joyously throwing her arms about him. Three and a half hours later, they exchanged their first words.

White House, Oval Office

Mikhail entered the office with his trademark lack of fanfare. The President greeted him warmly and briefly discussed their two country's mutual desire for peace then introduced Eric Danis.

"It's an honor, sir," Danis replied while he shook Turgenev's hand. Foremost in the CNO's mind, details of *Steelhead*'s final moments, but that would have to wait. "And congratulations on your successful coup."

"Thank you, Admiral. With the people and military backing us, things happen rapidly. And thank you for the fine accommodations in *Steelhead*. Picking me up off Severodvinsk demanded exceptional bravery. I shall ever be grateful to Captain Maddock and his dedicated submariners. For the lost members of *Steelhead*'s gallant crew, my deepest condolences."

"Thank you, Mr. Turgenev. I shall be sure the crew survivors and every *Steelhead* dependent receives your compassionate message."

"Please, Admiral, Mikhail will suffice. Highest rank I achieved in the Soviet Navy was captain."

The platitude exchange concluded, *Dempsey* asked, "Mikhail, is your great-grandfather's novel *Fathers and Sons* a good book? Ashamed to admit I haven't read it."

A rare smile engulfed Mikhail Turgenev's face. "Neither have I, Mr. President."

Glossary

1MC – General announcing system

21MC – Tactical intercom system

585 – *Skipjack*-class nuclear-powered submarine

637 – *Sturgeon*-class nuclear-powered submarine

688 – *Los Angeles*-class nuclear-powered submarine

7MC – Intercom connects Bridge, Attack Center, Torpedo and Maneuvering Rooms

ADC – Acoustic Device Countermeasure

ADCAP – Advanced Capability MK 48 Torpedo

Akula – Soviet *Typhoon*-class ballistic missile submarine, world's largest

AMS – Auxiliary Machine Space

AN/BQQ-5 – Listening sonar

ASW – Antisubmarine Warfare

Baffles – Area directly behind the ship where sonar is virtually deaf.

BCP – Ballast Control Panel

BN – Ballistic Missile Nuclear-powered Submarine

Boomer – Ballistic Missile Nuclear-powered Submarine

BQR – Listening sonar

BQS-14 – Forward and upward looking sonar mounted on the sail front to determine presence of downward-hanging ridges and thickness of ice above

Burke-**class** – Arleigh Burke class Destroyer

Can – Slang for battery

CNO – Chief of Naval Operations

COB – Chief of the Boat

COM – Commodore

Conning Officer – Officer in charge of controlling the ship while submerged

CONUS – Continental United States

Convergence Zone – 32 miles

CPO – Chief Petty Officer

DCNO – Deputy Chiefs of Naval Operations
DD – Destroyer
Delta-**class** – Soviet attack submarine
Doc – Universal nickname for ship's hospital corpsman
Dogface – Navy slang for U.S. Army soldier
DR – Dead Reckoning
DSRV – Deep Submergence Rescue Vehicle
ECM – Electronic Countermeasure
Exec / XO – Executive Officer
FBM – Fleet Ballistic Missile
GDU – Garbage Disposal Unit, used for getting rid of waste
Gertrude – Underwater telephone
Goat Locker – CPO quarters
Grays Harbor – Fishing port on Washington State Pacific Coast
Helo – Helicopter
Icepicking – Submarine stopped, resting with top of sail pressed tight against the overhead ice
JCS – Joint Chiefs of Staff
JO – Junior Officer
Kip – Rest
LLER – Lower Level Engine Room
LT – Lieutenant
LTJG – Lieutenant Junior Grade.
MK 46 – Lightweight antisubmarine warfare torpedo
MK 50 – Advanced lightweight torpedo for use against fast, deep-diving submarines
MK 117 – Digital Fire Control Computer
NKVD – Soviet Secret Police
NLM – Noise level monitor
Operation Clear Seas – Code name assigned to defense of a sea lift operation between the United States and Britain
PCO School – Prospective Commanding Officer School
Petard – Explosive device
Pitometer – aka Pit Log, measures speed through the water in nautical miles per hour

Pitstop – Submarine base hastily put together on west coast after nuclear attack

Polynya – A stretch of open water surrounded by ice (especially in Arctic seas).

POW – Prisoner of War

QMOW – Quartermaster of the Watch

RADM – Rear Admiral

RPM – Reactor Plant Manual

Sail – Coaming around submarine conning tower

Sea Lance Missile – Rocket-propelled long-range submarine-launched missile with MK 46 or MK 50 payload.

SECNAV – Secretary of the Navy

Shaft Boot Seal – Emergency inflatable device to temporarily stop flooding through the ship's main propeller shaft.

Shchuka-**class** – Soviet attack submarine, Victor III

SOA – Speed of Advance

SOB – Son of a bitch

Soviet Boomers – *Typhoon* and *Delta* class ballistic missile submarines.

SPM – Secondary Propulsion Motor.

SSBN – Ballistic Missile Nuclear-powered Submarine

SSMG – Ships Service Motor Generator

SSTG – Ships Service Turbine Generator

Streamer – Sinking salmon fly

SUBGRU – Submarine Group

Tango-**class** – Soviet attack submarine

Tippet – Variable weight line tied between leader and fishing fly

Tovarish – Comrade

Towed Arrays – Listening hydrophones at end of long cable

TPES – Turbine Pump Ejection System.

USET-80K – Russian defense mechanism - ASW torpedo, sensor, on/off switch

Williamson – Rescue maneuver for man overboard or low visibility

Zampolit – Soviet Political Officer

Zhukov – *Akula* class attack submarine.

About the Author

Author D. M. Ulmer enlisted in the U.S. Navy in 1947. In two years, he was promoted to third class electronic technician onboard the submarine USS *Clamagore (SS 343)*. Six months later, he was advised he would be transferred to the Naval Academy Prep School. When Ulmer asked his captain "Why me?" The skipper replied facetiously, "I don't think you're smart enough to make second class and I need the bunk space."

Ulmer returned to *Clamagore* in 1967 as Commanding Officer. He then became one of the few, if not only, to have served in an enlisted status and as commanding officer in the same warship.

Captain Ulmer's 32 year Navy career included:

1949 – Brief duty aboard German U-boat (U-2513), gifted to the United States Navy in 1945 as partial WWII reparation.
Mar. – Sept. 1949 USS *Clamagore* (SS 343).
1954 United States Naval Academy graduate.
July 1954 – 55 USS *Fremont* (APA 44).
July –55 US Navy Officers' Submarine School.
Jan. 1956 – June 58 USS *Halfbeak* (SS 352).
June 1958 – Sept 59 USS *Barracuda* (SSK 1).
1959 – 60 Aide to Commandant, 8th Naval District.
July – Oct. 1960 Polaris Weapons School, Dam Neck, VA.
Dec. 1960 – July 62 USS *Patrick Henry* (SSBN 599).
1963 – 65 Staff, Commander Submarine Squadron 14.
Nov. 1965 – July 67 Executive Officer USS *Corporal* (SS 346).
July 1967 – Mar. 69 Commander USS *Clamagore* (SS 343).
1969 – 72 Office of Chief of Naval Operations.

1972 – 77 Naval Sea Systems Command.
1977 – 79 Trident Project Manager Staff,
April 1979 – Retired.

A versatile author, Captain Ulmer has 11 published novels. He is also the tour guide in the DVD, *Tour of the USS Clamagore, Patriot's Point, South Carolina.*

After a 32 year career in the United States Navy Submarine Service, D. M. Ulmer was employed by the Boeing Company (1979-96). He currently is a docent at the Seattle Museum of Flight and volunteers at a local hospital.

A Series of Submarine Classics
by D.M. Ulmer

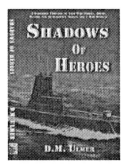

Fiction Titles

D.M. Ulmer, Author
Silent Battleground
Shadows of Heroes
The Cold War Beneath
Ensure Plausible Deniability
Missing Person
The Roche Harbor Caper
The Long Beach Caper
Count the Ways
Where or When
Skagerrak
Shared Glory

DVD
Brett Kneisley, Author
Tour of USS Clamagore at Patriot's Point, South Carolina

Nelson O. Ottenhausen, Author
Civil War II
The Blue Heron
The Killing Zone
The Sin Slayer
Jugs & Bottles
The Naked Warrior
Little Hawk & Lobo

B.K. Bryans, Author
Those '67 Blues
Flight to Redemption
The Dog Robbers
Arizona Grit
Brannigan Rides Again

Roger Chaney, Author
Carquinez Straits

Paul Stuligross, Author
The Donkey

Jack Verneski, Author
Scarecrow Season

Tom Gauthier, Author
Mead's Trek
Code Name: Orion's Eye
Die Liste

Dari Bradley, Author
Hickory Nuts in the Driveway

Non Fiction Titles

Paul Sherbo, Author
*Unsinkable Sailors: The fall and rise of the last crew
of USS* Frank E. Evans
Fish Out of Water

Art Giberson, Author
The Mighty O

Ralph McDougal, Author
A Cowboy Goes to War
Mules to Missiles

LTC Peter Clark, Author
*Staff Monkeys: A Stockbroker's Journey through
the Global War on Terror*

Joseph C. Engel, Author
Flight of the Silver Eagle

Hannah Ackerman, Author
I Kept My Chin Up

Hal Olsen, Author
Up An' Atom

Robert & Billie Nicholson, Authors
Pearl Harbor Honor Flight: One Last Goodbye